THE CURSE OF MYCENAE

ALSO BY THIS AUTHOR

The Curse of Mycenae

Ella Mortimer

MY THANKS TO

My brother Martin, fellow author and companion on this writing journey, an invaluable resource as proof reader, marketing consultant, confidante and friend.

MYCENAEAN GREECE
c.1200 BCE

LEMNOS
HEPHAESTOS

•TROY
ILIUM

MYSIA

LESBOS
TEUTHRANIA

EUBOEA

•DELPHI

•AULIS
•THEBES

•ATHENS

ACHAEA

•PISA

•MYCENAE
•ARGOS

•SPARTA
LAKEDAIMON

•KNOSSOS

CRETE

CONTENTS

1

An Army of Suitors

Klytemestra's sister was fair of hair, with creamy white skin and a voice of liquid gold. A shining beauty that reduced Klytie's own dark hair and brown eyes to the drabness of a shade.

Rumour said that her mother had lain with the great Zeus himself, to produce the sublimely beautiful Helene. Klytie had no idea how her father felt, being cuckold to a god, but of all Queen Leda's children, two had been fathered by Zeus.

Growing up with this paragon of beauty for a sister, Klytie was forced to watch while the world doted on Helene. Beside her, Klytie felt positively plain, ordinary beyond belief. Her whole life, she had languished in the shadows, lost behind the blinding light of her divine sister. Poor Klytemestra. The mortal one. The normal one. Now this.

There before them filling the megaron, the King's audience chamber, were Helene's suitors, clamouring to win her hand. There were so many they masked her view of the great round hearth in the centre of the room, its four flanking pillars barely visible above the heads of the throng. Klytie gazed over a sea of eager faces, princes all.

Some were young and fair of face, some old and needy, but most were hardened with the rigours of battle. All were eminently suitable, all begging for the chance to prove they were worthy. Not one of them came for Klytemestra.

Klytie watched as her brothers pushed their way through the crowd, enforcing order. One rippled with muscle, his strength writ on his frame for all to see. The other was thin and wiry but with eyes that glowed with power and an unearthly beauty that rivalled even Helene.

Castor, mortal like Klytemestra, true son of Tyndareos, had trained hard to meet the physical prowess of his divinely empowered half-brother Polydeuces. Klytie alone knew what her brother had suffered.

She related to him on a level like no other. He too had to struggle in the shadow of a child of Zeus. He spent long hours building muscle, pushing himself to the limit of his mere mortal strength to keep up with "the little Pollox", who had no need of physical training to best every opponent.

Castor winked at his favourite sister as he approached, and Klytie stifled a laugh.

"Father, the men are getting restless. They want your decision," said Castor.

"I haven't decided," said King Tyndareos with a frown. "I don't intend to."

A murmur rustled through the crowd at this statement.

"Then what do you intend to do?" said Pollox.

"I intend to let Helene decide."

The murmur grew louder.

"Father, do you think that's wise?" said Castor.

"You question me, son?"

"No, Sir, of course not, but... it's not..."

"I understand your concern, my boy. I know it's more usual to take political considerations into account when choosing a husband for a daughter, but in this case I see no solution that won't bring jealousy and recrimination down on my own head."

Castor tilted his head. "How would letting her decide

make any difference?"

"I have a plan," Tyndareos said with a wink. The King raised his voice to address the milling throng.

"My lords, take heed!" Tyndareos cried. "I propose a contest. Each of you will be given a certain amount of time with my daughter, in which you have my permission to woo her. Use your time wisely, let her get to know you and convince her that you'd make the best husband."

The assembled suitors grumbled, exchanging looks. Klytie almost laughed aloud at the undisguised calculation in their expressions, some openly hostile and others closing in with a shifty gleam behind hooded eyes. This was going to be interesting. The King held up his hand.

"I won't tolerate plotting of any kind. You will behave amicably toward each other. There will be no fighting and no attempts at sabotage. Any such behaviour will result in instant dismissal from this contest and expulsion from Sparta."

The men grumbled.

"How much 'time' will we have?" called Elephenor, son of Chalcedon.

"As much time as my daughter needs to decide if you're worthy or eliminated."

"You mean it won't be an equal time? That's hardly fair!" cried Aias from Salamis.

"It's completely fair," countered the King. "If you can't impress Helene quickly, why should we continue the pretence? That wouldn't be fair on the others, making them wait longer than is necessary. If she likes you enough to continue associating with you I would think it good for your chances."

There were more grumbles.

"What happens to the 'worthy'?" said Menestheus from Athens.

"Those Helene considers worthy will be invited to continue proving their worth. To help her decision they will be assessed on the quality of their nuptial offerings and they will take part in a physical contest, a series of games to determine the winner."

"Which wouldn't be fair to those older or less wealthy," grumbled another.

"If you doubt your chances, Protesilaos, you can leave now and save us the bother."

This brought more raised voices, more bickering.

"That's an insult to all of us here!" cried Protesilaos. "Who's she to say any of us are not 'worthy'?"

A polite cough from the midst of the throng caught the King's attention.

"Yes, Odysseus, you have something to say?"

"Might I offer a suggestion?" he said, raising a hand before the King could reply. "With a price."

Tyndareos narrowed his eyes at the Prince of Ithaca. "What... price?"

"I'll step back, give my place to another, and offer my help to you. On one condition."

The King crossed his arms and stared. "Well?"

"I want your oath that you'll aid my cause and win me the hand of your niece, Penelope."

The King's eyes widened. "A bold proposal, Odysseus. What makes you think I can achieve such a match?"

"I'm no fool, Tyndareos. I know you can."

"Very well," the King said with a nod. "Now what's your suggestion?"

"There will be a treaty, drawn up by your legal advisors, and signed by each and every man here. Whoever wins Helene will also win alliance with all of them. They will all swear fealty to the winner, here and now, whoever that winner may be."

"I like it," the King mused. "It shall be done."

"But Father," said Pollox. "There are more suitors arriving every day. Are you saying they will be turned away?"

"Not at all. Each new arrival will be required to take the oath just as these here have done."

"Then the contest will never end!" cried Aias with a frown.

"It will end when Helene makes her final choice."

"But you said everyone has a chance with her. What if she decides before she's seen everyone?" said Protesilaos.

"So be it. That's the risk you must take in signing this agreement. Helene's decision ends the contest."

The grumble grew to an angry roar.

"Accept my terms, or leave now!" cried the King.

The crowd grumbled but every man stood his ground. Every man but one. Stepping forward, he addressed the King.

"My lord Tyndareos," he said.

"Tantalus," said the King.

"I wish to make a counter proposal."

"Speak, my friend."

"I'm a practical man. I am not a young sprite puffed up by arrogance and pride. I know I have no chance in this company of fine young princes."

"Tantalus, we've been friends a long time, and you are anything but old."

"Perhaps, but I'm getting there. I'm past my thirty-fifth year and I have no wife, nor heir to follow me. I can't pin my hopes on such a contest."

"Then what do you propose?"

"My lord, you have another daughter."

Klytie's head snapped up. Before her, was a man in his mid-thirties, a warrior hardened by training and damaged by battle, with the confidence and bearing of a king. She turned to her father, wondering what his reply might be.

Tyndareos laughed. "You have an arrogance at least as strong as these others here. Why not take your chances in the contest?"

"I know I won't win, and I suspect your daughter feels the same hopelessness. She is at least as beautiful as Helene, yet she is cast aside and forgotten. She deserves her time in the sun."

The King turned to his daughter. "What say you, Klytemestra? Would you agree to this man's proposal?"

"I..." Klytie spluttered.

"Speak, child, ask him anything you wish."

Klytie looked about. Suddenly the attention of the whole gathering was on her. She caught the look of disdain in her sister's eye, the smirk on her mouth. Klytie felt the old anger simmering just beneath the surface, her calm threatening to break.

How dare Helene look at her that way, as if she, Klytemestra, were nothing. As if it were only fitting that she give up her own dream of love to marry the first man who noticed her, because maybe nobody else ever would. It was too much. She turned to the man before her.

"You say I'm beautiful?" she whispered.

The man smiled and his face changed, the care-worn lines of life fading away and the green eyes gleaming.

"Yes," he murmured.

"Even with my sister right there, shining as she does, you say that?"

"I admit, shining is a good word, but her beauty is nothing to yours."

"And you say you have no chance," Klytie snorted. "You're a champion of charm and persuasion. But I know what you say is untrue. I'll never compare to my sister."

"I mean every word. Helene is blessed with the ethereal

beauty of her heritage, but I don't want a goddess for a wife. She can have any man she wants with a wink of an eye. How long will it be before her beauty takes her from me and into the arms of a younger, more tempting man?"

"I..."

"You, on the other hand, have something much more. Yes, you are beautiful, but it's a real beauty, as perfectly human as Helene's beauty is divine. You may not shine, but you burn with a fire that I for one would be honoured to treasure."

Klytie felt flushed, unsure how to receive the first compliment she had ever heard. Her practical side took over. She looked out across the crowd, all there to woo Helene, and felt a warm glow growing from deep inside.

If she agreed, she would be married first. Her perfect sister would be left to deal with all those suitors while she, the plain one, would be a married woman with a house of her own and a future secured. It was so very tempting.

"But... I don't love you..."

"Perhaps in time you will," he shrugged. "And I'll never stop trying to win you. I want to spend the rest of my life caring for you."

Klytemestra looked to her father for guidance.

"Your choice, my dear," he smiled.

She turned to the man. She took a deep breath, swallowed down a feeling of trepidation, and gave an almost imperceptible nod. Tantalus grinned, his face lighting up, and she could not help returning the smile.

Helene's choice was postponed until after Klytie's wedding, and all the suitors became guests at the wedding feast. Klytemestra wore a fine gown, its skirt pulled in at the waist and falling in banded layers of colour to the floor. Over it, she wore a figure-hugging jacket, with sleeves to the elbows, pulled in under her bare breasts and laced tightly at the front.

First, they enjoyed a fine banquet, with roast meats and flat loaves, dried figs and olives, spiced apples and many other delicacies from every corner of the world. Then, before the wine was watered, the gifts arrived.

Tantalus had scoured his small kingdom and presented a dazzling array of livestock and precious items for his new father-in-law. An official of the treasury sat beside the King to make account of the gifts.

As the first gift was brought into the hall, he rolled a ball of clay into a fat sausage, then squashed it into a small, narrow tablet. Picking up his stylus he began to write, inscribing the symbols in the wet clay. By the time the gift-giving was complete he had seven such tablets listing all the King had received for his daughter.

First, a mother deer and her newborn calf, a special offering to be given to the gods to ensure prosperity and fertility. Next was a fine gold tripod and matching libation bowl, followed by a beautiful set of ivory carved musicians each playing their own instrument including a harp, flute and lyre, from the Cyclades. There were spices from Sumeria, far to the east, and papyrus from Egypt in the south.

At the conclusion of the gifting ceremony, the wine was watered for the men to enjoy, and the new bride was escorted from the hall by her maids. In her chamber, Klytie sat for the ritual cutting of the hair. With vision blurred and a small moan of loss, she watched as her long dark tresses fell to the floor, symbolising her new birth as a married woman.

When it was done, she ran a hand over her bare scalp and stifled a sob. Her head was covered with a beautifully embroidered linen veil and her maids gathered up the possessions of her childhood. Her toys and her child's clothing would all be offered to the goddess Hera, a sign that she had left childhood behind.

The last remaining maid helped her dress in a simple linen shift with matching pins holding the shoulders and a leather belt keeping it closed at the front. With the veil concealing her shaven head, the maid helped Klytie climb onto the bed and left the room. Klytemestra lay quietly, staring at nothing, her mind in turmoil.

What had she done? Agreed to a marriage, with a stranger more than twice her age, for what. Pride, arrogance, something she could hold over her perfect sister. Now she felt trapped, terrified, dreading the night to come.

She did not have long to wait. When he came to her, bathed and sober, he stood and looked at her for what seemed an eternity, a small, almost shy smile on his face. Then he sat on the edge of the bed and she shivered in fear, wishing she could bury herself down under the thick woollen under-blanket and burrow into the skins beneath.

He hesitated, one hand hovering over her shoulder pin.

"You needn't be afraid," he murmured. "I won't hurt you."

He bent closer and kissed her. Klytie resisted the urge to pull away, exploring the sensation of his mouth on hers, and decided with surprise that it was not so bad. Curious now, she allowed him to remove the pins at her shoulders and to untie the belt at her waist.

As he explored her youthful form, first with his eyes and then his hands, she shivered again. But he kept his promise. He was gentle. Kind and loving, carefully helping her to accept him without fear and find some pleasure in the experience.

When it was over and he lay spent and snoring beside her, Klytie stared into the darkness, mind racing. Nothing could have prepared her for this and she thought, not without a sense of wonder, that maybe she was lucky. She could have done worse than a kind and gentle man for a husband. With a little sigh of contentment, she pulled the woollen blanket over her nakedness, curled up and went to sleep.

Klytemestra woke slowly, coming out of slumber to the unshakeable feeling that she was being watched. Allowing her eyes to flutter open she saw in the dim room a man, her husband, propped on one arm studying her. The shutters were still closed and the early morning light filtered through, giving the room a curious glow.

"Good morning, my dear," he said gently.

She smiled and he covered her smile with his own, his kiss stirring her to a repeat of the enlightening events of the night before. But, in the midst of their mutual enjoyment, her mind settled on one nagging thought. When he lay beside her once more, she forced her tongue to form the words.

"Do you really think I'm beautiful or was it a ploy to get me to agree to this marriage?"

Propping himself up once more, he sighed. "Why do you find that so hard to believe?"

"I've spent my whole life being compared to my sister. When you came here, it was for her, not me. I can't believe you saw me and thought me the better catch. There has to be another reason."

"I won't lie to you. I did come here to try my luck with Helene. But it wasn't really important which sister I married. I wanted either one. Until I saw you."

"You can't possibly tell me you saw me and wanted me more than her," she snorted.

"That's exactly what I'm telling you. You are the most

beautiful girl I've ever seen."

"Now I know you're lying," she laughed.

"No, I'm not, but you're right. You are not the most beautiful girl because, as you say, there is your sister. But everything I said in that room was true. You are most definitely the most beautiful mortal woman I've ever seen. You don't need divine blood to impress me. I wanted to catch you before some other man there realised it too."

She dropped her gaze in embarrassment, feeling the warm flush of pleasure his statement brought. But something he had said stuck in her mind.

"You said... you wanted either one of us. So you had another motive."

"I see I caught the smarter sister," he chuckled. "I won't lie to you. Your father is the King of Sparta, commander of the greatest army in the world."

She shook her head in confusion. "Why do you need an army?"

"For my father, of course."

Klytie felt even more confused. Here was a political tangle far out of her experience. Seeing her puzzled gaze, he smiled indulgently.

"It all has to do with the family curse," he said. "Did you know that twenty years ago my father was the King of Mycenae?"

"Mycenae? But I thought he was king of Pisa?"

"He is, now. When we were thrown out by my uncle, we eventually found our way to Pisa, which was once my grandfather's home. The queen was recently widowed and childless. She took us in, and in time my father became king."

"I still don't understand. You say you were thrown out. What does that mean?"

"It's a long, sorry story," he sighed. "In Mycenae, it is

known as the curse of Atreus, but really it goes back further than that. Have you heard of Pelops?"

"Didn't he hold the first games at Olympia?"

"That's right. He created the games in honour of his father-in-law Oenomaus, King of Pisa. He's also my grandfather. He's the one who was cursed. He failed to reward the charioteer, Myrtilus, who fixed the chariot race so that Pelops might win the hand of Hippodamia, my grandmother. Instead, Pelops betrayed the man by throwing him off a cliff. As he fell, Myrtilus cursed my grandfather and all his descendents."

Klytemestra felt suddenly cold. She had married a man under a curse. But she had to hear the rest of it.

"What happened then?" she whispered.

"Pelops married Hippodamia and they had many children, including twin sons; my father, Thyestes and my uncle, Atreus. After some strife involving one of their brothers, the twins were banished. They came to Mycenae, where Thyestes became king and he and my mother had four sons. Thyestes and Atreus fought over everything, including the Kingdom of Mycenae. Atreus accused my father of seducing his wife, Aerope. I have no idea how true this accusation was, but it was the excuse he needed to kill my younger brothers and cast my father out of Mycenae, claiming the crown for himself."

"How did you survive?"

"I was fifteen and had just joined the ranks of the army. My troop mates protected me and helped me escape."

"And now you want to go back?"

"No, but my father has given me an offer. If I secure a bride, with an army from her father, he'll lead us to Mycenae and, once his throne there is restored, he'll give Pisa to me. He wants revenge on Atreus and he needs troops to do it."

*

Klytie set out for her new home on a bright summer's morning, her few remaining belongings squeezed into the spaces between the other more important items in the two wheeled cart, lumbering along at the head of a train of supply carts. She sat in the rear of the leading cart, ensconced between a large wooden crate and an even larger earthenware jar, with only a few cushions for comfort.

The driver stood on a small platform at the very front, wielding the reins with practised ease, keeping the four horses on course as they wound their way down the long track, following the ridge of Sparta to the road below. He said nothing to Klytemestra. In fact, to him she was little more than cargo.

Their small military escort marched alongside without a glance in her direction, and the two maids she had been allowed to bring from home were riding in another cart somewhere behind. With no company and little comfort, Klytie settled in to watch the world crawl by.

The heavy wooden wheels of the cart rolled ever on, somehow finding every bump and divot in the rough surface of the road, jarring and bruising at every moment. Klytie held on, watching the soldiers strolling casually alongside and thinking she could walk faster than that blasted cart. But when she tried to alight, she was told firmly to remain where she was.

Smiling to hide her frustration, Klytie seethed inside. She was a Spartan princess, no ordinary woman. She had trained alongside her brothers, learning to swing a sword and ride a horse. She should be riding with her husband. She determined to take him to task on the matter, if this damned thing ever caught up with him.

The carts rolled inexorably onward, without stopping. Even the noonday meal was passed to her over the side of the cart, a small stale loaf with some hard cheese and warm beer. It was dark when they finally approached the army, the lights of hundreds of campfires twinkling through the trees.

Tantalus was there to meet her, ready to help her down. Trembling with fatigue and groaning as her cramped muscles protested against movement, Klytie could do little more than fall into her husband's waiting arms, allowing him to carry her into his command tent.

She had little energy to consume the hearty broth he presented her, hardly noticing the richness of the tent as she sank gratefully into the soft mattress of skins on the low camp bed. She murmured her thanks as she sank into a deep sleep.

When she awoke to the sounds of the army pulling down their camp, Klytie did not forget her resolution of the day before and when her husband led her toward the cart she voiced her protest, refusing to climb aboard.

"Can't I ride with you?" she moaned.

He blinked. "This is the way all ladies travel."

"Not Spartan ladies! I've been riding since I was five."

"Oh," he said, nonplussed. "I just thought..."

"Please, husband, I can't take another day in that thing. Please find me a horse, let me ride at your side."

"Of course, my dear. Whatever makes you happy."

Riding beside Tantalus at the head of the army Klytemestra felt invincible. Travelling west with her new husband, she felt the power of the army at her back. Thousands of sandalled feet marched in time, sending a rhythmic thud that could be heard for miles, vibrating through the body of the horse beneath her.

She heard the clang of armour, breathed the tang of sweat and warm metal and, when she turned in her seat to watch, saw the flash of sunlight on bronze like burnished gold. If this was how it felt to lead the march to battle, she could understand why so many men were seduced to a life of warfare.

Finally, they reached the top of the pass and began the descent to the plain of Messenia, hemmed in on three sides by mountains and by the lonely coast to the west. Striking out across the plain, they veered northwest toward Pisa and Klytie's new home.

They rounded the northern tip of Messenia's mountain spine at midday, and by early afternoon they could feel the salt breeze off the western sea. On a scorching mid-summer evening, as the sun dropped to kiss the water, Klytemestra had her first glimpse of the town of Pisa.

Modest houses clustered along the river, and there on the first ridge of the northern mountains, silhouetted against the unbroken sea, squatted the citadel. Travel-worn and weary, Klytie finally entered her husband's house.

She was immediately ushered off to a small bathing room off the megaron, where her maids joined her. The small, one-person bath was already filled with hot water warmed by the palace furnace, and Klytie allowed her maids to remove her clothing. She stepped up onto the small external platform, whitewashed to match the bath itself, then reached for a steadying hand as she slowly dipped a foot. Stepping down into the knee-deep water, Klytie settled herself with a sigh at one end.

Toward the middle of the bath, where both sides narrowed to form a generous shelf, were a collection of soaps and perfumes, soft cloths for washing, a goblet of watered wine and a small plate of sweet treats. As the maids scrubbed away the dust of travel, Klytie eagerly set to work demolishing the unexpected repast.

She thought again how lucky she was to have found such a considerate husband, feeling certain this attention had been ordered by Tantalus. She sat back and closed her eyes, feeling the welcome warmth seep into her aching bones.

Klytemestra had no chance to meet her new father-in-law. Very early the next morning her husband woke her with a light touch to her cheek.

"I'm sorry, my dear, but I have to go. My father wants to get an early start for Mycenae. He is nothing if not eager. He has waited a long time for this chance."

"Oh," she sighed.

"I wish I could stay with you but my father needs me. But this is your home now, it's yours to explore."

Klytie sighed again, thinking of the strange new world in which she found herself and feeling deserted. She would be alone in an unfamiliar town, with none but her maids for company.

"I really am sorry, my dear," he continued. "Please, my home is yours, as are my servants and staff. They will cater to your every wish. And I promise I'll be home by winter."

* * *

2

THE CURSE OF PELOPS

The servant stood by the King, waiting for orders. He could hear, muffled by stone and distance, the sounds of battle outside the citadel wall. This siege must end soon. The people were starving; the defending army close to revolt.

The servant saw King Atreus wince at a loud rumble of falling masonry, followed by screams and the clash of bronze. The servant observed and waited, just as he had always done, but somewhere deep inside he exalted. He had dreamt of this day every waking moment of his life.

A scuffle outside, a clamour of armour and pounding feet, brought the King's eldest son, fresh from the battle. The servant seethed quietly, reliving a lifetime of torment at that man's hands; demeaning him, beating him, calling him slave.

"Father, you must leave, the wall is breached."

The King smiled. "No, my son, I will await my doom. My brother will hunt me down, and I have no desire to spend my last years running."

"Father, you need to go," cried the King's other son, rushing in on his brother's heels.

"I will stay," said the King in a hard voice. "But you boys must escape, live to fight again."

"We won't leave you here," the eldest protested.

"Yes, you will. You will gather your allies, build your

strength, and return to avenge me."

The servant held his breath. Would the brothers stay to be killed alongside their father? Oh, he hoped they would. But he could see they were itching to be away.

"Father, we can't just leave you here to be killed!"

"Yes, you can. Pelops' curse has come to take me, but you have long lives ahead. Plenty of time to return and retake the city, fulfil the curse yet again."

The sounds of battle were closer now, raging through the streets below the palace. The servant melted into the shadows, held his breath, heart thudding in his chest. Stay... he prayed. Stay and meet your death!

"Father, come with us!"

"No, my son. Please, go now, before it's too late."

The brothers looked at each other and seemed to come to a decision. A cry from outside broke the moment and the brothers rushed for the door. Too late.

A warrior strode into the hall, bronze armour dulled with dirt and blood. Tall, with grizzled beard and piercing green eyes, the man snarled. Behind him, a second man entered, younger but with a likeness to the first that was striking.

The King's sons reacted instantly, rushing at the intruders with cries of rage. They met in battle with a great clash of bronze on bronze, swords flying. The servant stood out of sight, watching with bated breath.

Could it be that all his hopes might be accomplished in this one vicious fight? The younger brother let out a cry, clutching at a leg caught by an enemy sword, and the watching servant felt a fluttering of excitement.

With a great roar, the King surged forward, forcing his way into the fray. He engaged with both enemies at once, pushing his sons back.

"Go!" he screamed to his sons. "Get out while you still

can."

The brothers backed away, watching their father holding his own, hesitating still.

"I order you!" the King roared. "Escape now, that you may have your revenge!"

The brothers turned and ran. The servant groaned, his disappointment like a knife in his soul. The battle raged on. Outside he could hear the invading army wreaking havoc in the city below. His hand rested on his belt and the dagger that lay concealed beneath his kiton.

His father's ceremonial dagger, kept secret and safe since he was a babe. He fingered the beautiful weapon, sliding his hand along the flat of the blade, its gold inlaid scene living in his mind, a thrilling lion hunt. His only proof of his birthright.

Now was the time, his life's ambition about to be fulfilled. He fumbled with the folds of fabric, drawing out the knife. Stepping from the shadows, the servant watched the fight. The King was tiring, but he was still holding firm against the attackers.

They circled him like two wild cats, stalking their prey. The King struck, feinted and dodged in, striking a lucky hit. The younger warrior stumbled and fell, clutching at his side.

"Now face me alone, Thyestes," the King snarled.

"With pleasure, brother," said the other.

The King screamed and fell into a ferocious attack, driving the intruder back. The invader was growing more tired, his face wet with sweat, grunting with effort. The servant licked his lips, waiting for his chance.

Suddenly the intruder stumbled and the King stood over his attacker. He lifted his sword for the final blow. Blood boiling, the servant rushed forward unseen, holding his knife in both hands.

He let out a cry of wordless rage, a lifetime of oppression and pain bursting out of him. Lifting the knife high he drove it into the King's back. He saw the intruder's eyes widen in surprise. Then the King fell to his knees as the servant drove the knife in deeper.

He clung to the hilt, dragging the King down, teeth clenched, forcing him to the floor by sheer will power. With a gurgling groan, the King finally hit the floor, his last rasping breath forced out of him by the weight of the servant on his back.

Standing and squaring his shoulders, the servant pulled the dagger from his victim's body and faced the newcomers. The younger man had regained his feet and the servant caught his eye. It was almost like looking in a polished bronze mirror.

He saw the man's surprise, thought he glimpsed a puzzled recognition. Then he looked at the older man, now standing before him. Long had he awaited this moment, and he studied the man in wonder. Then the servant smiled, and caught his breath.

"Welcome home, Father," he said.

* * *

Klytie settled into her new home without her husband to make her feel welcome. The residents of the palace were all as helpful and respectful as Tantalus had promised. She began training to take on a queen's duties as potinia, the priestess of the lady.

She spent long hours wandering aimlessly, and the small town market soon became familiar and uninteresting. She found her steps more often taking her down the little rocky track to the sanctuary of Olympia, to the west of the town, where she found peace and solitude in the sacred grove.

When her boredom became too stifling, she would take

her favourite filly and ride west, easily covering the miles to the western sea, to spend the morning walking on the shore, gazing out over the water.

The sea filled her with awe, its majestic power at once inspiring and exhilarating. She loved the feel of the coarse sand between her toes, the smell of the salt spray that left its taste on her lips.

Her gaze drifted out over the water, stretching so far into the distance it met the sky, merging with it in a haze of vapour that shimmered in the air. In all her life she had never seen such a sight, never dreamed the sea was so vast.

She stared out over that great expanse, her eyes drinking in the distance with wonder. Two months into her lonely exile, Klytemestra discovered a new joy, a secret pleasure that grew as the weeks progressed.

She wished Tantalus could be there to share it with her but, as month after month passed, she began to worry that he would miss the wonderful event. As she stood on the citadel wall, staring east into the dark of night, she hugged her growing stomach and wished he would come home soon.

The cold winter wind whipped her hair, and she pulled the woollen cloak more tightly about herself. Her evening vigil had become a customary end to her solitary days but, as she stared out toward the distant peaks, she squinted, trying to see into the darkness. Something was there, a cloud of dust almost invisible in the dark night.

A lump formed in her throat and she clambered her way down the stairs to the street below, stumbling in her haste to reach the inner courtyard behind the gate. Careful now, she chided herself as the child kicked within her. She waited, breathless, hearing the clamour of horses outside the gate. Then the great wooden doors swung inward and Tantalus strode through.

*

Later, Klytie lay propped up on a pile of cushions, staring at her husband as he told his story.

"My father is now the happiest king alive thanks to you, my dear," said Tantalus with a grin.

"So the campaign went well, then?"

"Well? It was perfect! The Spartan troops besieged the citadel and starved them out. Atreus was completely unprepared. He didn't know what hit him. The city had no stores to last out a siege; they hadn't even begun the late harvest for winter. When it became clear that the residents were losing heart, we stormed the citadel and took it in a day."

"What happened to King Atreus?"

"My father faced him in the megaron."

"So, the curse of Pelops has struck again," she sighed. "What happened to his family?"

"His sons fled the city as soon as the citadel fell. They didn't even stay to see their father die."

"They knew they wouldn't be spared," she said shrewdly. "I'm sure their father filled their heads with horror stories about their uncle Thyestes, just as your father did with you."

His eyes narrowed. "I wouldn't have expected you to take their side. Such disloyalty isn't becoming in a wife!"

"Hush, husband, I'm not taking their side. I just think this curse is a little too convenient an excuse. If you could just stop this family feud, the deaths and coups would be a thing of the past."

"The insult dealt my father by his brother Atreus can never be forgiven," he frowned.

"I'm sure his sons feel the same way about your father Thyestes. This curse will come again. The sons will avenge their father."

"You worry too much, my dear. They have no troops to

lead and no allies to call upon. I'd wager they won't be back in a hurry."

"They'll find a way. And when they do your life and that of your father are forfeit. Can't you see that?"

"I haven't told you the best part," he chuckled. "I'm not alone in support of my father. His silent allies have appeared as if by will of the gods, men who've lain in wait all these long years while Atreus sat his usurped throne. And with them, someone we never expected to see alive."

"Who?"

"My brother!"

"Your... brother?" she gasped. "But you said they'd all been killed."

"We thought they were. But the youngest was only a babe, barely older than a newborn. He was taken and exposed on the mountain behind Mycenae. We never saw his body."

"Are you saying he was found and taken in? How can you be sure it's really him?"

"A woman, who was working in the palace as a maid at the time, witnessed it. She saw Atreus' slave take the babe from his mother's bed while she slept. She followed and, when the deed was done, she took him and kept him. Her husband was a goat herder. She fed him on goat's milk and raised him as her own."

Klytie shook her head. "It's such a fantastical story. What proof do you have, other than this woman's word?"

"He had father's long lost ceremonial sword. Besides, you only have to see him to know it's true. He and I could be twins we're so alike. Stand him next to our father and there can be no doubt."

On a cold and blustery day as winter waned, a messenger arrived on horseback from Sparta. The man strode into the megaron, and approached the throne on the right hand wall. Klytie sat up straight, eager for news from home, as Tantalus motioned for him to speak.

"I'm charged by my lord Tyndareos to inform you that his daughter, Helene has chosen the most eligible suitors. You're invited to attend a contest of skill between the selected princes to determine the winner. The games will begin on the first day of spring and continue until all but one are eliminated."

"I thank you and in return I charge you to tell your master that we would be honoured to attend."

The messenger bowed and hurried from the room as Tantalus turned to his wife.

"I assume you do wish to attend? Or do you think the babe will be too young to travel?"

"He won't be long now," Klytie smiled, running a hand over her very full stomach. "He should be fine as long as I keep him close."

"Then we'll set out once you're recovered and the weather breaks," he smiled, reaching over to caress her belly. His grin widened as the baby kicked at the pressure of his hand.

"I can't wait to meet him," he whispered.

Less than a month later, Klytemestra and her husband Tantalus entered the crowded megaron at Sparta. Turning to her right, Klytie could just see her father deep in conversation with one of the suitors. She felt a tug at her side, heard a deep chuckle and felt strong muscular arms encase her in a stifling hug. The babe, cuddled in a sling at her breast, protested the rough treatment and she was released.

"Little sister, you grace us with your presence. It's good to see you."

"Castor!" she cried, returning the smile with delight. "Where's Pollox?"

"Right here, sister dear," said Polydeuces at her ear.

"Come, let's get you through this rabble," said Castor with a wink.

The boys set to clearing a path, pushing the men aside and glaring when they protested. Klytie and Tantalus followed at a cautious distance. Finally, the crowd opened up and she found herself in front of her father's throne. Tyndareos beamed at her, rising to embrace his daughter.

"Welcome home, my dearest," he murmured, planting a kiss on her cheek.

"Father," she smiled, opening the sling to reveal the sleeping babe. "Meet your grandson."

As if on cue, the boy child opened his eyes and stared at the bearded face peering down at him. Then he screwed up his face and let out a piercing wail. The King laughed delightedly as his daughter hushed her newborn son.

"What ails your husband?" said Tyndareos, looking over her bowed head.

"What do you mean?" she said absently, turning to look.

Tantalus was half way across the room, frozen where his steps had faltered, and he stood wide-eyed, mouth twisted in anger as he stared past his wife. Klytie followed his gaze to see a man by the throne, the suitor her father had been addressing. She saw the man lift his eyes to her husband, and saw his expression change.

Recognition flashed briefly in his eyes, quickly engulfed by an expression of pure hatred, the fury lending fire to his eyes as his face turned red. Then, before anyone could stop him, he charged at Tantalus with a wordless growl of rage. Tantalus watched unflinching as the man came.

"You!" cried Tantalus, his anger barely controlled.

In a flash, Klytie's brothers were there in front of him,

catching the irate man by the arms before he could reach his target. The man fought wildly, screaming his anger, but the boys held firm, needing little effort to keep him back. Tantalus stared at the snarling man.

"What are you doing here?" he whispered.

"How dare you," the man spat. "Murderer!"

Tantalus shook his head and brushed past the struggling man, striding forward to address Tyndareos.

"What's he doing here?"

"I'm sorry, my son, I had no choice. He came asking asylum and you know the law. Xenia dictates I give him shelter. I tried to turn him away, but then he claimed to be coming as his brother's champion to compete for Helene. He would not be swayed."

"Where's his brother?"

"In Argos, I think. He says he was wounded and fell ill with a fever, brought on by the cold and possibly an infection."

"He should have stayed in Argos too," Tantalus said.

Tyndareos nodded. "I suspect he has another reason for coming here."

"Of course he does, he wants your army, to return and retake Mycenae!"

"Who is he?" Klytie whispered.

"My cousin, Agamemnon. Son of Atreus."

"I told you, husband," she gasped. "I said he would find a way!"

"He won't get his way."

"He will if he wins Helene!"

"I'll do just that," said Agamemnon in a voice of thunder. "My brother Menelaos will take Helene to wife and I'll claim her sister for myself." He looked Klytie over, a covetous gleam in his eye.

"Now, Agamemnon, you presume too much," said

Tyndareos with a raised hand. "My daughter Klytemestra is already married to Tantalus."

Agamemnon raised an eyebrow. "So that's why he's here. No matter. When I avenge my father I'll have her anyway."

Klytie felt her blood run cold.

3

A Prize For the Taking

The first day of spring was a bright, blustery day, with puffs of white cloud skipping across a blue sky. Klytemestra joined her husband and father in the megaron, ready to walk out to the great courtyard, where the field had been set for the games.

Helene bounced with excitement, her brothers watching on indulgently. Klytie moved to her husband's side and took his arm with a smile.

"I thought I told you not to come," he murmured.

"Why shouldn't I come?" she retorted. "Father, tell him!"

"Are you really going to let the women watch, sir?" said Tantalus with a frown.

"My girls have done more than watch in the past," said the King with a shrug. "Klytie can hold her own in armour and you know what a talented rider she is. And Helene runs like the wind."

"And you let them? Women don't take part in the games and they never watch!"

"This is Sparta, my son. Just try to stop them."

"But the boy!" said Tantalus. "The throng of the games is no place for a babe."

"Nonsense," Klytie said haughtily. "He will be a warrior himself one day. Besides, he needs to be fed."

*

Twenty men milled about in the middle of the field while the spectators gathered. Helene clapped her hands appreciatively and turned to Tyndareos with a gleam in her eye.

"Can we go down and inspect them?" she whispered. "Please, Papa!"

The King nodded with a smile and Helene jumped up and down like a little girl. Klytie frowned at her sister's childish exuberance, but then Helene grabbed her hand and Klytie allowed herself to be pulled along.

Soon she was running with her sister, the babe in his sling gurgling in delight at the sudden rocking motion. Married propriety forgotten in her love of the games, Klytie wished she could be competing, but this was Helene's moment, the contest that would finally reveal her future husband.

Down on the field Klytemestra and Helene surveyed the suitors. Helene fluttered and gasped, whispering to her sister as they approached. The men stood silently, bare chested, oiled skin glistening over rippled muscle. Their hands were padded and bound in himantes, long strips of leather, ready for the first event, the boxing.

"Aren't they beautiful," Helene gushed. "Oh, Klytie, which one is going to win?"

"Which do you wish to win?"

"Oh, I don't know! They're all so perfect."

"Then it doesn't matter who wins."

"No, I suppose not," she sighed. "But oh, I hope he's young..."

At a call from their father, the girls returned to the seats placed for them at the head of the field. Castor and Pollox made their way among the men, pairing them. A horn blew and the boxing began, each pair circling and looking for an opening.

Klytie watched as a very young man eyed his mismatched opponent, tall and heavy set. She felt sorry for the poor boy and determined to berate her brothers for making such an unfair match. At one swing from the much larger man, the boy squealed and ran from the field.

Another bout ended almost as quickly, the loser defeated more by his age and rounded frame than his wily opponent. The younger man ran about in circles, keeping just out of the older man's reach, forcing him to spin and throw fists at thin air. With no punch yet to meet its mark, the poor old man held up his hands in surrender.

Three more bouts ended in quick succession, leaving five pairs still on the field. More evenly matched, the men sank into the rhythm of thrust and dodge. A lucky hit saw another bout over while the grunts of effort continued. Another ended, and another, leaving only two pairs in the field.

The two couples included Agamemnon against his friend and neighbour, Diomedes from Argos, and Askalaphos of Orchomenus against a young man Klytemestra did not know. She watched with interest. Askalaphos was said to be the son of Ares, god of war. He was bound to be an excellent fighter. She wondered how the hero's young opponent had lasted so long.

Askalaphos seemed to be sauntering about his opponent, expending little effort to keep him at arm's length, his swings wide and lazy but with a menacing strength that suggested this bout could have ended much sooner. Finally, with a grimace of disdain, the son of Ares gave a mighty swing, catching the young man full on the jaw and sending him sprawling.

Then Askalaphos laughed and swaggered from the field. As the young man was helped to his feet, Klytie noticed the other bout had also ended. Diomedes had conceded to his friend, and Agamemnon was leading him off the field with an arm about his shoulders.

The winners of the first round were presented with a gold coin each, which they secreted in leather pouches, made for the purpose. These coins would be tallied at the end of the games to find the winner. Then, with barely a few moments for rest, the second round began, the winners of the previous round paired off again, making five bouts on the field.

Aias dispatched his opponent in an instant and strode from the field. Elephenor finished off Idomeneos almost as quickly. Menestheus and Antilochus circled warily, testing each other with random thrusts before throwing themselves into a flurry of blows.

Out of that mess, Menestheus somehow emerged as the victor. Two pairs remained on the field. Once again, Agamemnon remained with his evenly matched opponent, Protesilaos, while Askalaphos faced a young warrior named Patroklos.

Patroklos held his own against the son of Ares, but Askalaphos parried easily, his expression calm and his face showing no sign of effort. Once again the son of Ares played, until the boredom settled on his face and with one swing, he despatched his worthy young opponent.

Agamemnon and Protesilaos traded punch for punch. There was no obvious leader, no way to guess at the outcome. With the whole field to themselves, the bout ranged all over, taking on a life of its own.

The battle ebbed and flowed, sometimes furious, other times lulled as they took a mutual breath. Each searched for signs of weakness in the other, looking for that opening that would give them the match.

In the end, a misplaced foot sent Protesilaos to the ground, and the victory went to Agamemnon. The five winners collected another coin and, after a short rest, gathered once more on the field.

This final round would be a less formal affair. The first two were chosen at random and the winner would stay in play for the next opponent. The first man to stay in action for three successive bouts would be the winner.

As the other four men took their turns, Agamemnon held back. He was fiddling with his himantes, the leather binding on his hands. Klytemestra peered down the field, trying to see what he was doing.

When he finally stepped in for his turn, his hands hung heavily by his sides. His first opponent stepped up and he swung an arm in a long, slow arc, grunting with effort. He connected and his opponent's head snapped back, his body following as he landed with a sickening thud.

The next opponent met a similar fate and in no time, the third had stepped up and been felled. Agamemnon strode from the field, unwrapping his hands as he did so, and claimed his third coin.

He bundled the leather himantes and passed them to a slave, murmuring something with a fierce look, and the slave ran off. Then he sauntered to where the King and his family sat among the spectators, stopping in front of Klytemestra and her husband.

"Your murderous father will not keep his stolen throne for long," Agamemnon sneered.

"His throne was stolen by your father first," Tantalus retorted.

"He deserved it, for stealing my mother's virtue. My father took what was his by right, his due payment for his wife's adultery."

"My father was innocent!"

"My mother confessed, right before she died trying to birth a bastard."

"You lie!"

"You weren't there."

That night, in her old room, Klytie tried to reason with her husband.

"You must be careful," she cried. "He has murder in his eye."

"What can he do? I'm not unprotected. I can hold my own in a fight, and your brothers are always at my side. He wouldn't dare."

"I think he would dare, and he'd succeed. He's only waiting for the right moment."

"I think you worry too much, my dear."

The next day, the suitors paired up for the wrestling. In a contest of pure brute strength, where the winner was the first to force his opponent to the ground, the mismatched bouts ended quickly while the more balanced pairs took longer. Arms linked, pushing each other back and forth, the pairs grimaced as muscles bulged.

In the second round, Menestheus and Patroklos quickly despatched their opponents, leaving three pairs on the field. Agamemnon faced Idomeneos, his mother's cousin from Crete, who raised his hands in surrender, allowing Agamemnon to win without a fight.

A few moments later, Aias won against Antilochus, leaving Askalaphos against Diomedes. The son of Ares held his strength in check as the spectators followed his every move. He smiled as he drank in the adoration of the crowd.

The only warning of the strike was a slight change in expression as his evident enjoyment of the attention gave way to boredom and he twisted, forcing his opponent to the ground in one bone crunching thud.

The final round was again a revolving contest of five.

The first to wrestle were Patroklos and Menestheus, with Patroklos the clear winner. Then Askalaphos stepped up. He approached his opponent, face showing his determination. He linked arms with Patroklos and, in a sudden movement, the younger man was on the ground.

The son of Ares turned to the next contender, holding his arms wide, welcoming the charge of Aias. His god given strength unshackled, Askalaphos clashed with Aias. After a brief struggle, the son of Telemon was on the ground at the feet of the son of Ares. Askalaphos beckoned to Agamemnon.

With a snarl, Agamemnon charged and the two clashed. The momentum of his charge pushed the son of Ares back, but he soon rallied and leant into the challenge. The two grunted with effort and the crowd hushed. They seemed evenly matched, despite the divine prowess of the son of Ares.

Agamemnon bristled with brute power, his thick shoulders bulging with effort. Askalaphos gritted his teeth, forcing his opponent back with difficulty. The bout lengthened, both contenders struggling to stay upright. Askalaphos growled, giving in to his anger that some mortal man might actually best him in his favourite sport.

Agamemnon pushed him back and the son of Ares almost faltered. He screamed his frustration, gave an almighty shove and Agamemnon lost his grip. But he did not fall. As Agamemnon charged in again, Askalaphos raised his eyes to the sky and yelled one word.

"Father!"

Darkness settled over the sky. Askalaphos seemed to tower over his opponent, power emanating from him like a black cloud. His arms grasped his opponent, blessed with super human strength, lifting him off his feet.

With a casual toss, the son of Ares dashed Agamemnon to the ground. He raised his darkened eyes to the crowd, the power of the god lingering for a moment. Then the darkness left him and he seemed to shrink a little, his human eyes dancing in his victory as he walked from the field.

Agamemnon clambered to his feet and rushed from the field. As he passed the King and his family, Tantalus called out to him.

"Not so cocky today, are we?"

Agamemnon scowled. "If that daddy's boy hadn't called for help I would have won."

"Then you're repaid for your weighted hands yesterday."

"Are you calling me a cheat?"

"I call it as I see it."

With a wordless snarl, Agamemnon charged at him, but Castor and Pollox were there, appearing out of nowhere to block his advance.

"Enjoy your protection while you can," growled Agamemnon as he stalked off.

Klytemestra watched him go with fear in her heart, rocking the babe to hush his startled whimpers.

"Why must you bait him so?" she asked her husband. "You're asking for trouble."

"I'm sorry, my dear," he shrugged. "Sometimes I just can't help it."

Over the next few days, more events were contested. The armed combat, in which the combatants fought in full armour with swords until the winner scored the first cut, was eventually won by Aias. The discus, a large iron disc thrown in a whirling motion, went to Protesilaos, the contestant who threw the furthest.

Agamemnon, known throughout the land as the greatest spear thrower, won the javelin. His swagger as he taunted her husband set Klytie's teeth on edge.

"The contest isn't over yet," Tantalus said.

"It's as good as mine, now. I have the lead and I won't lose it for anyone."

"You're not the winner yet and, if I tally true, Aias is equal with you, with at least two others very close behind."

"Aias?" he spat. "That boy might have done well in the strength events, but he's no racer."

"Don't be so sure, the footrace is next and I know you're not as fleet-of-foot as some others here."

"We shall see," he growled.

"And if you win, your brother gets a wife. How very noble of you."

"You think I'm incapable of helping my brother simply because he needs me?"

"We both know you have your own plan."

Agamemnon laughed. "You're afraid I might win! Then I'll take your borrowed army from you and claim my prize."

"What prize?"

"Why, nothing less than a kingdom and a bride."

"I won't allow it!"

"You won't stop it!"

Seated together in the megaron at the end of another day of contests, Tyndareos and his daughters held a light banter with their guests. Tantalus stood to one side, close by his wife, ignoring the scowls of his cousin and refusing to be drawn into an argument.

A commotion at the doorway caught Klytie's attention and her brothers, Castor and Polydeuces, hurried to enforce order as a newcomer, fair of hair with a muscular frame and an air of haughty self-confidence, made his limping way toward the King. Agamemnon rushed to his side, offering a hand, and Klytie heard her husband curse under his breath.

"Who is it?" she whispered.

"Menelaos," Tantalus replied.

"My lord Tyndareos," Agamemnon boomed. "I'd like to present my brother, Menelaos, arrived safely from Argos."

"You are welcome, Menelaos," said the King. Klytie heard a hiss from her husband and calmed him with a hand on his arm.

"Thank you, my lord, I'm glad to be here at last," he said as his ice blue eyes roved over the two princesses, his injured leg no impediment to his lithe, athletic stance.

"And is this the beauteous Helene?" he said with a broad smile. "My lady you are fair as the fleece of the golden ram that once graced my late lamented father's herd. You shine like the sun and we are all rendered dull in your presence."

Helene leaned over to the King, an eager hand clutching his arm. "Oh, Papa, I want him!" she murmured in excitement.

"Hush, girl," said Tyndareos with a frown. "Menelaos, your brother has championed you well, but now you're here do you intent to take his place in the contests?"

"My lord, as you can see, my injury would prevent my success in any athletic event but, if you permit, I will compete in the chariot races."

"But Papa," Helene cried. "Must we continue now? I've made my choice!"

"Be quiet, child!" the King snapped. "We can't cancel the contest, it would be unfair to the other suitors. He must follow the same rules as everyone else."

But Klytemestra was not so sure. She felt certain these brothers had no intention of following any rule but their own.

4

To the Victor Go the Spoils

The footrace was divided into four heats of five each. At the end of the heats, four finalists would race to find a winner. The first three heats saw some strong contenders eliminated. Menestheus, Patroklos and Diomedes all fell to the likes of Askalaphos, Elephenor and Protesilaos.

The contenders of the fourth heat lined up at the head of the track. In their number were Antilochus, Idomeneos and another Klytie did not know. At either end of the line stood Agamemnon and his chief rival, Aias.

As the horn sounded, the runners sprang forward, heading at speed down the track, toward the post at the other end. The contestants began to spread out as the slowest fell behind. Aias and Agamemnon jostled for the lead, Idomeneos a step behind.

At such distance, Klytie could not see their faces, but she could see Idomeneos closing the gap, coming up behind Aias, breathing down his neck. The younger man faltered, shrugging at the annoyance at his back.

As they neared the post, Agamemnon took a sharp turn, cutting across the path of his opponent. The younger man veered to the side in an attempt to avoid a collision, but the turning post was in his path.

Idomeneos came up behind, forcing him forward, and suddenly Aias was on the ground, rolling in the dirt as

Agamemnon took the lead on the return run. Idomeneos jogged after him, but made no effort to catch him as Agamemnon sauntered across the line.

Beside her, Klytie heard her sister squeal with delight, and heard a low, murmured reply. In a blatant expression of favouritism, Helene had invited Menelaos to sit with her to watch the foot races. Klytie glanced across to see Helene jump up and throw herself at Menelaos, clinging to his neck in an unseemly show of favour. Menelaos laughed, arms about the girl, enjoying her attention.

The four finalists lined up. Askalaphos, Elephenor, Protesilaos and Agamemnon. At her side, Klytie felt her sister's excitement, heard her girlish chatter and the deep, whispered replies of the man at her side. Any one of the finalists could win this race. Agamemnon was ahead in the tally, but any of his nearest rivals could catch him now.

Agamemnon sneered across at his opponents. Askalaphos stood still, eyes skyward as black clouds blotted out the sun. The horn sounded and the race began. At first, the field seemed even, but two contestants began to creep forward as they neared the post. Agamemnon pushed ahead, legs pounding the earth.

Without warning, Askalaphos surged forward, reaching the pole first, launching himself into the turn. One hand grabbed at the pole, body swung into the curve, legs flew in a graceful arc. Hand grasping the pole, the son of Ares flung his body around the corner, completely leaving the ground with the momentum of his turn.

Legs came forward and hand released the pole. Askalaphos flew forward, landing mid-stride and racing headlong down the final stretch toward the finish. He had left the competition far behind, the strength of the god speeding him on to victory.

Helene jumped to her feet, her face contorted in anger.

"How dare he! He cheated, using a god's power to win."

"Now, Helene, you have no proof of that," said her father.

"No Proof? You all saw it!"

"I saw an athlete perform a trick of training, nothing more."

"How can you say that?" she fumed.

"Calm yourself, child."

"I won't be calm. If he can do it, so can I!" she cried and stormed off.

The night was late when Klytemestra was awoken from her slumber by a hungry child. Gathering up the boy from his cradle by her bed, Klytie settled into the cushions with the babe at her breast. She hummed a little in contentment while the boy fed. Glancing at her sleeping husband, she smiled through bitter tears.

Tantalus refused to see the danger ahead, the murderous intent of the sons of Atreus. There was a curse on her husband's house and she sensed it coming with a keen edge at the corner of her mind's eye.

When the baby slept again, Klytie gathered her cloak about her and slipped out of the room. She had intended to take some air on the wall, but a light flickered in the courtyard and she followed. Someone was making their way silently out of the palace, across the courtyard and out the gate, heading for the temple complex.

Heading across the ridge, Klytie saw the figure slip into the shrine of Zeus and hurried to follow, thinking she knew who it was. Who else would be sneaking into the house of the great god in the middle of the night? But why?

Klytie pushed the door carefully, slipping through the small gap and closing it again. A small light flickered at the altar. Helene was there and Klytie watched from the shadows as she pulled something from under her robe and placed it on the altar, stripped off her nightdress and stood naked before the altar. She raised her arms and Klytie saw light flash on the bronze knife.

Bringing the knife down, Helene sang praise to the god as she raised blood-drenched hands and spread the dark stain across her breasts and torso, covering her face and arms, all the while mumbling something under her breath. Then she stood still for a long time, eyes closed. When she finally stirred, Klytemestra came forward. Helene jumped when she caught sight of her sister.

"What are you doing here?"

"I was about to ask you the same thing," said Klytie dryly.

"What does it look like I'm doing? I'm praying to my father."

"Why?"

"To ask him to make Menelaos win tomorrow."

"Oh, Helene, why?"

"I should think that was obvious. I want him to win."

"But he's our enemy..."

"I don't know what you're talking about."

"Don't you realise what will happen if he wins?"

Helene shook her head. "What do you mean?"

"His brother intends to kill Tantalus and take me as his own."

"Why would he do that?" Helene snorted.

"As revenge. He blames my husband for his father's death."

"And so he should."

"Helene, you don't know the whole story."

"I know enough to see that you hate him... for no good reason."

"For every reason!"

"You just don't want to see me happy!"

"Helene, please..."

"No! I won't listen to your slander. Leave me be!"

In four heats of five contestants, the two-horse chariot races were run. Menelaos limped out onto the field for his heat, leading his team into position. The crowd murmured and the other contestants watched, some friendly and others unimpressed.

For months, these men had conducted a civil rivalry, taking their chances with Helene with good grace on the most part and building a bond that would last a lifetime. But this man was a stranger, represented until now by his abrasive brother. Taking a moment to check the rig, Menelaos appeared to be unwilling to engage with the other men.

He clambered up into the light racing chariot and stood at the ready. Klytie had to admit he was an arresting figure, standing tall and athletic, his injury no impediment now. He held the reins with a casual confidence and spared a wave for Helene. The girl squealed and waved in return.

A horn blew and they began to move, sedately at first while the barrier, drawn by a team of four horses ahead of the pack, held them back, keeping the pace steady. Then when all were on the move, the team at the barrier pulled to the side, away from the pack and, one by one, the chariots surged forward. A second horn blew and the race was on.

The teams raced headlong down the track toward the post, Diomedes the first to reach it and make the dangerous turn, his chariot flinging itself around on one wheel behind the pounding hooves.

The next two attempted the turn together. With a clash of metal and a ripping of wood the wheels locked and the braces tangled, sending both chariots tumbling.

Menelaos took the turn next, with the final contestant

some distance behind him. He carefully navigated the wreckage littering the corner, and straightened into the final stretch. Diomedes was some distance ahead, but Menelaos slapped the reins and gave a loud cry to his team.

With an astonishing burst of speed, the chariot seemed to fly toward the finish, coming closer to the leader. Beside Klytemestra, Helene screamed at the heavens, jumping up and down in her excitement. The lead chariot seemed to falter, the horses stumbling.

By the time Diomedes had righted his team, Menelaos was upon him. The two raced neck and neck toward the final post. Menelaos yelled to his team and Helene screamed in entreaty to Zeus. At the very last moment, Menelaos edged forward, passing the post a nose ahead of his rival.

"One more race and the prize is ours," crowed Agamemnon from the crowd near the King's chair.

"One more race and you will lose your lead," Tantalus retorted. "He races with the best of the best. You won't win."

"Oh, my brother will win. There's no better chariot driver than Menelaos."

Four finalists lined up at the head of the track. This time, they each drove four horses pulling a heavy war chariot, and they would race twice around the posts. Menelaos, Askalaphos, Elephenor and Aias. Menelaos held the lead, but the contest was so close now, any one of the others could force another race if they won.

The horn blew and the chariots lumbered forward, the guide rig pulled out of the way. The second horn had barely begun to sound and the contestants were already on the move. The first leg was vicious as the four finalists jostled for position. Nearing the first post, someone had to give way. But none would give ground.

The larger chariots needed to slow to round the post

safely. The first to enter the turn was Aias, carefully turning his team in a wide arc. Elephenor sped into the turn with Askalaphos close behind. The son of Ares forced his team onto the inside, squeezing through the narrowing gap. Too late, Elephenor realised the danger and tried to pull up. His team shied and the nearside horse clipped the rear of Askalaphos' chariot. With a squeal, the horse went down, pulling the whole team with it. Elephenor jumped clear as his rig toppled, rolling with the momentum of the missed turn, horses screaming.

In the rear, Menelaos swung wide and negotiated the turn, spurring his team on in an attempt to catch the others. Far ahead, Aias was already rounding the starting post and heading back up the straight. Menelaos sped after Askalaphos and the second turn.

At the far post, Elephenor was tugging at his shattered rig, trying at least to save his horses from the war chariot now bearing down on them. At the last moment he jumped out of the way as Aias came thundering down the track, heading for the post.

Elephenor had managed to pull most of the rig off the track, but as Aias came into the turn his inside wheel hit a stray piece of wreckage. Once overbalanced the heavy chariot was impossible to right, and the whole rig toppled sideways in a tangle of broken wood and flailing hooves.

Askalaphos approached the carnage at full speed, heading wide and taking a long circular path around the turn. Menelaos followed his lead, but at the crucial high point of the turn a horse shied and his chariot pitched. Unable to maintain his balance on his injured leg, Menelaos fell from the chariot as his team continued through the turn.

Rolling in the dust, Menelaos came to his feet. He lifted his fingers to his lips and gave a piercing whistle.

His team turned unguided, crossing the centre of the field and coming back into the turn. Swinging aboard as they passed, Menelaos spurred his team after the son of Ares. In the crowd, Helene pleaded with the heavens.

The two chariots sped down the track. Helene sat with her family, watching eagerly and bouncing on the edge of her seat. Klytemestra felt almost embarrassed by her sister's behaviour. She sat forward in her own chair in fear.

He could not win, Klytie prayed. It would spell the end of everything. The brothers would seize the army of Sparta and exact their revenge on Tantalus and his father.

As Menelaos tore down the straight it seemed his final dash was futile. Askalaphos was almost at the final post. Helene screamed entreaty to the sky. Without warning, there was a loud crash of thunder, and in an instant the lead chariot fell apart.

The son of Ares was on the ground as his team stumbled at the sudden lightening of their load. He raced to catch his horses, unharness the nearest and swing up onto its back. But the delay had been all Menelaos needed to close the gap. As he thundered past, Askalaphos screamed his divine father's name.

A flurry of black wings, a cloud of large feathered predators, soared across the path of Menelaos and his team. The horses reared as the birds flew into their faces and the chariot wheels broke in the melee. It was Menelaos' turn to unhitch a horse and make a last dash to the finish.

Askalaphos was almost there. Klytemestra heard her sister scream to the great god. There was a violent flash of light and a great clap of thunder, and once more Askalaphos was on the ground. Menelaos passed him, but again the black birds attacked.

Thrown from his horse, Menelaos clutched at Askalaphos as he tried to run past. Catching his rival's arm, Menelaos swung a fist and landed a heavy blow across the side of his jaw. As Askalaphos fell to the ground unconscious, Menelaos limped slowly past the post.

Amongst the spectators, two voices rang out. Helene, squealing in delight, ran out onto the field to throw herself at her new husband-to-be. But the other voice was more sinister. A deep laughter, building into a great roar of victory. Agamemnon turned on the King and his family. Raising one hand, he pointed straight at Klytemestra's husband.

"Now your army is mine!" he crowed.

"They'll never follow you," Tantalus retorted.

"When I claim my bride they'll have no choice."

"You'll have to kill me first!"

"That can be arranged!"

5

A Kingdom in Flux

With her father on one hand and her husband on the other, Klytemestra tried to ignore the giggles of her sister at her father's other side. Helene's new husband charmed and flattered, but Klytie knew it was an empty gesture. He may revel in the attention of his beautiful young wife, but the sugar coating of his manner hid something darker.

Lifting her eyes to the crowd, Klytie caught the gaze of the other son of Atreus. Agamemnon had kept a covetous watch all evening. Klytie felt his eyes pricking at her, forcing her to look again. She tried to ignore him and engage her husband, but he too was watching Agamemnon. Klytie shivered, feeling the sinister mood come buffeting at her from that black stare.

"My son," said Tyndareos, leaning in. "Take that frown off your face and welcome your brother."

"No brother of mine, my lord," Tantalus hissed.

"I know there's bad blood between you, but you are blood kin nonetheless, now kin by marriage as well."

"My lord, you were led into this marriage treaty by deceit and trickery, I'll have no part of it."

"I saw no deceit, no trickery, my son. Menelaos and his champion competed alongside all the other suitors and won the hand of Helene. I am honour bound to adhere to the agreement laid down at the beginning of this contest."

"If you didn't see it, you're blinded, my lord."

"He doesn't see it because it's not there," said Agamemnon from the crowd.

"It's there," Tantalus growled. "And I'm not blinded by you."

"You're blinded by your own prejudice and a refusal to believe in me."

"No, I refuse to believe your lies. You came here with the express purpose of winning an army, with falseness on your tongue and murder in your heart."

"Spoken by one who knows."

"What's that supposed to mean?"

"Didn't you come here with the exact same purpose? Isn't that the very reason you chose your bride?"

"Of course not!" he said with a glance at his wife. Klytie smiled and touched his arm, remembering his confession.

"Ah, but it is. How soon after your marriage were you marching with an army to Mycenae? With the express purpose of murdering my father and taking my kingdom."

"Your father did the murdering first. Your father took the Kingdom first. Mycenae should have been mine."

Klytie clutched his arm. "Be careful," she whispered.

"In whose world?" Agamemnon spat. "Your father seduced and defiled my mother, why should he have kept his throne?"

Tantalus shrugged off his wife's hand, lurching to his feet. "You have no idea what your father did to us."

"Nothing that wasn't justified by his wife's adultery. Your father deserved everything he got."

"Children killed, kingdom stolen, cast out from our rightful place?"

"Yes! I grew up without a mother!"

"And I grew up without a home."

"Then you know how I feel."

Tantalus gave a mocking laugh. "When you have lived in exile, denied your birthright for twenty years, then you will truly know how it feels."

"You got everything you deserved."

"Your father murdered my brothers, and served them up as meat for the dinner table!"

Klytie gasped. Why had he not mentioned that?

"That's a lie!" Agamemnon growled.

"I was there! I saw their little fingers dressed up on the platter..."

"How dare you! What you suggest is..."

"It's the truth, cousin," Tantalus said. "Your father was a monster."

Klytie hissed. "Sit down, husband, you're playing with fire."

"Woman!" Agamemnon roared, pointing an accusing finger at her. "You keep silent and remember your place."

"You leave her out of this," Tantalus said.

"She's at the heart of this. She gave you the power to commit murder."

"My actions were justified."

"As is my revenge," Agamemnon yelled.

"My father is finally restored to his rightful place, and I will not allow you to jeopardise that."

"Not allow? You'll have no choice," he screamed.

"So you keep saying. You're all bluff, Agamemnon. You don't have the guts to follow through!"

Agamemnon roared his anger, reaching for his sword.

"So what do you intend to do with that? Slice the ewe from the spit?" Tantalus sneered.

"If you are the spit and your wife the ewe," Agamemnon roared.

Pulling his arm back, a great scream of rage ripping out of him, Agamemnon hurled the sword. It flew hard and fast.

Klytie screamed as her husband was hit in the chest, the sword driving through his body, the momentum throwing him back. He hit the wall, leaving a slick red trail as he slid down to the ground and was still.

"I should have done that a long time ago," said Agamemnon with satisfaction.

Through a haze of tears, Klytie saw her brothers closing in on Agamemnon, too late to stop the horror. Vision blurred, she saw the sneer as he shook off their hands. She covered her mouth, hiccupping as the sobs threatened to burst out of her.

"I have the right of revenge, you can't touch me," Agamemnon snapped, breaking free of the brothers' grasp. "And, by the right of victory in single combat, I claim my prize."

With that, Agamemnon approached the table, vaulted over and took the seat next to Klytemestra. She shrank back from the smell of wine and the leer in the man's eye.

"Smile, my dear, this is your wedding day," he smirked, raising his voice to address the incredulous crowd. "Drink hearty, my friends, this is now a double wedding!"

Klytie stirred at the muffled sound of a crying babe. Dragging herself painfully out of the bed, she stumbled to the next room to find her maid. She paced the room, rocking and bouncing, the little boy protesting loudly in her arms. Klytie reached out her arms for him.

"I'm sorry, my lady, I tried to keep him happy, but he's hungry."

"You should have woken me."

"I didn't want to disturb you, my lady, after..."

"The less said about that, the better," Klytie mumbled.

Settling into a chair, Klytie put the babe to the breast and sighed as she sank back into the cushion. The maid fussed over her, clicking her tongue and shaking her head.

"Let me go and find a salve for those bruises, my lady..."

Klytie shook her head, shifting position slightly as the weight of her growing son put pressure on her sore arms.

"No, you've done enough for one night," Klytie murmured. "You can go to bed now."

The maid cocked her head dubiously, but then nodded. Finally alone, Klytemestra crumbled, her calm veneer vanishing as the tears fell. She stared down at her little boy as he fed, the tears dripping on his face, and rocked him gently.

Through her sobs, she relived the events of the night before. The face of her dead husband swam before her eyes, the blood pooling about him and the bronze sword standing upright in his lifeless body. She saw her brothers taking the body away, leaving a gruesome trail through the hall.

She tried to suppress her sobs, dreading the thought of waking the man now in her bed, who had dragged her screaming from the feast. She had pleaded with her father, but even he had been powerless to stop him.

She had fought him, but it had only made him more determined to have her. She was his property now. In her heart, she would never call herself his wife.

The boy was grumbling again. He was so hungry, made to wait for hours while his mother was... She coughed down that thought and switched him to the other breast, groaning as her aching muscles protested.

Her life with Tantalus had been so promising. She had been happy with her fate. But now, here she sat, widowed at fifteen, taken unwillingly to wife by her husband's murderer, with no recourse to the law.

She may be a Spartan princess, but to the rest of the world she was just another woman, fated to be married off to the richest or most powerful, or indeed taken by force.

What would life bring to her now?

When Klytie awoke, she was still in the chair, the sunlight breaking the dimness in bright pinpricks through the shutters. She moaned softly, lifting a hand to her aching head, realising with a jolt that the baby was gone. She stood carefully, muscles stiff and sore, calling for her maid.

"Where is my son?" she asked when the woman entered.

"My lady?"

"Did you come and get him this morning?"

"No, my lady, I haven't been here."

"Then where is he?"

"I... I'll go see..."

Klytie moved stiffly to the window, pushing the shutters wide and letting in the morning sun. When she turned from the window, she froze in place, staring. Agamemnon stood in the doorway, the bright light falling on his face, capturing a look of pure disdain.

"Did you think I would leave a cuckoo in the nest to stain my house and threaten my future?"

Klytemestra gasped as her heart thudded in her chest. "What have you done?"

"Only what was necessary," he shrugged.

Fear sank like a cold stone in the pit of her stomach as a wail worked its way upward, threatening to rip its way out of her. She ran headlong from the room, calling frantically for her father, her brothers, anyone who might help her find her son.

The palace servants searched to no avail. Castor and Polydeuces led a small group of soldiers out into the rocky countryside. By the time the little boy was found, high on an exposed hilltop, stuffed into a crevice between two boulders, it was too late.

Klytemestra was given no time to mourn. She stood in

her favourite brother's arms, eyes dry as the shock of recent events took hold. Pollox stood close beside them, his blue eyes troubled.

Together they watched as the wagons were loaded, watched Agamemnon strut before the army he now commanded. Soon, Agamemnon strode over to drag his new wife away. Castor held her even more tightly.

"Stop this unseemly display, woman," he sneered. "Get to your place in the wagon."

Klytie stood tall, pride forcing an angry retort. "I will not ride in that wagon. Get me a horse!"

Agamemnon roared and grabbed at her. He lifted her bodily and slung her over his shoulder, ignoring the protests of her brothers and dumped her, kicking and screaming, into the wagon.

"You'll do as I say!" he huffed.

As Klytie's brothers rushed to her aid, Agamemnon turned to face them, arms up in an effort to appease them.

"I promise you, your sister won't be harmed if she learns to curb her tongue and swallow her pride."

The boys stopped in their advance, sharing a dubious look.

"Come now, boys," the man purred, his gruff manner tempered by a honeyed slickness in his tone. "We're family now and families look after their own."

"What are you plotting now?" Castor frowned.

"No plot, but I do have a proposal."

"Oh?" mumbled Polydeuces.

"I hear you boys like a bit of adventure..."

"What makes you say that?"

"My dear Pollox, you can't deny it. I heard what you did when Helene was taken by Theseus a few years ago. You chased him to Attica and took her back, and put Menestheus on the throne. You two have built quite a name for yourselves."

"So?" Castor said.

"So, I could use a little of that spirit. Once long ago a ram with fleece of pure gold graced the herds of Mycenae. My uncle seduced my mother and made her give him the ram so that he might be king. My father cast him out, but he took the ram with him and it was never seen again. I hear that Pelias, the King of Iolcus, is funding a voyage to find my father's lost treasure, the fleece of the golden ram. Perhaps you could join them and somehow bring the fleece back to Mycenae rather than letting Iolcus have it."

"Castor, don't do it," Klytie cried. "He's only trying to get you out of the way. Please, Pollox, don't listen to him!"

"Be quiet, woman," Agamemnon snapped. "You sit there and wait, the carts will be leaving soon."

Klytie could see her brothers were intrigued. Their love of adventure would get them killed one day, she thought. She watched in trepidation as Agamemnon led the boys away.

Klytie's cart rattled and bumped along the road ahead of the supply train as they lumbered slowly north toward Mycenae. She was ignored by everyone around her, but she did not notice. She stared at nothing, numbed by grief.

The miles passed with little to break the monotony. By midday, Klytie slumped in a daze. She ignored the meagre meal offered by the cart driver, took only a few sips of the tepid water. Baked in the hot sun, the front of her dress soaked in the milk that dripped from her painfully engorged breasts, she was sorely bedraggled by the time the cart finally reached camp some hours after dusk.

Agamemnon lifted her bodily from the cart and took her straight to his command tent amid jeers and whistles from his officers. He pointed her to a small basin of water.

"Get yourself washed, you stink!" he said ungraciously.

Klytemestra held her tongue and staggered to the water, taking a long drink before stripping off her rancid dress to wash. Then she attempted to wash the dress in what remained of the water. Before she could finish she found herself lifted off her feet and dumped unceremoniously on the camp bed in the far corner of the tent.

She gritted her teeth as her brutish husband forced himself on her, stifling her own cries as his crushing weight pressed against her breasts bringing white-hot pain shooting through her torso. She squeezed her eyes shut, but the tears came anyway and the screams fought to break out between teeth that bit down on lips in an effort to stop them.

With a curse, Agamemnon rolled off her. "What in hades is wrong with you?" he growled.

"You're hurting me!" she cried, unable to keep silent.

"If you'd show me proper respect and do your duty as my wife without protest it wouldn't hurt so much!"

"I'm not talking about that, you oaf!" she screamed.

"Then what's your problem?" he shouted.

"This," she said, gingerly cupping her tender breasts.

"What are you talking about?"

With a stifled curse, she reached out and grabbed his hand, placing it on one engorged breast. He looked at her in bewilderment and shook his head.

"Feel it," she growled.

He squeezed slightly and she swallowed a sharp intake of breath. His eyes narrowed as he realised something was not normal. He lifted his other hand to feel the other breast and Klytie bit her lips again. Agamemnon looked at her in astonishment, really meeting her eyes for the first time.

"Why are they so hard?"

"They're full of milk."

"What?"

"What did you think would happen when you stole my baby?" she said bitterly. "He should have fed several times today."

He shook his head again.

"He didn't feed," she said through gritted teeth. "They're full."

"Oh!" he said finally. "What can you do about it?"

"I can't do a damned thing. I can squeeze out some, but it won't do much good."

"So I'm going to have to put up with your screaming every time I bed you?"

"Until they dry up, yes."

He paced. "There must be another way."

"There is. But I don't suppose you have a suckling baby somewhere in your retinue?"

He shook his head.

"So someone else has to suck it out."

His face screwed up. "You can't be serious. I'm not letting some slave touch my wife! Especially not... like that."

"Then you'll have to do it."

He stared at her, dumbfounded.

"It's your choice," she shrugged. "Or you could leave me alone for a while..."

"You'd like that, wouldn't you? I know how much you dislike me."

"So, give me a reason to like you. Ease my pain."

He hesitated, looking her up and down. "Much as you may think me a monster, I do care." With that, he stepped up to her and clutched her to him, bending to take one swollen nipple.

"Gently," she moaned, stifling a scream.

He lowered her to the bed as he suckled one breast then the other. Klytie felt her agony dissipate as the flesh softened. Finally, relaxed into submission, she allowed him to have her.

"Thank you," she whispered when it was over.

"I could have had your sister for myself, you know," he replied. "I chose to give her to my brother. I wanted you for your beauty and your fire, though you never gave me the chance to tell you so."

"You came to Sparta with one purpose. You had murder in your heart from the moment you saw Tantalus."

"I had right on my side. I was justified."

"My husband was a good man and you killed him in cold blood. I concede you had the right of revenge. But didn't he have the same right?"

"Enough, woman! You shouldn't speak to me like this. You've been taken in by his lies and I'm your husband now."

"I don't doubt that you feel you were justified. If you'd stopped there, I might have been more willing to accept you. But you took my son, stole him from my arms as I slept, had him taken out and left to die. That I can't accept and will never forgive."

6
A City Reclaimed

Another day trapped. Forced to stay put inside the command tent, Klytemestra paced. Day after day of heat and stale air, eyes accustomed now to the dim light broken by a small brazier in the centre, which only served to make the tent more stifling. Outside she could hear the soldiers moving about, the daily routine unchanged. But today, something was different.

There was a lightness in the voices as they called across the camp, a new urgency in the footsteps hurrying past. And the sounds of battle coming from the walls were gone. A sudden shaft of light burst into the dim tent as the door flap was flung open and Agamemnon strode in. Klytemestra rushed toward him.

"What's happening? Please tell me."

"Today the city will fall," he crowed.

"How do you know?"

"The sappers have finished their tunnel, the fire is lit. Soon the wall will be breached and we will win through. Today I finally come home."

As he strode from the tent once more, Klytie sank down into the cushions. At least she would be out of this damned tent, and maybe she would get a proper bath soon. But what would happen to Thyestes, the father-in-law she had never met, kin no more.

She somehow knew this would be his last stand, that he would not survive this day, and it made her sad. Klytie had no idea how long she had been cloistered in the commander's tent. She had lost track of the days. Weeks, she thought.

She put a hand to her stomach, the awareness of new life still a private treasure. She hoped this family would end its feud now. She hoped this child would be born in peace, that the curse would not come again.

Sometime in the late afternoon, Klytie heard a loud rumble, followed by a colossal crashing roar. There were cheers and hurried footsteps, thousands of feet pounding the earth as they ran to the breach. Klytie settled down to wait, listening to the receding sounds as the army entered the city.

At the head of the defending army, the King and his son rallied the troops and tried to push the invader back toward the breach. The Spartan mercenaries, so recently loyal to Thyestes, swarmed into the city at the order of the King's greatest enemy.

His son stayed close by his side, desperate to keep his newfound father safe. But the King knew this would be his last battle. At the head of the enemy, he saw his dead brother's son surging forward, his great war cry echoing through the city.

"Captain!" the King yelled.

"Yes, my lord?"

"Get my son out of here, get him to safety."

"No, father," his son cried. "I can look after myself. I want to see that man killed!"

"It won't happen today, son. Look at him. He's too powerful for either of us."

"Then we'll face him together."

"No! You're young and inexperienced, I'm old and tired and he's a warrior in his prime. The most I can do is to give you the chance to get away."

"I'm not going anywhere!"

The King turned his back on the approaching enemy. He put his hands on his son's shoulders, gazing into his face, heedless of the battle raging around them.

"Son, listen to me. These past few months have been more wonderful than I ever dreamed. To find you alive after all these years, to regain my throne. I can't imagine a better way to end my life. But it's over; we're defeated. I need to know you're safe. You need to vanish into the background, go back to your old life, hide away until you're strong enough to vanquish him and avenge me."

"Father..."

"No, I won't listen. I won't allow you to risk everything for me. If he sees you now, your life is forfeit too. If he ever discovers your identity, he'll destroy you without a thought. You need time to plan, time to plot his downfall. Promise me, you won't rush needlessly to your death."

"I can't do it, father. I can't go back to that. I can't go back to living under his thumb, at the mercy of his cruelty. I can't do it."

"You can and you must."

"Come, my lord," said the Captain. "Let's go."

"Father, please don't make me do this."

"Goodbye, my son. Remember me."

The King turned away as the Captain dragged his unwilling charge out of the fray. Thyestes lifted his sword, ready for the clash of his enemy's rage. If this was the end, he would face it with honour, and show that upstart son of Atreus his true worth. He may not defeat him, but he would see him humbled before the end.

*

After what seemed hours of near silence, broken only by the occasional cheer or crash of falling masonry, Klytie's seclusion was shattered by a rabble of soldiers rushing into the tent.

They gathered her up and ushered her outside, settling her unceremoniously in a sedan chair and lifting her, chair and all. The chair was not so much a gesture of respect to her, she thought, than a symbol of prestige, a display of Agamemnon's power and an announcement to the city that his queen had arrived.

As the chair was carried slowly up the hill toward the citadel, Klytie gazed in wonder. She sat back and stared at the approaching walls, honeyed limestone shimmering in the late afternoon sun. The famous golden walls of Mycenae.

The sheer size of the fortifications took her breath away. Finally, they reached the level of the wall, with its immense stone blocks laid so perfectly she could hardly tell where they met. The soldiers turned into the final approach, the road flanked by massive walls. Ahead loomed the great gate. Klytemestra held her breath in awe.

Surrounding the gate, a great sandstone wall glistened in the setting sun, which cut a shaft of light down the shadowed approach. The wall shone, the tiny grains in the rock catching the light and reflecting it, making the rock seem golden in truth.

Four massive golden limestone blocks surrounded the huge wooden doors of the gate. Carried closer, Klytemestra stared upward with a shiver. In the relieving triangle above the lintel, flanking a classic Minoan column, two enormous carved lions reared up, roaring down at her, daring her to come further.

As they neared the gate, a guard gave a call and the doors swung slowly inward, pulled from the inside. Her valiant escort stepped up to the gate, taking the passage carefully and heading up the processional ramp, past buildings and shops and a large circular enclosure to the right.

Half way up, they turned left to cross between rows of buildings until they reached a higher path where they turned right again to follow the line of the hill and continued on toward the palace.

At last, they reached the top of the ramp, coming out into a flat, irregular courtyard flanked on one side by the huge citadel wall and ending in front, where it met the high, imposing edifice of the palace itself.

To the left, at the grand entrance to the palace, the soldiers lowered the chair and Klytemestra stood. She was led up a long staircase, turning at the landing and continuing upward until she reached the first in a series of staterooms. The soldiers turned right, and led her out into another courtyard where many more soldiers and servants were milling about.

Klytie felt their eyes on her as she made her way through the crowd, following her guides. Crossing the courtyard, they stepped between two columns and up onto a low porch. They entered the antechamber and crossed into the megaron, with its central hearth and four columns.

There, only a few soldiers and a handful of servants gathered. Klytie approached the King's seat on the right wall, where Agamemnon regarded her approach with hooded eyes.

"Welcome, wife," he boomed.

Klytie looked around apprehensively. Every eye in the room was on her. She nodded to Agamemnon but held her tongue.

"Slave," he motioned. A young man stepped forward, green eyes flashing as he stared at her. "Escort my wife to my private chamber."

"Yes, my lord," the slave mumbled.

"May I visit the bath first?" Klytie blurted.

"You'll do as I bid," Agamemnon snapped. "My generals and I will bathe first. You'll wait in my chamber until summoned."

Klytie ground her teeth, biting down a bitter retort. The slave motioned for her to follow, eyes boring into her, a gleam of anger barely masked. The man looked as if she had done him an immense disservice! But behind those eyes was something familiar.

She walked after the young man, who moved stiff-backed out of the room without looking to see that she followed. They came out onto the porch and turned right, taking a small set of stairs and moving right again to a well presented reception room beside the megaron, with a bench to one side and beautifully painted frescoes imitating curtains. As the young man hurried down the adjoining corridor toward another flight of stairs, Klytie quickened her pace in an attempt to keep up. But she soon fell behind, unable to match his long stride.

"Wait, slave," she called.

He spun to face her. "I'm no slave!" he spat. "I'm a paid servant of the palace."

"Oh!" she breathed as she caught up. "But Agamemnon..."

"He calls everyone slave. He makes no distinction."

"I'm sorry I offended. But please, slow down."

He grumbled and turned to continue up the stairs toward the King's chamber, but he slowed his pace as he stared ahead.

"Why are you so angry?" she asked.

He flashed her a look from the top of the stairs, but did not answer.

"I've been here less than a moment. What's your gripe with me?"

"You're Agamemnon's wife," he snapped. "What can I possibly have to gripe about?"

She stopped him with a hand on his arm. "But I'm not Agamemnon."

He shook his arm free and strode on, turning a corner taking them into a new corridor. Klytie hurried after him as he opened a door and motioned for her to enter. As she brushed past, she stopped and stared up into his face. She had to say something, and she thought she knew where his problem lay.

"I see you're angry," she said. "Were you here before, when Atreus was killed?"

"Yes," he mumbled.

"Then you witnessed the return of Thyestes. Was he a good king? Is that why you're angry now?"

He said nothing, mouth set in a hard line.

"Please, let me prove I'm not like my... like Agamemnon. I promise, I won't report you."

He hesitated, those eyes that seemed so familiar flicking over her, masking something Klytie could not read.

"Things were better with Thyestes," he murmured.

She nodded. "I can believe it."

"If you need anything, my lady, just ask," he mumbled and hurried away.

Moving to the window, Klytemestra leant on the sill to watch the blaze of orange sky as the sun set just out of view. A light breeze tickled at her hair and she lifted her face to accept its cooling touch, but it did little to cool the room. She climbed up on the sill and sat with her back to one open shutter, closing her eyes.

Floating up from the megaron, Klytie could hear laughter and voices. She tried to close her ears too. She wondered what her life would be like in this new palace, ruled over by a gruff and arrogant king like Agamemnon.

She could understand why the servants might be apprehensive. She tried to imagine what the city had been like under Thyestes. Was he as good and kind as his son had been?

She remembered her husband's face, tried to imagine his father sitting in that megaron now. The kind green eyes of Tantalus swam before her mind's eye and she sighed. Then her eyes snapped open.

She suddenly knew why the young servant had seemed so familiar; those eyes so like her husband's had been. But it could not be...

The room was dark and the night had deepened when Agamemnon stumbled into the room. Klytie still sat in the window dozing in the cool night air. The King clutched at her, pulling her from her perch, then reached through and pulled the shutters to with a slam.

He dragged her to the bed and clambered on, ripping at her clothes, his wine-soaked breath hot in her face. Klytie closed her eyes again, gritting her teeth against his weight upon her, and waited for it to be over. She had learnt not to fight him, but it did not mean she had to welcome him.

Some time later, she lay in the dark staring at nothing, hearing the snore beside her. She slipped from the bed and pulled on a light linen shift. Moving silently to the door, she opened it a crack and squeezed through. Then she stopped, looking either way and wondering how to find the bathing chamber.

It would be downstairs, so she headed back toward the stairs and down. At the bottom, the reception room was ahead of her, and to her right was a small chamber, leading to more rooms.

She knew she had not passed the bathing room the previous afternoon, so she turned the other way. From the smaller chamber, she could see there were two more doors further along, coming off the hall.

As she hesitated, wondering if one of those rooms held the bath, a servant appeared from the farthest room. It was the young man she had met earlier. With a sigh of relief, Klytie hurried forward.

"Is that the bathing room?" she blurted as she approached.

"Ah, yes, my lady," he spluttered. "But... I'm sorry, my lady, but the maids have all retired."

"No matter, I can look after myself."

"I'm sure you can, but..." he hesitated. "The King and his generals made quite a mess earlier and I've been cleaning in there. I'm afraid I've already opened the drain..."

"Oh," she sighed, her disappointment overwhelming. "Well, thank you anyway." She turned, shoulders slumped and weary feet taking her unwillingly toward the stairs.

"My lady, wait," he called.

She turned to face him, squaring her shoulders again in an attempt to appear composed.

"The main pool is empty, but I can fill the King's personal bath, the one he uses when he's not entertaining."

Klytie's eyes widened and she smiled. "Would you?"

"It might take a while, I'll need to collect more water from the main cistern, if you don't mind waiting, and there may not be any hot water."

"Oh, well, I don't want to keep you. You've done enough tonight if you've been cleaning all this time."

"It's my job, my lady, I don't mind. And I'd like to do it... for you."

"Well then, thank you," she smiled.

"You can wait in the reception room just down there, if you like."

*

Klytie was dozing on the cushioned bench when the servant finally came to her. He led her back down to the bathing room and opened the door to enter. The room was cool but, in the hot summer night, that was a blessing.

The entire floor was thick white plaster, still damp from the water that had recently filled the room. Set against the far wall was a more modest bath, the kind she was used to, and she saw steam rising. Somehow, the young man had managed to heat the water for her. She felt thankful tears welling as her vision blurred.

"Thank you," she murmured.

"It's my pleasure, my lady. I'll wait outside until you're finished."

"No," she said suddenly. "Please, stay and talk with me."

"My lady, you know that's not allowed. Only your personal maid should be with you as you bathe."

She shrugged. "Everyone's asleep, and I'm not suggesting anything improper. I just want some company."

He hesitated, but nodded. "Alright, then."

Klytie proceeded to undress and the young man turned his back in embarrassment.

"Don't be silly," she laughed. "Help me in."

Eyes averted, he held her hand as she climbed in and sank into the water.

"I'm fully covered," she said. "Now sit and talk to me."

He perched on the edge of the bath as commanded and stared straight ahead. "What do you want me to say?"

"Tell me about yourself."

"There's not a lot to tell, my lady. I was born here in the palace, and I've worked here my whole life, except when I wasn't working with the herds."

"What's your name?"

"Aegisthus, my lady."

"Strange name," she murmured. "Suckled by a goat?

That's what it means, yes? How did you come by such a name?"

"It's accurate, in a way," he chuckled, flashing her a look. "I was raised by a goatherd and his wife. She fed me on goat's milk."

"She wasn't your mother?"

"No, I have no memory of my mother. I don't really know who she was, but I've heard stories. Some say she was a slave, or my father's legal wife, or my father's brother's wife, or even my own sister."

"You don't know the truth?"

"My foster mother told me my real mother died, and I was given to my sister to suckle because she had lost her own child."

"Do you believe her?"

"She served my family and was there when it happened. Soon after, I was taken and left on the mountain to die. She found me and took me in."

"You were exposed? Why?"

He shrugged. "It doesn't matter."

"Of course it matters. Who were your parents? You said you were born in the palace."

"I don't want to talk about that, my lady."

"But surely you wonder? I'd want to know why my family didn't want me."

"It wasn't my family. I was stolen."

"But why?"

"It's not important."

"But it is important. My son was stolen," she murmured, voice catching. "But there was no goat herder's wife to save him."

He stared at her, meeting her tear-filled eyes. She wondered at those green eyes of his. He looked so much like her first husband, only much younger. He seemed closer to her own age, just a few years older than herself. She remembered Tantalus saying the resemblance was unmistakeable.

"You are the son of Thyestes," she blurted.

His eyes widened. "What makes you say that?" he whispered tremulously. "Who told you that?"

"Your brother, Tantalus."

"You know my brother?"

"He was my husband," she murmured. "Until Agamemnon killed him."

"Tantalus is dead?" he said, his face white. "I should have known. How else could Agamemnon have taken control of the army?"

"Does he know who you are? Is that why he treats you so poorly?"

He shook his head. "No, I've been very careful about that. My foster mother was a maid in the palace, so I grew up among the servants. Agamemnon has known me his whole life, but he doesn't link me with that stolen baby."

"But Tantalus knew you..."

He sighed. "I did a foolish thing. When Atreus was killed and the princes were banished, I came forward and revealed myself to Thyestes."

"Why was that foolish?"

He laughed bitterly. "I dreamed of regaining my heritage. I thought I could step back into the life I'd been denied. But I failed. The other servants wouldn't accept me as their superior, even though most of them knew the story. Now that Agamemnon is back I've tried to return to my old position but it's been difficult."

"Why?"

"They don't trust me anymore. They think I rose above my station and was knocked down accordingly."

"Is that how you feel too?"

"It will be a long time before they accept me again. I must resign myself to my fate and move on with my life. I must always remind myself that it was never meant to be."

"Surely you don't believe that? You are the son of a king!"

"Once a goatherd, always a goatherd," he sighed.

Dressed once more in her linen night shift, Klytemestra slipped out of the bathing chamber on her way back to the King's bedroom. As she headed off toward the stairs, she came face-to-face with Agamemnon.

"There you are!" he exclaimed. "What have you been doing?"

"I was taking a bath."

"Alone? No maids to help?"

"No, one of the servants filled the bath for me," she said.

At that moment, Aegisthus came out of the room behind her and Agamemnon frowned.

"You let a male slave help you bathe?" he growled. "I thought I made it clear I didn't want slaves touching you."

"He didn't touch me," she snapped. "He filled the bath and stood guard so I wasn't disturbed. He was a model of propriety."

Agamemnon frowned. "You should not be consorting with males who are not your husband. Especially not slaves."

"I wasn't consorting," she bristled.

"I'll be the judge of that," he snapped. "Get back to my room while I deal with this impudent slave."

"Don't punish him! He did no wrong."

"You hold your tongue and keep in your place! Go!"

When morning came, Klytie joined Agamemnon in the megaron, ready for her introduction to the household and to take charge of the servants allowed her as potinia. She was looking forward to her duties as priestess of the lady. She relished the challenge of organising the religious and ceremonial life of a big city like Mycenae.

When the servant Aegisthus appeared, Klytie gasped. He wore the simple loincloth of the slave and his back was criss-crossed with welts from the whip. He refused to meet her gaze, but she caught a glimpse of a dark bruise around a swollen left eye.

"I asked you not to hurt him," she accused.

"He needs to learn his place," Agamemnon retorted. "Now, choose your servants."

As potinia, priestess of the lady, Klytemestra was allowed three servants of her own, to be completely under her control. She did not hesitate. She named the two maids she had brought with her, and Aegisthus. Agamemnon frowned, but Klytie knew there was no reason for him to object. It was her right to choose.

* * *

7

A SEMBLANCE OF CALM

The potinia sat in her carved wooden chair, watching as the last of the supplicants filed out after a hard morning of judging augury, distributing festival funds and dispensing rations to the temples. At the desk in the corner, her scribe finished rolling the last clay finger and flattened it to begin inscribing the final judgement of the day.

Klytemestra sat back in the hard chair, its small, flat cushion barely softening the seat, and sighed. She looked about the room, its red walls meant to symbolise the womb of the lady, offset nicely by the border of rosettes around the floor, and the red and blue striped border around her chair.

She had redecorated the room herself, not long after she began work there as potinia, a position often assumed by the king's wife. The red walls were required, but the roses were her own design. It seemed so long ago, the room now a familiar haven from palace life.

"All done, my lady," said her assistant.

"Thank you, Aegisthus, you may go now," she said, hearing the little giggles of her daughters from the antechamber.

"I'll wait for the children, my lady," he smiled.

They burst into the room, Iphigenia in the lead as usual. At six, she was a bundle of energy, always into mischief. She launched herself at her mother.

"Mama, I've been learning to ride!" she yelled. "And I didn't fall off once!"

"Lower your voice Gennie, you're not in the training ground now."

She giggled and threw her arms about her mother. Four-year-old Elektra squealed and climbed up beside her sister, elbowing her out of the way. Her ice-blue eyes flashed and her red hair tossed. Iphigenia slid off, lower lip trembling.

"Mama, she pushed me!"

"Now, Gennie, she doesn't understand."

"Mama Mama," little Krisothemis wailed, clutching at Klytie's skirts.

"Down now, Elektra. Your sister needs a feed."

Lifting the toddler onto her lap, Klytie allowed her to find the nipple, the ceremonial dress that left her breasts bare making it easy for the child to latch on. At five months shy of two, little Krissie would soon be weaned and Klytie had to admit she would miss it, even though it meant her chance of falling pregnant again would increase.

Elektra slumped on the floor and sulked. But Gennie bounced over to her mother's assistant.

"Gissus!" she cried, throwing her arms about his neck. "Do you want to see me ride?"

"Of course I do, sweetie. As soon as I pack up these tablets."

"Mama, can I ask Papa too?"

Klytie frowned. "You know your father doesn't approve of girls riding."

"He won't stop me," she pouted. "Can you ask him? Please?" she wined.

"Alright, when Krissie is finished, I'll try."

Crossing the courtyard, the girls skipping along in her wake, Klytie shared an apprehensive look with her assistant.

"Do you think he'll come?" said Aegisthus.

She shrugged. "It depends what kind of mood he's in."

"She'll be so disappointed if he refuses..."

"I know," she sighed. "The girls are lucky to have you, Aegisthus. You care for them as if they were your own children, even though you have every right to hate their father."

"Their father is nothing to me," he murmured. "I love them because they're your children too."

She smiled. "You're a good friend."

He looked away, silently took the children in hand as Klytie stepped through the columns of the porch and into the anteroom.

Taking a deep breath, Klytemestra stepped through the door into the megaron. At her entry, the King's audience parted, watching her approach silently and allowing her through to the throne on the right hand wall. Agamemnon looked up and smiled. Klytie sighed in relief.

"Potinia, how may I assist you?" he said reverently. She was still wearing the ceremonial robes of the priestess, she realised with a jolt. No wonder they were all being so respectful.

"My lord," she began. "The Princess Iphigenia requests your indulgence."

His smile deepened and his eyes twinkled. "What does my little scamp request?"

"My lord, she would like you to attend her in the training ground. She has... something she would like to show you."

"By all means," he chuckled. "My friends, I beg your pardon, I'll return when I've dealt with this matter." He motioned for the potinia to lead the way.

In the courtyard, Iphigenia squealed. "Papa!"

She ran to her father, who swept her up and spun her around, laughing with her. Then, setting her down, he ruffled her hair.

"What have you got for me, little scamp?"

"Papa, I've been learning to ride! Come see!" She pulled him by the hand.

"To ride?" he murmured. "Well then, let's see..." He straightened as Iphigenia skipped ahead. He looked at Klytie, eyes suddenly narrowed and dark. "I thought we were clear on this," he hissed under his breath. "This is not Sparta."

"It wasn't my doing," she snapped. "I had no idea, she did it herself."

"Then you need to control her better!" he growled.

"Papa, come on!" the child called.

"Coming, little scamp," he smiled at his daughter, then turned to hiss at his wife. "We'll talk about this later."

Klytie stood still for a moment as he stomped away, her hands clenched to fight the tremble, and her mouth set in a hard line. When the servant put a hand on her arm, she jumped. She scooped up little Krisothemis and held her like a shield.

"Come along, Elektra," she said quietly as she followed after Gennie and her father.

But Aegisthus would not be dissuaded. "He shouldn't talk to you like that. Especially near the children."

"He's gruff and full of pride, you know that. But when he stops to notice, he's a good father."

"You shouldn't defend him."

"And you shouldn't judge me."

The potinia was often summoned to the megaron. She was expected to work with the King on all matters, and the pair were seen publicly as a team, governing together. But in her heart, Klytie dreaded those meetings.

She was becoming sick of the farce. All decisions went his way, whether he was right or wrong, and Klytie's opinions were at best tolerated and rarely heard. This summons was unusual, outside the normal schedule.

Klytie entered with apprehension. She had no idea what to expect. The room was strangely quiet, only a few servants attending the King.

"There you are," said Agamemnon gruffly. "I need you to prepare for a journey."

Klytie stared. "Where am I going?"

"We," he said, "are going to Sparta."

"Oh!" she smiled. "What's the occasion?"

"Nothing good, I'm afraid. My grandfather in Crete has died. Menelaos and I must travel there to organise the rites and set up a new king. My brother has asked for you to attend his wife while we're gone."

"Keep her in line, you mean."

"I didn't say that," he frowned.

"No, but I know my sister. She's vain and improper and an incorrigible flirt. Menelaos is no fool. He wants her watched."

"Well spotted, my dear," he murmured.

"May I take the children?"

Agamemnon frowned. "It's a difficult journey. I would prefer they stay here."

"But who will look after them? They need their mother!"

"They have maids."

"But Krissie still feeds!"

"It's about time she stopped!"

Later, in her private sitting room, Klytemestra cuddled her children, fighting back tears. She allowed Krisothemis to feed, perhaps for the last time. Elektra sat beside her, clinging to her arm and staring up at her, those big blue eyes wide and worried. Iphigenia huddled against her other side, sobbing softly.

THE CURSE OF MYCENAE

"Why must you go, Mama?" she wailed. "Why can't we go with you?"

"It's your father's wish that you stay here, where you're safe."

"But I want to see Hermione!"

"I know, Gennie, you miss your cousin. It's been so long since you've seen each other. I can't understand why your father forbids it this time."

"It's not fair!"

"Mama, don't go..." Elektra whispered.

"I won't be gone long," Klytie lied. She knew it could be months, even longer, before the King and his brother returned from Crete. "You have the maids to look after you, and Aegisthus will protect you."

"Don't want Gissus," Elektra pouted.

At that point, the servant entered. Iphigenia jumped up and ran to him, sobbing.

"Gissus, tell Mama she can't go!"

"I'm sorry, sweetie, I don't think she has a choice."

"You will look after them, won't you?" Klytie said with a catch in her voice.

"You know I will, my lady."

"You do so much for them already. It's not fair. You should be having children of your own. When I get back, I'll set you free."

"You'll do no such thing, my lady."

"But..."

"I'll hear none of it. I have no wish to be anywhere but here, my lady."

"One day, you'll want to have a family."

"This is where I belong, my lady. I'll never leave you."

Early the next morning, Klytemestra walked with her children down the great stair to the lower courtyard, where a small retinue of soldiers waited with Agamemnon. The King approached and offered her the reins of a young filly.

"You're allowing me to ride?" she whispered.

"We're in a hurry," he grumbled. "I don't want to wait for the carts to catch up."

Klytie bent to hug her daughters, letting them cling to her for a moment and resolutely removing their clutching hands to mount up. With eyes blurred, she offered them a smile, trying to ignore their sobs. Then, before she had a chance to do more than wave, the small force set off down the hill toward the citadel gate.

Three days later, the King, his wife and their small escort entered the city of Sparta. Moving at a careful walk, they rode along the ridge above the river, winding their way slowly to the peak. Nearing the top, they passed around the palace wall, coming almost full circle before they reached the gate.

They rode into the huge courtyard in front of the palace, where they dismounted under the shadow of the ancient north wing, crumbling into ruin. Entering the palace, Klytemestra followed Agamemnon down the short corridor leading directly to the megaron.

There a small family group waited, including Tyndareos in his seat flanked by Helene and Menelaos on one side and Klytie's brothers on the other, close in conversation with two women, one nursing a young child and the other heavily pregnant. Klytie rushed forward eagerly.

"Castor!" she grinned as her brother met her, arms wide. "I didn't know you were back." She smiled over his shoulder at Polydeuces, waiting for his turn. "Pollox!" she said, accepting his more sedate embrace.

"Back and gone and back again, sister dear," Castor beamed.

"We'd like you to meet our wives, Phoebe and Hilaira," said Polydeuces with an equally wide smile.

"Wives?" said Klytie with a grin. "When did that happen?"

"Last year, soon after we returned from Iolcus," said Polydeuces.

Castor leant in close and whispered. "We stole them from our cousins, Lynceus and Idas."

Klytie frowned. "One day your mischief will get you boys in trouble. Weren't they terribly mad?"

"Oh yes," said Castor with a smirk. "They've vowed to get their revenge, but I assure you the girls came willingly. Any stories you may hear of us carrying them off against their will are grossly exaggerated."

"Besides," said Polydeuces. "Idas and Lynceus have plenty of other beautiful girls to chase in Thebes, they won't miss two."

The brothers ushered her toward the throne, where her father sat, looking pale and old. Klytie sobered, forcing a smile.

"Father," she sighed, bending to kiss the papery skin of his cheek.

He beamed, eyes glassy and staring, trembling hands clutching at her. "It's good to see you, my dear," he whispered, voice thin and weak.

As Klytie hugged her sister, Agamemnon greeted his brother before turning on Castor and Polydeuces.

"Well, boys, did you find the fleece?"

"Yes, after many troubles, we tracked it down to a place called Colchis in the Black Sea, in the possession of King Aetes. But he had no intention of parting with it."

"I hope you convinced him."

Castor shrugged. "He threw some mighty challenges in our path. He made us tame fire-breathing beasts, use them to sow dragons teeth as seeds, then fight the dread warriors that emerged from the soil."

"I see you survived," said Agamemnon dryly.

"But he still wouldn't part with the fleece," Pollox murmured. "He kept it under the guard of a beast from hades, a dragon that never sleeps."

"Come now, you boys are braver than that. You didn't give up, surely."

"No," said Castor. "By a stroke of luck, the King's daughter took a liking to our leader, Jason. Medea betrayed her father and brother to help us obtain the fleece. She charmed the dragon."

"And you got the fleece and escaped," said Agamemnon dismissively. "So where is it?"

"It wasn't that simple, sir," Polydeuces said. "The trip home was even more dangerous that the journey to Colchis. We almost lost everything more than once. The only thing that saved us was the help of Thetis, the sea nymph. She's married to Peleus, one of our comrades, you know. Not to be confused with Pelias of Iolcus of course..."

"Yes, yes, enough blathering," Agamemnon snapped. "Where's the fleece?"

"In Iolcus, sir," said Castor.

"What's it doing there? I charged you with bringing it home to me!"

"Yes, I know, sir. We had it all sorted, we had an agreement with Jason that we would help him regain his throne and then he would give us the fleece. But we were betrayed at the last moment."

"Betrayed? By Jason?"

"No, no, sir," Pollox cried. "It was Acastus, another of our comrades."

"Acastus? Who's he when he's at home?" Agamemnon groaned, flustered.

"Sir, it all has to do with the house of Iolcus," Castor

explained. "They have a long running feud, not unlike your own family curse. Jason's father was supposed to be king, but his half-brother, Pelias, seized the throne. So Jason was sent away for his own safety."

"When Jason returned to claim the throne," Pollox said. "Pelias sent him off to find the golden fleece, offering the throne as prize."

"But while we were gone," Castor continued. "Pelias arranged the deaths of Jason's father, brother and mother. When we got back, Medea went into the city dressed as a witch and convinced the daughters of Pelias to kill him for us, claiming she could make him immortal."

"With Pelias gone, we were able to take the city," Pollox said.

"So you won, then," said Agamemnon. "But you said you were betrayed."

"Yes, Sir," said Castor. "Acastus is the son of Pelias. He had the support of the people and the soldiers of Iolcus. He grew up there; he knows them. Jason had no chance. Acastus cast us all out, took the throne himself, and claimed the fleece as well."

Agamemnon cursed. "Jason just let him? You had all the greatest heroes of our time right there with you on that ship. You couldn't stop one little overgrown princeling?"

"Sir, our numbers were halved. Our greatest warrior was Herakles, and he had already run off on his own adventure months before. Jason was distraught, his family dead and his half-brother a traitor. He took Medea and left the throne to Acastus, and there were none left strong enough to oppose him."

"I suppose it's what I get for sending boys to do a man's job! When I return from Crete, I'm taking you two and the Spartan army and getting my property back."

X

A FOLLY OF PRINCES

Klytemestra sat once more at her father's side, but it was bittersweet. At the King's other hand sat Helene, hand on chin, all sighs of boredom and yawning petulance. Klytie watched Tyndareos surreptitiously. He stared vaguely, barely hearing and rarely understanding when addressed.

The court still accepted petitions but no business was concluded. The megaron slowly filled with disgruntled supplicants and confused servants as the business of running the city ground to a halt.

Klytie realised how much the reins of government must have been taken in hand by Helene's husband in recent years. Her brothers sat oblivious, drinking wine and carousing with their wives, two unpromising young women who giggled and flirted outrageously with vapid converse and fluttering eyelids.

Another useless day, another group of supplicants turned away unheard, grumbling in their displeasure. Into this stale and stagnant assembly entered a pair of angry young men, one thin and wiry and one huge, towering above the crowd. Breezing into the megaron with studied purpose, they blew away the cobwebs of idle banter with their flustering.

"Castor!" came the cry from the anteroom.

"Pollox!" another voice cried in tandem with the first.

"Oh dear," Polydeuces murmured.

Castor laughed. "At last, some fun!"

The two men stalked their way into the gathering, the tall one pushing away the arms of the guards and parting the assembled supplicants with a look.

"Idas," Castor smiled. "And Lynceus too! Welcome to Sparta, dear cousins."

"How dare you, wife stealer!"

Castor held his hands out wide as a flustered Hilaira hid behind his muscular frame. "Come now, Lynceus, you know we did no such thing."

"You did almost as much," growled the other. "You know they were betrothed to us."

"Idas, they were free to choose," said Pollox, arm about Phoebe. "They chose us."

"They were seduced by you," Lynceus snarled. "Hardly a fair choice."

"They wanted nothing more than to get away from your licentious advances," said Pollox with a grimace of distaste.

"How dare you," Idas roared as he charged forward.

"Wait, cousins," Castor smiled, one hand raised. "Perhaps we can settle this with a little contest."

Idas paused. "Contest?"

"What did you have in mind," said Lynceus eagerly.

Castor pretended to consider. "My captains have brought news of an incursion into our lands, a herd of cattle, unclaimed as yet by any of our neighbours."

"So?" said Idas dismissively.

"So, we ride out and get them. If you succeed in catching them all before us, you take them with our blessing, as a gift and an apology."

"And if you win?" said Lynceus.

"Then we keep them and the girls and you drop the matter and go home."

Idas frowned. "So you get the girls either way?"

"You get the cattle if you win..."

"I suppose I can live with that," said Lynceus.

So the boys set off on their foolhardy escapade, and the boredom of a neglected court became even less bearable. An ailing king and four young women held court to an increasingly disgruntled people.

"Papa, can't we do something fun?" Helene whined.

"What would you do, my dove?" the old man murmured.

"I know!" Helene bubbled, clutching the King's arm. "Let's have a party. We can invite people from all over; have a great feast like we used to have. Please, Papa!"

Tyndareos smiled indulgently. "Anything you like, my dove."

Helene squealed. "Oh thank you, Papa! Come, Klytie, let's make a list. Who might we invite?"

Klytemestra shrugged.

"Oh, you're right, let's just invite everyone. Let's make this the biggest feast since our wedding day!"

"I'm not sure your husband would approve..."

"Menelaos isn't here," she snapped. "Besides, he's such a spoilsport, he never lets me have any fun. I'm sick of sitting around, I want to enjoy myself."

"Just remember, you're married now, you can't flirt with every prince who catches your eye."

"Don't be silly, would I do that?"

"You used to."

"Oh, I'm not going to do anything. I love my husband, even if he is a bore."

Klytie raised an eyebrow. "Do you really?"

"Well of course I do," Helene cried. "My dear sister, what must you think of me to say such things?"

"I think you've forgotten you're a wife and a mother and

a party such as you suggest is no longer appropriate. Think of your daughter, would you have her exposed to that kind of drunken revelry at her tender age?"

"We attended father's parties at her age, and younger."

"Yes, and you were taken off by Theseus to be his child bride and would have been lost to us if Castor and Pollox hadn't rescued you."

"I wish they'd left me there. Then I wouldn't be sitting here arguing with a prude of a sister when I could be enjoying myself."

Klytie sighed. "All I'm saying is be careful. You don't want to be accused of infidelity when Menelaos gets back."

"I won't do anything like that. It's just a bit of fun. I promise."

In the great courtyard before the palace, Klytemestra watched as her young niece put her beloved pony through its paces. Half the courtyard had been sectioned off and posts had been set up at either end. Hermione raced toward the far post, taking the turn in a skidding of hooves and a cloud of dust.

Then she dug in her heels and galloped toward the finish. She came in at break-neck speed, heading straight for the wall. At the very last moment she pulled back on the reins and skidded to a halt. Klytie laughed at the expression of pure joy on her face.

"You're becoming more like my brother Castor every day. You're a fine rider."

"Aunt Klytie! I didn't know you were there."

"I came to find you. I notice you spend very little time in the hall."

"That stuffy place? Why would I sit cooking myself by the hearth, watching Grandpapa snooze, when I can be out here?"

"I remember saying something very similar when I was your age."

"I wish Gennie were here. Why didn't she come?"

"I'm sorry, her father wanted to get here quickly."

"Couldn't she have ridden with you?"

"Her papa doesn't approve of girls riding. He only agreed to me riding because he was in a hurry."

Hermione frowned. "Why shouldn't girls ride?"

"Here in Sparta it's not a problem, but elsewhere..." Klytie sighed. "Most women never sit on a horse."

"That's too bad. I know Gennie would love riding."

"Oh she does, and her papa just barely tolerates it. I'm surprised your papa allows it."

"He wouldn't dare stop me. Besides, he knows Uncle Castor is the best horseman in the world. He knows I'm well taught."

"Yes, you are, by what I just saw."

"Why did you want to see me?"

"Your mama is planning a party."

"Oh!" she grinned. "I love parties!"

"Do you now?"

"Well... sometimes. But mama's parties can be boring, just people talking and eating mostly, and... icky stuff. I much prefer games. I wish mama would hold games instead."

"Now you remind me of myself," Klytie chuckled.

"Aunt Klytie," said Hermione with head tilted to one side. "Would you take me riding sometime?"

"Of course I would. I'd love to, any time you want."

The megaron bustled with servants and supplicants, joined now by the first of the visitors. Helene sat deep in giggling conversation with three young men, her sisters-in-law taking a keen interest. Klytemestra hung back, watching her sister make a fool of herself.

Tyndareos dozed in his chair as the afternoon wore on. Klytie was torn between playing chaperone to her sister and attending her father. She would much rather be riding with her niece. She had tried to admonish Helene, but she waved her away with a dismissive laugh.

"Oh, Klytie, get a sense of fun, will you? It's been so boring around here, and the boys are only talking."

Klytemestra stared dubiously. Her sister had always been an outrageous flirt, ever since she came back from Athens after being kidnapped at eight years old. She had been so innocent, a pleasant and shy girl, but the experience had changed her. Klytie shuddered at what she must have been exposed to at her captor's hands to come back so altered.

From that time on, Helene had liked nothing better than to chase boys. She loved male attention and always would. Klytie sighed. How could she protect her sister from indiscretion with all these attractive young princes arriving for the ill-advised party?

A commotion at the door brought Klytie out of her reverie. Who was arriving now? The crowd parted reluctantly and a tall young man made his way toward the King and his family. Klytie heard her sister gasp, then giggle delightedly.

"Klytie, who's that?" Helene whispered loudly.

Klytie shook her head as the newcomer approached, blond and tanned, oozing self-confidence and more than a little haughty arrogance. His bronze armour sparkled in the firelight from the central hearth, and his hair shone.

"I have no idea," Klytie replied.

"He's beautiful," Helene sighed.

Klytie touched her father's arm to wake him, and the King stared at the man.

"Ah!" said the King. "Another guest? Welcome to the

party, young man."

"Party, sir?" the man said, voice soft and vibrant, bringing another sigh from a besotted Helene.

"You're not here to join my girls in their revelry?"

"No, sir, this is the first I've heard of it."

"Then who are you?" Klytie said.

"My name is Paris Alexandros. My father is king of Troy."

"Troy? I don't think I know that city..."

"I would be surprised if you did. It's far away, in the land of Ilion, where the rising sun sends its benediction over the wine-dark sea."

Klytie raised an eyebrow. Such poetic words from such a beautiful stranger. This man was dangerous.

"Why have you come?" Helene asked breathlessly.

"To meet you, my lady," he murmured.

"Me?" Helene breathed.

"Word came to me that here, in the fabulous city of Sparta, in the land of Lacedaemon, lived the most beautiful woman in the world. I see the rumours were true!"

Helene giggled and blushed, fluttering her eyelids. "You came all that way just to see me?"

"Just so," he whispered.

"Why?"

"Would you like to hear a story?" he murmured.

Klytie coughed. "Would you like some refreshment, sir? Maybe a bath to wash away the dust of the road?"

Paris straightened. "I suppose I should, though I'd like nothing better than to sit here with you beautiful ladies."

"We'll still be here when you return, with something to ease your thirst and calm your hunger."

"Then how can I refuse?"

Late in the afternoon, as the assembly milled about, waiting for the meal and the anticipated story of the strange prince from far away Ilion, a commotion broke the quiet. Four young men blustered into the hall, laughing and chatting raucously. Klytemestra watched her brothers approach, their cousins Idas and Lynceus in tow.

"Castor," she said with a smile. "Have you all had your fun?"

"Sister, dear, we've had a wild adventure. We've sallied forth together to capture the herd, we've fought over the spoils and we've toasted the victors. All in all, a great diversion."

"I'm glad. So who won?"

"We did," said Idas with a smirk. "Or should I say... I did."

"You cheated," said Castor.

"He reinterpreted the established conditions of the contest," said Lynceus.

"Dare I ask what happened?" Klytie frowned.

"We each captured half the herd," said Pollox.

"But then we had to decide who would take the entire lot," said Castor.

"Your brother decided we should slaughter one cow," said Lynceus. "Then cook it, divide it, and eat it, to see who could finish their portion fastest."

"The brothers who finished first would win the whole herd," said Pollox.

"But they cheated," said Castor. "Idas the giant ate his own portion and then his brother's, finishing before us."

"It was a fair interpretation of the rules," said Lynceus with a shrug.

"He's a giant," said Castor. "It took him three bites to finish his own and the same for yours. We made it barely half-way through our own portions."

Idas shrugged. "Nobody said we couldn't do it that way."

9

THE JUDGEMENT OF PARIS

The visitors gathered around, princes and servants mingling, an expectant quiet falling as the newcomer gazed at his hostess with a twinkling eye. His voice, barely more than a whisper, fell into the hush with the softness of silk. It gathered the crowd in with its lush timbre and wrapped the women up in its embrace like a secret lover.

"My lady, my story begins many years ago, when I was very young, just married, precocious and pretty," Paris smiled and the women sighed. "In fact, the story goes back further, and begins in Olympus. There is a goddess, child of the sea, who was victim of a dread prophecy. Her name is Thetis, and it's said that any son of hers will become greater than his father. Now this goddess was desired by two of the greatest gods in Olympus, Poseidon and the great Zeus himself."

Helene laughed. "My father always did like the girls."

"And a good thing, my lady, for now we have you!"

Helene giggled and fluttered her eyelashes.

"Now these two great gods quarrelled over Thetis. Both wanted her, but they were also both frightened of the prophecy. In times past, the gods in Olympus overthrew their fathers. What would happen if their children were to do the same? It couldn't be allowed to happen. So they decided to marry her off to a mortal man called Peleus, thus ensuring that her children would be less powerful than the gods."

"My father is nothing if not wise," Helene smiled.

"Now at first, Thetis wasn't willing. She ran, she fought, but eventually Peleus won her virtue, after which she relented and agreed to marry him."

Castor chuckled. "I remember the story," he said. "Peleus regaled us with the tales of her conquest in the quiet times on the Argo. He said her father Proteus told him how to bind her while she slept so that she couldn't escape by shifting form. He was finally able to keep her still long enough to win her over."

"Forgive me, sir," said Klytie with a frown. "But what has all this to do with you?"

"I'm getting to that, my lady," Paris said with a bow. "The marriage of Thetis and Peleus was performed on Mount Pelion, outside the cave of the centaur Chiron. All the gods were there, Apollo playing his lyre and the muses singing, with feasting and great gifts. But one goddess was not invited. Eris, the goddess of strife."

"Why was she not invited?" whispered Helene. "Was she terribly angry?"

"She was excluded in an attempt to prevent discord at the wedding. And yes, she was furious. She turned up unannounced, with a golden apple from the garden of Hesperides. She threw the apple into the crowd, crying 'for the fairest!'."

"Who did she mean?" Helene gasped.

"Nobody knows. But that was the whole point. She did it specifically to cause strife, as she is wont to do."

"Who got the apple?" Helene breathed.

"Well, three goddesses sprang forward, all wanting to claim it, all believing they were the fairest."

"Who?"

"There was Hera, Athena and Aphrodite. A fight broke out, all three giving as good as they got. Scratching, biting and screeching... utter chaos, just as Eris intended."

"Who won?"

"None, yet. When they eventually wore themselves out, they turned to Zeus to decide. He was placed in an unenviable position. He was being asked to choose between his wife Hera and two of his many daughters."

"And who did he choose?"

"None. He decided not to choose."

"So what happened?" Helene breathed.

"Not long before that, I had hosted a tournament, with bull sports and games. In a competition for the best bull, the field was reduced to two, my prized bull and another. I awarded the prize to the outsider, against my own bull. That outsider turned out to be the god Ares in disguise. By reason of that unbiased decision of mine, Zeus decided that I would be the judge, that I would decide the fairest of the three goddesses."

Helene squealed, clapping her hands together like a little girl. "Who was it?"

"It was a very difficult decision, as you can imagine. The three stood before me. Hera is by far the most beautiful of face, but hardly fair of character. She is shrewish and jealous, full of prickly accusation. No wonder great Zeus finds solace in other women."

"I don't wonder she is such a shrew," Klytie said. "Zeus brings it on himself by constantly cuckolding her."

"Nevertheless, my lady, her accusing eyes and fiery tongue detract from her beauty."

"What about the others?" Helene whispered.

"Athena is sublimely beautiful, in a strong, martial kind of way. She is athletically slim and has a clever mind."

"And Aphrodite?" breathed Helene. "The goddess of love.

Surely there is none fairer?"

"Aphrodite," Paris sighed. "She is all curves and voluptuousness. She is soft and sensual, charming and brazen at the same time. She has a way of putting a man completely at ease while sending him to the height of expectant fervour with a mere glance. She stood before me completely naked and totally unashamed..."

"And so you awarded her the prize," Klytie scoffed. "Just like a man to choose the woman who flashes her bits at him."

He chuckled. "No, my lady, I didn't choose her for that."

Klytie raised an eyebrow. "No? Forgive me if I don't believe you."

"Oh, Klytie, hush," said Helene.

"Allow me to explain," said Paris with a smirk. "As the three great ladies stood before me, each as beautiful as the others in their own unique ways, I found I couldn't decide. That was when they began offering something more, a prize of sorts."

"What did they offer?" Helene sighed.

"Hera offered me a great kingdom, thinking I might be swayed by fame and power. But you see I'm already prince of a great kingdom, with all the luxury and power that comes to a royal house, so her offer was not as tempting as she had hoped."

"What about the others? What did Athena offer?"

"Athena promised wisdom and military prowess. Now, as a prince with a kingdom to earn I am already well trained in warfare, skilled at arms and experienced in military strategy. So what did she offer that I do not already have?"

"And Aphrodite?"

Paris smiled, a gleam in his eye. "What did Aphrodite offer?" he murmured as he moved in close to Helene. "For choosing her," he whispered. "She promised me the most beautiful woman in the world."

Helene's eyes opened wide. "But... that's me!"

He chuckled as he took her hands in his. "Yes, my lady, it most certainly is."

"But..." she whispered. "I'm married!"

He shrugged. "So am I."

She giggled. "Sit by me," she whispered.

"Helene," Klytie hissed. "Remember your place; you're in no position to entertain a suitor."

"Hush, Klytie, there's no harm in being friendly."

Klytie frowned. "There's something that puzzles me, sir."

"And what is that, my lady?"

"You say this all happened many years ago. Why did you take so long to come here?"

"Well," he shrugged. "I knew what my prize was, but not who, nor where she was. I began searching but no news ever came to me. I live so far from here, you see, my messengers never got this far. So I settled back into my life and waited for word. In time, I almost forgot."

"What changed?"

"Last year I had a visitor, a man exiled from his home, wandering the world. He told me a story about a young girl with so many suitors she held games to make her choice. A girl who was said to be so beautiful she shone like the sun, the most beautiful woman the world has ever seen. I knew it must be my promised bride."

"And here you are," breathed Helene.

"And here are you," he murmured in reply.

Klytemestra stood on the palisade outside her room, staring down into the central court. The party continued on, sounds of laughter and song wafting up from the megaron, the flickering light from the doorway spreading its glow out into the dark courtyard.

Moonlight broke the dark in silvery shafts across the shadowed flagstones and a light breeze ruffled her hair, cooling her brow. Klytie sighed. She had grown tired of the endless revelry, night after night of feasting and flirting, watching her sister make a fool of herself with Paris Alexandros.

She suspected their flirtation had progressed to something more, but she had no proof and she dreaded the thought that she may be right. Her frequent warnings had fallen on deaf ears. Helene was having fun and how dare she try to stop her.

A movement from the hall caught her gaze. In the brightness of the doorway two figures stood, laughing at some secret folly. As they spilled out into the courtyard, Klytie recognised her sister, heard her giggling laughter, drunk again. Helene stumbled a little as she crossed the threshold and the man caught her about the waist.

There in the half-light, the two fell into a passionate embrace, a kiss full of hungry, clutching desire. Klytie groaned and turned away. Oh Helene, why? Why could she not control her lust? Klytie knew she should not be surprised, but it had been her task to prevent this, and now she would have to explain how she had failed.

Another night, another feast, another guilt-filled evening for Klytemestra. Inside she seethed. Why should she feel guilty when it was Helene doing the deed? She could do nothing to stop it now, she could only watch as Helene and Paris conducted their affair in unfettered abandon.

It did not matter that the guests had formed their own attachments in the past weeks and most barely noticed. It mattered for the mutterings that only Klytie heard. It mattered for the spoiled reputation of her sister and her family. It mattered for the rage of Helene's cuckolded husband when he finally returned.

As Klytie sat steaming, chewing her nails in helpless rage, she noticed an absence. Her brothers were not present. Their wives sat giggling in a corner, and Klytie knew neither brother had formed a guilty alliance of their own.

She saw Idas and Lynceus, flirting outrageously with a couple of servant girls, making their beds for the night. Her brothers were not concocting some scheme then. Or were they?

She remembered overhearing their conversation of the night before. Castor had been bemoaning the lost cattle herd. He had been trying to convince his brother that some raid might be in order. She had thought nothing of it at the time, just another one of Castor's pranks. With a sinking heart, she made her way to where her cousins sat.

"Greetings, beauteous cousin," Lynceus beamed as she approached.

"Have you seen Castor and Pollox?" she asked.

Lynceus looked about. "No, not recently. In fact..." he frowned. "I haven't seen them all day."

"You don't think they could be up to some mischief?" asked Klytie.

"I wonder... Idas, do you think maybe we should find them?"

Idas nodded. "Let's go."

Klytemestra tried to put her brothers out of her mind. They could look after themselves. She gave up trying to pry Helene away from Paris. In resignation, she sat back and wondered what would happen next.

It was a breezy, early autumn afternoon, when a messenger arrived with the news that Menelaos was on his way home. Klytie shivered.

"Alright, that's it," she shouted into the crowd filling the hall. "This party is over. Time to go home!"

There was a murmur of dissent.

"I mean it. I need you all to pack up your things and prepare to depart. I want everyone gone first thing in the morning."

"Klytie, don't be so rude!" Helene cried from her lover's lap.

"That goes for him too," Klytie said.

She pointed an accusatory finger at Paris Alexandros, tangled up in Helene's embrace, just once showing her disgust at her sister's behaviour.

"Your husband is coming home," Klytie spat.

Helene stared dumbly for a moment. Then her eyes widened slightly as realisation hit home. She began to shake, her bottom lip trembling. Her hands clutched at her lover.

"He's going to kill me!" she whispered.

"Very likely," said Klytie.

"What are we going to do?"

"I don't know about you, but I'm going to get rid of these 'visitors' and try to clean up this place. I suggest you say your goodbyes and muster up some kind of dignity. Maybe we can hide what happened here..."

"Hide it? But everyone knows. Someone will tell him!"

"That's your problem."

"Klytie, please, don't make Paris go away... I can't go back to that..."

"I thought you said you loved your husband," Klytie said, feeling an absurd pleasure when Paris flinched.

"I know, but he's so boring, Klytie. He's like a wet fish, all slobber and gasp! I can't go back to him, not now that I know real love..."

"Real love? A few lustful tumbles and you suddenly know real love?" Klytie snorted. "You wouldn't know love if it hit you in the face!"

"And you would?"

"I know what it's not, and it's not..." she waved a hand dismissively. "Whatever this is."

Helene turned to Paris, clutching at him frantically. "Paris, you have to do something!"

"Don't worry," he murmured. "I'll think of something."

Early the next morning, Klytemestra stood watching the departing princes as they marshalled their retinues in the great walled courtyard outside the main palace building. The sky glowed pale blue in promise of a fine day, but the courtyard was in shadow, with the rising sun not yet visible behind the palace, and Klytie shivered in the cool morning air. Searching the crowd, Klytie could not see the prince from Ilion, nor her sister. She caught a passing servant.

"Can you find Prince Paris and see if he's ready to depart?"

The servant gave her a quizzical look. "My lady, he's already gone."

"Gone?"

"Yes, my lady, he left before sunrise."

"Does my sister know?"

The servant shrugged and hurried off.

Klytie went inside in search of a chambermaid.

"Is my sister awake?" she asked the first maid she saw.

"I don't know, my lady, I haven't seen her yet. Do you want me to wake her?"

"No," Klytie sighed.

She hurried down the corridor toward her sister's room, entered without announcement and stopped short. The room had been cleaned out, was empty but for the bed. The bed was neat and tidy, obviously unused. The shutters were open, the morning sun streaming in.

Klytie stood dumbfounded for a moment, her mind racing. Oh, Helene! What had she done? Had she really run off with him? She had taken everything. She had no intention of ever coming back. Klytie jumped at a gasp behind her.

"Aunt Klytie? What's going on?"

"Hermione!" Klytie turned, her heart wrenching at the confusion in the young girl's eyes.

At eight years old, Hermione would never understand this. How could Helene do this to her only child?

"Where's Mama?" the girl whispered.

Klytie suppressed a sob. How could she explain this? She opened her arms to the girl. Slowly, and with an expression of complete bewilderment, Hermione accepted Klytie's embrace.

10

A Brother's Sacrifice

Idas made his way down into the peaceful little valley where the cattle herd grazed. Beside him, Lynceus peered into the darkness, the sun almost gone behind the hill at their backs.

"There," whispered Lynceus.

Idas squinted, trying to see where his sharp-eyed brother pointed.

"I see Pollox by the herd, but where's Castor?" said Idas with a frown.

"Probably on lookout," answered his brother. "There, in the tree."

"I see him now."

They crept closer, the scene unfolding before them. Polydeuces had taken down the rope barrier and was moving about behind the herd, ushering them forward. Idas fumed. They were stealing his hard won cattle, going back on their deal. He rushed forward, a yell ripping out of him.

"Pollox!" he heard Castor shout.

Hefting his spear, Idas took aim and threw with all his strength. His massive arm sent the missile hurtling toward his treacherous cousin. He watched it sail to its mark and saw the man topple from his perch to hit the ground.

With a cry of triumph, Idas rushed forward to jump on the man, screaming his rage at his cousin's duplicity, pounding Castor's head with his huge fists.

"Castor!" shouted Pollox.

Idas barely noticed his brother rushing past to meet the son of Zeus. He looked up to see Lynceus crash into Pollox, who met him with a growl of rage. The two clashed with bare fists, Lynceus throwing all his strength into the fight.

But he was no match for the godlike Polydeuces. The power of his divine father shone about him and with a sickening thud, Idas saw his brother fall.

Screaming out his anguish, the huge man rushed at his cousin, fists flying. Pollox stood watching him come as the sky above rumbled with his divine father's anger. But, filled with rage at his brother's death, Idas barely noticed the crashing noise above.

Polydeuces met his charge with all the power of his heritage, but Idas held his own, his brute strength equal to the son of the god. The little Pollox would pay.

Idas would see that neither of the treacherous brothers would see their home again. But he took no heed of the rumbling thunder, unaware of the eye of Zeus fixed upon him.

Klytemestra sat beside her dozing father, staring blankly at the flames in the hearth. Smoke from the unbanked fire filled the megaron, but she could not raise the energy to call for a servant to scrape the coals. Hidden behind her glazed eyes, her mind raced.

Menelaos would soon return. How would he react to a missing wife, the only news of her the rumour of a torrid love affair? She gulped down the rising panic. It was all her fault. Menelaos had entrusted her with keeping Helene in line and she had failed. But it was not Helene's wronged husband who filled her with fear.

Agamemnon would be furious. Her fevered mind turned

the story over in her mind, turning toward self-preservation. Helene was gone and out of reach, but not Klytie. She would bear the brunt of both men's rage. How could she salvage this, and turn a story of elopement into something they could accept, and believe?

"Klytie!" a scream rang across the courtyard.

She patted her ailing father's arm and rushed out of the megaron, down the short corridor to the main door. Bursting out into the great court, she stopped. Her brother Pollox was struggling toward her, carrying the limp form of his much heavier brother Castor. Klytie gasped and ran forward.

"What happened?"

"It was Idas," he hissed.

"Idas?" she murmured. Then her head snapped up. "What did you do?"

"It was Castor's idea," he groaned. "He wanted to recapture the herd we lost to Idas and Lynceus."

"What? You mean this is all about that herd of cattle? I thought that was over."

Polydeuces shrugged. "We thought we could claim it back. Idas and Lynceus disagreed."

"I'm not surprised."

"They ambushed us and there was a fight."

"Where are the others?"

"Dead," he said. "I killed Lynceus myself, but Idas nearly got me too. He was struck down by my father's thunderbolt."

"Let's get him inside," Klytie murmured.

"Klytie, I think he's dying..." Polydeuces sobbed as they carried the unconscious Castor into the palace.

"Don't say that, Pollox! He's not going to die!"

"Idas got him a mighty blow with his spear and jumped on him while he was down, crushing his body and hitting him about the head..."

Klytie hissed instructions to the servants clustered about as Polydeuces took his brother into the megaron, quiet and warm. A servant returned with a blanket to spread on the floor and Castor was laid down beside the hearth.

"What's going on?" the King mumbled, staggering to his feet.

"Don't worry, Papa," Klytie said, forestalling him. "The boys have been getting into mischief again. You sit while I deal with it."

At that moment, a wail filled the room. A distraught Hilaira hurried to her husband's prostrate form, followed by her sister Phoebe. Pollox stopped his wife with a look as Hilaira sank to the floor beside Castor.

"Castor?" she cried. "What happened?"

"He got in a fight with Idas," Klytie whispered.

"Why won't he wake up?" she sobbed.

"I'm sorry, Hilaira. He might not make it."

"What?" she sniffled. "No!" she cried. "Castor, you must live! Anagon needs his father, you mustn't go!" She collapsed in a heap over her husband's battered form, her wails cutting the quiet and waking Tyndareos. Klytie watched Hilaira grieving over Castor and realised there was more to this woman than the silly giggles and flirting she had witnessed so far. She really cared for her husband, and this was no time to condemn her vapidity. Klytie felt suddenly guilty for misjudging her.

"Klytie, what's that noise?" the old king said.

Klytemestra could not hide the truth any longer. "Papa, Castor is badly hurt. He may die," she sobbed.

"Klytie," Pollox moaned. "What are we going to do?"

She took a deep breath and straightened her shoulders. "First I need to see his injuries, then I'll know what offerings to make, and to whom."

"Should I get the potinia?"

"No, Pollox, I can do it."

She gently removed Hilaira's hands and quickly unhooked the shoulder pins on his blood-stained kiton and bared his torso, ignoring his wife's gasp at the extent of his injuries. Klytie felt his ribs, finding several breaks, but none seemed too far out of place. The spear had left a jagged hole in his side and she pressed carefully on his stomach, exploring by feel. The usually soft flesh was hard and distended, suggesting further injury.

"I think he's bleeding inside," she whispered. "If we don't make an offering soon he'll fill with blood and die."

As she continued to probe his gut, Castor moaned and his eyelids fluttered.

"Klytie, I think he's waking up!"

She moved to his head, prying open his eyes, but he would not focus. His mouth moved and she called for water.

"He may have something wrong in his head too," Klytie said.

"What can you do?"

"His worst injuries are all inside. I can't sprinkle remedies on them or wrap them as I would for a sword cut. I can wrap his wound, but it won't stop the bleeding in his gut. The best I can do is to make offerings to Asklepius. Maybe the god of healing will take a hand to save him..."

Pollox groaned. "I can't lose him, Klytie!"

"I'll do my best, Pollox. I don't want to lose him either!"

Feeling useless, Klytie did the only thing she knew, calling for servants to bring the libation bowl and tripod. She ordered a series of small animals to be brought for sacrifice and prepared to perform the ceremony right there in the megaron, beside her beloved brother's failing body.

Klytie hurried to her rooms to change into her ceremonial robes, the tight open-front jacket and flounced skirt. She tied the sacrificial apron around her waist and made her way downstairs.

The servants had set up the wooden table ready for her, the double axe standing upright to one end and the rhyton in the shape of a lion's head waiting to catch the sacrificial blood. She took a deep breath and approached the table.

A young girl came toward her, holding a cane basket. Klytie removed the lid and looked in on the two snakes coiled inside. These were not her own familiar serpents, but they were well fed and sleepy. She hoped they were also well handled. They may not be dangerous but they could still give a nasty bite.

Slowly she reached into the basket and grasped a snake in each hand, holding them just below the head. Bringing the snakes out, Klytie brought them to her face, murmuring soothing words and letting their flickering tongues taste her face. Then she planted herself before the table and held the snakes aloft as they writhed in the firelight.

"Oh great gods on Olympus, hear the servant of Potinia," she cried. "Accept these offerings in the name of the lady. I call on Asklepius, the great healer. Once you were human. Now you watch over the sick and injured. Watch over this man now."

She lowered her hands, holding them out toward the hearth as the snakes calmed their writhing and wrapped themselves about her arms, right up to her shoulders and down her torso. She released her grip on the serpents' heads and they settled into position on the backs of her hands. Then she called for the first sacrifice.

A servant led in the first animal, a goat, tugging at the rope and bleating piteously. Klytie reached a hand to the animal, calming it with a touch to the head.

"In the name of the lady, we thank you for the gift of life," she said to the goat.

She grasped the double axe, one side sharp the other

blunted like a club. With a practised sideways swing, she brought the club down on the side of the goat's head, just hard enough to stun it, and the animal was silenced. The snakes hissed a little but remained entwined about her. She motioned for the servant to lay the goat on the sacrificial table.

"Oh great healer, accept this offering in the name of the lady."

She raised the axe, sharp side this time, and brought it down cleanly on the goat's neck, severing the head, which fell into a basket on the floor beside the table. The snakes reared up, hissing and spitting.

A girl stepped in with the rhyton as the animal bled out, the bright red arterial blood pumping from the neck and running into the channels carved into the table. The girl held the rhyton beneath the table to catch the blood as it ran into the spout. Then she passed the vessel to Klytie.

Turning to the golden bowl on the tripod, Klytie raised the rhyton to the heavens, the snakes resting their heads on the rim.

"Asklepius, healer of the sick, I offer the blood of this animal, who gave his life for you. Hear my plea and heal this man."

With that, she poured the blood into the libation bowl in a long red stream, symbolically feeding the god. She passed the empty rhyton to the girl and raised the bowl. She carried it to where Castor lay. Dipping a hand into the liquid, she drew a line on her brother's brow.

The snake uncoiled and slithered down her arm, wrapping itself about Castor's head and shoulders. Its flickering tongue tasted the blood trail and it rested its head on the sick man's forehead.

Next, Klytemestra dipped the other hand in the bowl and traced a circle of blood across Castor's stomach. The second snake slid down off her arm and coiled itself on the man's torso, resting its head next to the wound in his side. Standing, Klytie called for a servant to take the bowl and its contents.

"In the name of the lady we give this blood," she intoned. "Take this to the shrine of Asklepius and place it on his altar," she ordered the servant.

"What now?" said Pollox as his sister wiped her brow.

"We ready the next sacrifice, and we continue offering until we see an improvement or..."

"Or he dies," he said through gritted teeth.

Klytie nodded with a sigh. She called for servants to remove the goat and bring the next sacrifice, this time a ram. She performed the ritual and poured the blood, calling again on Asklepius, and sent the second bowl to the shrine. Castor lay unresponsive, his breath weak and his flesh pallid. Klytie bit back a moan of fear, unable to do more than shake her head at Hilaira's pleading eyes.

"It's not working," Pollox groaned, pacing the floor. "Klytie, he's not responding. Asklepius hasn't come..."

"I'm not done yet, Pollox. Bring me a fawn."

After a short wait, a young deer was let into the room, hooves skittering on the flagstones and eyes wide in fear. Klytie touched the baby deer with a gentle hand, looking deep into its huge brown eyes.

"I thank you for the gift of life," she murmured. "May you bring the spark of new life to one that is failing."

She gently cupped the head in her hand and brought the clubbed side of the axe to the fawn's temple. She completed the ritual and poured the libation, holding her breath for a favourable result. But she was pulled from her trance by an ear-piercing shriek.

"Klytie!" Hilaira screamed. "He's not breathing!"

Klytie gasped and dropped by her brother's side. In

the midst of the ritual, she had not heard his rattling last breath. The god had chosen not to heal him. She hung her head.

"No!" Pollox cried. "I will not accept this. Bring me a bull!"

Klytie's head snapped up.

"Pollox, what are you doing? A bull is too powerful for healing!"

"It's too late for healing now. I'm going to a higher power."

"Pollox..."

"Don't try to stop me, Klytie."

A clamour and a loud bellowing heralded the arrival of the bull. Two men led the powerful animal with ropes tied about its neck, their hands clutching its long, slightly curved horns. The great beast snorted its rage and tossed its head, flinging one man off his feet.

The other held tight, catching the horns with both arms and pulling downward with all his weight. Polydeuces took the sacrificial axe, holding it aloft in both hands, and gave a mighty overhand swing. It came down between the bull's horns, narrowly missing the terrified servant, and crashed through the beast's huge skull, lodging in the brain.

The servant jumped free as the bull fell to the floor, hooves flailing for a moment before it lay still. Ripping the axe out of the animal's crushed skull, Pollox lifted it once more and brought the sharp blade down on the thick neck, slicing through skin and bone but not quite managing to sever the head.

He raised the axe to swing again, with all of his greater than human strength, and somehow managed to break through the spine. Scrambling through the spreading pool of blood, he grabbed the rhyton and held it against the spurting artery, catching the crimson stream. The vessel filled quickly, but still the animal's life-blood flowed, the floor slick with it. Scrambling to his feet, Pollox lifted the rhyton above his head.

"Father!" he screamed. "I call upon Zeus, father of gods and men, if you ever cared for your son, come to me now!"

There was a sudden rumble of sound, a great clap of thunder. Zeus was listening.

"I give you this bull as a sign of my resolve. I call on you to save my brother."

The rumble came again and Klytie held her breath as she watched Pollox pour the libation.

"Father! In my veins runs the divine gift of your blood, while my mortal brother dies. I have no need of immortality without him. Take my divine half and give it to my brother that he may live!"

This time the thunder rolled on and on, growing louder and stronger, reverberating through the floor and rattling the bones.

"Please, Father!" Pollox cried.

There was an almighty crack and a blinding light. Blinking as she lifted her eyes from behind her shielding arm, Klytie saw Pollox lying on the floor beside his brother. She scrambled toward him to find him staring upward unblinking, eyes fixed on nothing and mouth moving silently.

"Pollox!" shrieked his wife, Phoebe.

"Pollox?" Klytie whispered.

Then Pollox sat up, eyes on the heavens. "Father," he cried. "I agree!"

"What?" Klytie snapped. "What do you agree to, Pollox?"

Pollox met her anxious gaze with wild eyes. "I can save him, but only if I go too."

"What do you mean, go too? Pollox, you can't."

"I won't stay here for all eternity without Castor!" he

ELLA MORTIMER

cried. "Don't you see, Klytie? I am the son of Zeus; I have the lifespan of a god. But what good is it without my brother? I choose to share my immortality with him, but I must share it in the home of my father. My mortal half will die, and we'll share equal time in Hades and in Olympus, swapping places each day. It's the only way to save him."

"But that's not saving him! I'd be losing you both!"

"No, dear sister, you'd have us both forever. We'd always be with you, watching from Olympus. It's the only way."

"I don't want you to go," she sobbed.

"And what about your son?" whispered Phoebe. "You would leave Nesileos and me here?"

"You'll be fine, and so will he. You and your sister should go back to your father. You'll be loved and well treated there."

Phoebe sobbed and shook her head.

"My mind is made up," he said.

Pollox staggered to his feet and picked up the libation bowl once more. He raised it high.

"Father, I'm ready. Take me now."

He poured the contents of the bowl over his own head, blinking as the blood ran down his face. There was a roll of thunder, a bright flash of light and a shattering detonation.

When the light dissipated and the smoke cleared, both brothers were gone. Klytie sank to the bloody ground, a gut-wrenching groan squeezing its way out of her of its own volition. As Hilaira and Phoebe filled the room with their wails, Klytie dissolved in a heap, her breath hiccupping out around her sobs.

The King in his royal seat woke with a snort and blinked at the nightmarish scene of his daughter and his sons' wives sprawled in anguish in a sea of sacrificial blood.

"What's going on?"

11

A Home No More

Klytemestra stared at the flickering flames in the hearth, the red and gold light burning into her soul, seeming to find a match in her seething heart. Beside her, the King mumbled in his doze, occasionally waking with a snort to ask the same question yet again.

"Where are your brothers?"

"They're gone, Papa," she replied.

"On one of their escapades, I suppose."

"No, Papa, they've gone to join father Zeus."

"Don't be silly, child, I never believed all that."

"You don't believe in the gods?" she gasped.

"Hush, child, of course I do. But all that nonsense about Zeus and Leda? No, it never happened. Pollox is my son as much as his brother is, I'm sure of it."

"Oh, Papa, I saw them disappear, right before my eyes. Zeus took them because Pollox asked him to."

"They'll be back when they've got over their latest folly," he murmured as he sank back into his doze.

"No, Papa, they won't," she whispered over the lump in her throat.

The next time he woke was not much better.

"Where did you say the boys had gone?"

"They've gone to live with the gods, Papa."

"No, they're just off adventuring. They'll be home soon."

"No, Papa, they're gone forever."

But he was snoring again. Klytie stared into the fire once more, gulping back the tears and waiting for the next time.

"Did you say the boys are with the gods?"

"Yes, Papa."

"Are they dead then?"

"As good as dead, yes."

"No, they'll be back."

Klytie sighed. She heard a clatter outside in the corridor and slowly stood. Heavy footsteps heralded the brothers, Agamemnon and Menelaos, returned from Crete. Tyndareos woke with a snort.

"Ah, here they are, I told you they'd be back."

"No, Papa, these are not your sons, they're your sons-in-law, Agamemnon and Menelaos."

"Ah. And Castor and Pollox? When will they be back?"

"I told you, Papa, they're gone forever."

"Are they dead, then?"

"Yes, Papa," she sighed.

"What's happened here? Where is everyone?" said Menelaos, approaching the King and his daughter.

"My brothers are with Zeus, never to return," said Klytie tonelessly. "Their wives have returned to their father, taking their sons with them."

"And my wife?" said Menelaos. "Where is Helene?"

"She is... gone too," Klytie murmured, taking a step back in anticipation of his anger.

"Gone? What are you talking about, woman? Gone where?"

"She..." Klytie licked her lips, eyes darting away. "There was a stranger, who appeared out of nowhere from a faraway place. She..."

Agamemnon stepped in front of his brother, grabbing at

his wife's arm, eyes boring into hers.

"What did they do? Did you allow her to be seduced by this man? After you were brought here specifically to prevent it?"

Klytie shook her head desperately. How could he have guessed the truth so quickly?

"No," she whispered. "I swear I tried."

Menelaos groaned. "Did my wife run off with this man?"

Klytie stared from one to the other, watching Menelaos carefully. She saw the rapidly crumbling expression on his face, her mind racing. Then her eyes widened and she shook her head.

"It wasn't like that," she lied. "She loves you, she told me so herself."

Menelaos gave a shuddering sigh at her words.

"He came with a wild story," she continued. "About how Helene had been promised to him by Aphrodite. He said he came specifically to claim her."

"And he seduced her," said Agamemnon. "You were supposed to watch her."

She flinched and shook her head again, rushing on with her lie. "No, he took her," she continued. "He stole her, took her away by force."

"He kidnapped her?"

"Yes!" she cried, nodding vehemently. "He dragged her away in the night, spirited her off. By the time we knew she was gone, it was too late. We searched and searched, but..."

"Gone..." Menelaos whispered as he sank into the chair beside the King. "Where?"

"Over the sea to the east, a place called Ilion."

"Gone," sighed the King.

"What do we do?" said Menelaos, looking to his brother with haunted eyes.

"We go after them," snarled Agamemnon. "And we make

him pay."

"How?"

"What do you mean, how? You have an alliance with every prince in the world, all the suitors of Helene."

"My sons are gone," murmured Tyndareos "You are all that's left."

Menelaos shook his head. "I can't! I don't have the will..."

"But I do," Agamemnon snarled. "Let me lead them for you."

Menelaos nodded. "Yes. We must get her back."

"Get her back," said the King. "Bring her home to be your queen..."

"What did you say?" said Menelaos, finally hearing the King's murmurings.

"My sons are gone, you are all I have."

"My lord," Menelaos began.

"No, I'm a sad old man. You're my lord now," he whispered. "Find my daughter."

The old man let out a sigh and his eyes closed, amid a stunned silence. Klytie lifted his blanket from the floor and spread it over his legs. He was quiet, not even a snore, and his chest was still.

"Oh, Papa," she whispered. "Sleep well and go in peace."

In her private chamber, Klytemestra sat in the window, staring out into the night. Soon Agamemnon would come. Once he had finished plotting with his brother, planning the invasion of Ilion.

They would talk well into the night, drinking wine, making lists and strategies, composing messages to all the princes of Achaea. Then he would find her. She did not doubt he saw through her lie. He knew she had failed to keep her sister chaste and she shivered in anticipation of his displeasure.

With a sinking heart, she crawled into bed, snuggling under the blankets and trying to sleep. She was awoken by the crash of the door and the roar of his drunken voice.

"So, wife, what did you get up to while your sister was betraying her husband?"

Suddenly wide awake, she tried to escape his clutching hand. He dragged her out of the blankets, pulled her up to his chest and pinned her, one hand clasping the back of her neck painfully as he forced her to meet his eyes.

"Who were you cavorting with, that you could miss it?" he growled.

She tried to shake her head, gasped at the smell of wine on his breath. His snarl struck terror in her heart.

"Don't play the innocent with me, wife. How could you not know what was happening? I've heard the servants' whispers; I know she wasn't stolen. Though I must say it was the perfect excuse, I have to applaud you on that. I knew you were the smarter sister."

"I don't know what you mean," she whispered.

He chuckled. "Keeping true to the story, are you? How long was he here, seducing her, before they ran off, hmmm?"

"I swear, he took her..." she said, voice cracking.

"Did he now? Or did they elope when they heard we were on our way? Oh don't worry, I won't tell my brother the truth. His revenge is justified and I'd do nothing to dissuade him from going to war."

Klytie could say no more, shaking her head in fear. He relaxed his grasp, but took hold of her arms, gripping them painfully and giving her a shake.

"But you," he whispered. "You watched it happen. You did nothing to stop it, which makes me wonder. Who caught your eye? Who took your attention away from your task?"

"Nobody!" she cried. "I swear."

"No? Why do I find that hard to believe? Your father has

other daughters, those daughters committed adultery too. I hear the stories; I know there was a curse on your father's house, that all his daughters would betray their husbands. What makes you any different from your wanton sisters?"

"I've done nothing wrong," she said, straightening her back indignantly.

He released her and sat back on the bed. She sank into the blankets, her stomach roiling and her limbs like water.

"Not yet, perhaps, but you will. How am I to be sure, now that I have an army to gather, and a war to wage? I could be gone for years."

She shook her head again, but he would never believe her.

"I intend to take you back to Mycenae and leave you with a chaperone. I'll hire musicians and entertainers, to keep you occupied and to watch you while I'm gone. People I trust, and who won't be swayed by you. You'll have no chance to betray me like your sister did my brother."

As the sun peeked its pinprick beams through the shutters, Klytemestra pulled the blankets up over her head, groaning at the ache in her arms. She stretched carefully, her whole body protesting and closed her eyes tight on the tears.

Agamemnon had hurried downstairs before dawn, not before waking her to have his way again, rekindling the pain of the night. Now, she buried herself down, blocking out the day. Today she would bury her father and tomorrow she would head for Mycenae.

A small spark of pleasure battled fitfully through the fog of grief as she thought of her children, waiting for her return. They would be older now; she had been away so long. She felt a pang of regret at what she had missed.

Iphigenia would be showing signs of growing up. Elektra

would be ruling the roost. And little Krisothemis... Klytie stifled a sob. Would Krissie even remember her?

There was a tap at the door, a light footfall, and Klytie groaned.

"Aunt Klytie?" came a hesitant voice.

Klytie sighed and pulled the blanket off her face, blinking in the light as she dragged herself up against the pillows. "Yes, Hermione?"

"What happened?" Hermione gasped. "Your arms are bruised."

"It's nothing," Klytie murmured, drawing the blanket up to her neck. "What can I do for you, dear?"

"Well," Hermione hesitated. "You're leaving tomorrow, aren't you?"

Klytie nodded.

"I wondered if you might... take me with you."

"Oh! I... don't see why not, but you should ask your papa. Why?"

"I don't want to stay here," she whispered. "Mama's run away, Uncle Castor and Uncle Pollox are gone, Grandpapa is dead..." she took a gasping breath. "When Papa goes to war there'll be nobody left. I'll be all alone."

Klytie's heart melted. "Oh, Hermione, of course you can come with me. I'm sure your papa won't mind."

Klytie dragged herself out of bed and dressed for the funeral procession, in her ceremonial gown once more. She was happy to step back and let the resident potinia take charge of proceedings and took her place behind the litter on which her father had been laid out.

He was dressed in his finest kiton and wore the gold mask of death. Behind her walked a long line of slaves, carrying offerings and treasures for his tomb. The procession filed out of the main gate, leaving the courtyard and walking across the ridge, covering the short distance at a slow, measured pace.

They made their way through the temple precinct and approached the ancestral tomb, buried beneath a little hill to the west of the palace. Moving around the base of the hill, the procession began to climb.

The King's litter entered the long, sloping approach to the tomb, high walls closing in as they neared the monumental doorway. Klytie looked up at a blue sky framed by stone, the morning sun throwing the hill's shadow over the doorway, and shivered.

Here her father would be laid to rest, the first step on his journey to the underworld. Klytie passed through the stone doorway, under the relieving triangle, and stepped into the dark interior. The old king's litter was laid on the floor in the centre of the room. The flickering light of one lonely torch barely dispelled the gloom and the high vaulted roof loomed in darkness above.

The dim light cast shadows on the walls and licked at the tantalising remnants of previous burials, which had been moved aside for the tomb's new resident. Outside the tomb, Klytie could hear the priestess of the lady, invoking the gods of the dead as she slaughtered the live offerings.

The libation bowls, full of sacrificial blood, were brought in and laid about the dead king. The animals would be prepared for the funeral feast. Then the singing began, young slave girls raising their voices in a wailing dirge for the deceased. Klytie clenched her fists, feeling only a desperate need to leave this place of death.

Finally, the procession began to move away and Klytie hurried out of the darkness, rushing past the line of mourners, retreating from the walled approach until she emerged into the sunlight and stood gasping for breath.

She stared out over the valley and the river far below,

following the line of the ridge along which the ancient city clustered, clinging to the slopes. The city of Sparta in the land of Lacedaemon. Her home. But no more.

Once she had felt exiled, trapped in Mycenae, far from her home and the people she loved. But it was all over now, her loved ones dead or gone, and all she wanted was to get away, back to her beloved children.

Klytie endured the burial feast, watched through a haze the hastily arranged games, the contestants a few local princelings who had managed to attend. But the frivolity only served to drive her further away.

Finally, she made her way wearily to her chamber, leaving Agamemnon to plot and scheme with his brother and the first allies to arrive at his call. She clambered into bed and huddled down in the blankets, eyes fixed on the shutters as she waited for the first sign of dawn to herald her escape.

It was with a sense of relief that Klytie approached the great lion gate at last, Agamemnon in the lead and her niece Hermione at her side. They had ridden together at the head of a small retinue, pushing the pace as they strove to put Sparta and the sad events of the past few months far behind.

Clattering up the hill, they approached the palace wall at last. Glancing up, Klytie could see a small group clustered on the wall above, staring down at them. Dismounting in the small outer courtyard, Hermione raced up the great staircase with Klytie close behind.

"Mama!" she heard from the court above.

Reaching the top of the staircase, where Hermione had paused uncertainly, passing the familiar rooms of the potinia, Klytie turned toward the large palace courtyard. As she stepped into the light, she was nearly bowled over as a tall, wiry girl thudded into her chest. With tears pricking at her eyes, Klytie wrapped her arms about her eldest daughter and buried her face in her hair.

"Oh, Gennie," she murmured. "I missed you so much." Klytie pulled back and held her at arm's length. "Let me look at you. You've grown so tall."

"Mama, why were you gone so long? You missed my birthday! I'm eight now."

"I know, sweetie, I missed everyone's birthday," Klytie said with a little sob.

"Is that Hermione?" Gennie whispered, staring over her mother's shoulder.

"Yes, dear. She's been eager to see you."

Gennie grinned. "Hermione, what are you doing here?"

"My mama ran away, and my papa's preparing to go to war to get her back."

"Really?"

She nodded. "Your papa's downstairs."

"He is? Come on then!"

The girls hurried off, chatting and Klytie smiled at their exuberance. It would be good for them both to have a friend in each other. She stepped out into the courtyard to see her two younger daughters waiting with their loyal servant Aegisthus.

Elektra stood to one side, arms folded and lower lip thrust out in a pout. Klytie forced down her desire to clutch her baby out of the servant's arms, and approached her middle daughter. Elektra turned her back on her mother.

"Elektra?" Klytie said softly. "Can mama have a hug?"

The child shook her head vehemently. Klytie moved around in front of her and knelt down at her level but she turned her back again. Klytie sighed.

"Please look at me, Elektra."

The girl turned her head slightly to peek over one

shoulder. Then she turned half way around, big blue eyes glistening with tears and jutting lower lip trembling.

"I'm so sorry, Elektra. I'm sorry I was gone so long."

The little girl's face screwed up and she rushed at her mother, burrowing into her chest and clambering up into her arms, forcing her back and onto the ground, where she settled into her lap, sobbing quietly. Klytie stayed there for a long time, cuddling Elektra as she cried herself out. Finally, the girl relaxed her grip and pulled back.

"I missed you, mama," Elektra sobbed.

"I missed you too, my lovely girl," Klytie whispered as she held her tight.

Looking up as a shadow fell across them, Klytie saw the servant standing with little Krissie in his arms. The toddler stared wide-eyed, little hands clutching at the servant's kiton. Klytie untangled herself from Elektra and stood. Elektra clutched at her legs as she held out her arms for Krisothemis. The baby burrowed her head in the servant's shoulder.

"Krissie, it's your mama," Aegisthus whispered. "Don't you want to say hello?"

The little girl lifted her head to stare. Klytie held her arms out but Krissie withdrew again.

"Now, Krissie, we talked about this," said Aegisthus. "I know your mama's been away, but she still loves you. You remember how we talked about your mama every day. She's home now, give her a hug."

He brought the child in close and pried her fingers loose, passing her to her mother. Klytie took the child carefully as her little fingers grabbed at Aegisthus, and the servant stepped away. Krissie settled in her mother's arms and gazed at her.

The baby face Klytie remembered was gone. She was growing into a little girl, losing her baby fat and thinning out into a lanky toddler. Almost three, Klytie realised with a pang of regret.

"Mama?" the child whispered.

"Yes, my sweet."

"Papa!" Elektra squealed, running for the stairs where Agamemnon had appeared with a chattering Iphigenia.

The King lifted up his middle daughter, swinging her around, blowing away her sombre expression. The girl giggled.

"Come inside, Papa, tell us a story."

"I can't, my pretty miss. I need to leave straight away."

"Why?" Elektra pouted.

"I only came to see your mama home safely. I have a war to plan."

Klytie spend most of the afternoon with her daughters, just sitting and talking, cuddling and smiling under the watchful eye of Agamemnon's paid musician Neohippos, who played his lyre and sang away the day while he regarded her with narrowed eyes.

But eventually the children left her to play in the courtyard and she attempted to slip up to her chamber. The minstrel followed close behind and she spun to confront him.

"Are you really going to follow me to the closet?"

"No, of course not, my lady," he spluttered. "Just see you come straight back."

Klytie shuddered and hurried off, heading up to her room. She settled herself in the window and watched the clouds scudding across the sky. After all the madness of funerals and homecomings and chaperones, this solitude was a blessing and a curse.

She had been able to keep busy but now it was all over and she was left alone to pick up the pieces of her heart and carry on. She took a shuddering breath. No, she would not cry. That would solve nothing.

"My lady?" came a voice at the door.

She jumped. "Yes, Aegisthus?"

"I've just filled the bathing room for the girls, would you like to join them?"

"Yes, I would. Thank you," Klytie smiled.

He hovered in the doorway.

"Was there something else?"

"Yes, my lady. Did I hear your niece say her mama ran away? And that there was a war coming?"

"Yes, that's right," she sighed.

"What happened?"

Klytie shook her head. She had no wish to relive that. She heard him approach and stared resolutely out the window.

"Please tell me. What did Helene do?"

"She..." Klytie hesitated. Should she tell the truth or the lie? "She ran off with her lover rather than face Menelaos."

"And that's what this war is about? Menelaos seeking revenge?"

"Something like that."

"Was she unchaperoned? Where were your brothers?"

Klytie took a gasping breath. "Gone..." she choked on the word, bit her lip and stared resolutely at the darkening sky.

"Gone where? Off adventuring again?"

She nodded. "They came back after she left, but they're gone for good now."

"What are you talking about? Have they gone after her?"

"No," she sobbed. "Just gone."

"I don't understand."

She sighed and stubbornly pulled herself together. "There was a fight, Castor was wounded and dying. Pollox appealed to Zeus, to take his immortal life and give it to Castor that he might live. Zeus took them both instead."

"They died?" he gasped.

"In a manner of speaking."

"And your father? How did he take it?"

"He... gave up," she whispered around the lump in her throat. She felt her resolve breaking, the pent up emotions threatening to overwhelm her. She clutched her hands in her lap, rocking slightly.

"What do you mean gave up?" he pulled at her arm, forcing her to face him. "Talk to me, help me understand."

"It happened a few days after," she whispered. "He couldn't take it. His heart just... gave up."

"He died too?"

Klytie nodded, her vision blurred.

"By the gods, Klytie, why didn't you say something?"

"I..." She felt herself falling into despair. She had been holding it in for so long.

"Come here," he said, coaxing her down from the window. "You shouldn't keep things to yourself. I'm here for you, you know that."

He pulled her into his arms, murmuring soothing words, stroking her hair. Klytie crumbled against him.

"They're all gone," she wailed. "I've lost them all, there's nobody left... I've got no-one," she sobbed.

"You've got me," he murmured.

She clutched at him, her grief squeezing out of her in aching sobs despite her efforts to stop them.

"There now, hush my love," he whispered.

Klytie stiffened, pulling away. "Don't," she gulped.

"I... I'm sorry, my lady."

She clenched her hands, almost collapsing again. Human comfort was such a powerful need but she must not give in. Not to him.

"Don't be sorry, just don't do it again."

She saw the flash of hurt in his eyes, the flair of anger, and felt a pang of regret.

"Don't worry," he said coldly. "I know I can't compare to the great Agamemnon."

She bit her lip, the tears coming unbidden. "You're as much a prince as he," she whispered. "You deserve so much more. But I can't give it to you..."

"Because you love him?" he shook his head. "I find that hard to believe."

"No!" she spat. "Because I know what he's capable of. If his spy gets even a hint of something going on..."

"Is that who that man is? Your chaperone?" he cursed.

She sighed, sitting on the bed. "Agamemnon believes I'll betray him like my sister did Menelaos. I won't prove him right."

"So where does that leave me?"

"Perhaps you should go away."

His face hardened. "Is that what you want?"

She could not answer. She blinked back the tears that threatened again, involuntarily shaking her head.

"I'll never leave you," he whispered. "You need me here as much as I need to be here."

She watched him turn and head for the door, shoulders squared, but a small figure stood in the doorway.

"Elektra!" Klytie gasped.

The child stared at her. How much had she heard? Her face showed a confused frown and she had her arms crossed.

"Hello, little miss," said Aegisthus. "I was just telling your mama about the bath."

Elektra shook her head. "No you weren't," she snapped.

"Elektra..." Klytie said again.

"The bath is waiting, Mama," the six-year-old said.

She turned on her heel and disappeared. Aegisthus made to follow but turned in the doorway.

"There's something else you should know," he said.

"What's that?" Klytie whispered.

"I missed you too, my lady."

Then he was gone. In his place, the minstrel stood, suspicious eyes flicking from her to the servant and back. Then Neohippos stepped into the room.

"My lady, what are you doing up here?"

"Is that any of your business?" she snapped.

"It's your husband's business, and it's my job to watch you. There'll be no hiding away like this."

"I can't even snatch some privacy in my own room?"

"Not if you're sharing that privacy with a man, servant or otherwise."

"He was informing me that the bathing room is ready! Am I not allowed to bathe with my children?"

"Of course, my lady, just as long as I am witness."

Klytie gasped. "You want to watch me bathe? How dare you!"

"No, of course not," he spluttered. "But I must stand guard at the door. I must know where you are and who you're with at all times. Those are my orders."

Klytie stormed past, turning toward the stairs, eyes blurred by a fog of anger. This was too much.

12

A Thousand Ships

Watching the girls chase each other about the courtyard, Klytemestra smiled. Gennie and her cousin Hermione, inseparable friends, teased the younger girls. Elektra screamed, ready to throw herself into a rage. Krissie was crying because she could not catch them. Klytie's little son sat cradled in her lap, clutching her hair in his pudgy fingers.

"They're growing up fast, my lady," said her loyal servant at her side.

"My beauties," she sighed.

"They take after their mother."

"Maybe how I once was, but I'm older now, a matronly mother. Any beauty I had is long gone."

"Not true, my lady, you're only twenty-five. To me you're more beautiful now than you were when I first met you."

She glanced quickly to where the minstrel Neohippos sat, playing his lyre as usual. That kind of talk would get them both in trouble.

"You're too kind to me," she smiled. "I wish you could be happy, find a wife and family of your own."

"I am happy," he murmured. "I have all the family I want right here. I love them like they were my own."

"Will I ever convince you that I don't deserve your loyalty?" she whispered.

"Never," he replied.

A clatter of hooves below the wall made her jump and the girls ran to the parapet to look over. Elektra clambered up onto the wall and little Krissie jumped up and down, raising her arms to Gennie to be lifted up.

"Who do you think that might be?" said Klytie, feeling almost resentful of the intrusion.

"You've had no message? No warning of visitors?"

She shook her head. Then Hermione squealed.

"Papa!" the girl cried. "My papa's here!"

"Mama," Gennie called. "Papa's home!"

Klytie stood slowly, soothing the little one, heart thudding painfully. What was he doing home? Was the war over already? She felt an intense desire to run, but chided herself for her irrational reaction. She should be happy. The servant had melted into the background, the easy companionship broken. She cast him a glance, noticing his bitter expression, and sighed.

"Come on, Elektra," cried Gennie, heading for the stairs.

"Mama," said Krissie. "Can I go too?"

"Of course, dear," she smiled.

The girls ran down the stairs to meet the men, and Klytie could hear their excited chatter floating up from below. She stood quietly waiting, flinching at the sound of Agamemnon's big booming laugh echoing up the stairs.

Finally, they emerged, Gennie leading the way with Elektra clutching her father's hand and Krissie in his arms. Behind them, Menelaos emerged with his arm about Hermione, the girl chattering up at him with adoring eyes.

"So are we going home now, Papa?" she was saying.

"Yes, my sweet. But I'll have to leave again soon."

As Agamemnon strode toward her, Klytie stood firm despite her shivers, holding the baby in front like a shield. The King stopped in front of her, studying her and the child.

"My Lord, I offer you your son," she said formally, holding the child out at arm's length.

The little boy kicked his legs and blew a spit bubble. Agamemnon's eyes widened in wonder. He put Krissie down and the girl ran to grasp her mother's legs. Then he took the baby, staring into the little face. Unabashed, the boy grabbed his father's beard in both hands, gurgling as he pulled. Agamemnon laughed.

"Welcome, little man," he murmured. "Have you given him a name yet?"

Klytie shook her head. "That's for you to do, my lord."

"Then I name him Orestes," he said with evident satisfaction.

"Papa," Elektra pulled at her father's arm. "Did you win the war?"

Agamemnon threw his head back and laughed in delight. "No, my pretty one, we haven't started yet!"

"But you've been gone for months," Elektra pouted.

"What have you been doing, Papa?" Gennie said.

"Let's get inside and I'll tell you everything."

Once in the megaron, the King sat on his great seat and his brother took the chair beside him. The girls sat about their feet, with little Orestes happily settled in his father's arms. Klytie sent for food and drink, standing to one side to listen.

"So where have you been, Papa?" said Gennie.

"Before any great war, little scamp, a general must gather his troops," said Agamemnon. "We've travelled through all the lands of Achaea, calling on the men who swore allegiance to Menelaos before his marriage to Helene."

"Where are they? Did they all come?"

"They're mustering at Aulis. Most have agreed to come, but some resisted. Some even went to extraordinary lengths to avoid coming, but we got them in the end."

"Who?" said Elektra. "How did you get them, Papa?"

"Well, pretty one, the first to resist was Odysseus. When we arrived in Ithaca, his wife Penelope welcomed us but said her husband had gone mad. Well, we found him in his fields, driving a plough with a donkey and an ox hooked up."

Elektra giggled. "That's funny, Papa. Why did he do that?"

"He thought it would make him appear mad. Being different sized animals, they made the plough go in circles."

Elektra giggled again. "Then what?"

"Now, I knew he was faking, but how could we prove it and catch him out?"

"How, Papa?" said Krissie, wide eyed.

"I sent Palamedes to Odysseus' wife, to bring his little boy out to the fields. I told Palamedes to take little Telemachus and sit him in the path of the plough."

Gennie gasped. "Papa, how could you?"

"It's alright, scamp, I knew he wouldn't hurt his son. Odysseus saw him and swerved the plough, proving he wasn't really mad."

"You're so clever, Papa," said Elektra with a sigh.

"Not half so clever as Odysseus," said Agamemnon. "That's why we need him."

"But why didn't he want to come?" said Gennie.

"He said he had been to see the priest Calchas for an oracle. He was told that if he went to war he would not return for twenty years. Naturally, he didn't want to leave his wife and son for that long, so he tried to get out of it."

"Then what? Did you punish him?" said Elektra.

He chuckled. "No, my pretty, I just gave him a quest, to find Achilles."

"Who's he?"

"He's the son of Peleus, king of the Myrmidons, and the goddess Thetis. He's very young, but he's said to be the greatest warrior in the world."

"Don't be silly, Papa, you're the greatest warrior in the world!"

Agamemnon roared with laughter. "If only that were true, pretty miss. No, the prophet Calchas gave another oracle. He said we couldn't win without Achilles. But when we went to his father's home, we found his mother had spirited him away. She didn't want him going to war, you see. He's only a boy, really."

"Did you find him?"

"Odysseus said he did, though he hasn't joined the muster yet. He found him in the house of King Lycomedes in Scyros, hidden amongst the King's daughters, dressed up like a girl."

The girls all giggled at that. "That's silly!" said little Krissie.

"Yes, little one, it is."

"Who else wouldn't come, Papa?" said Gennie.

"Well, there was one other. King Cinyrus of Cyprus. He promised faithfully, swearing on my shield, that he would send fifty ships."

"What happened?" said Gennie.

"When I got to the muster, after visiting every one of the allies and drawing out their promises to come, I found Cinyrus had sent his son on one ship. When I asked about the rest of the promised fifty, he produced a wooden chest. Can you guess what was inside?"

The girls shook their heads.

"Forty-nine little toy boats, with tiny crews and soldiers to match."

Krissie giggled, clapping her hands.

"What a nasty trick," frowned Elektra.

"Yes, it was," said Agamemnon.

"What now, Papa?"

"Now, I have to gather my troops, from all over Argos, and take them to Aulis. Menelaos has to go to Sparta and collect the armies of Lacedaemon. Then, when we are all gathered at Aulis, we set sail for Ilion."

Klytie sat in the chair by the bedroom window, giving her son his last feed for the night. The girls had gone to their beds and the voices from the megaron were settling down. Agamemnon burst through the door, striding to her side to stare out the window.

"Is he really my son?" he said, dangerously calm.

Klytie blinked. "Of course he his. Why would you say that?"

"How do I know he's not the result of some... fling, with whoever took your attention off your sister."

Klytie bristled with anger. "I told you, there was no-one! I tried to stop her, but she wouldn't listen."

He turned, leaning back against the sill as he gazed at her.

"How can I be sure?"

She pulled the child off the breast and lifted him to his father.

"Look at him," she said. "How can he be anyone else's?"

He took the child, cradling him as he stared into those slate blue eyes, fingering the wild crop of dark hair on his little head. Klytie knew the resemblance was too strong to be denied.

"You're right," he whispered. "I believe you."

He passed the sleepy boy back to finish his feed.

"I'm sorry for how I behaved, back in Sparta," he said quietly. "I should not have doubted you. You are not your sister."

"No," she said. "When my sister was taken by Theseus all those years ago, she came back changed. Awakened too soon, she never learned to control her lust. I'm not like her, and I can't stop her."

"Menelaos is a fool. He should not be chasing after a harlot. But I won't deny him his pride."

"So you're leaving again?"

"Before dawn tomorrow. I must visit every city in Argos and collect my forces. I'll head straight to Aulis when I'm done."

* * *

A blustery wind scudded across the sand and pushed the patchy clouds across a grey sky. The long, pointed prows of hundreds of ships lined up along the shore, wooden hulls black with tar to keep the water at bay. On the bluff behind the beach, thousands of men had made camp, huddled about their fires to ward off the unseasonal cold. A young warrior strode through the troops, looking for one man.

"Agamemnon!" the young man yelled. "Come and face me!"

In his command tent, Agamemnon heard the call and groaned. His generals grinned, exchanging looks of exasperation.

"I said you wouldn't avoid him forever," said Odysseus with a grin.

"That boy needs a good lesson in humility," Agamemnon grumbled. "I don't have time to pander to him."

Odysseus laughed. "Maybe so, but we need him."

"And he knows it. I have a good mind to leave him behind if he doesn't settle down and let us get to business."

"He's still smarting at being caught out and forced to come here. When I found him, he was in a very cosy position, living with the girls of Scyros. From what I hear he had even infiltrated the virtue of the king's daughter."

"Infiltrated? You make it sound like a military campaign. The boy got himself a bit of skirt. So what?"

"So, he's young. Nothing is more important to him right now. He has nothing but lust in his head."

"That and no small amount of arrogant pride. He thinks the world should bow down and worship him."

"Agamemnon!" the cry came again.

"You may as well go out and speak to him. He won't shut up until you do."

Grumbling, Agamemnon strode from the tent to confront the little twerp. The young warrior stood there pouting, tossing his fair hair out of his eyes and glaring at him. Agamemnon sighed.

"What do you want, Achilles?"

"I want to know why you dragged me here to this forsaken place and why we're sitting here doing nothing when I could be warmer elsewhere."

"Neither of which are important questions right now."

"Not important? I'll have you know..."

"What?" Agamemnon snapped. "You're the great Achilles, son of the goddess Thetis? So what?"

"So, I deserve your respect. I deserve to know what you're planning."

"You deserve nothing until you've proven your worth. You're among great men here, none of whom look on you as any more than an upstart child. We go in search of a daughter of Zeus!"

The boy bristled. "At least tell me, when do we leave?"

"We leave when we're good and ready. I suggest you go back to your men, sit down like a good boy and wait."

Agamemnon turned his back on the fuming lad and strode back to the command tent, stepping into the dim interior. The assembled generals almost fell over themselves with laughter.

*

The prophet Calchas set up his sacrificial table by a tree at the edge of the field. Above his head, a brood of sparrows chirped as they waited for mother sparrow to bring their food. The gathered warriors watched silently as Calchas opened the basket, reaching in with both hands.

Two snakes, his own personal serpents, faithful companions through many a ritual offering, slithered up his arms to lick his face. He began the ritual, stunning the sacrificial goat with the blunt end of his axe and laying it out on the table. Lifting his serpent clad arms he invoked the gods.

"I call on the gods of Olympus to hear and respond. I call Athena, the martial beauty to bless us with her guidance. I call on Ares the god of war to bless us on the eve of battle. I call mighty Zeus, father of gods and men, and father of the woman who inspires this war. I call on the divine twins, Apollo as giver of oracles and his sister, the huntress Artemis. Give us your guidance and protection."

Then he brought the axe down, severing the head of the animal. The snakes on his arms hissed and reared their heads. Calchas caught the blood and poured it into the libation bowl. One of his serpents slithered up to rest on his head, coiled there, and stared upward.

The other snake slid down the prophet's arm, across the corpse of the goat and down the leg of the table. It slithered quickly across to the tree and made its way up the trunk, heading for the nest where the baby birds still called for their mother.

It moved out along the branch, lifting its head up above the nest, rocking from side to side as the men watched in awe. The snake darted in, clutching one baby sparrow in its mouth, raising up high and biting the bird, pulling it further into its mouth.

In three quick gulps, the snake had swallowed the baby bird. Then it dipped in and grabbed another, and another. Each chick was swallowed in turn, and still the snake took another, eight little sparrow chicks in all went into the serpent's maw.

As the last chick disappeared, the mother returned, diving to attack at the killer of her children. The snake reared up and snapped, catching her in mid-air, drawing her into its mouth and eating her too.

The last sparrow was gone and all was silent. No more chirping brightened the day. The sated serpent curled up in the nest that had once held the brood of sparrows and was still. Calchas reached a hand up to call the snake back to him but it did not move. He made his special clicking noise, a call that the snake never ignored, but it still did not move. Calchas sighed and lowered his hand.

"What does it mean?" whispered Menelaos.

"The snake is dead. Apollo the oracle giver has spoken," said Calchas. "The sparrows are years, the snake is Ilion. Nine years will be eaten in this war with the men of Troy. In the tenth year, Ilion will fall."

Some weeks later, in a far-away land, as the sun rose over the high cliffs, a lone scout rode through the camp, searching for the commander. He finally found the large command tent and stepped inside.

"My lords," he said.

"Report," Agamemnon replied.

"There's not much around, but follow the river a small way inland and you will find a walled city."

"Do you think it could be Troy?" Menelaos whispered.

The scout shrugged. "I really can't tell, but it's busy, lots of people coming and going, and it's well fortified, with guards patrolling the walls."

"It sounds like they're prepared for a fight," said Agamemnon. "It must be the place."

"Then let's go," said Menelaos stiffly.

Agamemnon nodded. "No point delaying."

Together the commander and his generals rallied the troops and began the march, coming across the city late in the afternoon. They set up camp to await the dawn, and at first light began their assault.

Leading the charge, Agamemnon and his Argives ploughed forward to the gate. To one side, Menelaos led the men of Laconia and to the other Achilles and his Myrmidons struck terror into the defenders.

The small force that came out to meet them fought viciously, managing to keep the Achaeans at bay. But by early afternoon Agamemnon felt sure the day was won. As his loyal men drove the defenders back to the wall, the gate opened and a relief force surged into the fray.

A cry from their commander brought Agamemnon up short, a familiar accent striking shock into his chest. That man was Achaean!

As the Argives slowed to a stop behind their commander, the men of Athens continued on from the side, pushing in close to the wall. Agamemnon could see their king, Thersander, tall in his chariot, leading them on. The two armies came together with a clash of bronze and a bloody melee ensued.

The leaders rushed at each other. As Agamemnon watched, Thersander jumped down to meet the defender hand to hand. In seconds, Thersander was cut down by the enemy's spear and Agamemnon groaned.

From the left he heard a great cry of rage as Achilles and his Myrmidons surged forward. The great hero, shining in his bronze inlaid with gold, charged at the enemy commander, meeting him head on.

Agamemnon pushed forward, trying to get closer, hearing the enemy cry retreat to his men in that oddly familiar voice. That man was Achaean. Who was he? Seeing Achilles cast his spear, Agamemnon cried out.

"Wait!"

Achilles turned in his chariot to look at the commander, not seeing his spear meet its mark, catching the enemy in the thigh. Agamemnon ordered his driver to bring his chariot alongside Achilles. The defenders were in retreat, their commander huddled in his chariot as his army ran for the gate.

"Achilles," Agamemnon gasped. "That man is Achaean."

"What?" said the hero with a frown.

Agamemnon called across to the enemy. "Who are you?"

The commander pulled himself up against the wall of his chariot, staring at Agamemnon.

"I am Telephus," he cried. "Son of Herakles."

Agamemnon heard Achilles gasp. Stifling his own surprise, he addressed the man again.

"You're Achaean? We had no idea. I'm Agamemnon and this is Achilles. We're looking for a man named Paris Alexandros, and a city called Troy in the land of Ilion."

"You have not found it here! This is Teuthrania, in the land of Mysia," Telephus hissed. "We admit defeat, now search for your quarry elsewhere."

13

ANOTHER CAMPAIGN

Klytie sat rubbing her temple as she listened to the tedious ramblings of the elderly priest. In the corner of the room, the ever-present minstrel snored. At least he was not playing his lyre. The man just would not let up, following her everywhere, watching her every move, pretending not to listen to her every word.

Months had turned to years and still her life was not her own, shadowed by the watcher. Klytie wondered how long she would have to endure the intrusive presence of Agamemnon's spy.

Even after admitting he was wrong, Agamemnon had still insisted she needed a chaperone. She sucked down the resentment at his lack of faith in her. She yawned and tried to focus on Apollo's head priest.

"Potinia, will you please intervene with the lady, to bring the people back into our temple. Worship has fallen to almost nothing, and the sacrificial offerings have dried up. My priests are starving."

Klytie sighed. "How many more supplicants, Aegisthus?"

"This is the last one, my lady."

"Then find me a goat and follow me to the temple of Apollo," she sighed. "I will come now," she said to the flustered priest.

Following the old man to the door, she paused by the

supine body of Neohippos the minstrel and glanced up at her servant. He put a finger to his lips and winked. Stifling a giggle, Klytie slipped past the sleeping musician and hurried down the stairs.

At the temple, her servant appeared with the required animal and a basket holding Klytie's own ritual serpents. She performed the sacrifice quickly and with all due ceremony, feeling relaxed and free for the first time in many moons.

No matter how much she had become used to the minstrel's presence, it was still nice to be without his watching eyes. With Aegisthus as her assistant, she worked through the ceremony. He held the goat for her stunning blow, and he held the rhyton for the blood as she severed the animal's head.

She caught his eye as she took the full vessel from his hands, a small smile coming unbidden. Then as she invoked the lady and called on the god, she poured the blood into the libation bowl that he placed on the tripod.

When it was finished the priest eagerly claimed the carcass and sent it to be butchered and cooked for the priests of the temple. He thanked her profusely and hurried off, in obvious anticipation of the coming feast.

"Did you notice," she whispered to her servant. "He couldn't care less for the sacrifice. He just wanted the free food."

"I noticed nothing but you, my lady," he murmured.

Feeling her face grow hot, she turned away. "We should get back."

"We don't have to. It's nice to be out without a follower. I miss spending time with you."

She sighed. "Mister Minstrel will be writing a scathing report about me."

"Do you really care what he thinks?"

"No, but I care what he says."

He sighed and took her by the hand, leading her back up the hill toward the palace. She smiled as she followed, happy to be led. For a brief moment, she allowed herself to enjoy the warmth of his hand, the comfort of his presence.

But too soon, the palace wall loomed ahead. A lone figure stood in silhouette on the wall, and she pulled her hand away. Approaching the stair, she noticed the watcher had disappeared, and as she entered the stairwell the minstrel Neohippos was there to meet her.

"My lady, where have you been?"

"I had to perform a sacrifice for a struggling priest."

"I should have come with you."

She shrugged. "It wasn't far and I wasn't gone long. It seemed a pity to wake you."

He frowned his disapproval.

"Are you going to stand there all day blocking my path?" she snapped. "My servant needs to fill the bathing room. I have sacrificial blood all over me, in case you hadn't noticed."

The minstrel spluttered and moved aside.

As another year deepened into another winter, the children spent more time in the warmth of the megaron with their mama and the servants. Even the business of the potinia was carried out in the main hall, a luxury that would never have been allowed if the King were in residence.

Gennie and Elektra sat quietly by the hearth playing a game with counters, while Krissie chased her little brother around the room. Orestes squealed, bouncing along on his chunky little legs and Krissie giggled. Close by the chair where Klytie watched her children, Neohippos strummed slowly on his lyre.

"Play something faster," cried Krissie as she passed by.

"Now, Krissie," said her mama. "I think you're loud enough without loud music too."

"Gissus play!" squealed Orestes, pulling the servant out of the corner by one hand.

Aegisthus laughed, snatching the little boy up. "Hush, little man," he said.

"Yes, yes!" cried Krissie. "Please play something, Gissus."

"You play?" said the minstrel dubiously.

He shrugged. "I'm not much of a player."

"I didn't know you could play," said Klytie, surprised.

"I play for the children sometimes, but I'm not very good."

"Yes you are," said Gennie, looking up from her game. "You're very good."

"You've never played for me."

"No, my lady."

"I'd like to hear," she said.

He bowed. "Anything for you, my lady." He stood before the minstrel. "Do you mind if I borrow your lyre?"

Neohippos looked dubious, a frown creasing his brow. Reluctantly, he handed over the instrument, standing to offer his chair. Aegisthus gave a nod and sat, strumming the lyre thoughtfully. He began to pluck, picking a charming melody out of the air, and Klytie sat up straight. He really could play! Then he began to sing.

"Beautiful maidenly
        Koré, the corn-tressed
                Daughter of Dem'ter.

"Fair as the spring, ever
        Chaste and pure, never
                Shall mortal tempt her."

Klytie swallowed hard. Even with the forced shortening of Demeter to fit the metre, the song was beautiful. After all these years, how could she not have known? She held her breath as the song continued.

"Great god of death, rises
    Drawn to her flame, Hades
        Comes, hungry for love.
"Takes maiden down into
    Hell, while the great Zeus
        Gives blessing above..."

"That's not what you usually play, Gissus," said Elektra with a pout.

"Hush," Gennie whispered. "This is for Mama."

"Koré the fair one
    Falling, her heart given
        Dread devil Hades.
"Thus, even death gives
    Way to the light, finding
        Love in the shadies..."

Krissie giggled. "That's a funny word!"

"Hush," Gennie hissed. "It's beautiful."

Klytie gave an involuntary sigh, entranced by the song. Aegisthus raised his eyes to meet hers, singing as if just for her.

"Lost in the dark, deathly
    Cold in my soul, waiting
        Here all alone now.
"Bring me the sun, blooming
    Here in the dark, sharing
        Love with my heart's vow."

Klytie's eyes widened and her heart pounded in her breast. He was singing about her! He had taken on the persona of Hades, compared her to Persephone in her role as Koré, goddess of the underworld, calling her to join him in his forbidden fantasy. She licked her lips, compelled to hear the end.

"Living for you, asking
    Fate to be kind, hoping
        Soon you will be near.
"Hiding my soul, never
    Showing my love, giving
        All of my heart here."

Klytie began to tremble. She knew he cared for her, but he had never dared state it so brazenly before. He spoke treason, and he intended to pull her down with him.

"Mama?" Elektra said. "What's wrong?"

Klytie stared through a haze of guilty tears. A part of her wanted to run to him, throw herself at his feet and accept his offer, with all the danger it entailed. Instead, she lurched to her feet, forced her legs to move and told herself she had to get away.

Ignoring the worried hands of her children, she staggered past them all, fighting the pull of her servant's eyes. Out in the hallway, the cold air hit her hot face and she gasped. Her blood boiled as she rushed for the stairs, toward the only sanctuary she knew. In the privacy of her own room, she paced, allowing the desperate tears to flow. But a step behind her made her spin.

"Are you alright, my lady?" the minstrel said, eyes narrowed. "You look like that song affected you a little too much..."

She felt the anger bubbling up, clenched her hands at her sides, clinging to calm. How to throw him off?

"Am I not allowed to miss my husband?" she spat.

"Oh," he mumbled. "I hadn't thought of that."

"No, you just jumped to the worst conclusion, like you always do."

"I... suppose I did."

"Get out."

He nodded and left the room. Moving carefully to the

door, Klytie watched to see that he went down the stairs, leaving her finally, really alone. Then she flopped on the bed and buried her head in her arms, pulling her knees up to her chest.

Moments later, she felt the overwhelming sensation of being watched. Lifting her head from under her arms, she slowly uncurled and sat up, breath catching in her throat.

"I'm sorry, my... lady," he whispered.

"How could you?" she moaned. "All those years keeping out of trouble and you do this?"

"I..."

"Declaring yourself like that, in front of the whole court? What were you thinking?"

He bristled. "It was just a song, my lady."

"You and I both know that was more than just a song."

He hung his head. "Nobody noticed."

"I noticed," she whispered.

He looked up under hooded brows, a small smile playing on his lips. "So I got your attention, then?"

"Oh, Gissus, you've always had my attention."

He grinned then. "So what's the problem?"

"The problem is... how many others' attention did you catch?"

"I don't care."

"I do."

"Yes, I suppose you do," he said bitterly. "Always worried about your reputation."

"I couldn't care less about that," she cried. "It's you I care about... your safety."

"Oh, you care about me do you?" he smirked.

"Stop it. Don't you know why I've kept myself closed off from you for so long?"

He straightened, took on a more serious tone. "You're scared of your husband."

She made a noise of disgust. "There's nothing he can do to hurt me more than he already has. I'm scared of what he would do to you."

"Bring it on. I can hold my own. It can't come soon enough as far as I'm concerned."

"Don't even joke about it," she sobbed. "He would crush you!"

"You seem to have a very poor opinion of me," he snapped. "Just because I didn't run to join his ill-fated crusade."

"You're not a fighter."

"No?" he barked. "Who killed Atreus?"

"Thyestes did, what's that got to do with it?"

He came in close, shaking his head. "No. It was me," he growled. "And I'll do the same to his son the first chance I get."

"You?" her eyes widened.

"Got your attention now, then."

"But..."

"Just because I'm a goatherd, I never held a sword? I trained. I studied. My foster father made sure I was ready to reclaim my birthright. And one day it will come to me."

"Just like all the rest of your family. I thought you were different."

"What's that supposed to mean?"

"That damned curse. Tantalus was just the same. Couldn't wait to get to Mycenae to get rid of Atreus. I thought you would be the one to let it go."

"I should be king! Why would I let that go?"

"For me?"

He paused. "Oh no, my love. For you, I would do it twice over."

She gasped, feeling a heavy tangling deep in her gut. "I think you should go now. And I think you should leave the palace. It's time for you to get that life I keep suggesting."

"I'm not going anywhere. I'll leave you alone now, but I'm not leaving the palace. I have reason to stay now."

"Why?" she breathed, stomach twisting in knots.

He moved in closer, with a broad smile and a sparkle in his eyes. She fought to stand her ground against the intense desire to run.

"I know you care about me now," he whispered.

He took her hand and lifted it to his face, kissing her palm and the inside of her wrist. She licked her lips, feeling her resolve crumbling. She gathered all her strength and pushed him away, finally finding her voice.

"Get out," she stuttered.

He chuckled as he dropped her hand. "One day, my love," he murmured and sauntered from the room.

With a shuddering sob, Klytie stood for a moment, looking about her unchanged room in confusion. She sat slowly on the bed, staring out the window as the tears fell.

Klytemestra rolled another clay sausage and squashed it down with hands cracked with dry clay. She picked up the stylus and paused, hand hovering over the soft clay tablet. She concentrated, trying to remember the symbols correctly.

"Mama, when will you be finished?" Elektra pouted from the door of the potinia's audience room.

"I'm sorry, Elektra, I have to finish up here first. I have to make all of the records myself, and I'm out of practice."

"Why? Where's Gissus?"

"I don't know, sweetie."

"Leave it, that's scribes work, Mama. Let him do it when he gets back."

"He can't, he wasn't here to take notes and I don't want to forget anything."

"Please come, Mama. Orestes is riding and he's so excited."

"What?" Klytie's head snapped up. "He's too young! He'll fall!"

"Gennie's riding with him," Elektra scoffed. "Come see."

Klytie sighed, eyes roving over her reports, a pitiful attempt at best. She knew it was useless. They would need to be redone anyway.

"Alright, Elektra, I'll come."

She followed her daughter out into the courtyard, passing the guard at the door without a glance. Neohippos had finally started trusting other people to watch her, but it was still an intrusion she had to live with. At least she did not have to listen to his constant lyre playing.

In the training yard, Gennie sat astride her favourite chestnut filly, little Orestes squealing in front of her as they rode in a long, slow circle.

"Mama, look at me!" Orestes cried in excitement.

"I see, my clever boy," Klytie smiled.

She leant against the stone parapet, watching her children. Letting go of the long, frustrating day, she turned to look down into the town. There below her, in the marshalling yard beneath the palace wall, stood two figures, heads close as they talked.

The girl stared up into the man's eyes, lips parted in a secretive smile. Klytie recognised one of the kitchen maids, who sometimes collected the meat from her sacrifices to prepare for cooking. The man's soft chuckle floated up to her and she caught her breath, recognising the voice of her missing servant.

Klytie gulped down an irrational stab of jealousy. She should be glad he seemed to be finally getting on with his life, instead of wasting away with her. She watched as he sent the girl upstairs with a hand at her back. As if feeling

Klytie's eyes on him, he turned and looked up at her, meeting her gaze.

Klytie snapped around, back to the wall, gasping. She steeled herself for his inevitable appearance at the top of the stairs.

"Gissus!" Krissie cried, running to meet him.

Klytie forced herself to breathe deeply, glad of the distraction. She had to appear calm. The minstrel had reappeared when she was looking over the wall. Damn the man for being so ever-present.

"Well hello, my little miss," she heard the reply.

"Where have you been?" Krissie cried.

"I had some business in town," he said with a laugh.

Klytie held her breath, holding herself steady, staring at her little son and her daughter riding slowly toward her.

"Gissus, look at me!" Orestes called.

"Look at you, little man."

"You should have been working," Elektra snapped. "Mama needed you and you weren't here."

"Elektra," Klytie hissed.

"It's true, Mama," Elektra pouted. "He's your servant, he should be here."

"I'm sorry, my lady," he said.

She bit down an angry retort and said nothing, unable to trust her voice.

"It won't happen again," he said, eyes searching for hers.

"No matter," she snapped. "You'll just have to take notes as I dictate."

Moving past him toward the potinia's rooms, she clamped her mouth against the more bitter words that threatened to spill out. She did not meet his eyes and did not look back to see that he followed. She heard the children run off giggling and stepped into the potinia's rooms with a sigh.

"My lady, I want to explain, I..."

He broke off as the minstrel stepped in, ready to watch. Cursing under his breath, Aegisthus settled into his chair.

"Did you do these?" he said, examining her poor attempt at record keeping.

She did not reply, sitting in the potinia's grand seat.

"They're very good," he smiled. "Hardly an error, if a bit hesitant in places."

"Can we get on with this?" she growled.

On a balmy spring afternoon, a lone messenger rode up to the walls of golden Mycenae. He passed the guard with a word, clattered his way up the hill and clambered clumsily up the stairs to the courtyard on his one good leg and a spear shaft as a crutch.

Crossing painfully to the porch he entered the megaron without ceremony or announcement. There sat the queen, as beautiful as he had been led to believe, her haunting dark eyes staring unblinking under soft lashes. Behind him, a gaggle of children burst in, almost knocking him over and rushing to their mother with excited chatter.

"Mama, is it news? Is Papa coming home?"

"Hush, let the man speak," she said. "Bring him a chair," she gestured to a nearby servant.

The messenger sighed as he sat before the queen and her family to begin his story, as he had for every city in his path all the way home.

"When I left the army, almost six months ago," the messenger began. "They had been sitting in siege outside a walled city on the Eastern Aegean coast. Commander Agamemnon hoped to find his quarry inside."

Gennie squealed. "So Papa's coming home soon?"

"I don't know that, my lady," he said. "The battle was fierce. I was injured, unable to fight, so the commander charged me with bringing news to the families waiting at home. But I really have little to tell. We claimed several towns in our search for Ilion, but as yet there is no sign of the woman or her kidnapper."

"So no real news at all," Elektra sighed.

"I can tell you the city did not harbour the fugitives. In the final battle, the King himself came out to meet us at the head of his survivors. His name was Telephus, a son of Herakles. The great Achilles injured him before the end."

"Telephus?" said Klytie. "So it wasn't Ilion at all?"

"No, my lady. I'm afraid we still haven't found that elusive place. We now know it was Teuthrania in Mysia, not Troy in Ilion. At the end of the siege, the fleet set sail once more and I began my long journey home."

"So, my sister is still not found," Klytie sighed.

"And your husband is still far away..." Aegisthus whispered at her side.

She hushed him with a look, worried that the minstrel Neohippos might have heard.

"There's one more thing," the messenger said. "As I sailed east with the rest of the grievously injured, our ship was buffeted by the tail of a storm. We were very nearly sunk before we escaped."

"How is that important?" said Klytie in exasperation.

"Because the brunt of the storm was behind me, in the path of the fleet. I don't know how they fared but I fear for their safety. It was a monstrous storm."

"Oh, Papa!" cried Gennie with a sob.

"Hush, dear," said Klytie. "I'm sure he's fine."

"Unfortunately," Aegisthus murmured under his breath.

Klytie shot him an admonishing look and he smirked, giving her a wink.

"Mama, what if he's not alright?" whispered Elektra.

"Don't worry, sweetie. I'll offer up sacrifice for his safety."

"Alright, Mama," she sighed.

14

A Moment of Weakness

The potinia sat in conference with the palace advisors, arranging funds for the spring festivals and approving plans for appropriate offerings in each of the temples. In his usual place, the servant took the records.

In the warmth of the afternoon, Klytie yawned, lulled by the tedious proceedings. In a corner, the minstrel strummed lazily. Into this somnolent atmosphere, a young woman burst through the door, shaking off the hands of the guard.

Klytemestra raised her head to see the young kitchen maid she had seen with Aegisthus. She frowned. Her unwelcome presence was not only an annoyance, it was inappropriate. Klytie opened her mouth to protest but the girl forestalled her.

"I'm sorry, my lady," she stammered. "Gissus, you need to come, right now!"

Klytie raised an eyebrow. The insolence of the girl, striding in here and giving orders. And using the pet name Klytie's own children had invented. She would have to see the girl was disciplined. But the servant stood without hesitation, his scribe's tools forgotten mid-tablet.

"I'm sorry, my lady," he echoed. "I really must go. I'll return as soon as I can."

"Wait a minute..." Klytie began, but he was already out

the door.

The assembled advisors looked at each other in astonishment as Klytie rose explosively from her ritual seat. Looking about at the confused faces she slowly sat, realising she was not free to chase after them. The minstrel had stopped his strumming and was watching her with a calculating stare.

"My lords, I think we should break for today. We'll continue tomorrow," she murmured, bewildered.

Standing in the marshalling yard, leaning on the wall, Klytie stared down into the city below. The spring sun beat down on her head, bringing beads of sweat to her forehead, but she did not notice. She could hear her children laughing as they chased each other about the courtyard to the ever-present sound of the lyre, but her ears strained for another voice.

It had been days since Aegisthus had run off, with no sign and no word of him. Klytie hated to admit that she was worried. She denied it even to herself, and of course, she did not miss him at all. She just hated not knowing what had happened.

"Mama!" Gennie jumped up to sit on the wall. She sobered at a look from her mother. "You're worried about Gissus, aren't you?"

Klytie shook her head. "I'm sure he's fine."

"But you miss him, don't you?"

Klytie frowned, levelling her daughter with a look. "He's just a servant, Gennie. I've already started interviewing for a replacement."

"Well, I miss him," Gennie sighed. "And I'm worried about him too."

"He can look after himself."

"Maybe," Gennie shrugged. "But you'd never replace

him."

Klytie's gaze landed on a young woman hurrying up the long ramp toward the palace. She was sure she recognised the young kitchen maid and her heart skipped a beat.

"Isn't that his sister, Philadora coming now?" said Gennie.

"Is it?" said Klytie.

"Yes, I'm sure it is. I'd bet she has news. Let me know what she says."

Gennie hopped off the wall and ran to join the other children. Klytie watched the young woman approach, her breath catching in her throat. His sister? Now she understood why he had run off with her so willingly.

She took a deep breath, feeling somehow lighter but not admitting it was from a sense of relief. At least she would know what had happened, she told herself. Pausing in the courtyard below, the girl looked up to meet Klytie's eyes.

She gave a little smile and hurried up the stairs. Klytie stood still, fighting the urge to run to the girl and beg her for news. She gripped the parapet with both hands, heart pounding in her ears. She hardly heard the girl approach and jumped when she spoke beside her.

"My lady, I bring a message."

Klytie turned to face her silently, not trusting her voice and hoping she appeared calm.

"My brother, Aegisthus wishes you to know he is safe and well, but he cannot return to you just yet."

"How can he be your brother?" Klytie said. "He is the last surviving child of Thyestes."

"I didn't realise you knew that, my lady," Philadora smiled. "He was raised by my parents, so we grew up together as brother and sister. He's kept that secret very close to his chest. But then, he speaks very highly of you, so I shouldn't be surprised."

"He does?"

"Of course. He loves you very much, my lady."

Klytie felt her face grow hot. "Oh," she breathed.

The girl cocked her head to one side, eyes narrowed. "Forgive me, my lady, but... I have to ask..."

"Yes?"

"I've watched my brother waste his life waiting for you. I need to know if you care for him too."

"I don't think that's an appropriate question. I'm your queen! And I'm a married woman who can't entertain such a fantasy. I've told him many times to go find a wife."

"Yes, I know all that. But none of that matters if you love him."

Klytie tried to draw breath, clenching her hands against the trembling that shivered up and down her body. She glanced around to see the minstrel occupied on his lyre and blinked back tears of frustration.

"I can't," she whispered.

"But you do," the girl murmured in return. "I know you are watched, my lady. I'm sorry I made you answer, but I had to know. I'll help you if I can."

"There's nothing you can do."

Philadora winked. "You just watch me."

On a dark, stormy afternoon, Klytie and her children had retreated to the megaron, taking warmth by the hearth on an unseasonably cool day. The minstrel entertained them with a jolly song while the girls danced. Klytie sat on the king's great seat, chewing her nails.

"Gissus!" Krissie squealed.

Klytie's head snapped up. Her youngest daughter threw herself at the servant and he laughed, catching her up. Klytie sat up straight, a smile tugging at her lips despite her attempts to stop it.

He looked drawn and sad, and her heart melted. What hardships had he been through? The minstrel stopped playing, eyes flicking from the queen to the servant and back again.

Behind Aegisthus, his siter Philadora entered, moving purposefully across the room to where the minstrel sat. Klytie watched as she planted herself on the minstrel's knee, wrapping her arms seductively about his neck.

"Why don't you put down that lyre and play with something else for a while," the girl said.

Klytie gasped, eyes wide, as the minstrel's beloved instrument hit the floor with a clang. She saw the covetous sparkle in the minstrel's eye. She watched the young woman plant her lips on the minstrel's mouth, saw his arms slide around her waist.

Klytie stared at Aegisthus, head full of questions, but he put a finger to his lips and gave a wink. Then he smiled and gestured for her to come.

Klytie slid from the chair and sidled past the amorous couple, hurrying to the door where the servant waited. Aegisthus took her by the hand and led her silently away. Outside, she found her children had already slipped out into the courtyard and were playing in the fading light.

"What's going on?" Klytie stammered. "Are you really going to let that man defile your sister?"

"She won't let it get that far. She's old enough to look after herself."

"Does she have a husband who might object?"

He chuckled. "Still standing up for propriety? No, she's not married. Her papa needed her too much to let her go. But that won't be a problem now."

"What are you talking about?"

"You'll see."

He called the children over. "Gennie, I need to steal your

mama for a while. See that Neohippos isn't disturbed, let the diversion work for as long as you can. Perhaps you can see the others settled for the night?"

"Of course, Gissus, whatever you say," Gennie said.

Klytie allowed him to lead her across the courtyard and into the stairwell. He slipped into the potinia's rooms and returned with a lidded basket.

"Why do we need my serpents?"

"I need the potinia," he replied.

"I'll get my gown, then..."

He tapped the basket. "Already have it."

Bewildered, Klytie followed him down the stairs and out into the city.

On the slopes below the city, the servant led the queen to a small cottage surrounded by goats. Entering the dimness of the main room, Klytie looked around. Sparsely furnished and humble, the hut spoke of a long life of hardship. On a low pallet in the corner lay the body of a lowly goatherd.

"Who is it?" she whispered.

"My papa," he said.

Klytie stood and watched, completely at a loss as Aegisthus knelt by the dead man's side, head bowed. Finally, he rose and gestured to a curtained doorway. Without a word, Klytie took the basket and slipped into the tiny bedroom to get changed.

When she emerged, dressed in her ceremonial robe, she saw that Aegisthus had set up a table for the offerings, and a small group of villagers had gathered to witness the funeral rites.

She was relieved to see Philadora standing with her brother, and shook off a sense of fear for the girl's safety. But she could not shake the thought that the minstrel was now unoccupied and probably searching for her.

Klytie closed off her scattered thoughts and damped her emotional turmoil, ready for the business at hand. She lifted her snakes from their basket and raised her arms to speak the invocation.

Then the first animal was brought, a large billy goat. Aegisthus held the animal by the horns and she swung the axe, to stun the animal. When it was laid on the table in front of her, she performed the sacrifice quickly and cleanly, moving on to the next animal without delay.

A nanny goat followed, then the first of two kids. She closed her mind to the bleating and thanked the baby goat for its gift of life. But when the servant reached for the second kid, it somehow broke free of his grasp and skittered away, escaping through the door. Klytie invoked the gods a final time and thanked them for the omen.

"Be assured," she said to the gathering. "The gods have given their blessing; the life of the kid has been spared as a symbol of the continuance of life even after death. The beloved father may be gone but his child lives on to pass on his legacy."

The audience gave a collective sigh. A woman stepped up to accept the sacrificial meat, and two young girls helped her carry it away to be prepared for a funeral feast. Then the pallet was lifted by two strapping lads and the goatherd was carried out onto the hillside.

A small procession followed the boys with their burden, moving along the ridge to a natural cave, where the man was laid on the bare rock floor. The potinia sang the last hymns to send the dead man on his way, and the ceremony was done.

Back at the cottage, Klytie changed out of her ceremonial garb and packed it back in the basket with the snakes. When she emerged from behind the curtain, she paused, transfixed. In the middle of the room stood Aegisthus, a baby goat cradled in his arms as he murmured soothing words. He looked up and smiled at her, gesturing for her to approach.

Moving closer, Klytie reached out a hesitant hand to touch the soft fuzz of the little animal's head, feeling the stubs of horns. The kid nuzzled at her hand, attempting to suckle her fingers, and she laughed softly.

"I thought the children might like to raise her for me," he said then.

She smiled radiantly. "Oh, Gissus, they would love that."

"I'm glad," he whispered. "You looked so beautiful tonight. You amaze me every time you conduct a ceremony."

She blushed, hanging her head.

"I want to thank you, for sending my papa on his way. I know you don't usually perform rituals for the poor."

She smiled, lifting a hand to stroke the little goat. "He was more deserving than many richer men."

"Why do you say that?" he said, cocking his head.

"He took you in, raised you as his own. That makes him noble in my eyes."

He stared for a long moment. "Do you really mean that?"

"Of course I do," she said, finally meeting his eyes. "I only wish someone had done that for my little boy, all those years ago."

He reached out with his free hand to brush the lone tear gently from her cheek. She closed her eyes, leaning into his hand. Then she felt his lips brush hers and responded instinctively, seeking more.

As the little goat struggled to jump free, the servant's arms closed about her, sending shivers up her spine and sparks into her belly. She melted into the kiss, his crushing embrace holding her up as her knees turned to water.

Somewhere in the fog, Klytie heard a cough, but she ignored it. The cough came again, louder, more insistent. Gissus pulled back reluctantly.

"Umm, do you really think I should stay with you, brother dear? Wouldn't you two rather be alone?"

Gissus looked at his sister. "Of course you're coming, you can't stay here."

"I just thought..."

Klytie untangled herself from his arms and gathered up her basket. "Don't let me intrude, I'm not staying."

Aegisthus reached out a hand to Klytie, only the slightest tremble in his fingers betraying his calm exterior.

"Let's get back to the house. We'll talk about it there."

Aegisthus led Klytie back up into the city, his sister following with the kid wrapped in a bundle of clothing, cradled in her arms. Heading into the upper terrace, they approached a large building with an impressive facade.

"Whose house is this?" Klytie asked.

"Mine," he replied. "My father Thyestes gave it to me."

Entering the richly decorated antechamber, Klytie looked around. It was such a contrast to the cottage they had just left. She wondered how Aegisthus had coped with such massive contradictions in his life. Raised in a hovel, given such opulence by a father he hardly knew, now relegated once more to the role of servant. No wonder he was bitter.

"Show me where I'm sleeping and I'll get out of your way," said Philadora with a smile.

Klytie stiffened. Now that she had had time to clear her head, she knew she had to get back to the palace. She had let things go too far already.

"You don't have to rush off. I'm heading back to the palace now."

"Why? You don't have to go," said Aegisthus.

"You know why. What did you think I was going to do, fall into bed with you after one moment of weakness? Nothing has changed."

"Everything has changed," he said, pulling her close. "You love me."

She pushed him away, shaking her head. "I can't love you."

He winced. "There are no watchers here."

"No, but there is one who will be searching for me as we speak. Or had you forgotten?"

"Damn that minstrel to hades!" he cursed. Grabbing her hand, he pulled her to the door. "Come on then, let's get you home, my lady," he snarled.

Moonlight shone across the parapet as they approached the palace wall. As they crossed the deep shadow of the lower courtyard, heading toward the stairwell, they were stopped by a low chuckle near the wall.

"I thought I'd catch you two slinking back if I waited long enough," said a snarky voice.

Klytie gasped. Gissus touched a calming hand to her arm.

"I knew something was going on. You certainly hid it well, I must say. Just think what Agamemnon will say when I tell him."

"Nothing was hidden," said Aegisthus. "Because nothing's going on."

"Now why don't I believe you?"

"The potinia was conducting funeral rites at my request."

"Was she now? Forgive me, but that's a convenient excuse, a spurious alibi at best. Given her family history, I have no doubt that slut couldn't wait to get her husband out of the way."

Klytie heard a low growl from Aegisthus and a heavy thud as the servant ploughed into the minstrel, slamming him against the wall and holding him there in the darkness.

"That's your queen you're insulting," he growled. "And the most virtuous woman you'll ever meet. She'll never betray her husband."

Neohippos laughed nervously, a strident, jangling sound. "This from the man who's already soiled her so-called virtue?"

"I've done nothing of the sort," Aegisthus hissed, pressing his face close to the minstrel's. "Do you think I haven't tried?"

"Are you saying she refused you? You expect me to believe that?"

"I expect it because it's true."

He released the minstrel with one last shove against the wall and backed away.

"I'll be watching you," said the minstrel. "Twice as closely from now on. You won't be able to blink without me knowing."

"You do that," Aegisthus said with a hollow laugh. He turned to Klytie with a hand on her arm. "Come, my lady, let's get you in out of the cold."

Neohippos the minstrel followed behind the queen and her servant as they climbed the stairs. He thought about what Aegisthus had said. Could it be true that their obvious attraction was unconsummated? He did not know if he should believe it.

He had to be sure. He hung back, watching as the servant took the queen's snake basket from her hands and took it into the potinia's rooms while she waited outside. Then they continued out into the courtyard. He let them cross the darkened yard to the porch and watched them move to the small steps leading into the private rooms. Then he followed.

Reaching the reception room, he found it deserted. He continued to the stairs, climbing slowly so as not to catch them. At the top, he saw them enter the queen's chamber. The servant paused at the door, searching the shadowy corridor for any followers.

Neohippos ducked out of sight and held his breath. Then when the servant disappeared into the room, the minstrel sidled quickly up to the door to listen.

"Do you think he believed you?" said the Queen in a tremulous tone.

"Not likely," the servant replied.

"Oh, Gissus, what are we going to do? What if he does tell Agamemnon?"

"He has no proof. You're completely innocent, and Agamemnon will see that."

"Will he? Don't you see, he'll act first and ask later? He won't care about the truth."

"Don't worry, my love."

"Stop it you mustn't call me that, what if he hears?"

"He already believes you're an adulteress, what difference would it make?"

"It would confirm his suspicion."

"I don't think he needs any confirmation. In his eyes we're already guilty."

"All the more reason why you need to stop this. I should be totally above suspicion."

"As you wish, my lady," he said harshly.

The servant burst out of the room, and the minstrel scurried backward. Neohippos met his eyes for one chilling moment, the servant's cold stare sending shivers up his spine. The servant took a menacing step toward him and he turned and ran.

His mind racing, the minstrel flew down the corridor, taking the steps three at a time, stumbling at the bottom and righting himself to continue his flight. It was true, they were innocent, and yet... He suspected, from the tension in their voices, it was only a matter of time before the Queen gave in. The King had to be warned.

In his small cell, Neohippos found a tiny pebble of kohl, scraped a scattering of black dust off it and added a drop of water, took out his only piece of Egyptian papyrus, given to him by Agamemnon himself for just this purpose, and his wooden pen. He knew what he had to do.

He would write the truth, being careful to state clearly the danger, and the King would come running. He dipped and thought. Then he began to write slowly and carefully, tongue caught in his teeth for concentration.

When he was done, he sat back and read over what he had written while the ink dried, nodded in satisfaction and rolled it, sealing it with a blob of clay and pressing his seal into it. Then he headed out into the night, hoping his contact would still be waiting.

It was late, but he was paid to wait by the gate until midnight every night. He might still be there. Neohippos hurried down the hill to the city gate. He could see the guard, lounging by the gate and hear the man's snores as he approached, but there was no sign of his contact. Maybe he was too late after all.

The minstrel hesitated for a moment, searching the shadows, but no messenger stepped out to meet him. He turned with a sigh and stopped. There behind him, a hooded figure had appeared on silent feet. The figure reached out a hand and the minstrel passed over his precious scroll without question. The man broke the seal and unrolled the message.

"Hey!" cried Neohippos.

"Papyrus?" said the man. "That's a bit rich, isn't it?"

"What's it to you, you're just the messenger."

The man stepped forward out of the shadows, uncovering his head as he did so, and the moonlight hit his face. "You need to learn to be more observant."

The minstrel gasped. "You!"

"Me," said the man. "I'm afraid I can't let you destroy my lady with this nonsense. I didn't want it to come to this but you leave me no choice."

"What are you talking about?"

"Your snooping is getting out of hand. Accusing the Queen like this with no proof is just going too far."

"What are you going to do?"

"I can't let it continue."

"How dare you threaten me!"

"Oh, I'm not threatening. I'm doing."

The minstrel took a step back, sudden fear gripping his heart. The maniac was going to kill him! He tried to run, but found his arms gripped by two burly thugs, keeping him in place.

"You'd kill me just for a quick tumble?" the minstrel snorted, putting up a brave front.

"She's much more to me than a quick tumble."

The minstrel sniffed. "You're drunk on the idea of bedding a queen. You couldn't care less about her."

"Oh, I do care. Very much, if you must know. I'd let her go on pretending she doesn't care about me if it meant she'd be happy, but I need her."

"Ha! Lust after her maybe..."

"You really don't know what you've gotten yourself into, do you? She's my ticket to the crown."

"You? You're a servant. You're not king material!"

"My dear Mister Minstrel," the servant scoffed. "You

might be a talented musician, you might even be an effective chaperone, but you're no spy. You have no idea who I am."

"Oh, I checked. You're a peasant, the son of a goatherd."

"Foster son," the servant laughed. "Any spy worth the name would have known that, and gone looking for the truth. A real spy would know my real identity."

"And what's that?" said the minstrel, cold fear gripping him.

Aegisthus stepped in even closer, bringing his face in front of the minstrel's in the darkness, eyes boring into him.

"I am the last son of Thyestes," he whispered. "I am your rightful king and you, my friend, have just committed treason."

The minstrel's eyes widened. "I don't believe you."

He felt his hands being wrenched behind his back, only then realising the servant was not alone. His wrists were quickly tied, far too tightly.

"No, you seem to make a habit of that," Aegisthus said.

"So kill me then."

"Oh, I'm not going to kill you. I'll let the vultures do that."

"Vultures? What...?"

"There's a tiny island off the Argive coast, populated only by a few birds. My friends here are charged to take you there for a little... holiday. I'm afraid you might be a bit tied up, so I expect you'll be staying there for... oh, the rest of your life."

"You're mad!"

"Not at all. I'm only doing what's necessary."

"You won't succeed. Agamemnon will kill you."

"We'll see about that."

15

THE ANGER OF ARTEMIS

The commanders watched as the lone ship made its way into the sheltered bay at Aulis. It was most likely another survivor of the storm that had scattered the fleet across the Aegean. It had taken years for them all to gather once more. As it came close to shore, the men of the army pointed and shouted, their agitation clear.

"It's a Trojan ship!" cried Menelaos.

A murmur rippled through the troops as they recognised the enemy. The captains clustered near the command tent, eager to speak to their generals.

"Calm down," said Odysseus. "It's one ship. I hardly think it can take down our fleet on its own."

"When it lands," said Agamemnon to the nearest officer, "bring its captain here."

"Yes, sir!"

The generals returned to the command tent, settling themselves to wait for the enemy captain. Agamemnon ordered wine and cheese, creating an air of calm unconcern, letting the men lounge at ease. They spoke little but let a lazy somnolence grow, giving an outward appearance of complete ease despite their concern.

When the Captain finally arrived, he faced a wall of hostile stares. He limped into the tent, made his way painfully to the centre of the gathered men and stood, staring at the commander. His injured leg oozed through the bandage, and he leant on a headless spear-shaft. Agamemnon recognised the Teuthranian king. He seemed drawn and jittery, a gleam of desperation in his eye.

"Telephus," said Agamemnon.

"My lord," Telephus inclined his head.

"Why are you here?"

"I come with a request and a proposal.

The generals stared silently.

"My lord, I come not for my city but for myself alone."

"Go on," said Agamemnon.

"When you sacked my city, I was injured by the warrior Achilles."

"I remember."

"My wound suppurates, it will not heal."

"I fail to see..."

"Let me finish, my lord. Unable to affect a cure, I consulted the oracle and asked what might be done about the wound. The reply was this: 'He that wounded shall heal.' And so I am come in search of Achilles, that he might heal me."

Agamemnon frowned. "And if Achilles is able to perform this miracle, what gain is there for us?"

"I'll lead you to Troy."

Agamemnon raised an eyebrow. "You'd betray your country for a cure?"

The man nodded.

"It's a generous offer," said Agamemnon. "With one flaw."

"What's that, my lord?"

"Achilles isn't here. He's yet to rejoin the fleet."

The man's face fell. "When do you expect him?"

Agamemnon shrugged. "We have no idea where he is. He could be shipwrecked or dead for all I know."

"He couldn't be!" cried Telephus. "Why would the oracle send me here if he were dead?"

"True," Agamemnon mused. "You're welcome to stay and wait."

"My lord, is there no way to find him sooner?"

Agamemnon shrugged again. "I've no idea where to start. Perhaps one of my generals can come up with a plan, but I really can't promise anything."

"Perhaps I can make a suggestion," Odysseus mused.

"What did you have in mind?" said Menelaos.

"You remember how the boy acted when we first conscripted him? He was loath to leave his cosy little nest in Scyros. Remember, he objected mightily."

"He did, like a spoilt brat," said Agamemnon with a sneer. "What's your point?"

"He's young, full of lust and arrogance. Think back to when you were that age. What was your first thought in the morning and your last thought at night?"

Agamemnon chuckled. "Girls."

"Precisely. And who is waiting for him back in Scyros? His little bit of skirt."

"You think he went back there?"

"I'd bet my life on it."

"And you'd win," chuckled Agamemnon. "Well, Odysseus my friend. Off you go, then. Bring the little brat back."

Agamemnon trudged through the brush at the head of the hunting party, scouring the trees for something to fill the bellies of his men. He bent to check another snare, untangled the small animal from the trap and threw it into the cart. Another meatless rodent, not fit for a dog, but the army had to eat.

He longed to try his spear on something larger, maybe a boar or a wolf, but those that had escaped the cook fires were too smart to stick around. He would even try his hand at a lion if he thought he could win.

To his left he saw Menelaos bend to check another trap, coming up empty handed. He caught his brother's eye and gave a shrug. At the edge of his vision, he saw a flash of movement through the trees ahead. He raised his hand for quiet and the thrashing footsteps of the men behind fell silent.

"What's that?" he heard Menelaos whisper.

"I think it's a deer," Agamemnon hissed.

He hefted his spear, feeling its weight and squinting to gauge the distance. A flicker of shadow, something breaking the light shafting down through the canopy. Behind, he heard the men getting restless and raised a hand again. A lone soldier thudded forward ahead of the others, heavy footsteps resounding through the wood, and the animal darted away.

"Damn!" Agamemnon swore.

He saw the flickering again, further away this time as the animal bolted. He lifted the spear, settling it in the crook of his arm, and moved forward at a jog. He could hear the men following behind, but he ignored them, all thought centred on the quarry ahead. The deer had slowed, head turned back to look for signs of pursuit. A lone soldier surged forward, past his commander, yelling in idiotic abandonment.

"Stand your ground!" Agamemnon growled.

Too late, the deer was all but gone, flitting through the trees in a lithe, twisting path that no warrior could match.

"Damn!" Agamemnon cursed again. "I'll be damned if I'll let my dinner get away because of some fool foot-soldier..."

He searched the forest ahead for any sign of the deer. He could see, barely visible in the faraway shadow, a mere fluttering of movement. The animal was still there, but it was spooked now. No chance of catching it by stealth.

He held his breath, assessing the distance, trying to judge the lie of the land, plotting a path. Moving another few steps, shifting his hold on his spear in the crook of his arm, he took up his jog once more.

The animal was there, looking straight at him, brazenly watching him come. Leaning into his stride, Agamemnon leapt into a run, crashing through the trees, straight at his prey. The deer broke cover, bounding away, but the King kept on, straight as an arrow.

The deer criss-crossed through the wood, moving first one way then the other, flitting across his path, but Agamemnon kept on. He was closing the distance steadily and the animal was slowing.

Almost in range, Agamemnon hefted his spear, shifting its weight and readying his aim. The deer bolted again, but to the side, closing the distance in its confusion. Agamemnon almost laughed. Raising his arm in front, lifting his spear arm behind, he took aim, still running full pelt.

Then in one massive overhand thrust, his spear arm shot forward, releasing the spear to fly in a high, graceful arc. He slowed to a walk, watching the spear chase the deer, flying fast and true.

The animal had no idea what was coming, running valiantly but in vain as the bronze point met its mark. The heavy spear hit the animal clean on the back of the neck, slicing through flesh and bone, driving the animal down with the force of the throw.

The sheer weight of the thrust sent the deer head first into the ground, breaking its neck. Agamemnon let out a war cry, a great roar of victory as the men finally caught him up, lifting him on their shoulders and running with him to find the kill. Standing over the fallen prey, the King crowed.

"Who's the greatest hunter in the world?" he cried. "I declare that even Artemis could not beat such a throw!"

The men yelled their support as he revelled in his victory, but they fell silent when the ground began to rumble and a great wind grew up around them. But Agamemnon continued to exalt in his victory, unaware of the tremors beneath his feet.

"I am the mightiest hunter!" he crowed in his victorious ecstasy.

"Brother, have a care," said Menelaos, staggering up to his side. "You bring down the anger of the goddess. You must rein in your pride!"

Agamemnon paused, noticing the abrupt change in the weather. Another rumble from deep in the earth almost threw him off his feet. He laughed nervously.

"You worry too much, Menelaos," he said.

Standing at the prow of his ship, his Myrmidon fleet trailing behind, Achilles stared ahead at the gathered armada of the Achaeans. It was the last place he wanted to be, with his new wife and young son left behind at Scyros. But he had made his choice, glory over long life, and he would not shirk his duty now.

With the cold wind of a storm at his back, the ship buffeted in the swell, the great warrior rode the gale into the beach. An immovable figure, appearing solid as the ship itself as it pitched and rolled, he held himself upright with one hand on the side. At the first scrape of sand under the hull, Achilles jumped over the side, landing in a crouch on two feet and rising to stand staring at the assembled army.

Not one captain or general waited to meet him. With anger simmering, the young warrior strode toward the command tent, ready to let loose on the commander who showed him so little respect. One day he would show them all. He knew they needed him to win this war, but they treated him like an insignificant child.

Bursting into the tent, Achilles faced Agamemnon. The commander gave him a dismissive look and went back to his conversation. Behind Achilles, the tent flap opened to admit Odysseus, who had chased him down and brought him back here like a truant boy. He would keep, one day he would pay for such an insult.

"My lord, I bring Achilles," said Odysseus in that condescending tone he so hated.

"So I see," said Agamemnon with a shrug. "Where is the patient?"

Achilles frowned. "Patient? What are you talking about, Agamemnon?"

From behind the commander a man stepped out of the crowd, a man familiar in his arrogance yet strangely subdued now.

"What are you doing here?" said Achilles with a sneer.

"Waiting for you," Telephus replied with a bow.

"Come to take another beating?"

"No, my lord, to beg your pardon and seek your aid."

"You'll get no such thing from me."

"My lord, I received an oracle that sent me here, seeking healing for my wound, a wound you yourself inflicted. A wound that only you can heal."

"I'm a soldier, not a physician," Achilles snapped. "Is this why you brought me here, Agamemnon? To listen to this coward snivel?"

Agamemnon chuckled. "No, boy, I brought you here because he thinks you can heal him, and in return he will lead us to Troy."

Achilles raised an eyebrow. So that was it. Once again, they needed him, but they twisted it to suit their own pride.

But he had no wish to heal the fool.

"I'm sorry Telephus, but I can't heal you."

"But the oracle said…"

"I don't care what some oracle said! I don't know…"

A loud cough caught him mid-tirade. "My lord," Odysseus said. "Might I have a word with the boy?"

Agamemnon nodded, and Odysseus gestured to Achilles to follow. The young warrior gave a shrug and followed the older man from the tent. Once outside he opened his mouth to give him a piece of his mind, but the cunning Odysseus held up a hand.

"Calm down boy. I know you have some skill at the physician's art. You trained with Chiron the centaur. Why would you refuse to heal him?"

"He's a traitor," Achilles spat. "He fought against us in Mysia, pitting Achaean against Achaean. Why should I heal him?"

"I understand your bitterness, boy. But take advice from one with more experience than yourself."

Reluctantly, Achilles nodded.

"It just so happens," said Odysseus. "I know exactly how to heal Telephus. Any man could do it. But he believes only you can, so I'm going to tell you how."

Achilles nodded again.

"First, put your sword in the fire."

"What?"

"It won't hurt it, it was made in fire."

"But…"

"Just do it. Trust me."

Achilles drew his sword dubiously. At a reassuring nod from Odysseus, he walked hesitantly over to the nearby watch fire. Taking a deep breath, he thrust the sword deep into the centre of the flames, leaving it standing upright. Then Odysseus raised his voice and called.

"Bring Telephus out here, my lord!" Then he turned to Achilles. "Now, boy, we need to make him believe. The words are very important. Remember your training..." and Odysseus began to coach him in the ritual farce he was about to perform.

When the commander and his generals emerged with Telephus in their midst, Achilles was ready. He motioned for Telephus to approach.

"Sit," he said.

Telephus sat in the dirt and Odysseus stepped forward to unwrap the bandages and reveal the infected wound. Then at a nod from Achilles, Odysseus took hold of the man from behind.

"This is going to hurt," said the young warrior. "Your wound is infected and needs to be cauterised. You need to hold still even as it burns."

Achilles stared into his victim's wide staring eyes, and a part of him revelled in the power he held over the foolish man. He turned to the fire and reached into the flames to grasp the leather bound hilt of his beautiful bronze sword.

The hilt was hot, very hot, but it was bearable, and he had to appear calm and untroubled. He drew the sword from the fire and turned to face his audience. Holding the sword before him, its blade blackened and smoking, Achilles gazed at the injured man, saw the fear in his eyes.

"May the blade that injured now heal," Achilles cried.

He thrust forward, bringing the flat of the blade down on the wound, holding it there while the flesh sizzled. Telephus screamed, fighting against the pain but somehow keeping his leg still.

The smell of burning meat rose from the gruesome blade. Finally, Achilles withdrew the sword, its point cooling rapidly, and stood before his enemy in triumph. The wound smouldered as the man moaned.

"Bring salves and bandages," said Achilles. "The infection is vanquished and the wound will now heal."

Stepping over the injured man, Achilles strode to face Agamemnon.

"I'll set my camp. I await your order to sail."

Then he strode off, back to his ships. Behind him, he heard the commander's order to the generals.

"Tell the men. As soon as this storm passes we set sail for Ilion."

But the storm did not pass. Three weeks after it began, the bad weather continued unabated. Striding through the camp, Agamemnon tried to bolster the men, but still the fights broke out, still the dissent in the ranks grew.

"We have to do something," said Menelaos at his side. "We'll lose this war to mutiny before we even get to Troy."

"The storm will pass eventually."

"I don't think it will pass. This storm isn't natural."

"What are you talking about?"

"I think it's a divine storm. I think Artemis is still angry about that deer."

"Don't be ridiculous," Agamemnon scoffed.

"I'm not," said Menelaos. "You committed hubris, brother. You called yourself better than a god. She won't forget it in a hurry."

"Supposing you're right," Agamemnon said. "What do you propose we do?"

"Summon Calchas, request an oracle."

Agamemnon sniffed haughtily. "Do you really think that's necessary?"

"If nothing else, it will show the men you're looking for a solution. It might just hold them at bay for a while."

Agamemnon nodded. "For that reason, I'll do it. Not, mind you, because I believe your theory."

"Of course not," Menelaos laughed.

Calchas set up his table in the command tent, out of the weather. He had with him his helper snakes and a collection of small animals the hunters had found and brought in alive for the sacrifice.

"I call on the gods to give answer," he cried, arms raised and snakes hissing. "Help us vanquish the storm that keeps us tied to this place."

One by one, he killed the little beasts, letting the blood flow and laying them out along the table. When he had enough blood to poor, he emptied it into a bronze libation bowl and dipped the fingertips of both hands in the sticky fluid. He lifted his hands to his eyes, painting the blood on his closed eyelids and murmuring.

"Apollo the seer, give me the sight."

Then he raised his snake-clad arms to the heavens. For a moment, he stood still, silent while the men watched with bated breath. Almost imperceptibly, his arms began to tremble.

The snakes reared their heads and flicked their tongues, as the shaking grew more violent. Soon his whole body resonated with power, shaking and convulsing as his mouth made strange disconnected sounds.

Suddenly the shaking stopped and his head snapped forward, eyes open, glowing red. One hand stretched out in front, the fingers working knots, finally settling into a fist. A finger flicked out and pointed, the red eyes blazing as they gazed on Agamemnon.

"You!" a strange disembodied voice came from the prophet's mouth. "You must atone!"

"What have I done?" Agamemnon gulped.

"You offended the huntress. Her anger must be appeased."

The crowd murmured.

"I told you," hissed Menelaos.

"What must I do?"

"Artemis needs a blood sacrifice. A personal gift from you alone. No ordinary gift will do."

"Tell me what I must give."

"The one you prize above all else, your most valued possession. The first flower of your house."

The priest collapsed over the altar, the spirit gone from his body. Lifting his head, he stared at the commander.

"The god has spoken," he whispered.

"What did it mean?" said Agamemnon. "Calchas?"

He glanced at Menelaos, silent at his side. His brother stood transfixed, a look of horror etched on his face.

"I'm so sorry, brother," Menelaos moaned.

"What? What does she want?"

"It was quite clear. The first flower of your house!"

Agamemnon shook his head in confusion. Then the meaning dawned on him and he shook his head more vehemently. It could not be true. How could the goddess ask that?

"I won't do it! I refuse."

"If you refuse," said Calchas. "You condemn the fleet to rot here, and you guarantee the failure of this war."

"I'll never get my wife back," said Menelaos. "You must do it."

"How can you say that? What's your wife, a harlot, to my Gennie? I will not kill my own daughter!"

16

A Necessary Evil

Watching the children play in the great courtyard, Klytemestra felt a peculiar sense of freedom. She looked around for the minstrel or one of his spies, but it seemed she was unwatched. Finally, blissfully free. Yet she worried. Where had the man gone?

"Have you seen Neohippos today?" she said to her servant, standing close by her side.

"Not today," he shrugged.

"I wonder where he could be."

"I wouldn't worry. Just enjoy the peace for a change."

"I can't. What if he didn't believe you? What if he's gone to take his suspicions to Agamemnon?"

"I really doubt that, my lady. He wouldn't go without proof."

"How can you know that?"

He shrugged again. "Maybe he's just given up. Finally realised there's nothing going on."

"After all these years? I find that hard to believe."

"My lady, I promise you, everything will be alright."

"It's just so out of character. I can't help thinking something bad has happened."

"Why do you care? He's been the bane of our lives every waking moment since your husband left. I should think you'd be glad of the reprieve."

"Oh, Gissus, I am... but what if..."

"Stop worrying, my love," he whispered.

"I told you to stop calling me that."

"I'll call you whatever I want, when we're alone. My love," he purred.

"The children..."

"What about them?"

"Just... don't," she snapped, moving toward the porch.

A clatter of hooves from the lower court echoed over the wall and Klytie stopped.

"Whoever that is, send them into the megaron," she said, continuing onto the porch.

"Yes, my lady," said Aegisthus with an exaggerated bow.

In the hall, Klytie sat in the king's seat and waited. The servant arrived ahead of a man dishevelled and weary from the rigors of travel.

"A messenger, my lady," said Aegisthus.

"Come forward," she said to the man.

"My lady, I bring a letter from the commander of the Achaeans. They sit on the beach at Aulis, trapped by bad weather and rough seas. He requests that you meet him there and bring your eldest daughter with you."

Klytie held out a trembling hand to take the scroll from him.

"Thank you," she murmured. "Please accept a meal and a bed. Tell the kitchen staff I sent you."

The man nodded and left the room. Klytie shared a look with her servant and hastily broke the seal.

"Come sit by me..." she whispered. "What can this mean?"

She shivered, dreading the thought that maybe this summons was a call to account. Maybe the minstrel's news had reached its mark. But no, it was far too soon for that. She read the words slowly, deciphering them with difficulty.

What she read was so outlandish it was beyond belief. She shook her head, handing the letter to her servant.

"Read this for me, Gissus. I fear I can't make sense of it. Tell me I'm not reading it right..."

Aegisthus took the scroll and read aloud.

"To my wife, the lady Klytemestra from your husband and commander of the Achaean fleet, Agamemnon, greetings. I write to bring news of a momentous occasion, that being the marriage of our daughter Iphigenia with the great warrior Achilles, son of the goddess Thetis and the hero Peleus. As is the case with most such events, this is an alliance between two great houses, as specifically requested by the aforesaid Achilles in exchange for his aid in the current war. I charge you to bring our daughter to me in Aulis so that the nuptials can be performed, ensuring the cooperation of Achilles in our campaign against Ilion. Bring the boy too; he needs to learn what it is to be a warrior."

By the time he had finished reading, Klytie trembled from head to foot.

"My Gennie," she whispered. "My poor baby girl..."

"It's a good match," Aegisthus said. "Quite a coup for Agamemnon."

"But she's a child, hardly old enough to marry."

"My lady, you forget. She's no younger than you were when you first came to Mycenae, with your second husband. Gennie is growing up fast."

Klytie sighed. "I suppose you're right."

"Shall I get her?"

Klytie nodded, bemused. But when Aegisthus brought Gennie into the megaron, Klytie took a deep breath and presented a happy mask to her daughter.

"Good news, my dearest," she said. "Your papa has found you a husband."

Gennie's eyes widened. "A husband? You mean I'm to

be married?"

"That's right. He's a great warrior by the name of Achilles. It's a very good match."

Gennie smiled, a gleam of excitement in her eyes. "Oh, Mama, I hope he's handsome!"

Aegisthus chuckled. "From what I hear of him, I'm sure you'll be pleased."

"You know of him, Gissus?" she breathed.

"His mother is a goddess."

"Oh," she sighed dreamily. "When can I meet him?"

"We'll leave as soon as you're ready," Klytie said. "We should have a gown made."

"Don't you have a ceremonial dress from when you were married, Mama? Would that fit me?"

"I think I still have it. We can try it if you like, but I thought you'd want something new."

"Oh no, Mama, that would take too long!"

The Achaean camp stretched for miles. Klytemestra and her daughter, riding a cart for the last leg of the journey, felt curious eyes on them as they slowly made their way through the ranks.

Orestes clambered about the cart, hanging over the side while he took in everything, eyes darting about. Men came out of their tents to gape at the women, some even clinging to the side of the cart. Klytie caught snatches of their comments as they passed.

"Is it her? Is it the daughter?"

"She came! I can't believe it!"

"Now we'll see some action..."

"He won't do it, he doesn't have the strength."

"He must, or he'll pay..."

Klytie sat stoically, staring ahead, arm about her daughter while Iphigenia huddled next to her, eyes wild.

"Mama, what are they talking about?"

"Don't listen it's the gossip of soldiers, nothing more."

Finally, nearing the centre of the great army, they could hear upraised voices. Klytie shivered as she recognised the voice of Agamemnon in full outrage. The other she suspected was his brother Menelaos. As the cart drew near, she caught sight of the men outside a large tent. The nearest soldiers went about their business with shifty looks at the arguing pair.

"I won't do it," yelled Agamemnon. "You had no right to stop my letter."

"I had every right! You've been given a directive from the gods. Your pride got us into this, now it's your responsibility to do whatever's necessary to get us out."

"My pride? I'm not the one chasing after a fallen woman. Why must you have her back if not for your wounded pride? You could get another wife. Why must my child pay for your desperate attempt to save face?"

"You agreed to lead this campaign, you angered the goddess, now pay your due!"

"I refuse," Agamemnon growled.

"Fine! Do as you wish, but look around you. Look at this great army gathered about us. They sit here at your order, waiting for months on end to set sail. For what? Your hubris, your refusal to honour the gods. They grow restless; they gather in secret to plot against us, and before long they'll act. Is it worth losing your life over?"

"So disband them, send them home and forget this war. Leave your slut wife to her fate and get another. Would you willingly give your own daughter? I think you would not."

"My daughter?" Menelaos paused. "My Hermione? I would never... I... Oh, I'm so sorry, brother. I suddenly realise what I've been asking you to do. You're right, let's just give up. Send them all home."

"Yes, but... You're right about the mood in the camp. They already know what we planned. What will they do if we back out? I don't think they'll go willingly. We've been building them up to this for so long, promising an end to the raiding from over the sea. They've been kicking their heels here, waiting for the word, waiting for the storm to break, waiting for months, getting more and more restless. I fear they'll turn on us."

Menelaos looked about, noticing the curious looks on the faces of the men. Then he saw the cart and the two women watching in confusion. He touched his brother's arm and Agamemnon turned. His face blanched, his shock stifled quickly but not before Klytemestra felt a cold shiver of foreboding.

"Welcome!" called Agamemnon, his cheerful tone sounding forced.

"Papa!"

Agamemnon strode quickly to the cart and helped Gennie down, clutching her in his arms. He offered a hand to his wife and Klytie alighted with dignity.

"What was that argument about?" she asked.

He shrugged. "It was nothing. I'm glad to see you both," he said flatly.

"Papa, I'm so happy!"

"I'm glad, little scamp," he said.

"Then why are you so sad?"

Agamemnon took a deep breath and gave a false smile. "I have the weight of war on my shoulders, scamp." He looked at Klytie. "Will you wait in my tent? I've something I need to take care of."

"Of course," Klytie smiled.

"Orestes, get down off that cart and come with me," Agamemnon barked.

The little boy glanced at his mother uncertainly and

she nodded. Orestes jumped down and took his father's offered hand timidly, walking with him with head craned back to stare at his mother. Klytie smiled reassurance and he trotted along beside the commander as they disappeared into the milling camp.

Inside the stifling heat of the tent, Klytemestra sat with her daughter, slowly combing her hair. The girl was putting on a brave face but Klytie remembered the sick knots in the stomach she had before her own wedding to Tantalus so many years ago.

She had been lucky then, catching a kind and loving husband. She hoped Gennie would fare just as well. Outside, the occasional shout or clash of armour would make the girl jump, betraying her nervous mood.

Klytie soothed her with calming words, but inside she worried. Another shout rang out, and she recognised the name of the Commander. She sighed, hoping this waiting was soon to be over. The shouting grew louder as whoever it was approached the tent.

"Agamemnon! Where are you? What's all this delay? My men sit by their ships and stew, waiting for you to give the order. Agamemnon!"

The man stopped, his tirade ending just outside the tent. Klytie held her breath. A soldier, coming across two women alone in a tent would be the height of impropriety, and downright dangerous.

"Agamemnon! I need to know what's going on, come out and tell me why we still sit here. My men are on the brink of mutiny. If you won't come out, I'm coming in!"

With that, the tent flap swung back and a magnificent young warrior strode in. He stopped, blinking in the dim light, and then stared.

"Oh!" he gasped. "I'm sorry, my lady, I was looking for

Agamemnon."

"So I heard," said Klytie dryly.

The man looked from one to the other.

"Forgive me, but... who are you?" he said. "And why are you here?"

"I am Klytemestra, wife of Agamemnon, and this is my daughter Iphigenia. We came when summoned. My daughter is to marry Achilles."

The man blinked. "Excuse me?"

"Agamemnon called us here, in order that the marriage ceremony might be conducted at once."

"I don't understand," the man frowned. "What marriage?"

Klytie sighed, exasperated. "Why, the marriage between my daughter and the warrior Achilles."

"But... I'm Achilles."

Gennie gasped.

"Oh!" said Klytie with a smile. "Then welcome!"

"Thank you, but... I'm afraid there's been some kind of mistake. I'm not expecting a bride."

"You're not? But it was set out quite plainly in the letter..."

"What letter?"

"The letter Agamemnon sent!" Klytie cried, angry now.

"I'm sorry, but someone has played a dreadful trick on you. I've made no marriage arrangement with your husband. In fact, I'm already married."

Gennie sprang to her feet. "No! Mama, what's going on?"

"I don't know, Gennie!"

"Wait," said Achilles. "Let me find your husband. We'll soon get this sorted out."

He stepped out of the tent, calling for a runner. Gennie sat down slowly, a dazed look on her face. Klytie put an arm about her shoulders.

"So... does this mean I'm not getting married?" the girl

whispered.

"I don't think so, sweetheart."

Outside, muffled voices floated through the canvas of the tent, the voice of Achilles as he questioned the soldiers. Klytie strained to hear.

"Where's Agamemnon?

"I think he's with Calchas, preparing for the sacrifice."

"What sacrifice?"

"The girl, where have you been? It's all over camp."

"What are you talking about? I've been waiting for orders, keeping my men happy while they sit…"

"There's going to be a sacrifice, to appease the gods and get rid of this never-ending storm. He's giving his daughter to Artemis."

"Find him! I need to speak with him right now!"

"Mama!" Gennie whispered. "Did he say he's giving me to Artemis? What did he mean?"

"Hush, Gennie. I'm sure it's nothing," she said.

"But Mama, he said sacrifice! Papa wouldn't do that would he?"

"Of course not," she whispered, but a cold wind blew across her heart and she shivered with an uncanny premonition that maybe he would.

The tent flap opened again and Achilles entered, face dark as a thundercloud, his mouth clamped in a thin line.

"Did I hear right?" Klytie whispered. "Is he really planning a dreadful sacrifice?"

"My lady, it appears you've been tricked into coming here for the most gruesome purpose."

Klytie groaned. "Oh, why would he do this? He promised marriage, but planned a murder! What can we do?"

"My lady, my name has been used to bring you here and for that I apologise. It's unforgiveable."

"Achilles, I beg you, do something."

"What can I do?"

"Use your army. Force him to let us go. Call on your mother to help. It's your own name on the line. He used you, now punish him for it."

He nodded. "He has shamed me yet again, and I won't tolerate it any more. I promise you, I'll stop this. I won't allow it. Let me speak to my men."

The young warrior rushed from the tent. Klytie clutched her daughter to her, hushing the girl's frightened sobs as all her hopes tumbled around her.

"Hush, my Gennie. When your father gets back I'll give him a piece of my mind."

They did not have long to wait. The tent flap was thrust back and an angry Agamemnon stormed in. Gennie squealed and hid behind her mother.

"I heard Achilles was here, looking for me," Agamemnon said.

"Yes, he was here," said Klytie through gritted teeth.

"What did he want?"

"Does it matter?"

"Well of course it matters. I'm too busy to be mucked about like this. Where is he?"

"Where's Orestes?"

"Playing soldier, he'll be fine. Now where's Achilles?"

"He went back to his men, to arm himself against you."

"Against me? What are you talking about?" His eyes narrowed. "What did he say?"

"Enough for me to know you lied about a marriage."

He looked askance. "What else?"

Klytie straightened her back, her anger giving her strength. "We know, Agamemnon, we know what you planned. How dare you! How can you come in here all fatherly and have murder in your heart?"

His face blanched. "You know?" he whispered.

"Oh, Papa," Gennie sobbed. "Please don't kill me, Papa!"

"Gennie, I..."

"Don't speak to her, you brute. You don't deserve such a daughter."

"Do you think I wanted this? I tried to stop it. I tried to send a letter, a second one, telling you not to come. I sent it within hours of the first."

"We never received such a letter."

"I know. It was stopped. My brother caught the messenger and took the note. By the time I found out it was too late. I tried. I swear I tried, Gennie..."

"You made me so happy, Papa. I thought I was going to be married. But it wasn't true. You want to kill me! What did I do wrong, Papa?"

"Oh, little scamp you did nothing wrong. It was my fault. I was weak, I couldn't say no to the others. They concocted this plan together. My brother, with Odysseus and the other generals, they made me write the letter. But then I tried to stop it."

"I don't believe you," Klytie spat. "I know you're quite capable of murder. I've seen it! You killed Tantalus, and my baby, now you want to kill my little girl. I did everything right, I acted like a good wife to you, I never complained. Haven't you hurt me enough?"

Somewhere in the distance, a roar of voices floated through the camp, angry men yelling, the noise coming closer. A small body hurtled through the flap, a terrified Orestes. He hurled himself on his mother.

"Mama, the soldiers are fighting! Mama, I'm scared."

"Don't you see?" said Agamemnon. "We're surrounded by the biggest army the world has ever seen. And they're angry, angry to be away from their homes, sick of being kept here waiting, hungry for lack of food, wanting to go to war. If I don't do this, they'll kill me and do it anyway. I can't stop it."

The noise was growing, coming closer. With it, a great jangling of bronze and thudding of sandals on the hard packed dirt, rumbling through the ground.

"You're a coward, Agamemnon, and a fool," Klytie spat.

He bristled at that. "How dare you speak to me like that, woman. I did what was right for my country, without thinking about myself and what I wanted. I did it for my brother, too, to get Helene back. And we can't do this without appeasing Artemis."

"So you put a slut higher than your own beloved daughter? You really are twisted, Agamemnon."

"No! I planned this to save us all from the marauders, to stop them plundering our cities and stealing our women. Helene is nothing to me, but she's everything to the Achaeans. She may be a whore but she's a symbol of all the women who have been stolen from their beds."

"Let her rot! Find another symbol."

The yelling was close now, one voice rising up above the mob in protest.

"Listen to them," Agamemnon cried. "They'll kill us all! Then they'll take out their revenge on Mycenae. If I don't do this we're all dead."

"If you do this, I'll never forgive you. You'll never be welcome in your own home. I hope you never return from this cursed war."

The door flap burst inward, the whole tent rattling with the force of the man's entry. Achilles saw Agamemnon and screamed his rage, lifting his sword ready to strike.

"I'll kill you for what you've done! You've turned my own men against me."

Suddenly, Iphigenia stood before her father, shielding him from the sword.

"Please, Achilles, don't hurt my papa."

The warrior lowered his sword, a look of bewilderment shadowing his brow.

"Tell me what happened," said the girl.

"They turned on me. I tried to explain that I was doing the right thing by you, an innocent girl bound to me by a promise of marriage. They laughed. They jeered and called me a slave to a pretty girl. When I told them I was going to stop the sacrifice, they called me weak. They've lost all reason; they threatened to kill me. Me!"

Outside the tent, the army screamed its rage, bashing swords on shields and stamping feet.

"Bring out the girl!" a voice cried.

"Stop hiding like a coward, Agamemnon."

"Bring her out and do as you promised, free us to go to war!"

Achilles screamed defiance. "I will not allow this!"

"Achilles, take my daughter, escape with her," Klytie whispered. "Save her please..."

Achilles nodded and took Gennie's hand, but the girl resisted.

"No, Mama, I won't go."

"Gennie, you must."

"No," said the girl stubbornly. She turned to her father and took his hands. "I understand now, Papa," she whispered. "I'm going to save you, Papa. I'm going to save everyone."

"Gennie!" Klytie cried. "You've got to go now."

"I'm not going, Mama. Give my love to Elektra and to Krissie."

"Gennie, stop this," Klytie sobbed. "I'm taking you home with me."

"No, Mama, I have to do this."

She bent to hug her brother. "Orestes, you must be strong for Mama. Take care of her while Papa is away, and try to help her not be mad at him."

She turned to Achilles, slipped her arms about his waist and hugged him.

"I want to thank you, Achilles. You're so kind and good. You tried to help me even though I came for a lie. You respected my disappointed hopes and tried to atone for them, when you owed me nothing. I would have been proud to have you for my husband."

Achilles took her face gently in his hands, bent down and kissed her softly on the lips. "Iphigenia, I would have been proud to have you for my wife," he replied.

"Now, take my hand," said Gennie. "Papa, take my other hand. Lead me to the altar."

"No!" Klytie cried. "Gennie, please, you don't have to do this."

"I do, Mama. My life is nothing compared to all of you. I want to do something to help, and if my death can send the army to war to save my country I'll go to it gladly."

"Gennie, don't believe them. It's all a lie!"

"Don't follow me, Mama. I don't want you to see."

"Gennie!" Klytie cried.

Iphigenia turned, walked toward the door, holding Achilles by the hand on one side and her father's hand on the other. Together they made their way out of the tent to meet the mob. As they emerged, a great roar went up.

"Gennie!" Klytie screamed. "Gennie!"

She sank to the ground in a huddle of anguished screams, her chest aching as the sobs heaved out of her. Orestes stood by his mother, one small hand on her back as she sobbed.

Walking toward the place where the priest Calchas had set up his sacrificial table, deep in the wood behind the camp, Achilles glanced down at the girl walking so calmly beside him. He could not believe she was willingly going to her death. Her courage made his own brave deeds seem small and petty.

Her soft hand in his made not a tremble, her steps did not falter. This maiden who had done no wrong, sacrificed for her father's pride, would rather die than see that father killed. Even as the darkness of the wood settled around them, Iphigenia walked without faltering to her doom.

On her other side, her father Agamemnon walked, face set in a hard stare. That one, too, showed a dreadful determination to carry out this heinous act. Something was terribly wrong in a world where father could kill daughter for the sake of war.

Achilles sent a silent thought to the heavens, calling on his mother Thetis. If only she might save the girl, take up her side against the goddess Artemis. Oh Mother, he thought. If you can hear me, save this poor innocent girl. He knew what her answer would be, felt it in his bones as if Thetis herself had placed the knowledge fully formed in his mind.

She would try, but she was only a nymph, no match for a great goddess like Artemis. Ahead, in a clearing in the trees, sunlight slanted down, beams spreading a soft glow over the table. Stopping at the edge of the light, Achilles watched as Iphigenia hugged her father.

"Don't be sad, Papa," she said.

Then the girl walked calmly up to the table, standing before Calchas, lifting her chin in defiance of her fate. The priest helped her lie on the table and spread out a cloth to cover her, draping it over her slim young form and covering her face. Achilles glanced across at Agamemnon. Was he really going to go through with this?

The commander was standing stiffly, his grim face wet with tears. But he made no attempt to stop the priest.

Calchas raised his arms to begin the prayer to Artemis, but Achilles heard none of his words. His mind was racing. They were really going to do it.

The nearest soldiers squeezed in close, all wanting a look, while those behind climbed on their backs to get a better view. Further back in the trees, voices could be heard mumbling their displeasure at being excluded from the spectacle.

By the gods, this was a young girl, not some feast day attraction. Calchas reached for his axe, lifting it high and taking aim. Unable to watch, Achilles gazed at Agamemnon, watching the commander's face. His eyes were squeezed shut, his jaw set in a hard line while his hands clenched in fists at his sides.

Stop it, Achilles thought. Why doesn't he stop it? He tried to make him stop it by sheer force of will, but to no avail. The commander said nothing, head in hands, shutting out the inevitable.

Calchas screamed the benediction and the axe came down with a sickening thud. Achilles jumped. Agamemnon flinched, a horrific groan escaping him and his shoulders shaking with his sobs. Then the men let out a great roar, followed by cheers and cries of joy.

"A miracle!" Calchas cried.

Snapping around to look at the priest, Achilles gasped, blinking to clear his sight. He hurried to Agamemnon's side, catching his arm.

"My lord!" he gasped. "Look!"

Agamemnon shook him off, insensible in his grief, but Achilles tried again.

"Sir, please, you must see."

Agamemnon raised his ravaged face to look at Achilles. The young warrior nodded and gestured with his eyes. The commander looked askance at the table where his daughter had been. Then his eyes widened at the blood soaking the white cloth, pouring into the channels and filling the bronze rhyton.

Following the path of the blood, he gasped at the sight of two magnificent horns rising up from under the cloth where the girl's head was still covered. He shook his head to clear his vision, and then looked again. The body lay still, wrapped up in its sheet. He thought he saw the bottom of one sandal. Or was it a hoof?

"It's a boon from the gods!" a soldier cried.

"Artemis has blessed us with a feast!" called another.

"No!" cried Agamemnon. "Don't touch her!"

"A deer for the fire!" another soldier yelled.

As Agamemnon tried to move toward the body on the altar, the army surged forward, pushing their commander out of the way in their eagerness.

"Wait, let me see!" the Commander screamed.

Before he could do more than cry out his denial, the body was swept up in the tide and carried away.

In the Commander's tent, Klytemestra heard the cheers of the soldiers, the sounds of celebrations wafting over the camp, and crumpled in a heap on the dirt floor. Her son tried to comfort her, sitting helplessly beside her as she groaned and sobbed.

When the tent flap opened to admit the Commander, her head snapped up, a snarl of rage on her lips. She flew at him screaming, fists flying, pummelling at him. Agamemnon grabbed her wrists, holding her at bay as she kicked at him. She twisted out of his grasp.

"I hate you!" she snarled.

"I hate me too," he murmured. "Would it help if I tell you there was a miracle? Our daughter lives with the gods."

"What?" she snapped.

"At the moment the axe fell she was taken, replaced by a deer. Artemis took her. She never died."

"Do you really believe that?" Klytie shook her head. "Did you see the body?"

"I... saw the horns, but I couldn't get close. They took her away."

"You let them take her?" her voice rose in pitch.

Klytie felt her gorge rise, gagging on the acid rising up from the pit of her stomach. A deer? To be dressed and roasted to feed the starving army...

"Is that really what happened," she whispered. "Or is it a convenient excuse?"

"What are you talking about? Didn't you hear me? She was taken by Artemis and a deer was left in her place."

"But you didn't see her! How do you know?"

"I saw the horns... She lives. She's been blessed by the gods and will live forever."

"Even if I believe it, she's still dead. I'll never see her again. And you let the only proof get taken away to be butchered! I can't even bury her!"

"I thought you'd see the good side. She's living with the gods."

"What will I say to her sisters? While you go off to Ilion, I have to relive this over and over again with your other children. I have to see her in her sisters' faces, walk past her empty room, and miss her laughter every day."

"I don't expect you to forgive me, but at least you can be happy knowing our daughter was saved."

"Happy? Happy that you have an excuse to salvage your conscience and justify yourself? You've taken my daughter, ripped her from me and sent her to the gods," she sobbed. "I'll never forgive you. I hope you rot in Troy!"

17

A Wish Fulfilled

Riding up to the great lion gate of Mycenae, Klytemestra shivered. Little Orestes, cradled in front of her, stared at the stone beasts glaring down at them.

"Mama..." he whispered. "I'm scared."

"Don't worry, they're not real."

"But they're looking at me."

"No, they're just carved that way. They're meant to strike fear into the heart of any invader. They warn you not to come any further, and dare you to come closer."

The little boy shivered and twisted around, burying his head in his mother's chest. Klytie wrapped him in her arms, as much for her own assurance as her son's.

"We'll be through soon and then you won't see them anymore."

They passed through the gate and began the long climb up to the palace. Settling in her arms, the boy gazed up at the walls high above. Klytie hugged him closer, biting back tears at the thought of the scene that awaited her.

"It's alright, Mama," Orestes said. "I'll tell them if you want."

"No, Orestes," she said with a pang of guilt.

The boy should never have been made witness to the events in Aulis. He was so young, he would never understand, and she prayed he would one day come to terms with it all.

In the lower courtyard, they dismounted and passed the horse to the bodyguard for stabling. A cry from above made Klytie look up to see the girls waving down at her. She smiled in spite of her melancholy and waved back. She hurried up the stairs, meeting them half way.

"Mama! Oh I'm so glad you're back," said Krisothemis.

"Welcome home, Mama," said Elektra, a smile beneath her serious expression.

"Oh my girls," Klytie smiled. "It's good to be home."

"Come on up and tell us all about it," said Krissie. "How was the wedding? I bet Gennie was beautiful."

"Yes, she was," said Klytie with a sigh.

"What's wrong, Mama?" said Elektra as they emerged into the upper courtyard.

"Nothing, my dear, just missing her."

"Me too," said Krissie. "Do you think we might be able to visit when she's settled?"

"No, I don't think so."

"Why not?"

"Gennie turned into a deer!" Orestes piped up.

"Hush, Orestes," Klytie hissed.

"Oh, don't be silly," said Krissie.

"It's true, Papa took her and gave her to the goddess and she became a deer."

"Orestes!" Klytie snapped.

"What's he talking about, Mama?" said Elektra.

"It's nothing, dear, just stories. Our Orestes spent a little too much time with the soldiers, that's all."

"And Gennie? Did she like her husband?" said Krissie.

"Oh yes, she liked him very much. He's very nice."

"Do you think she's happy?"

Klytie sucked in a breath, held her voice for a moment before answering. "I'm sure she's living in bliss," she said with a catch in her throat.

"Oh, I'm glad," said Krissie with a happy sigh.

"Come inside, my lady," said her servant from the porch. "We have a meal waiting and a bath prepared."

Klytie smiled. "Thank you, Gissus," she murmured. "Can I eat in the bath?"

"I don't see why not. I'll have a table set up."

"Come on then, children," Klytie said, trying to lighten her mood. "Let's all go, like we used to do."

Orestes ran ahead and the girls followed, one on each side of their mother, pulling her along. Soon they were gathered in the bathing room while Klytie and Orestes shared the small bath and they all shared the meal that had been set up against one wall. Keeping the mood light, Klytie steered the chatter away from any mention of the real events in Aulis, instead making up a pretty story about a beautiful wedding.

"But Mama, that's not what happened," Orestes said.

"Hush, Orestes," she cried. "Let's not spoil it."

The boy grumbled but held his tongue.

"Now, it's getting late," said Klytie. "You've had a long day and it's time for bed."

"But Mama!"

"No buts, Orestes. Bed. Now."

The boy grumbled but clambered out of the bath, calling for the servant. As Aegisthus bundled him up in a robe and led him off to bed, the girls turned more serious, sitting on the edge of the bath to talk to their mother.

"Are you going to tell us the real story, now?" said Elektra.

Klytie sighed. "Oh, I will, I promise. But not now."

"Please, Mama," said Krissie. "That story was a lot of fun, but we know it wasn't true. Orestes was all head shakes and frowns."

"I know, but I can't. Not today, my dears."

"Alright, Mama," said Elektra. "When you're ready then."

"I promise."

"Then we'll go to bed too," said Krissie with a smile. "You look like you need some quiet time."

The girls hugged their mother and headed out of the bathing room. When they were gone, Klytie let out a long, shuddering breath. Then, leaning back against the end of the bath, she drew her knees up to her chest and hugged them against her, dropping her head into her arms.

Now that she was alone, it was easy to sink back into despair, giving in to her grief. Telling her daughters would not be easy, but it was still so raw, so easy to relive the events over again in her mind, and she needed to tell them with calmness and resignation.

She knew, if she had tried, she would have broken down, and the girls did not need that from their mother. A cough brought her out of her fog. She looked up through a haze of unshed tears.

"My lady? What's wrong?" said Aegisthus.

She drew a shuddering breath, sinking deeper into the bath. "Nothing," she whispered.

"Now, I know that's a lie," he said. "Something happened that you're not telling us."

"Please don't," she said, voice catching. "I just can't. Not yet."

He shrugged and sauntered over to the bath. He sat behind her on the edge, hands on her shoulders, massaging. She sighed and relaxed a little, sitting up to make the treatment easier. Swinging his feet into the bath, he leant in closer, hands too gentle for a real massage, caressing and comforting.

"It seems every time I come home I'm followed by tragedy," she whispered. "And you're always here, to pick me up."

"And always will be, my love," he murmured.

Slipping into the bath behind her, he continued his gentle massage, arms slipping about her as his lips brushed her neck. Klytie leant back against him with a sigh, closing her eyes.

He always seemed to know when she needed comfort, pushing his suit when she was at her most vulnerable. She knew she should be angry with him, but she did not care. He brought a hand up to her face, turning her chin toward him as his mouth sought hers.

She gave in to the kiss, relishing the shivering sensation as his arms pulled her close against him. Why had she fought him for so long? She knew she should stop this before it went too far.

Much as she hated Agamemnon, she was still his wife, and she had no right to entertain even the idea of a lover. She was not her sister. She would not be tarred with the same brush. Pushing against him with her hands, Klytie tried to break away, but he only held her more tightly.

"No," she groaned through his kisses. "Let me go!"

His arms released her and she exploded from the bath, clutching for her robe and rushing from the room. She left him there and ran for the only safe place she knew. Entering her room, she quickly dressed, knowing he would not be far behind. She had to get herself under control. She had to build up her defences against him. Too soon, he was in the doorway, rubbing at his wet clothing with a bath sheet, a look of hurt in his eyes.

"I wish you'd stop running away," he said.

"Stop chasing me, then," she snapped.

"Never," he murmured. "Klytie, you know how I feel about you. I know something is wrong and I need you to tell me."

"Not now," she said, voice strangled. "Not here."

"Not here?" he said. "Alright, then."

He crossed the room and grabbed her hand, pulling her toward the door. "You're coming with me."

"Where are we going?" she gasped.

"Somewhere you can't run away from me."

She pulled against him. "I won't go! It's dark outside, where are you taking me?"

He said nothing, mouth set in a hard line. His hand gripped hers painfully as he pulled her down the stairs and out into the courtyard, across to the great stair and down into the city. She soon stopped fighting, knowing it was impossible.

He was so determined. She was sobbing by the time they reached his house. Taking her inside, across the hall and upstairs, he did not allow her to stop until they entered a small room, sparsely furnished but richly decorated. He closed the door behind her and slid the bar across.

"Whose room is this?"

"Mine."

She turned to the door in a panic, but he caught her.

"Sit," he said harshly, pointing to the bed.

She did as she was told, holding her breath on the sobs.

"Now. You're going to tell me what happened in Aulis."

Klytie stared. What could she say? There was so much to tell, all of it painful. She had no idea where to start. She shook her head.

"Alright," he said. "Let me help you. How was the wedding?"

She took a deep breath. "There was no wedding."

"No wedding? Then where is Gennie?"

"The wedding was a ruse."

"A ruse for what? Klytie, you need to tell me. Do I have to drag every sentence out of you?"

She sucked in a shuddering breath. "Do you remember when I said he couldn't hurt me anymore?"

He nodded.

"I was wrong," she whispered. "The wedding was a lie."

She proceeded to tell him the whole story, haltingly at first but growing stronger as the anger took over from the grief. She watched his manner change as the story unfolded, his own anger clear on his face. When she finally got to the end, he was pacing, face red and fists clenched.

"And so," she finished. "Gennie is with the gods and the army is on its way to Troy."

"With the gods," he spat. "A fine euphemism for dead!"

"I have to believe it," she sobbed. "I can't let her be dead. I can't have her wasting away in the dark of Hades. Or worse. My baby girl is walking the halls of Olympus with Artemis."

"Worse? What can be worse than dead?"

"What do we do with our sacrifices?" she whispered. "They were starving..."

"Oh, gods, no!" he gasped, face white. "You can't be suggesting... He's not that kind of a monster, surely..."

"His father was," Klytie hissed. "I know he's capable of it. He let them take her; he didn't even try to stop them."

"Oh, Gennie! Poor little miss, taken before time by her own father, her helpless body defiled... How can you defend him now?"

"I can't," she hissed. "I hate him more than ever now. He can never be forgiven."

He sat beside her, an arm sliding about her shoulders and pulling her close. She buried her face in his chest, the warmth of him seeping into her battered soul and loosening her hold on her heart. She sobbed quietly as he held her close.

"Do you see what this means, my love?" he whispered.

"You owe him nothing now, least of all your loyalty. He doesn't deserve you."

She pulled back to look at him, eyes wide. His face was wet with his own tears, but he was smiling. Her gaze flickered over his face, her mind racing. He was right. For so many years, he had watched over her, standing back and letting her be, respecting her wishes. Yet he loved her.

He had waited for her without any hope of ever winning her, yet here he was. His hand was under her chin, lifting her face to his. This time she welcomed his kiss, her arms sliding about his neck as she melted into his embrace. Then his mouth explored her, his breath hot on her neck and she arched her back.

"Let me love you," he whispered huskily into her ear.

Then his mouth found hers again and she responded with an unexpected eagerness that bubbled up from deep in her belly. His caressing hands brought fire where they touched, tingling down her arms, across her thighs and under her clothing.

No man had touched her like that, not even Tantalus, who had been kind and loving in his quiet way. She had never dreamed love could be so overwhelming, sending her into a place of intense pleasure. She allowed him to push her down onto the bed, lost in the sensation of his touch.

Waking slowly, Klytie allowed her eyes to flutter open on an unfamiliar room. She stared at the closed shutters, pinpricks of sunlight making star-like patterns across the floor. She drew in a deep breath and felt arms tighten about her, listened as the slow breathing at her back quickened.

"Good morning, my love," he murmured.

Klytie's eyes widened as the memory of the night before washed away the fog of sleep. She sat up, pulling the woollen blanket up to her neck.

"What's wrong?"

She shook her head, mind racing. She should never have allowed it to happen. Now, in the light of day, she knew it was a mistake. It could never work. She had to get back to the palace. The children would be looking for her. She slipped her legs over the side of the bed.

"Wait," he said, clutching at her hand.

She hesitated, his touch sending sparks up her arm. She sucked in her breath, surprised by the sudden fluttering in her stomach, cursing her traitorous body for its instant reaction. She had to get away. But he had both her hands now, pulling her around to face him.

"You're not thinking of running away again, are you?"

"I..."

"Because I won't let you. Not now."

"The children..."

"Can look after themselves. We'll be home soon enough."

She licked her lips, avoiding his gaze. "It can't happen again."

"Klytie, look at me," he said. "There's no going back to how things were."

"There has to be..." she whispered. "We can't do this."

"Why? What are you afraid of?"

"I..."

"Your husband?" he spat.

She gasped at his sudden change in tone. "What if he comes back, survives the war... What then? He'd kill us both if he knew."

"We'll deal with that when it comes. We could have years together before that happens."

"And then?" She shook her head again. "No. I won't do it."

"Are you saying you don't want me?" he frowned.

His face blurred and she swallowed hard, trying to

speak around the lump in her throat. "I don't want... I can't love you only to lose you," she whispered.

"I'm willing to risk it."

"You are?"

"Oh, my love, how many times can I say it? You're my whole life, and now that I have you I won't give you up."

Her tears spilled over and she drew a sobbing breath as he pulled her into his arms, silencing her fears with his kiss. She responded almost against her will, her body's urgency overriding her protests and her mind subdued by the power of his caresses.

It was late morning when they finally returned to the palace. Klytie dreaded telling her daughters the truth about Iphigenia, but she had Gissus for strength.

"Mama, where have you been?" cried Orestes as they entered the upper courtyard.

"Your mama had some business with the priest of Apollo," Gissus lied smoothly.

"Dressed like that?" said Elektra with a frown. "You're not even wearing your potinia gown."

"It was a consultation."

"So?"

"It was an informal request. She wasn't there in an official capacity."

"Mama, is this true?"

Klytie nodded, unable to trust her voice. Elektra frowned again.

"What was the consultation about?" she said, eyes narrowed.

"That's not your concern, Elektra," Klytie snapped.

"Well sorry, Mama, forgive me for being concerned. What am I supposed to think when you disappear before dawn without a word?"

Klytie sighed. "I'm sorry, my dear. Please girls, come into the potinia's room, I'm ready to tell you about Gennie."

The girls ranged themselves either side of Klytie's official seat, with Orestes on the floor in front. Aegisthus stood close by, ready with a smile and a comforting word. Krissie accepted the news stoically, tears glistening in her eyes, but Elektra frowned, her face like a thundercloud.

"I don't believe you," she said when her mother was finished. "My papa would never do that. My sister is alive and living with her husband."

"Elektra, I'm sorry, but it's all true."

"I don't care what you say! You're lying."

"Elektra!" Klytie snapped.

"You've always hated Papa. You try to hide it but I can tell. Papa wouldn't hurt us like that," she cried, storming out of the room.

1X

Of Plagues and Priestesses

Telephus pointed to the small island on the horizon.

"That's Lemnos," he said. "Sacred to Hephaestos. From there it's just a small hop over to Troy. We should pull in at Hephaestia and take stock."

"Do you think that's necessary?" Agamemnon mused. "If Troy is so close, why not keep going?"

"It's your choice, but just outside Hephaestia is a sacred grove dedicated to the Kaviri, the children of Hephaestos and Kaviro. They're known to be protectors of sailors."

"Yes," Agamemnon nodded. "Perhaps it's right to give thanks for our voyage. We don't want another divine storm scattering the fleet again."

"True, my lord," smiled Telephus. "Take the fleet around the island to the north, there's a cove with a beach."

The Achaean fleet pulled into a little bay beside the town, their numbers too great to ride onto the beach. The commander signalled across to his captains to join him on shore, and just the leaders made landfall in their black ships. There waiting for them was a group of islanders, ready with gifts and praise.

"We welcome you, great lords, to our humble city. We hope you will accept these offerings in the spirit of friendship."

"You don't have to worry," said Menelaos. "We don't intend to sack your fine town. We wish merely to camp and visit your sacred grove."

"Please accept these animals for your sacrificial feast," the town's spokesman replied, pointing to a small herd of goats.

"We thank you for your kind offer."

The prophet Calchas performed the sacrifice and the captains sat themselves down in the sacred grove to partake of the sacrificial feast. The goats were slaughtered and roasted, to be eagerly shared by the various captains and commanders. Wine flowed and laughter echoed out over the bay. Hearing the noise of the feast floating on the breeze, Achilles ordered his ship to land. Enraged, he stormed into the grove, interrupting the party.

"Agamemnon!" he thundered. "How dare you feast without me. Will you never stop piling insult upon me?"

"Oh pipe down, Achilles," Agamemnon scoffed.

"Why wasn't I invited to this feast?"

"It was an offering to the gods, from the leaders of the Achaean fleet. You're a minor princeling, or had you forgotten in your arrogance?"

"I should have been included," the young warrior pouted.

"Oh shut up, you little toad, stop snivelling," cried Philoctetes from where he lounged by the fountain. "Can't you see you're not wanted?"

Achilles rounded on the man. "Why are you here? You're no better than me."

"I'm the heir of Herakles, I carry his bow and without me this war is over before it begins. What do you offer, little toad?"

Achilles bristled. "Without me Troy will never fall. It was

prophesied, or hadn't you heard?"

Philoctetes snorted his derision. But his expression changed and he let out a cry of pain.

"By the gods, I've been bitten!" he screamed.

"What?" said Achilles. "Don't change the subject…"

But Philoctetes was screaming now, clutching at his leg, his ankle already swollen and purple. Agamemnon sat up, staring at the man.

"What was it?" the commander said.

"Some kind of serpent," Philoctetes gasped. "It slithered off into the bushes.

"Probably a water snake," said Telephus.

"Is it dangerous?" said Menelaos with a frown.

"Not particularly. Some people are unaffected. But some people suffer a reaction that can be life threatening. Some take years to heal. Or die."

"You see?" Achilles crowed. "The gods agree with me. They struck you down mid-insult. I am vindicated!"

"Well, Achilles, since you're here," said Agamemnon. "You're the trained healer. Why don't you see what you can do for him?"

The next morning, Philoctetes lay feverish and barely conscious. Achilles had laid poultices over his injured leg and strapped it to keep it still as the man writhed in his agony.

"What do we do now?" said Menelaos to his brother.

"If he doesn't improve today, we'll have to go on without him," said Agamemnon.

"No!" cried Philoctetes in his delirium. "Don't leave me…"

"Perhaps we can wait a few days," said Menelaos. "We could take this opportunity to send a delegation ahead to Troy, see if we can't resolve this peacefully."

"I doubt it," Agamemnon snorted. "But I suppose we can try. At least find out if we really have found Troy. Wouldn't want a repeat of the debacle at Teuthrania."

Agamemnon raised his voice. "Telephus and Odysseus," he called.

"Yes, my lord," Telephus cried.

"How do we find Troy from here?"

"Round the point and sail due east," Telephus replied. "You can't miss it."

"Odysseus, take a delegation, sail to Troy and see if you can't get an audience with their king. Try to find a peaceful settlement."

"Of course, my lord," said Odysseus.

"I'll come too," said Menelaos. "But what will you do, Agamemnon?"

"We'll stay for a few days, then follow and make camp near Troy. If Philoctetes heals, fine. If not, he stays here."

"There's a small island just off the coast, called Tenedos," said Telephus. "You can anchor the fleet there until you know the outcome of the meeting."

"That's a good plan," Agamemnon nodded. Then he raised his voice again. "Achilles!"

"Yes, my lord," the boy said eagerly.

"Take your Myrmidons and harry the coast around Troy, conquer their neighbours and capture any cities you find. Let the Trojans see we mean business; take their allies away."

"Yes, my lord," Achilles grinned. "It will be my pleasure!"

As his black ship pulled up on the sand, Menelaos stared, past the cliffs, across a wide flood plain, to the immense walls of a great city. He held his breath for a moment, holding down conflicting emotions of rage and eager anticipation.

Somewhere in that city, his wife lay with another man. If this embassy were successful, she could be returned to him this very day. He somehow doubted that would happen. Who would willingly give up such a prize as Helene?

Jumping down onto the sand, he made his way up the beach, Odysseus close behind. Together they climbed the bluff and stood waiting while the chariots were unloaded. Then, with a small retinue of foot soldiers, they drove out onto the plain toward the imposing walls.

At the gate, a challenge echoed out. Menelaos raised his voice to answer.

"I am Menelaos, king of Sparta. I come to sue for the return of my wife, Helene. I seek audience with your king."

There was no reply. Menelaos waited anxiously, hoping the guard had conveyed his message. Eventually the gates opened and a small force emerged to escort them into the town. Moving through the gate, the Achaean delegation was led through the town amid hostile stares.

At the central square, outside a small shrine, Menelaos stopped as a woman caught his eye. Surrounded by maids, the woman had just come out of the temple, her fine golden hair shining in the sun. Menelaos sucked in his breath. Helene! He would have recognised her anywhere.

As he watched, the woman looked up, catching his eye. Her mouth opened as if she might speak, but instead she shook her head, an expression of immense sadness darkening her flawless face. Menelaos took a step toward her, but the Trojan escort prevented him, one soldier pointing a spear at his gut.

Odysseus took him by the arm and urged him on. The woman let out a cry and ran back into the temple. Blinking back tears, Menelaos allowed himself to be led, mind trapped in melancholy as he held onto the unexpected vision of his lost wife, dwelling on her unhappy expression. Was she sad to be trapped here with her kidnapper? Or was she sad to see him, unwilling to go home with him?

They entered the palace and finally came into the presence of the King and his retinue. A large group, many obviously family by their similarity of face, stared at the delegation. On the royal seat, an old man gazed at them with hooded eyes.

"I am King Priam," he said in his quavering voice. "Do I have the honour of addressing Menelaos of Sparta?"

"You do, my lord," said Menelaos. "And this is Odysseus of Ithaka."

"You seek the return of Helene, my son's beloved wife?"

Menelaos winced. "My wife first, my lord."

"I see. And what would I gain from this, besides a wounded son?"

"We would leave you in peace."

"Is that a threat?"

"My brother stands ready, a fleet of a thousand ships at his command."

The King raised an eyebrow. "You would attack my city for a mere woman?"

"Not just any woman," Menelaos hissed. "My wife, who your son stole against all the laws of decency."

"It was my right," a young man cried. "She was my promised bride, given to me by Aphrodite herself!"

Menelaos let his eye rove over the haughty looking man, noting his prideful stance and arrogant expression. He snorted with derision.

"So," Menelaos sniffed. "You are the one. Hand her over now or feel my wrath, princeling."

"You wouldn't dare," the young man snapped.

"I will crush you, wife stealer, and take her whether you like it or not."

"Never," he hissed.

"My lord, wait," murmured Odysseus, a hand on Menelaos' arm. "Let me see what I can do."

Menelaos frowned, but swallowed his anger to let Odysseus speak.

"My lord, what my friend says is true. We have a mighty fleet waiting for the signal to go to war. Perhaps you should consider the situation. If you hand over Helene and all the property stolen with her, we will leave you in peace, never to return."

The King frowned while his sons cried out in protest.

"Don't do it, father," yelled Paris.

"Father," said another. "We will support you in your decision, but we stand as one in this. Helene belongs here now. Would you see Paris shamed by this man?"

The King held up a hand. "Odysseus, you make a compelling case but I must ask. What will you do if we do not return Helene to Menelaos?"

"Then we'll have no choice but to bring bloody war down on your city. Deny us now and we'll be camped at your door by morning."

The King nodded. "I am inclined to support you if not for the harm it would do my son."

"I will not give her up," Paris snarled. "Hektor, you'll support me, won't you?"

"We all will, brother," said the man who had spoken before. "We stand together, the sons of Priam, to fight for your bride."

"Then we are at odds," said King Priam. "I must side with my sons. Antenor, see that these men are escorted safely from the city."

"You're letting them go?" screamed Paris. "Why not kill them where they stand?"

The King raised a hand. "They came in good faith, to parlay in truce. It would be the height of hubris to kill them now."

"I don't care," snarled Paris.

"Antenor, take them out," said the King. "Paris, control your temper. You will have plenty of chances to fight."

Another city had fallen under the warrior's hand. The great Achilles, proving his valour, raided and pillaged, sacking city after city. He thought back on his exploits and squared his shoulders in pride. Now those Achaean commanders would see his worth. Now Agamemnon would have to give him the respect he deserved.

Striding through the streets, Achilles saw men lying dead and women carried off to be given into slavery. The most noble would go to the commanders as concubines, prizes of war. Ahead he saw a temple, standing undamaged while the buildings around burned. On a whim, he stepped inside. A squeal of terror drew his gaze to the altar, where two young women cowered.

"I won't hurt you," he smiled. "What are your names?"

The elder girl straightened and sniffed. "I'm Chrysé, daughter of the priest of Apollo. This is Briseis."

Achilles gazed at the younger woman, her big eyes staring as she stood frozen like a startled doe. Her exquisite face sent a shudder of desire through him and his eyes rested on those soft full lips.

"You are priestesses?" he murmured.

"Yes," said Chrysé. "But Briseis is also the daughter of the King."

"You know the King is dead," he said. "I killed him myself."

Briseis flinched. "Yes, my lord," she whispered. "All my family are dead."

"And you know that you're now a prize of war?"

She nodded.

"Don't be afraid. You're both highly valued as priestesses, and your beauty will ensure you go to the greatest commanders of the Achaeans."

He reached out to take each girl by the arm. First, he took hold of Chrysé.

"You'll go to none other than the great Agamemnon himself," he murmured. "My gift to him and hopefully a sign of my regard, so that he'll give me the respect I deserve."

Then he stretched out a hand for Briseis. As his fingertips brushed her forearm, he felt a sudden spark, sending a thrill into his chest. He caught his breath as he enclosed her small wrist in his powerful hand.

"But you," he whispered. "Are mine."

The girl licked her beautiful lips, sensuous in her innocence. Achilles led them both toward the door, the thin wrist of Briseis somehow finding its way out of his grip as her small hand slipped perfectly into his own.

On the beach below Troy, a huge fleet of black ships rested on the sand. On the dunes above, the Achaean camp stretched along the shore. Around thousands of campfires, the men lay groaning. Not one in five were unaffected by the debilitating illness that left them lying in their own excrement, weak and unable to keep even water down.

"What should we do?" groaned Menelaos. "We're defeated by a miasma of the gods."

"We must sacrifice. Find Calchas," Agamemnon said vaguely to the air, knowing someone would take his message.

When the prophet arrived, he bowed before the commander.

"My lord, I don't need a sacrifice to know what must be done," he said.

"Tell me," said the commander.

"Your slave, Chrysé. She was a child of Apollo. Her father was his head priest at the temple in Lyrnessus. Now the god is angry."

"So it's Apollo who brings this plague on us?" murmured Menelaos.

"Yes, my lord."

"What must we do?" said Agamemnon.

"She must be returned, to appease the god. Maybe then he will lift the plague."

"Are you saying I must give up my prize?" Agamemnon snarled.

"I'm afraid you must, my lord."

"I won't! I'm commander of the Achaean fleet. I deserve my prize!"

"If you don't, we'll fail to illness before we get close to breaching those walls."

"Then I'll take another prize," growled the commander. "I won't be denied my right."

"You'd take someone else's prize?" said Menelaos. "Whose?"

Agamemnon mused. "Who's the least senior among my captains? Wait! There's one who's not even counted among the war council. Why did Achilles get a prize?"

"I think he felt that because he led the campaign he deserved it," said Menelaos.

"Nonsense. I'll have his prize."

"My lord, are you sure?" said Calchas.

"Absolutely. Find Odysseus, and tell him to bring her to me. Oh and tell him to prepare a ship to take Chrysé home."

"Yes, my lord."

Snuggled under the blankets in the arms of his willing young slave, Achilles felt a deep contentment that had eluded him since leaving his wife and child in Scyros.

Finally, he had the recognition he deserved, and a beautiful concubine to celebrate it.

Feeling an unaccustomed tenderness for his perfect prize, he dreamed of making her his new wife, to have her forever. He pulled her sleeping body close, enjoying the softness of her form. A noise outside broke him out of his reverie, and a sudden gust of cold air hit his face. A man stood over him.

"I'm sorry, Achilles," said Odysseus. "By order of Agamemnon I come to claim your prize."

"You what?"

"In order to lift the plague, the commander has returned his own war prize, the priestess Chrysé, to her home in Lyrnessus."

"That's his choice. What's that got to do with me?"

"The commander mustn't be without a prize. He claims yours."

"No! I won't let him. Briseis is mine!"

Odysseus reached out and flung back the blanket, dragging the girl out of the warmth and leading her stumbling from the tent. Achilles jumped up to follow.

"You can't do this!"

"The decision is made," said Odysseus. "I'm sorry, lad, but the war council have all agreed."

"I won't allow it! You have no right!"

"Achilles!" the girl screamed.

"I'll get you back, Briseis," Achilles cried. "I promise."

19

A TREACHEROUS AFFAIR

On the wall, above the great lion gate at Mycenae, the captain of the guard lounged against the parapet. He studied the man before him, dressed in the garb of a palace servant but exuding a level of confidence that belied his humble appearance. There was a spark in the man's eyes that he had not seen for a long time, not since the old king Thyestes had briefly regained power.

"We haven't seen you in the barracks for a long time," the guard said.

"No," replied the servant. "The queen keeps me busy."

"You need to keep up your training, if you're to take on Agamemnon when he returns."

The servant glanced about. "Be careful," he hissed. "You never know who might be listening."

The Captain shrugged. "Nobody would care. Besides, we all know how long you've waited, and how good things were under your father."

"That may be, but the King has spies everywhere."

"None we don't know about."

"True."

"I just don't know why you haven't made your move yet. With the King away, you could seize power easily."

The servant shook his head. "I need to be sure. I'm not strong enough and if I showed my cards now I'd be signing my own death warrant. He'll be returning with an army at his back, bonded to him by the glory of battle."

"And we'll be waiting at yours."

"That's good to know. But right now I'm working from the inside, building my influence in the palace."

"What do you mean?"

"Let's just say I have the... ear of the Queen. She'll back me when the time comes."

The guard raised an eyebrow. "What have you been up to?"

"Nothing at all, my friend. But the Queen is frightened. If the King is returning I need to know in advance."

"How do you plan to do that?"

"That's where you come in. I need to steal your men, probably most of the home guard."

"But who would protect the city?"

"Who would attack the city? Every soldier in Achaea is with Agamemnon, far across the sea."

"What do you need us to do?"

"We're going to set up signal fires, following the coast, hilltop to hilltop right around the Aegean, all the way to Ilion."

The Captain whistled. "That's... ambitious, my lord."

Aegisthus grinned. "As am I."

"What does the Queen say of this plan?"

"She doesn't know yet, but she'll agree. You can invoke her name without fear of reprisal. I want this to look like it came from the palace, straight from her."

"It shall be done, my lord."

The servant chuckled. "I like hearing that, but please keep your voice down!"

In the palace, Klytemestra paced her room. The children had gone to their beds and the stars twinkled in the night sky, but no sign of Gissus. She stopped by the window, wondering if any of those stars were her brothers or, bless her soul, her darling daughter. A step at the door, and she spun to see him standing there, a self-satisfied smirk on his face.

"Where have you been?" she cried.

"Just taking care of some business," he shrugged.

"I was worried."

"You were?" he chuckled. "Does this mean you finally admit that you care?"

"Of course I do," she blushed.

He held his arms out to her and she rushed into his embrace, welcoming his kiss with a fervour she had never thought possible. She was amazed how quickly she had become dependent on his love. Of course, she had been dependent on him for years, though she still could not quite admit it. With a contented sigh, she snuggled into his arms, resting her head on his shoulder.

"Mama?"

Klytie's eyes snapped open. "Elektra!" she gasped.

Letting go of her, Aegisthus spun. Klytie took a step toward her daughter but stopped at the girl's furious stare, her eyes shooting daggers.

"I knew it," she hissed. "How could you?"

"Elektra, I..."

"Oh be quiet, Mama," the girl spat. "I was talking to him."

"Elektra," Gissus began.

"I don't want to hear it. You had no right to seduce her. You're a servant. I've a good mind to write to Papa and have you punished, except that it would hurt Mama too."

"Elektra, let me explain," Klytie cried with a sob.

"No Mama," she said, turning on her heel.

"Elektra, please," Klytie rushed after her.

"Leave me alone, Mama!"

The girl stalked off.

Klytie rounded on Gissus. "You see?" she hissed. "This is why this has to stop!"

"No! We just have to be more careful. Elektra will get over it."

"She won't get over it. Elektra stores things up, holds grudges and throws it back at you when it suits her. Give her the right provocation and she will write that letter."

"Then we'll have to make sure that doesn't happen."

"Isn't that what I said?"

"I won't give you up," he said through gritted teeth. "I've waited too long. You're mine now."

"I'll never be yours," she cried. "I don't know why I let you talk me into this. We're just setting ourselves up for disaster. Can't you see that?"

"All I see is you, not willing to fight for us. You deserve to be happy. I was willing to love you in spite of everything, for as long as we may have. But if you don't want me, I'll leave you to your misery."

"What? What are you saying?"

"I'm going home," he sighed. "If you change your mind, you know where to find me."

"But..."

He turned away, walking slowly from the room without a second glance. Klytie caught at his hand, but he shook himself free and left her standing there. She watched him walk down the corridor to the stairs, her heart thudding painfully in her chest.

Klytie spent a sleepless night, the horrible scene running through her mind, twisting and growing in magnitude as her fears ran through all its permutations, dwelling on the last words of Aegisthus that dared her to give in and run to him. But that was what he wanted, to prove he had her in his power. She was not a wanton woman, hanging on the hopes of a doomed love affair. She was not her sister.

After an eternity of fevered wishes and half-dreamed imaginings, the dawn finally pushed its way through the shutters. Klytie made no effort to rise, even when the housemaid came in and opened the shutters, letting in the bright sunlight. She lay there, staring at nothing, blankets pulled up tight in her clutching hands.

After Elektra's accusations, there was no way Klytie could entertain her happy delusion any more. Her daughter's words had given her a slap in the face, bringing her out of her illicit fantasy and back into the cold world of truth. It was good that he had gone away. They could never go back to their easy friendship. She would have to learn to live without him. She caught her breath on a sob, her grief overwhelming.

A long time later, a small voice broke into her feverish ramblings.

"Mama?"

Krisothemis. Klytie sighed. She heard her youngest daughter moving across the room toward her. She stared resolutely. She was not going to let her see her pain. She would play sick and send her away.

"Mama, are you alright?" Krissie sat on the bed beside her mother. "Elektra told me what happened. She's very angry."

Klytie stared, biting her lips on the retort that tried to burst forth. Elektra was her child and very young. She had no life experience, nothing to teach her how to understand what she had seen. Klytie knew she should not be angry with the girl who had so suddenly destroyed her dreams.

"Mama, if it helps, I think she's wrong."

Klytie blinked and turned her gaze on Krissie.

"She thinks you have betrayed Papa."

"I have," said Klytie with a sigh.

"Yes, but... Elektra doesn't see the truth. It's just like when you told us about Gennie, when Elektra refused to believe Papa would do that."

"How is it like that?"

"Elektra refuses to believe that Papa could be bad."

"He's not bad, not really. Proud, arrogant, stubborn and self-centred, but not bad. He's a warrior."

"I know, but that's not how Elektra sees him. She remembers the fun things, but she forgets how little she actually knows him."

Klytie frowned. "I'm not sure what you mean, Krissie dear."

"I'm sorry, Mama, I'm trying to understand it myself. Papa's been away so long, I hardly remember him at all. But Elektra remembers just enough to worship him as a little girl would. All she remembers are the stories and the games."

Klytie smiled. "It's right that a girl should love her father. I don't blame her for that, and you're too young to understand what my life has been."

"But Mama, I think I do. I don't know what Papa was really like, but I know you. I know you've been unhappy for a very long time. I used to think it was because you missed Papa, but now I don't think that's it. I think it was Papa himself that made you unhappy."

"Krissie..."

"No, Mama, it's alright. It was Gennie, what Papa did to her, that made me start to think differently about him."

"I'm sorry, I should have left it with the happy story, not told you the truth."

"That's unfair, Mama. We needed to know, and I'm so

glad you did because now I understand you."

"Oh?" Klytie chuckled bitterly. "And what do you know?"

"I know that Papa didn't make you happy. I know that killing Gennie wasn't the first thing he did to hurt you. I know that Papa doesn't deserve you."

"And how do you know all that?"

"I know because I've never seen you as happy as you've been these past few days. And the only person that could have made you so happy is Gissus."

Klytie stifled a sob. "Whatever gave you that idea?"

"Now Mama, you've always liked him. If you love him, don't let him go away."

"Oh my sweet Krissie," Klytie murmured, tears pricking her eyes. "You're too young to be so wise. What do you know of love?"

"Absolutely nothing, except what I see in you."

"So what do you suggest?"

"Go after him. Love him while you can, because when Papa comes back you'll have to be sad all over again. Be happy for now so you can get through the bad times later."

"Who are you and what have you done with my little girl?"

Krissie giggled, suddenly a child again. "I want you to be happy, Mama."

After Krissie gave her a hug and skipped from the room, Klytie sat up, her mind racing. Memories of the furtive love she had found with Gissus ripped through her mind, sending shivers of longing down into the pit of her stomach.

How could it take a ten-year-old woman-child to make her see clearly? Did she really want to throw away her only chance of happiness just to avoid some pain when it had to end?

Down in the city once more, Klytie made her way toward

the house of Aegisthus. Fighting the nervous urge to run blubbering back to her room in the palace, she slowly approached. Lifting a trembling hand, she knocked on the gilded wood door and waited.

All was silent, the door remained closed fast. She carefully pushed the door open and stepped inside the empty antechamber, looking around for any sign of life. The house seemed deserted.

She stood there uncertainly, wringing her hands. She did not know if she should wait or go home. Perhaps she should seek him elsewhere. If she went home now, she might never build up the courage to try again. Perhaps he was at the farm, but... no, she should just wait. She paced the floor, her whole frame trembling in delicious anticipation. She did not want to wait. She needed to find him now.

Hurrying from the quiet house, Klytie made her way down the hill toward the postern gate. She slipped out onto the terraced fields, heading toward the small cluster of farmhouses near the river. She thought she remembered which cottage and, as she searched with her eyes, was mesmerised by the sight of a shirtless goatherd. She caught her breath in recognition.

Even from high up in the terraces, she would have known him anywhere. Rushing down toward the little goat farm, she tried to control her descent, stumbling in her eagerness. When she righted herself and looked up, he had seen her. He vaulted the fence and came toward her, face lit up in a smile that sent shivers down her spine and pangs of longing into her belly.

He caught her up in his arms without a word, covering her mouth with his. She melted into him, filled with a wild need that took her breath away. He scooped her up, carrying her into the small farmhouse, straight through the sitting room and through the curtain into the little bedroom.

As he removed the pins in her kiton with unexpected ease, letting her dress fall to the floor, she found herself fumbling with his scant clothing. He chuckled at her eagerness, his rich voice mumbling through his kisses, sending her deeper into desire. Together, they fell onto the little bed.

20

THE SONS OF PRIAM

On the walls of mighty Troy, Paris Alexandros stood, the beauteous Helene at his side. Behind them sat King Priam and the whole court, watching the battle ground below. The Achaeans were mustering for another day of fighting, but word had reached the Trojan princes that the great warrior Achilles had withdrawn from the field.

The mood in the city was elated and full of hope. All Trojans knew of the warrior Achilles, how he had attacked cities all over Ilion, killing the men and capturing the women. Without Achilles, the enemy would be crippled. Now was the time to drive them off the beach.

With a last tender word for his beloved, Paris made his way down to the gate, where his brother Hektor waited in front of the army. He did not look back to see Helene leaning eagerly on the parapet, searching the Achaean lines for a sight of Menelaos.

Secure in his own hold over the divinely beautiful Helene, Paris almost skipped his way to the front line, certain in his heart that today he would prove his right to keep her. The gates opened and the army roared, surging forward. Caught up in the excitement, Paris darted forward with them, almost dancing onto the field.

Oblivious to the imposing sight of the Achaean army ranged before them, Paris continued on when the rest of the

Trojans halted. The absence of Achilles and his Myrmidons made little impact on the Achaean lines. Paris faltered, turning to face his countrymen.

"Why the hesitation?" he cried. "The day is ours. All we have to do is take it."

He spun about, taking in the heady atmosphere, revelling in the excitement of all eyes on him.

"Who will fight beside me?"

Still the army hung back, waiting for the order from Hektor, their commander. Paris turned slowly, spreading out his arms, holding wide the leopard skin cloak draped over his shoulders, revealing the bronze cuirass he wore, causing it to shine like gold when it caught the sun.

"I will fight, with or without you!" cried Paris, drunk on his own presence. "I challenge any one of these Achaeans here. May the winner take the spoils and claim victory in this war. Come face me for the honour of Helene!"

Immediately, a great warrior stepped forward. Tall and powerfully built, red hair flowing free under his bronze helmet, he strode into the field. Paris felt his knees go weak, his hands trembling behind his shield. He swallowed on the bile that rose from his stomach.

"I will fight you, wife stealer!" yelled Menelaos. Behind him, his army cheered.

Paris scurried backward, rushing behind the Trojan lines, running from the terror of his greatest enemy. Behind him, Menelaos roared his anger and Paris kept running, until he smacked into the broad chest of Hektor. His brother caught him by the shoulders and shook him hard.

"Where is your pride, Paris?" Hektor scowled. "You called the challenge. You can't run from it now."

"But... look at him! He'll kill me."

"And win the day, according to your rules."

"I can't fight him! I can't lose Helene."

"Then why make such a declaration? You fool. Go out there and face him. And try not to get yourself killed."

Hektor dragged his snivelling brother out onto the field. He raised a hand and the two great armies fell silent.

"Paris has made a challenge," he cried. "Single combat between himself and Menelaos, for Helene and the war! The victor will take the woman and all her treasures. This war ends today! Do you agree?"

"I agree!" yelled Menelaos, and the army at his back erupted in a great roar.

"Then let us draw for the first throw."

In moments, the names had been written, and King Priam himself descended from the wall to draw the name. He raised his crumbly old voice to cry out.

"The first throw goes to Paris."

With that, the King retreated and the two armies stood back, clearing the field. Paris looked about, shivering in fear, facing his own death unwillingly. He gulped down his terror, turned to face his enemy, and raised his spear. Menelaos waited, his shield held solidly in front, face set in a hard stare. Paris pulled back and took aim, throwing with all his might.

The spear flew fast and true, straight at the great warrior, but at the last moment Menelaos stepped aside and the spear struck a glancing blow across his shield. Flying harmlessly past, the spear slammed into the ground. Then Menelaos raised his own spear.

Paris trembled behind his shield, watching the warrior take aim. The spear came and Paris held tight to his shield, hoping he could deflect the deadly throw. The spear slammed into his shield, splintering the wood and throwing him to the ground.

Paris saw the spearhead punch through the back of the shield, watched in slow motion as it kept coming, unable to halt its progress. So powerful was the throw, the spear broke through and continued on, catching Paris in the side, puncturing his cuirass and embedding its tip in his flesh, pinning him to his shattered shield.

Paris heard his own screaming as if in a dream. He pulled the shield away, taking with it the horrid spear and its deadly point, pulling it out of his flesh with an agonised cry. Before he could do more than throw the ruined shield away, Menelaos was on him, raining blows with his sword.

Paris parried weakly with his arms, catching the blows on his greaves, the bronze buckling under the onslaught. Then a mighty blow hit his helmet and the sword of Menelaos snapped in two.

Scurrying backward as he pulled out his sword, Paris tried to regain his feet, but too late. Menelaos had him by the plume of his helmet, pulling him along. Paris scrabbled in the dust, trying to get his feet under him, only to find himself dragged head first toward the enemy lines.

He clutched at the chinstrap digging into his throat, trying to release the buckle, gasping as it cut into his windpipe. Then, just as he thought he would black out from loss of air, the strap broke and Paris found himself free.

Gasping and sobbing, he scrambled away, running for his life and disappearing into the Trojan lines. He turned at the great roar that echoed over the field, just in time to see a furious Menelaos hurl his lost helmet away, to be caught by exultant Achaean hands. Consumed by mortal terror, Paris fled.

Out on the field, Menelaos roared his fury.

"Come and face me, wife stealer! Is this the quality of the Trojan hero? To run in the face of defeat? I claim victory! I demand my prize!"

Menelaos paced the field, searching the Trojan lines for

his quarry to no avail. Then, in mid tirade, the great warrior stumbled backward and a silence fell. An arrow stood lodged in his torso, shot from somewhere in the Trojan lines.

Menelaos stared at the blood spreading from the wound and flowing quickly down his legs. He staggered, backing into the safety of the Achaean line and was taken up by his men, carried swiftly away from the field. Behind him, a great roar rose up as the Achaeans surged forward to join with the Trojans in battle. There would be no truce now.

Standing at the parapet, the lady Helene watched as the armies clashed. She had watched in trepidation as her two husbands fought over her, deciding her fate. She had seen Paris flee from the wrath of Menelaos, and seethed at his cowardice. But when she had seen Menelaos carried off the field, her confusion mounted.

Here was her loyal husband, who had come all this way, fought for the best part of ten years just to get her back. If not for that over-zealous bowman, she would have been handed over, to return to her old life and the home she had almost forgotten. Now she watched as the uneasy truce fell apart and her fate hung once more in the balance.

"My lady..." a maidservant whispered at her shoulder. "My lord Paris is returned from the battle, he is in his room and calling for you."

"Why should I go to him? He's brought shame on my name, and on all of Ilion, running from the fight like that. I have no wish to pander to his vanity when he threw away the truce with no regard for my future."

"My lady, he's injured. His wound needs treatment."

Helene sighed, following the woman with great reluctance. A few hours ago, her path had seemed so sure. Paris would win this war eventually and she would be his forever.

But her friends here were few and she knew what they said behind her back, cursing her for bringing war down on their heads. Could she really be happy here for the rest of her days, unloved by all but a handful?

Now she had seen a side of Paris that she had never before suspected, the cowardly side, and her respect for him had suffered in response to it.

"So, you slink back from the battle, seeking comfort instead of standing up to your enemy?" she said as she entered the room. "How dare you run from the fight?"

"The fight was unfair! Menelaos had the blessing of the gods. It was flee or die."

"Don't invoke the gods to me. You forget whose child I am. He beat you fairly and you ran like a coward. Now you taint me with your cowardice. I wish you had died by his hand!"

"Helene! You don't mean that!"

"Don't I?"

"Please, Helene, I'm wounded."

Helene sighed. "Let me see."

With the help of the maid, she removed his cuirass and pulled up the blood stained linen shirt. Using a cloth dampened with water, she cleaned the wound. It was a small cut, the bleeding already slowed. As she dressed the cut and pulled his shirt down over it, two men rushed into the room.

"How is he?" cried Deiphobos, the second son of Priam.

"As if you care," said Elenos, his younger brother. "You just want to be the first to claim Helene for yourself."

"And you don't? Father already agreed that I would get her, you have no right to try to best me."

"I'm right here," said Paris with a scowl.

"And looking none the worse for your ordeal," sneered Deiphobos.

"As I predicted," said Elenos with a smirk.

"Oh yes, the great prophet. Handing out predictions even more ridiculous than your pompous twin."

"Cassandra is not pompous. Can you blame her for being bitter when no-one will believe her?"

"Whose fault is that? She's the one who tempted Apollo and then refused to bed him."

"Why should she give up her virtue just because a god wanted her? It's no reason to curse her."

"Stop it, please," said Helene. "You're supposed to be here for your brother. But nevertheless, the question is moot, since Paris will live. It's barely a scratch."

"Oh," said Deiphobos, trying not to look disappointed and failing.

"You see? She's not yours yet."

"She will be soon enough, coward that Paris is."

"Enough!" said a voice from behind.

"Hektor!" Paris cried. "Thank goodness, these two were fighting over my corpse."

"Too bad the corpse is still warm, coward," sneered Deiphobos.

"You're cowards all," said Hektor. "Standing around chatting while your countrymen die on the field of battle. Even Troilus is more keen than you, child though he is."

"Well said," cried Paris, bounding up and grabbing his cuirass. "Let's get going."

Out on the battlefield, the sons of Priam gathered their men and followed Hektor in his great war chariot as he took up the assault against the invader. Battle raged as the day wore on, warrior pitted against warrior, hero against hero, and the field grew red with blood.

The sun made its way across the sky and past its zenith, taking the downward path toward the horizon. Coming across Elenos mid field, Hektor pulled his chariot to a stop and stared. His brother stood as if in a trance, somehow shielded from the battle raging around him.

Hektor jumped down, absently parried a blow and gutted the attacker with his bronze spear without taking his eyes off Elenos. Bashing away another blow, Hektor made his way to where his brother stood and moved into his protective aura.

"Elenos?"

"The gods speak within me," he intoned.

"What do they say?"

"This is not your day to die."

"Well, that's good to know. What else?"

"You must create the same conditions under which your brother Paris failed. Tell them you offer single combat for the outcome of the war."

"How am I supposed to do that?"

"You must end this battle. Make the armies pull back from each other and take on a champion of the enemy single handed."

Hektor sighed. "How am I to end a battle? I'm one man against a mad rabble."

Elenos looked at his brother, eyes clear as the protective bubble burst and the sounds of battle broke in. "I don't know," he said.

Hektor looked about, searching for an opening. He stood in a natural clearing, where the ebb and flow of battle had left a space, and raised his spear to the sky.

Trusting in the gods to protect him from harm, Hektor waited, sensing a calm radiating out from the place he stood. When he thought enough soldiers had noticed his strange behaviour, Hektor raised his voice.

"Men of Achaea! Faithful Trojans! Hear me!"

The warriors close by hesitated in confusion, turning

their eyes on the Trojan commander. As those men stopped their fighting, the soldiers nearest them stopped too. In a wave that travelled toward the edge of the field, the men stopped, turned and lowered their weapons to listen.

"I call a truce!" cried Hektor. "I call a cessation to the battle, and request your indulgence. Please will the armies clear the field and take up opposing lines."

Miraculously, the armies did as they were told, separating from the battle and lining up in ranks on either side of the field. Hektor caught his breath and continued.

"This war has gone on long enough. My brother Paris may have failed this morning and our truce may have been broken, but I offer a new chance now, under the same conditions. I offer myself up for single combat. I will fight any hero the Achaeans see fit to pit against me. The winner will determine the outcome of the war."

A great cheer rose up from both sides.

"Who will fight me?"

Immediately, one warrior stepped out of the Achaean lines. Menelaos. As Hektor watched, the commander Agamemnon stopped him with a hand. Hektor strained to hear the exchange.

"No, Menelaos. You're already injured and would face certain defeat."

Menelaos scowled. "It's my honour, my war. It's only right that I accept the challenge."

"No. Just this once, let another be your champion."

Frowning, the great Menelaos stepped back into the protection of the Achaean lines. Hektor raised his voice again.

"Will no-one fight me?"

"Achaeans!" Agamemnon yelled. "Where's your courage? I step forward, who'll join me?"

After a short hesitation, another stepped out, a huge

man full of power and martial spirit. Then Odysseus stepped out, followed by Diomedes and several others behind them.

"My lord Hektor!" called Agamemnon. "Will you allow us to draw lots?"

Hektor gave a nod and watched as the Achaeans milled about, the contenders marking their names on clay potsherds and placing them in the commander's helmet. When they were done, Menelaos stepped forward and drew the name.

"I name Aias as champion!" he cried.

The big warrior crowed in triumph and stepped willingly forward. Watching the giant of a man stomp into the field, Hektor felt his blood grow cold. A brutal warrior, easily his match and better. Certainly a fitting champion, but an opponent who would be difficult to best.

Hektor forced himself to remember his brother's words. This is not your day to die. He had to take strength from that. He had to believe that he could defeat this great man. Drawing in a deep, calming breath, straightening his back and squaring his shoulders, Hektor stepped forward to meet him.

Raising his spear, Hektor took the first throw, pulling back and heaving the spear at the giant's great shield. With a solid crash, the spear hit the laminated hide of the big man's shield, tearing its way through the layers, halting just before it broke through.

Hektor watched as Aias raised his own spear and threw, the weapon coming hard and fast. He clutched his shield, waiting for the blow, knocked backward when it did come. The spear punctured Hektor's shield easily, the force of the throw sending it straight through and slicing into his tunic.

Twisting to avoid the deadly point, Hektor saved himself from injury by a hair's breadth. The two warriors pulled at the spears embedded in their respective shields, then crashed in close, ready to stab at each other.

Hektor's thrust bounced harmlessly off the bigger man's shield, and Aias jumped in at the attack. Hektor braced for impact, stumbling backward from the force of the blow. He felt the spear drive through his shield yet again and gasped as the point grazed his neck.

Rolling away from the onslaught, Hektor scrabbled out from under his enemy, one clutching hand landing on a large rock. Grabbing at it, Hektor spun around and threw, a loud clang ringing out as the rock hit the boss of the giant's shield and bounced away.

With a roar, Aias stooped and picked up an even larger rock, a heavy boulder. Arms bulging with muscle, the giant grunted as he threw. The great rock crashed into Hektor's shield, forcing him backward against the ground, his shield landing heavily on top of him as it buckled from the blow.

Hektor reached for his sword, exploding to his feet and rushing at his opponent, ready to take the fight to close quarters. Aias roared his challenge and rushed to meet him. Neither had any inclination to end the fight, certain this would be a battle to the death.

But from each side, a herald stepped into the fray, sent by the men to put a stop to the fight. With spears placed between them, and hands on their chests to push them apart, the two heralds ended the bout.

"We see you're evenly matched," said one. "And night comes close."

The other nodded. "Let's call a truce. Tomorrow the armies can face each other in battle again."

Hektor looked askance at Aias and the big man nodded. "Aias, I honour you. You're a worthy opponent," said Hektor.

"As are you," said Aias with a smile.

"Worthy warriors of Achaea," Hektor cried. "Loyal Trojans! We call a truce for this night. Rest, for tomorrow we take time to bury our dead! When all rites are performed and our fallen comrades are welcomed in Hades, we'll meet again in battle."

From both sides a great cheer rose up and the two champions left the field.

21

When Heroes Meet in Battle

Standing at the prow of his ship, staring out over a camp now overrun with Trojan soldiers, Achilles frowned. For many days, he had stood apart from battle, unable to forgive the insult heaped upon him by the treacherous commander Agamemnon. Now he almost regretted his decision as he watched the armies of the Achaeans pushed farther back toward their ships.

He longed to know what was going on down there, who lived and who had died. But he would not break his own resolution. He would not give in to their begging and he would not himself enter the battle. Let them see how sorely they needed him.

"My lord, I don't understand how you can stand there and see your allies suffer. Your heart must be hardened beyond imagining."

"Not hardened, Patroklos. Disheartened and sorely wounded."

"Then go to them. Lead your Myrmidons out into battle as they desire. Your men bite their nails and shuffle their feet, eager to take on the Trojans and drive them back."

"I will not help them. Not after what they did. They don't respect me and they turn on me. They don't deserve my help."

"What did they do that was so bad?"

"You astonish me, Patroklos that you don't remember."

"I remember some silly nonsense about a slave girl, nothing so drastic as to bring on this stubborn refusal."

"They took my prize, freely given and justly won, just to succour the pride of Agamemnon. Why should my reward be taken and given to him?"

"His slave had to be returned to assuage the anger of Apollo, the god she served. You know that. The whole army was riddled with plague, brought on by the theft of Chrysé, Apollo's priestess. Once she was returned the sickness abated, but the Commander lost his prize."

"That didn't give him the right to take mine!"

"But it did! He's the Commander and you're just a minor vassal. Why should he miss out on a prize when you keep yours?"

"Briseis was mine! I won her, I claimed her. He had no right."

"There are other slaves, other prizes to be won."

"None like Briseis."

"Why was she so special?"

"I loved her, Patroklos!" Achilles groaned. "I would have taken her into my home, kept her in the style of a wife forever."

"Then you're a fool, Achilles."

"I won't justify myself to you."

"No? Then at least explain to me why you won't fight."

"I should think I've given you reason enough."

"Even when you see them falling? Hear their cries of anguish as they fight hard up against the shore, driven well back from the walls of Troy by Hektor and his men?"

Achilles sighed. "Are there many gone?"

"A great many, my lord. And many more injured. Even our greatest leaders lie injured in their ships, awaiting the final defeat."

"Then we're surely lost."

"Not surely, my lord. Not if you lead your Myrmidons onto the field, lead a counter attack and drive the Trojans back behind their walls."

Achilles shook his head. "I won't do it."

"Then let me."

"You?" Achilles gasped. "No, Patroklos, you don't have the skill or the presence to lead them."

"You seem to have little faith in me, cousin. I'm not without skill. Besides, in your armour they'd never know. The Achaeans would rally and the Trojans would flee before me."

"I don't like it. You'd be killed. I can't bear to lose you, Patroklos."

Patroklos shrugged. "It's that or you drop your pride and do it yourself."

Achilles scowled. "I will not!"

"Then so be it." He turned to go.

"Wait!" Achilles cried. "If you must do this, promise me one thing."

"Anything."

"Don't cross the earthworks. Harry the Trojans and expel them from the camp but please, when you rout them, don't jump the ditch and give chase. Come back here and let the rest of the Achaeans follow them to the walls."

The Myrmidons swarmed out of their camp, ready to clash into the Trojans and join the Achaean defence. Riding at their head, Patroklos felt invincible. Wearing the glorious armour of Achilles, standing tall beside his driver, he cut an image of almost godlike wonder, and he knew it.

He felt the stares of the Achaeans and heard their cheers. He thought he saw the Trojans quail and fall back. Stabbing at an enemy soldier, Patroklos felt the resistance of flesh through the haft of his spear, and saw the bright splatter of blood as the point drove through his victim's shoulder, piercing his lung.

With a loud cry of triumph, his spear rained fury down on the enemy from atop his war chariot. And Trojan warriors fell before him. Leading the attack, Patroklos dragged the Achaeans from the jaws of defeat, forcing the enemy back. Around him, warrior killed hero and Achaean voices cried havoc at their foe.

The Trojan lines broke in retreat and Patroklos took his army after them, toward the dirt rampart and its deep ditch. Ahead, he could see the enemy foundering in the ditch, chariots broken and horses screaming as they trampled the men who fell beneath their hooves. Patroklos laughed as he plunged into the melee.

Directing his charioteer toward the deepest concentration of the fleeing enemy, Patroklos charged into them, mowing them down. Patroklos continued on, crashing into enemy chariots, sending their men into the dirt to be crushed under his wheels, his horses snorting and his bronze flashing.

His chariot clattered up the rampart, and the god-given horses of Achilles pushed off with their powerful hind legs, leaping over the ditch and bringing the chariot safely down on the other side.

Breaking through the enemy retreat, Patroklos turned his chariot, charging back into the Trojans as they fled toward him, pushing them back against the Achaean defences. Spear flying, Patroklos killed again, his spear piercing through a warrior's chest, pulling out again, stabbing in on an oncoming charioteer.

The spear sliced into the man's jaw, the force of the blow lifting the enemy over the side of his chariot to fall under the wheels. Another fell to a blow across the head. Patroklos killed and killed again, power filling him with the red haze of battle.

Ahead, he saw a great warrior jump down from his chariot and march in fury toward him. Crowing in victory, Patroklos jumped down to meet him hand to hand. The warrior came on, his men around him.

"You think to cut me down like you have my men?" the man yelled. "I am Sarpedon, son of Zeus!"

Patroklos pulled back and cast his spear, sending it into the belly of Sarpedon's man at his side. With a roar, Sarpedon answered the cast, but his throw missed its mark. Grabbing the spear that stood upright and quivering in his friend's body, Sarpedon threw again.

The spear passed harmlessly over Patroklos' shoulder as he bent to retrieve his enemy's first spear. Spinning around, using his momentum to add power to the throw, Patroklos cast again. The spear flew hard and fast, catching Sarpedon in the chest, piercing his heart.

As Patroklos yelled his challenge, his Myrmidons flowed in to take on the men of Sarpedon over the dead man's body. Bronze clashed with bronze, men fell in the bloody dirt and battle raged on.

Men fell under spear thrust, sword cut and stone to the head. And the Trojans began to fall back. Jumping back into his chariot, Patroklos gave chase, his Myrmidons leading the Achaean charge as the Trojans fled for the wall.

Coming hard up on the gate, Hektor turned his chariot to survey the battle. Rout more like. He saw the Achaeans, throwing themselves against the wall, only to be repelled by the archers above. He saw in their midst the glittering armour of Achilles and cursed. Why did the hero have to choose that day to rejoin the fight, when the men of Troy had victory in their grasp?

With a signal to his driver, Hektor took his chariot back

into the fray, aiming straight for the Achaean hero, the armour of Achilles shining out like a beacon to guide him. Hektor saw the great warrior jump down from his chariot, felt a brief confusion over his quarry's behaviour. Then the warrior rose up and spun, letting loose a deadly missile that flew at its target.

Hektor felt the impact through the body of his charioteer Kebriones, close by his side. The man fell over the side of the chariot into the dirt, his life taken by a great rock hauled by the dreaded Achaean. Hektor screamed his anger and vaulted out of the speeding chariot to land in front of his enemy.

He rose up and plunged at him, sword in hand. The two warriors clashed over the body of the charioteer. About them, their armies fell into vicious combat while the two heroes fought with bronze and fist. Scrabbling in the dirt, they clutched stones and threw, and dragged at the body of Kebriones.

Hektor was determined to protect his dead friend from the scavenging Achaeans. In rage, Hektor grabbed at a large rock in both hands, hefting it above his head to throw it at the enemy warrior. By some miracle, the boulder met its mark, striking the Achaean on the side of the head, dislodging his helmet.

The bright bronze helm of Achilles rolled toward him, the four horns on its brow making patterns in the dust, and Hektor bent to scoop it up in glee. Then he raised his eyes to crow his success at his enemy, but took in a sharp breath as he saw the man.

The warrior before him was not Achilles! The man stood there dazed, swaying slightly, eyes glazed over. His spear clattered to the ground and snapped in two. His huge shield slipped from his grasp and hit the ground with a loud clang. The ill-fitting linen corselet had slipped, exposing soft flesh open to attack.

As Hektor watched, the hero Euphorbus came up behind with his spear, cast it straight into the stunned warrior's back. Hektor scowled and Euphorbus pulled his spear away, stepping back with a grimace.

Moving in close with his own spear, Hektor looked the warrior in the eye, drew his arm back, and let his weapon slice into his belly, pushing through. The man stumbled and fell. With a foot on his chest, Hektor retrieved his spear. Then he bent down and began removing the shining armour of Achilles.

On the beach in front of the Myrmidon ships, Achilles paced, fear gripping his heart. He had seen from his vantage point on his ship's prow, watched the Achaeans fall back. He knew something had gone wrong. Patroklos had not returned after the first rout as promised.

There was only one answer. The fool had let pride and the heat of battle take him, chasing after the Trojans. He saw, hurrying along the beach toward him, the warrior Antilochus. Eager for news, Achilles rushed to meet him.

"What's happened?" he blurted. "I see the Achaeans are in retreat again, but I can't tell the reason."

"My lord, I am come direct from the field with dreadful news. I'm sorry, but there's no way to say it. Patroklos has been killed, and Hektor wears his armour, strutting along in front of his Trojans as if he's already won the day."

"Oh I feared as much!" Achilles groaned. "Carried away by excitement and the thrill of battle. Oh Patroklos, I told you to return to me," he moaned, heart aching.

"He acquitted himself well, my lord. He killed many Trojans before Hektor cut him down."

"Is that supposed to make me feel better?"

"No, my lord, I just..."

"How did it happen?" Achilles sobbed. "He deserved to live out the rest of his life far from the horror of war."

"Sir, I don't know the details, but I do know you're needed, to bring him back whole. Hektor rages, he intends to dishonour the body and put his head up on the wall."

"What? Who told you that?"

"Menelaos himself sent me to find you. He stands with Aias, holding the Trojans at bay, protecting the body until you can get there. Please, sir."

"How can I go to battle without armour?"

"You must do something."

Achilles paced, his grief settling like a black stone in his chest. Yes, he had to do something. He lifted his eyes to the heavens and silently prayed to his mother. Maybe she could help. But what could she do to prevail on the greater gods? Would they even listen to her?

"I need to see," he murmured, striding out across the camp toward the earthwork rampart.

Reaching the outer defences, he climbed the rampart and stared out over the battlefield. He could see the rout was much closer now, the Achaeans in full retreat. And there, hounded and harried at the rear, two men dragged a body slowly through the dust.

In their wake, the giant Aias spun and parried like a mad thing, deflecting the enemy harassment to allow them to escape. At the head of the attackers, Achilles recognised the gleam of his own god-given armour, now worn by the Trojan commander. Achilles raised his voice and gave a mighty shout.

"Hektor!"

Below, heads turned, warriors faltered in their advance. The Achaeans raised a cheer and doubled their efforts to achieve the camp. They were at the rampart now, scrambling through the ditch and onward toward the sheltering ships.

Achilles shouted again.

"Tomorrow you face me, Hektor!"

The Trojan looked up, pulling his chariot to a stop. Around him, his army slowed and milled about, staring up at the warrior on the earthwork.

"Do you hear me, Hektor?" Achilles screamed. "Tomorrow, you die!"

Hektor stared quietly for a long moment. At his back, the Trojan army hesitated in apprehension. Slowly, Hektor raised an arm and signalled the retreat. He stayed a moment longer, eyes locked on his enemy before turning his chariot and heading back across the field toward the city wall. From the Achaeans a great cheer rose up.

"I promise you, Patroklos," Achilles murmured. "I will kill every last stinking son of Priam, starting with Hektor."

With a heavy sigh, Achilles made his way down to where his friend had been laid. With tears staining his cheeks, he helped lift Patroklos onto a litter and walked beside him toward his ship, weeping all the way. And that night, slipping into his tent while the army slept, a small soft body gave him comfort; Briseis finally returned unharmed from the tent of Agamemnon.

Striding out of his tent at dawn, Achilles stood in the early light under the wondering gaze of his men. He basked in the glory of the sun blazing off his new armour, shining bronze inlaid with gold and silver, worked with the skill of the god Hephaestos.

"My lord!" his lieutenant gasped. "Where did that come from?"

"It was a present from my mother. Do you like it?"

"It's... incredible. But how?"

Achilles chuckled. "She called in a favour from the blacksmith of the gods. Isn't it pretty?"

"Nice to have friends in high places, my lord."

"Yes, it is. Now, let's set the fear of the gods in these Trojan dogs."

That said, he led his men out onto the field.

Surrounded by the clash of arms, Achilles searched for his quarry. He thought he saw him once, deep within the Trojan lines, but Hektor proved an elusive target. Achilles drove ahead, his Myrmidons in his wake, heaving about with his spear.

In front of the lead Trojans, a tall figure ran along the line, dark hair flying and muscled arms wielding the spear with power and grace. With a cry of triumph, Achilles sped after him. Lifting his spear and making the throw, he watched it fly straight and true, striking the runner in the back.

Moving closer, Achilles pulled out his spear and bent to remove his victim's helmet. Rolling him over, he groaned in disappointment. Not Hektor, but a younger version of him, barely more than a child.

Hearing a scream of rage, Achilles turned to see his quarry racing out of the crowd, spear raised. Hektor cast his weapon, but a sudden gust of wind sent it flying back. A cloud of dust rose up around, obscuring his vision as Achilles thrust at Hektor, missing his mark.

"Who was the boy?" he yelled into the dust.

"Polydoros," the angry retort came out of the dust. "My younger brother."

Then the warring armies enclosed them, taking Hektor away from him.

"That's one," Achilles murmured.

But it was a bitter victory. Above him, dark clouds blotted out the sun. Leading his men into the fray, Achilles drove on, chasing them as far as the river. Seeing men struggling through the water in an attempt to reach the other side, Achilles strode in after them, hacking left and right, cutting them down.

As the storm broke, the fighting grew desperate. Feet were sucked into the mud, water made its chilling way under armour, and the river became a torrent. Reaching the other side, Achilles watched a Trojan warrior battle his way up the bank and raised his spear to throw.

The man raised his eyes and recognition flashed. Achilles hesitated, surprise staying his hand. Then he scowled and made his thrust. The intended victim threw himself down under the path of the spear, scrabbling in the mud to clutch at Achilles' legs while the spear buried its point in the mud of the bank.

"Please, great lord!" he cried. "Spare me."

"I know you," Achilles replied. "I defeated you! I sacked your town and sent you off as a slave. How can you be here?"

"I gained my freedom. I'm just returned. Please, don't take me away again, think of my father."

"Oh I am thinking of your father. And the vow I made to a dead friend. No son of Priam will live. It's your turn, Lykaion. Let go of my knees and face it like a man."

"No!"

Achilles growled. Drawing his sword, he slammed its hilt down on the man's head. As Lykaion fell backward, Achilles thrust in, his sword making its way easily, sliding through his victim's stomach, the point bursting out from his back. Achilles pushed him off with a small grimace of distaste.

"That's two," he whispered.

As he stood there over the body, Achilles heard a deafening roar, punctuated by screams and cries of terror. Looking up, he saw a wall of water bearing down on him.

He yelled to his men.

"Out of the water! Use the flood to chase the Trojans back to the walls."

Then the wave hit him, and the great Achilles found himself carried along, inexorably driven downstream by the roaring flood.

Hektor raced along, the flood at his heels as his Trojans streamed across the field toward the gate. As he drew near, he saw the great wooden doors swing inward to admit the fleeing army. The Achaeans hot on their backs as they approached the wall, the Trojan army filed into the city.

Taking up the rear guard, Hektor waited by the gate, ushering the men through while the enemy came on like a wave at the head of the flood. Finally, Hektor allowed the gate to be closed, but stayed himself on the outside, one hand on the wood as the archers rained arrows down on the enemy, keeping them at bay.

Hektor stared out at the golden figure racing across the field. With his heart in his mouth, he watched Achilles come, his brilliant armour glittering as the clouds opened to let the sun shine down upon the bloody field.

Hektor swallowed hard on his fear. He should just slip inside the gate and deny his enemy the privilege of a fight. Yet his pride forbade it. He remembered his brother, the way Paris had lost his courage, and how Helene had denigrated him for his cowardice.

He must face Achilles, even though it meant certain death. He had no hope against the great hero. Again, Hektor drummed his fingers on the wood, chewing his lip in anguish. Was he really going to do this?

He thought of his beautiful wife, waiting for his return from battle, their baby son clutched at her breast. A son needed a father, a wife her husband. But what if he were to win? He could end this war right here, right now.

Still the warrior came on, closer now. Hektor itched to open that gate, slink inside like a coward. He could see Achilles in all his glory, hear his sandals thudding on the hard-packed battlefield, see the sweat on his brow and hear the gasping of his breath.

He was beautiful. The power of the gods shone in him, and Hektor felt humbled before him. And his courage left him. Losing all thought, Hektor dropped his huge round shield and ran. He left the safety of the gate and sped along the wall, under the watching eyes of his men.

He tried to rationalise, thinking maybe he could tire him. Achilles was already winded from running across the field, Hektor only had to keep ahead of him long enough... And Hektor was a great runner; he always won at the games. He could beat Achilles.

Hektor ran, under the wall, around the city. Pacing himself, he tried to keep one step ahead of Achilles, controlling his breathing with an effort. As he came around toward the gate, he considered slipping inside to leave his enemy outside and denied his prey.

But glancing behind, he saw how close Achilles had come, and knew if he were to open the gate now his enemy would be inside with him. He had no time to slow down, or Achilles would be upon him.

So he continued, around the walls again. His chest screamed in agony, his lungs fit to burst. His heart pounded in his ears and his legs threatened to crumble beneath him. But Achilles was struggling too. Hektor ran on, desperate to stay ahead.

As he rounded the wall the Achaean army took up a fearsome chanting, calling the name of Achilles over and over. On the wall, Hektor heard the cries of his own men, urging him on. Coming around to the gate for a second time, Hektor thought again that maybe he could escape. And again, Achilles was there, right on his heels.

Moving on, past the gate, Hektor trudged around again. With breath coming in gasps, his feet seeming to catch every bump in the track, Hektor still managed to stay ahead. He could feel Achilles behind him now, almost on top of him.

He could hear the warrior's wheezing; feel his hot breath on the back of his neck. He could almost feel the thud of his feet through the earth. Stumbling as his legs almost gave way, Hektor felt a spear thrust slip past his ear, and scrambled away to run again. His sides ached, his lungs burned, his heart hammered in his ears.

Approaching the gate for the third time, he saw a man standing there, waiting. Behind him, he heard Achilles falter. With gladness in his heart, Hektor recognised his brother Deiphobos. Certain that here was his rescue, Hektor staggered up to him, ready now to retreat inside the walls. But Deiphobos held him in place with hands on his shoulders.

"Hektor, you must stop," said Deiphobos. "Stop this cowardly running and turn to face your foe."

"What are you saying?" Hektor gasped.

"This running brings no honour to you or your house, Hektor. Don't prove yourself a coward now. Your family wouldn't thank you for it."

Hektor licked his lips, chest heaving with his laboured breathing. But Deiphobos pressed on his shoulders, turning him to face Achilles. With a pat on his back, Deiphobos handed him his shield and stepped away. Hektor straightened his shoulders.

Achilles watched, waiting for his target to find his courage. At last, this meeting would be resolved. Lifting his spear, Achilles threw. At the last moment, Hektor dropped to a crouch, letting the spear pass harmlessly overhead. Rising up, he crowed.

"You missed."

Then Hektor threw and Achilles held his glittering shield to catch the blow. The spear hit the centre of the magnificent shield and bounced away.

"Deiphobos, another spear!" Hektor cried. But his brother was gone, back inside the gate.

Seeing his enemy draw his bronze sword, Achilles scrabbled for the spear on the ground and leapt to the attack. Holding his shield in front, he levelled the spear, aiming at the point where the armour bared the neck by the collarbone.

Holding tight, Achilles ploughed in. There was a clash of bronze as his shield deflected his opponent's sword, and a satisfying resistance as his spear met its mark. Achilles savoured the feel of spear slicing flesh as his weapon drove its way into his victim's neck.

Hektor fell, bright blood spurting from his severed artery, his breath groaning out of his undamaged throat. His eyes glazed over and he fell backward into the dirt, his last breath coming in a gasp as he hit the ground, then a long sigh as the blood pooled around his head, soaking into the dust.

Achilles stood over him and raised his arms to the sky, a great cry of victory echoing over the gathered armies and finding its match in the anguished screams from the wall.

"That's three," Achilles murmured.

Bending to remove his victim's armour, Achilles piled it into a chariot brought by a silent lieutenant. Then he drew his sword and pierced Hektor's ankles between the bone and the great tendon behind.

He took the long leather strap from Hektor's shield and threaded it through the holes he had made. Dragging the body by the strap, he tied it to the back of the chariot and climbed aboard. He flicked the reins, heading back to the ships, pulling Hektor's body along behind with its head bouncing in the dust.

And the next day, Achilles dragged his fallen foe into the field, parading in front of the walls of Troy, day after day, letting the body follow like a dropped banner in the dirt.

22

A Short But Glorious Life

The old man shuffled across the field on cautious feet, only the moon's grey light to guide him. As he approached the earthen rampart of the Achaean camp, he paused, looking for the best way to proceed. The main gate appeared unguarded, but the old man was cunning enough to know the guard would be somewhere nearby.

Moving slowly forward, he listened for any sound, heard a faint rumble in the darkness beside the gate. Could it be? Perhaps the gods would favour him after all. Coming closer, he searched the darkness for the source of the sound. He was certain it was the guard, asleep at his post.

He crept forward, past the snores, and put a hand on the wood of the gate, pushing gently. Holding his breath, he slipped inside. He knew where he was going. His sons had pointed out his target from the city wall and they would know, having been down here in the thick of the fight.

So he moved without hesitation toward the ships of the Myrmidons and, in the midst of their camp, the tent of Achilles. Listening at the tent, the old man heard a low chuckle. The hero was awake, but not alone. The old man shrugged. Too late to back out now.

Pushing his way through, he entered without announcement. The man with Achilles burst from his seat, but the great warrior remained calm and motioned the old man forward. Kneeling before the god-like Achilles, the old man clutched at the man's knees and bowed his head.

"Please, old man," said the warrior. "Tell me how I may help."

Looking up, the old man raised a hand to lift the fold of cloak covering his head, pushing it back.

"My lord Achilles, I come not as a king, but as a supplicant. I come to beg for the body of my son."

"Priam!" Achilles gasped. "You take a great risk coming here alone, in the dead of night."

"I know. But I hear you are a good man, and I know you will see reason."

"Oh? You presume to know my heart? You know nothing, old man."

"I know you love your father."

"My father? What's he got to do with this?"

"Nothing, my lord, except this: Think of your father, waiting in his old age for you to return from this war. Think of your father, hearing the news that you are dead, your body held by the enemy, never to be returned, never to be buried in your native soil. Think of him mourning you, and think of the greater distress he would feel if you were desecrated and denied proper burial."

"Old man..."

"Think of him."

Achilles cursed. "You think I don't remember him every day? You must think me heartless indeed."

"No, I know you do, which is why I know you will let me take my son home tonight."

"This is unfair. To use my own father against me."

"My lord, I've seen you these past two weeks. I've watched from the walls while your men celebrate burial rites for your friend and all your fallen comrades. I watch the Achaeans paying homage to their dead and sending them on the path to Hades. Why will you not allow my son the same right? Stop dragging him behind your chariot day after day and give him the respect deserving of a warrior fallen before his time."

Achilles sighed. "You're right, my lord. I see how my actions have hurt you and I regret that I might cause such hurt to my own dear father, so far away. You may take him."

Priam smiled as his heart filled with relief. "Thank you."

"But first, you'll dine with me."

Priam nodded, and accepted the warrior's offered hand, allowing Achilles to lift him from his knees. Achilles guided him to a chair with all the reverence he might have shown his own father, and Priam was glad he had come.

He watched as Achilles gave orders to his man, heard something about meat, and something more about cleaning the body and laying it out properly. At last, the proper respect would be shown to his poor son Hektor.

Over a simple meal of meat roasted over the fire, the two men talked. Priam found himself liking this man, admiring his strength and courage.

"So, my lord Priam," said Achilles. "How will this truce end? Do we see an end to the war now that your commander is gone?"

"Hektor was my oldest son, and therefore most dear to my heart. But he was not my only son, and not even the best."

"No, it was another son of yours who started this whole affair."

"Yes, I always knew Paris would take my city to the brink of destruction. It was prophesied at his birth. But a mother's love is stronger than any prophesy and we thought we might have escaped the ill omen. Until he brought Helene here."

"You can't say he'll replace Hektor though, coward that he is."

"No, he is not a commander that is true. Nor is Deiphobos, though his pride would lead him to demand it."

"Then who? Elenos?"

"No, Elenos is a fine man, but his visions make him unstable."

"He's a seer?"

Priam nodded. "He has already told me how to save my city."

"A lucky thing for you."

Priam chuckled. "Not so lucky. It means putting my youngest boy in harm's way. The prophecy is that once Troilus reaches his full potential he'll be invincible."

"Really?"

Priam frowned, a cold dread hitting his spine. He had said too much.

"And now," he said quickly. "I must thank you for your hospitality, and take my boy home before your camp starts to wake."

"Of course," said Achilles. "How long would you like for your burial truce?"

"Oh, the usual two weeks will be acceptable. After that, we shall see which side is the victor."

With that, he hurried out of the tent and clambered up onto the cart outside, loaded with the body of Hektor. Heart in his mouth, Priam rolled slowly toward the gate and out of the enemy camp.

Skipping ahead of her brothers, Polyxena laughed at their worried calls. Silly boys, making danger out of nothing. The grove of Apollo was sacred; both armies knew that. It was a place where Achaean and Trojan could meet in peace. She was in no danger there.

Rushing forward, she raced into the grove, eager to reach the little fountain in front of the temple, with its deliciously cool water spilling into a little pool that promised immediate relief from the heat. Polyxena pulled up short.

Someone was there, an Achaean warrior, drinking from the fountain. She tried to pull back into the trees, but it was too late. He turned, fixing her with an appraising gaze, and she gasped. He was beautiful! Standing there in his glittering armour, bronze inlaid with gold and silver, his pale hair loose about his shoulders, Polyxena drank him in with her eyes.

"It's alright," he said. "I won't hurt you."

Polyxena blinked, her whole body reacting to his rich, silky voice. Heart pounding, she stepped forward into the grove, moving almost without volition, drawn toward him on feet that almost floated across the grass.

She could not take her eyes off him, his beautiful eyes probing hers, those full lips begging to touch hers. How could a stranger make her feel this way? She opened her mouth to speak, but the words would not come. She licked her lips, eyes flickering, studying every part of him.

"I'm Achilles," he murmured. "Who are you?"

"I'm... Polyxena," she whispered. "Priam's daughter."

"Ah," he said in that golden voice. "You should not be here alone."

"My brothers are coming," she replied, feeling acute disappointment at the thought of being disturbed.

"Then we should be quick," he chuckled, bending in close.

"I... I'm sorry about your friend," she stammered.

He raised an eyebrow. "I'm sorry about your brother. And for how I acted."

Polyxena felt a fluttering deep in her gut, her breath almost gasping out. Faint voices drifted through the trees from outside the grove.

She glanced about in panic, filled with an irrational need to get away, but not from him. She wished she had never told Troilus she was coming here. It was his fault they were all about to break in on her unexpected bliss.

"Your brothers are coming," he said.

"I know," she wailed, pleading with her eyes.

He chuckled. "Perhaps I should go."

"No!" she cried, and then blushed. "I mean... don't go just yet."

He chuckled, reaching for her. With a gasp of pleasure, she welcomed his embrace. She chided herself for her brazen behaviour, but the woman in her knew she might never see him again. Standing on tiptoe, she allowed her lips to brush his.

She was completely unprepared for his response, let alone her own. As his arms closed tightly about her, crushing her against the quilted linen of his corselet, she returned his kiss with a desperate fervour. Wanting more, she clutched at him, pulling him down to her, drowning in desire, eager for his touch.

"Polyxena!" her youngest brother yelled.

"Troilus, no!" she cried.

Pulling away, she placed herself in front of Achilles. But the warrior moved her aside, his gentle hands on her shoulders.

"Go inside the temple," he whispered in her ear. "I'll follow you."

Feeling tears pricking at the backs of her eyes, Polyxena did as she was told, rushing into the temple to wait out the fight she knew was coming. Why, oh why did she have to fall in love now? Stupid, stupid girl!

Turning to face Troilus as he charged, Achilles paused

to note the boy's uncanny likeness to the charming girl who had just tried, however innocently, to seduce him. Smiling at her youthful exuberance, he drew his sword and stood ready for the boy's attack.

He remembered what Priam had said, about Troilus having the potential to be invincible. He might have met his match here. But Troilus was still a boy, not yet close to that mighty potential.

Achilles braced himself, ready for anything. The boy came at him, all anger and arrogance and fearless invulnerability. A bit like Achilles himself had once been, he thought ruefully.

Troilus came on, charging straight at him, making no attempt at feint or dodge, sword levelled at his gut. Achilles stepped to one side and brought his sword down on the back of the boy's neck.

Troilus dropped, blood spurting about him, and was still, the boy's fine hair floating in the sticky ooze that began to pool at the base of the fountain. Achilles sighed bitterly. It had been too easy, the boy too ready to fall on his sword in his eagerness to do battle.

"That's four," he whispered sadly.

"Troilus!"

Achilles' head snapped up as an arrow whistled past his ear. The other brothers had entered the grove, and Paris was rushing at him, bow drawn for another shot, a look of pure hatred twisting his face. Achilles ran, heading into the temple.

Paris fired again as the Achaean scum ran, but his shot fell short, grazing the man's ankle. Kneeling by his fallen brother, Paris seethed. How dare he come here to this sacred place and commit murder?

He could not let this stand. Achilles deserved to die.

Paris sprang up and headed for the temple.

"Paris, no!" Elenos cried. "Not in the temple!"

But Paris ignored him. Elenos was too soft, always had been. Behind him, he felt his other brother following and smiled. At least Deiphobos had the guts to follow through. Together they broke into the temple to find Polyxena wrapped in the arms of Achilles.

Before the pair had time to react, Paris pulled back on the bow and let fly. The bolt buried itself in the warrior's side, in the hollow of his arm. Polyxena screamed.

"Let him alone!" she cried. "Don't hurt him."

"Stand aside, Polyxena."

Paris fired again and Achilles fell to the ground. Polyxena dropped to his side with a tragic scream.

"What have you done?" Polyxena sobbed.

"I've killed the enemy dog who just killed your brother," Paris snapped. "Now come here and behave!"

"No," she cried. "I'm not leaving him."

"Paris, leave her, you need to come," said Deiphobos.

"Paris, you've defiled the temple with murderous blood," said Elenos behind him.

"I don't care. He deserved it."

"Paris, someone's coming," said Deiphobos.

Paris nodded and turned for the door. "Come on, Elenos."

Elenos shook his head. "I'm staying with Polyxena, to see she gets home safely and to see he gets taken back to his men. They'll kill you if they find you here."

Paris and Deiphobos ran. Elenos moved to his sister's side and stared down at the fallen hero. The warrior's eyes flickered, blinking as he gazed up at them, a crimson froth forming on his lips.

Outside in the grove of Apollo, Odysseus and Aias saw

the two sons of Priam running from the temple and shared a look of bewilderment. By the base of the fountain, a body lay huddled in the grass.

"Something's not right," said Odysseus.

Aias nodded. "You were right to follow Achilles."

"He walks around believing he's invincible. But those two had murder in their eyes."

"Let's check the temple."

Bursting through the doors, they stopped at the sight of the tableau before the altar.

"Achilles!" cried Aias.

Odysseus groaned. Moving to where the hero lay, he knelt beside him, noting the girl's hand clutching his.

"I should have known there was a girl involved," he sighed.

Achilles grasped weakly at his arm and Odysseus leant closer.

"It was Paris and Deiphobos," he whispered, a trickle of blood bubbling out the corner of his mouth. "I killed Troilus out there and they came upon me in here with Polyxena. I was stupid. It's my own fault."

"Hush, don't talk, you're not dead yet."

"Oh, but I am," he gasped. "I knew it would come. A short but glorious life. That was my choice."

"Help him," cried Polyxena. "He can't die!"

"Dear girl," said Odysseus. "Despite the rumours, he is a mortal man. He's bleeding out, drowning in his own blood. There's nothing we can do."

Polyxena wailed, clutching at the warrior's chest.

"Polyxena," he whispered. "We only knew each other for a moment. Go home, live your life, find a husband. Don't mourn me."

Polyxena sobbed. Elenos lifted her up, holding her gently.

"Go home, Lyxie," he whispered. "I'll see that he gets back safely."

The girl nodded, wiping at her tears with a trembling hand.

"Go now, don't look back."

Sobbing loudly, the girl ran. Turning back to the Achaean warriors, Elenos took a deep breath.

"My lords, I offer myself as hostage, to atone for the crime of my brothers."

Arriving at the camp, surrounded by soldiers shocked and grieving, Aias handed his burden over to the Myrmidons. Then Odysseus led Elenos to the command tent. Agamemnon, deep in conversation with his brother Menelaos when they entered, looked up and frowned.

"My lord, bad news," said Odysseus without ceremony. "Achilles is dead."

"What?" Agamemnon grunted. "What happened?"

"He was beset in the temple of Apollo. Paris and Deiphobos. Two bolts from behind, from the bow of Paris."

"Damn! What was he doing there?"

"It's not important. He's dead and that's that."

"Now what are we going to do?" said Menelaos. "He was our greatest hope for victory."

"Not so, my lord," said Elenos softly.

"Who are you?"

"Elenos, son of Priam," he replied.

Agamemnon raised an eyebrow. "And why are you here?"

"My lord, I surrendered, to atone for my brother's crime. Paris desecrated the temple. I want no part in it."

Agamemnon nodded. "What did you mean just then?"

"Achilles was your greatest hope. But Troilus was our last. Achilles killed him in the grove, hence my brother's

ELLA MORTIMER

anger that led to his hubris in the temple."

"Troilus?"

"My youngest brother, my lord. It was prophesied that if he lived to maturity he would be invincible, and with him our city. But he's dead now, thanks to Achilles."

Agamemnon ignored the hint of bitterness, still confused by the man's surrender. "Prophesied by whom?"

"By myself."

"Ah!" Agamemnon chuckled. "And what do you prophesy for us?"

Elenos hesitated. "It's true, I have a message for you, but I want an assurance first."

"Assurance of what?"

"I'm about to betray my father, my lord. I want asylum."

"You shall have it. You have my word. But you'd really betray your people because of an act of heresy?"

"I admit it's not the only reason. But the rest is my own concern."

"Very well. What's your prophecy?"

"First the bones of the hero Pelops, progenitor of your house, must be brought to witness the greatest war of all time."

Agamemnon whistled. "That's a very specific request."

Elenos shrugged. "I only repeat the message, my lord."

Agamemnon frowned. "I'll send to my wife for the bones of my grandfather. You said first. What else?"

"Second, the hero Philoctetes must join the Achaean force, bringing with him the bow and arrows of Herakles."

"Odysseus, choose a force to find Philoctetes and convince him to join us."

"He won't come willingly," said Menelaos. "He may still be bitter about being left behind on Lemnos."

"He was injured. How can he blame us for that? He'll come. What else?"

"Third, the son of Achilles must fight for the Achaeans."

"Neoptolemus? He's a child!"

"He carries the blood of Achilles. That condition for your victory hasn't changed. Achilles is dead, you must find his son."

Agamemnon sighed. "Odysseus, it looks like you must also go to Scyros."

"Yes, my lord."

"Anything else?"

"One more thing," said Elenos. "The sacred idol of Pallas Athena must be taken and removed from the city. Only when this Palladium is outside the walls will the city fall," intoned the prophet.

23

A MAN ON THE INSIDE

Klytemestra and Aegisthus sat close together in the potinia's audience chamber, finishing the records for the day. Klytie rolled the balls of clay into sausages, squashing them into tablet form as Gissus required. Taking the next tablet from her, his hand brushed hers and a smile played on his lips. Finishing the last characters, he put down his stylus and looked up, eyes twinkling.

"I think we're done," he said.

Standing and stretching she nodded, a yawn threatening. His arms slipped about her waist and she shivered, a giggle bubbling out of her.

"What should we do now, my love?" he murmured.

She sighed. "Let's go home."

"Home," he smiled. "I like hearing you say that."

"I like saying it. I just wish it didn't mean leaving the children alone at night."

"They're not alone, they have their maids to look after them, and there are plenty of servants if they need anything."

"I know."

"So stop worrying," he chuckled.

"But..."

He covered her mouth with his, smothering her complaints. The eagerness burst forth, still breathtaking after all the months since they had given in to their feelings.

She felt the familiar shivering in her belly that set her knees trembling, the aching need still as sharp as the first time.

With his hand doing interesting things beneath her skirt, Klytie wanted nothing more than to let him have her, right there. But even as she moaned with pleasure, tearing at his clothing, something stopped her. A pact with herself, that she would never risk being discovered by her children.

"Mama!"

With a strangled oath, Klytie struggled out of his arms, smoothed down her skirt and turned to see Elektra, all angst and accusation, staring her down.

"There's a messenger waiting in the megaron," said Elektra, looking her mother up and down in disgust. "Whenever you're ready," she finished with a grimace of distaste.

"Elektra…"

But she was gone.

"Damn," Klytie groaned.

The messenger handed over the note without a word. Klytie signalled to a maid and suggested she guide the messenger to the kitchen for a meal. Then, with a worried glance at Gissus, she broke the seal on the papyrus scroll with a trembling hand. Mouthing the words, she frowned. Gissus took the scroll from her unresisting fingers and read aloud.

"To my wife, the lady Klytemestra from your husband and commander of the Achaean force, Agamemnon, greetings. I write in fulfilment of a prophecy, in order that the victorious Achaean army might finally bring the Trojans to their knees. It has been brought to our attention that in order to win we need the bones of my grandfather Pelops, to bear witness to our great undertaking and to influence the fates in our favour. I request the required artefacts be exhumed and transported by the hand of this messenger, direct to us in our camp outside Troy."

"What a strange request," Klytie said.

"He can't be serious," Gissus growled.

"Agamemnon never jokes."

"I know that," he spat. "But how can he ask such a thing? To defile a tomb to win a war. It's unheard of."

"We have to do it," she shivered.

"How dare he? Pelops was my grandfather too!"

"You forget; he doesn't know that. In his mind he has every right."

"I won't allow it," Gissus frowned.

"I don't think you have a choice."

"Of course I have a choice. Send the bones and he wins, to come back victorious, or don't send them, he loses and maybe gets himself killed. I know which option I prefer."

"Surely you see the flaw in that logic?"

"I see no flaw," he pouted.

She sighed. "You don't send them, he knows something is wrong and comes to investigate."

He stared at her from under lowered brows, face dark as a thundercloud.

"You and me," she whispered. "Would be over."

"Not if I can help it!"

"So send the bones. At least we'd have a few months longer together."

* * *

Menelaos and his brother Agamemnon stood on the beach by the command tent, watching as a lone ship pointed its long black prow at the shore.

"Do you think it's Odysseus?" said Menelaos. "Will Philoctetes be with him? He was pretty angry when we left him on Lemnos."

"I hope so. The last message from Odysseus said he'd

picked up Neoptolemus and intercepted my man with the bones of Pelops, and he was on his way to Lemnos. He wouldn't have returned without Philoctetes, willing or no."

"Not a moment too soon. We need to break this stalemate somehow."

"We've been lucky. The Trojans have lost the best of their leaders. Time to draw them out and get this wrapped up."

"What about the other thing Elenos mentioned. The statue of Athena? That's inside the city."

"We need to get in there. Perhaps Odysseus can come up with a plan. I'm afraid it might have to wait until we breach the wall."

"We'll never break through those walls."

"Now, now, it's not as bad as that," said Agamemnon.

"But I think it is," said Menelaos with a frown. The walls are so thick; the foundations must be even thicker. I think the rams are too low. We're hitting at the strongest part of the rampart."

"What do you suggest?"

Menelaos shrugged. "We have to do something."

As soon as the ship hit the beach, a group of men jumped down and came toward them as the sailors pulled the ship up onto the sand.

"My lords," cried Odysseus as he approached.

"Odysseus," said Agamemnon.

Behind Odysseus followed a tall man carrying an enormous bow, and a young lad, well built but beardless.

"Philoctetes," said Agamemnon. "I am glad to see you recovered."

"Not completely, my lord," said the man. "My wound still troubles me. I was hoping your doctors could help me."

"Of course, I'll see that they come to you after the meeting."

"My lord," said Odysseus. "This lad is Neoptolemus."

"I suspected as much, you're much like your father, boy."

The boy frowned. "When may I see my father's grave?"

"Someone can take you now, if you like."

Another man stepped forward, carrying a large round ceramic pot, with a wooden stopper sealed with wax. Without a word, he offered it to Agamemnon. The commander licked his lips and took it reverently, glancing at his brother.

"What should we do with it?" whispered Menelaos.

Agamemnon shrugged. "Take it to my tent for now, I suppose." He looked at the men gathered about. "Shall we all go to the command tent? We have a lot to discuss."

Stepping into his brother's tent, the command centre of this never-ending war, Menelaos shivered. His eyes rested on the silent figure of Elenos, standing in a corner, eyes catching everything.

He always felt a little uncomfortable in the presence of the Trojan traitor, who had been willing to betray his own family. He did not stop to think his wife had done the same thing when she came to Troy all those years ago.

"Now, first things first," said Agamemnon as he took his seat and motioned for the others to sit. "How do we draw the Trojans out? The truce is ended, yet still they hide behind their walls. Elenos?"

"They're demoralised, my lord," said the Trojan. "Their greatest leaders are all dead. Paris isn't well liked, for starting the war, and Deiphobos has made enemies of his own."

"How do we bring them out?"

Elenos looked down, shaking his head.

"What have you seen?"

The man was shivering, shoulders shaking. He tried to

turn away, but Agamemnon leapt from his chair, grabbing at his arm and turning the Trojan to face him, taking his shoulders and shaking him.

"You can't back out now," he snarled. "You gave yourself freely, accepted asylum for helping us. You must see it through."

Elenos shuddered. "Forgive me, my lord. You must understand this is my family..."

Agamemnon dropped his hands. "Tell me."

"Single combat," Elenos sighed. "Your bowman with the arrows of Herakles. Paris is the best bowman in all of Ilion, he won't be able to resist."

"No!" Menelaos cried. "Paris is mine!"

"You know Paris will never willingly fight you," said Agamemnon. "He's terrified of you, remember how he ran before. He'd never come out for you."

Menelaos frowned. He knew his brother was right, but his pride could not let go of the thirst for revenge. Paris had insulted him personally by stealing his wife. He had to pay, and Menelaos wanted to be the one to do it.

"Think of me as your champion," said Philoctetes then. "You can stand by me and watch him destroyed close up."

Agamemnon glanced at Elenos. "That's what you saw, isn't it?"

"Do I have to say it?" he whispered.

"What will happen?" Agamemnon growled.

"Paris will come out. He'll be..." he took a shuddering breath. "He'll die, and my father will send the soldiers out in force."

Agamemnon nodded. "Good," he said in satisfaction. "Then Neoptolemus will lead the Myrmidons in and drive them back against their own walls."

Elenos collapsed in a heap, hands over his face and shoulders shuddering with his sobs. Menelaos stared, his resolve to hate the traitor crumbling at his obvious distress.

"What about the palladium?" said Odysseus. "How do we capture it?"

"We need to get someone inside the walls," said Agamemnon. "Elenos? We need a way in."

The traitor curled into a ball, arms covering his head. Menelaos moved over to him, squatting beside him. He touched a hand to his shoulder and the man jumped.

"I'm sorry," Menelaos murmured. "I know this is hard. I can't imagine doing what you've done. How can I help?"

Elenos looked up, showing his ravaged face. "There's nothing you can do. I brought this on myself."

"I do feel responsible. This is my war. It's my fault you're in this mess now. Is there someone you want protected? You don't have to lose everyone when you take up asylum."

"It's a kind offer, my lord," he said. "But by the time this is over they'll all be gone. I've seen it."

With that, the traitor took a deep breath and clambered to his feet. He straightened his shoulders and cleared his face of all expression. Then his cold blue eyes turned on Agamemnon.

"My lord, I apologise for my weakness. May I make a suggestion?"

Agamemnon nodded, waving a hand for him to continue.

"To capture the palladium you need a man on the inside. I can be that man."

Agamemnon frowned. "How will you achieve this?"

"When Paris falls, I'll return with him into the city. Once inside I can let your man in to retrieve the idol."

"You expect us to trust you, after that display of remorse?" Agamemnon scoffed. "What's to stop you turning on us the moment you see your beloved family?"

"As I said, they can't be saved. Nothing I do will prevent it, so why fight it. I'd be grateful of the chance to see them one more time, but that's all."

Walking out onto the field with Philoctetes and his huge bow on one side, and Menelaos in full armour on the other, Elenos stared up at the walls of home. On the battlements, he could see people clustered. He thought he recognised his father, but it was hard to see from such a distance.

There were women there too, and he wondered if Helene were there. Finally, just outside of bowshot, they stopped, and the two Achaeans pushed him forward. With a nervous glance behind, Elenos stepped closer and raised his eyes to meet those of the watchers on the parapet.

He scanned the anxious faces, swallowing down the lump in his throat. There was his father, Priam, flanked by his surviving brothers and surrounded by the women of the castle, all looking down at him. It was time for the ultimate betrayal. He pushed his pain down and raised his voice.

"The Achaeans request a contest," he said. "A call to single combat, using the bow. They suggest you send a champion to face the Achaean bowman Philoctetes. Will you send your best archer?"

"You know very well, the best archer in Ilion is your brother Paris," cried Priam. "And we know who Philoctetes is, and whose bow he uses."

Elenos swallowed hard, his throat dry. "So do you accept?"

"No! It's an unfair fight, with no reward."

A sudden commotion set the watchers mumbling. Elenos knew his brother would never deny the contest, especially now that his father had forbidden it. After a few moments, the gate opened a crack and two men stepped out. Paris and Deiphobos. From above, Priam called out.

"Apparently... we agree."

Elenos stepped back, a sudden vision of his brother

lying in the dust, filled with arrows, clouding his sight. He wiped the tears away with an angry curse. Paris stepped forward, bow at the ready.

Raising his arm and taking aim, he pulled back and let fly. Philoctetes lifted his shield and the arrow slammed into it, the point breaking through the back, narrowly missing his arm. Elenos held his breath, praying that Paris could draw again before the great bow of Herakles sang.

But he had seen this all play out hundreds of times in his mind. Philoctetes dropped the shield, drew the great bow and released, all faster than Paris could reach for another arrow. The bolt flew, hitting Paris' hand and throwing his arm back, bones snapping under the power of its momentum.

Paris screamed, pulling at the huge arrow piercing his palm while the arm flopped lifeless from it. Another arrow flew, striking Paris through the right eye, lodging in his skull. Paris stumbled against the force of the blow and scrabbled backward, turning to run with the arrow bouncing in front of his face.

Elenos groaned, but he could not turn away, fascinated by the vision made real before his eyes. Elenos heard the bow sing again, another arrow, and immediately another. The first found flesh in Paris' left foot, pinning it to the ground. Elenos winced, hunching his shoulders.

Paris turned on the spot, pivoting on the pinned foot. The second arrow ploughed into the right foot. Paris fell backward, landing with a thud in the dust. Beside Elenos, Menelaos drew his sword and rushed forward. But Philoctetes was faster.

He drew and shot, the bolt flashing past Menelaos to strike Paris full in the chest, burying its point in the Trojan's heart. Elenos sobbed, a deep groan escaping him, his unwilling feet carrying him slowly toward his brother.

Menelaos rounded on Philoctetes, a snarl of anger on his face. He ran past Elenos, pulling his gaze, and flew straight at Philoctetes, sword raised. Philoctetes caught up his shield and blocked a wild thrust.

"You could have let me have the killing blow!" Menelaos screamed.

"I'm sorry, my lord, but the prophesy said the bow of Herakles would kill him, not the sword of Menelaos."

"I don't care what the damned prophecy said!"

Elenos turned away and dropped to his knees by his brother. The dead eyes stared at nothing.

"I'm so sorry, Paris," he whispered.

At a roar from behind, Elenos turned to see Menelaos coming at him. Pulling the sword from Paris' belt, he stood over the body, ready to stop the charge.

"Stand aside, Elenos," Menelaos yelled. "I will have his armour!"

"No! I'm taking my brother home!" Elenos cried.

Deiphobos stepped in beside him, sword raised. Elenos glanced at his brother, giving a look of gratitude, and he smiled.

"It's good to have you back," Deiphobos murmured.

Menelaos paused.

"Take him," Elenos said to his brother. "I'll hold these two off until you get under the wall."

"Are you sure?"

"Do it!" Elenos hissed.

Deiphobos shrugged, sheathed his sword and took Paris under the arms, dragging him back toward the gate. Elenos stood firm, eyes locked on those of Menelaos. He shuddered at what he must yet do.

The final betrayal, and the horror yet to come. But he was committed now, and the only thing left was to save himself the only way he could. When Deiphobos was out of earshot, he screwed up his face and growled one word.

"Midnight," he hissed with a groan.

Menelaos gave a slight nod, and Elenos backed away, moving in under the range of the bowmen on the wall. Then he turned and hurried to help Deiphobos, and together they carried their fallen brother through the gate. Once inside, Elenos looked around at the familiar faces, tears falling unheeded.

A woman pushed her way through the throng, golden hair falling from its pins where she had clutched it in her fear. Helene. She stood before the brothers, big eyes staring at the body. Elenos thought he saw a tiny smile playing on her lips, quickly hidden.

"No time for grief, woman," Deiphobos crowed. "Now you're mine!"

24

IF RAMS WERE HORSES

Trojan soldiers streamed out of the gate toward the Achaean lines, waiting to meet them. Standing before his men, Neoptolemus shivered in anticipation. Now was his chance to prove his mettle, to live up to his father's name.

These old men had no fight left in them, but he would show them how to win a battle. Standing in his father's glittering armour, the boy felt invincible. It did not matter that the cuirass sat loosely, even cinched to its tightest, or that the greaves hung uncomfortably off his calves, cutting into the tops of his feet.

The strap of the great shield cut into his shoulder and the sword hilt rubbed under his arm. Riding in his chariot, it did not matter that he could not run with the weight of adult sized armour on his not quite adult sized frame. He was big for his age. He could cope.

He only needed the spear anyway. He was good with a spear. He raised his arm and gave the signal to charge. He crowed as the chariot burst forward, revelled in the power of the horses pulling him into the fray. Beside him, the charioteer guided while Neoptolemus tasted his first blood, his spear raining havoc down on his foes.

In his mind, he felt a flush of pride, knowing his father was with him. It seemed too easy, as the Trojans fled before him. It never occurred to him that maybe it was the image of his father that swam before their eyes, forcing them back.

They saw Achilles reborn, and ran in terror from the impossible warrior. Neoptolemus returned from the rout changed, no longer a green boy with no experience. Now he puffed up with pride, sure that he had surpassed his own famous father that day.

Sneaking out of camp as the moon rose high, Odysseus and Diomedes hurried toward the grove of Apollo.

"Do you think he'll be there?" whispered Diomedes.

Odysseus shrugged. "We'll see."

"What if he takes us inside only to ambush us?"

Odysseus shrugged again. They slipped into the grove and looked around, searching the shadows.

"See? I knew he wouldn't be here," said Diomedes with a snort.

"Keep your voice down," someone hissed. "I could hear you a mile away."

"You see?" murmured Odysseus.

"And now I have to trust my life to a Trojan traitor?"

"You do if you don't want to get caught," hissed the Trojan.

Odysseus chuckled. "Lead the way, Elenos."

"Into the trap…" Diomedes murmured.

"Keep your voice down or I will," Elenos growled.

Mumbling under his breath, Diomedes followed the traitor and the fool, ready to run at the slightest hint of trouble. But they found their way quickly to a small sally port and slipped into the city. Keeping to the shadows, Elenos led them toward the centre of town and the temple of Pallas Athena. Once inside, Diomedes rushed forward to grab the small statue of Athena.

"Odysseus?" a woman's voice, low and cautious.

Diomedes groaned. He knew this was too good to be

true. Now they were caught.

"Helene!" Odysseus hissed.

Oh great, thought Diomedes. Now the bitch will run to her Trojan friends.

"Don't be alarmed," she whispered. "You're not without friends in the city. When the time comes, you'll have the help you need."

"How can we trust you?" Diomedes hissed. "You're the biggest traitor of them all.

"Diomedes!" Odysseus snapped. "Pull your head in."

"He's right," Helene moaned. "I don't know why you don't leave me here to rot."

"Helene," Odysseus whispered. "Are you saying you want us to win?"

"Of course I do!" she sighed. "But you have to get out, now."

Odysseus nodded. "We're going."

Diomedes breathed a sigh of relief, heading for the door.

"Diomedes, take it easy," Odysseus snapped. "Calm down or you'll get us all killed."

"Odysseus," Helene murmured. "Tell Menelaos I'm sorry, I..."

"Hush," said Odysseus. "Tell him yourself, when this is over. Let's go, Elenos, take us out."

Menelaos paced while the others sat about the command tent making plans.

"My lord, perhaps we could make the rams taller?"

"How do you propose we do that, Odysseus?"

"I'm sure our engineers can think of something."

"With Trojan arrows raining down?"

"We'll do it at night."

"And what then? We've done everything the prophet told us to do and yet the city still stands." Menelaos clasped his hands nervously behind his back. "It's been one great quest after another for nothing. What good will one more plan do?"

"Nothing," said Odysseus. "Unless it's a plan to win."

"Do you have such a plan?" said Agamemnon.

"Perhaps. But we must make sure every contingency is covered or it will fail like all the rest."

In the soft light of the coming dawn, Menelaos stared at the great battering ram, raised high on big thick posts looking for all the world like a beast's legs. In the shadowy light, the square sides of the canvas shelter housing the greater part of the ram took on a softness, as of an animal's body.

The great ram sticking out in front could almost be its head, crudely carved to increase the illusion, with the rear of the ram sticking out the back like a tail. Normally the ram would be swung by a troop of men hiding inside the shelter, safe from the arrows of the enemy.

Now, the men who climbed the ropes were fully armed and ready for battle. Menelaos turned to gaze out to sea, where the last of the fleet could just be seen rounding the point, led away by Agamemnon to take up a position near Tenedos and await the signal.

"Sir, you must get aboard," said Odysseus beside him. "Soon the sun will break and the shadows will dispel. We must be hidden, or the sentries will catch sight of us and all will be lost."

Menelaos nodded. "Do you think it'll work?"

"It has to."

Inside the ram, the men sat squashed in, many more than the shelter was designed to hold. Keeping hushed only by the threat of instant death if anyone gave them away, they listened in the dark for any sound from outside.

As dawn broke, there was a cry from the wall. Menelaos pictured the scene outside. The beach was empty of ships, the Achaean camp deserted. All that remained outside the wall were a few siege engines, including the one in which they hid, the mightiest ram of all.

The men listened as the Trojans came to inspect the thing. With the ropes pulled up, they could not climb into the shelter, but the sound of their voices seemed to continue for hours.

Inside the ram, the soldiers sweltered through the day, their grumbles barely quelled by the passing around of water skins, the liquid warm and fetid. Sometime around midday, the Trojans came again, but this time they brought an unexpected surprise.

"Menelaos!" a woman's voice.

Inside the canvas shelter, Menelaos gasped. "Helene!" he breathed.

Odysseus stopped him with a hand on his arm, a shake of the head almost imperceptible in the darkness.

"Mené are you there? They sent me to find you. They want to know if there's anyone inside this beast. Mené, I want you to be there! But I hope you're not, because they'll kill you if you are."

A groan escaped him as he listened, the sound of her old pet name for him sending a knife of grief into his gut. A small hope grew in his heart that maybe Helene might help, that she might willingly go home with him.

"Mené! I want to go home. They can hear me, but I don't care. The women don't trust me, and the men hate me for causing this war. But I can't come home if you're dead!"

Menelaos stifled a sob. His arm ached where Odysseus held him, crushing fingers digging into the muscle. Menelaos wanted to call out to her, but he bit down hard, feeling tears of joy pricking behind his eyes.

"Mené, I'm so sorry. Don't lose your life for me. I'm not worth it. They want me to beg you to come out. They think you'll surrender, for me."

A long pause, while Menelaos stifled his ragged breathing, a hand clasped over his mouth.

"I'll tell them you're not here; you would have come out if you were. I don't know whether to pray you're not there or hope that you are. I only hope it all goes well with you."

A short silence, then a man's voice raised in query. "Well?"

Menelaos heard Helene's reply. "It's empty, the Achaeans have gone. You've won."

Then another voice, calling to the troops. "Bring it in, bring the biggest engine inside. We'll celebrate our victory as we dedicate the wooden beast to the gods."

A long, arduous afternoon followed. There was a great noise of men, yelling, chanting, huffing in their progress, mercifully drowning out the occasional clatter of armour that the men inside tried to muffle, jostled and crushed together as the beast-like siege engine was slowly pulled toward the city.

Eventually, the rumbling movement slowed and stopped. There followed a long period of shouting and revelry, and the men trapped in the great war horse groaned in their hunger as the smells of a feast wafted into their prison. Cutting their hunger on meagre travel rations and more stale water, the men grumbled but kept to the plan, waiting for the word. Finally, late in the night, a voice hissed up at them in the darkness.

"My lord, it's me, Sinon!"

Menelaos shared a look with Odysseus. Had the man really managed to survive and carry out his part of the plan?

Or was it a trick of the Trojans? Odysseus put a finger to his lips and made his way to the tail end of the ram, cracking open the canvas a sliver to peek out.

"It's him," Odysseus whispered.

He threw the rope and slid down to meet the spy he had himself ordered into enemy hands. Menelaos followed. Once on the ground, he signalled to the watching men.

"Quickly and quietly," Menelaos whispered upward.

"My lord, the story worked," said Sinon. "I acted the part of a runaway just as you suggested, Odysseus, sir. They believed me and quizzed me as to the plans of the Commander."

"So they accepted that we had all left," said Menelaos. "That explains why they believed Helene so easily."

"Yes, sir. Now they're all feasted and drunk and settling down to sleep off their revelry."

"Is the fleet on its way?"

"I assume so, sir, I lit the signal before I came for you."

"Well done," said Menelaos. "Odysseus, you're in charge. Get the guards neutralised and those gates open. I'm going to find Helene."

Odysseus dispatched the sleeping guards without a noise, and his men rushed to open the gate.

"Hush!" he hissed. "We don't want them waking before the army gets back."

He slipped out onto the field and peered down toward the beach. He could see a few ships close to shore, and more out on the water, silhouetted against the moonlight. Heading back inside, he organised the men.

"Find the family," he ordered. "Priam and his sons, the women too. Round them up and bring them to the temple in the square. Quietly!"

The men hurried off, and by the time they had found

the King and his family the full Achaean force was making its way up the beach and across the field. They spread out through the town and snuck into homes, killing as they went.

Coming across Priam escaping from his captors, Neoptolemus saw a chance for glory. He chased the old man into the temple of Zeus, right up to the altar. The King ignored the boy, hands clutching at the altar and voice raised in prayer. Feeling the thrill of victory coursing through his veins, the boy raised his spear and threw, catching the old man in the back.

In the temple of Athena, the wives of the King and his dead sons were clustered, threatened by their captors. At the altar, Elenos knelt beside his sister Cassandra, watching her wild eyes taking it all in.

"I told them," she cried. "I told them all! Why don't they ever believe me?"

"Hush, Cassie. They wouldn't listen even to me."

"They take your advice all the time. It's me they won't believe. My curse brought this down on our heads. And there's more to come…"

In the house of Deiphobos, Helene huddled on the bed, hearing the sounds of death. Her new husband had slipped out of the room to see what was going on, but she knew. She swung her legs over and stood up, flinching at a woman's scream somewhere out in the darkness.

She padded over to the window, trying to see through the shadows, trying to hear a familiar voice. A crash from the outer room brought her back to her senses. Someone was inside the house, someone who could be here to kill her, or worse.

She wondered where Deiphobos had gone. He might be arrogant and selfish, making her skin crawl every time he touched her, but at least he cared. He would protect her. She dressed hurriedly, slipped on her sandals and crept out of the room. A cry stopped her in her tracks.

That was Deiphobos. Moving slowly, she crept down the stairs. In the reception room at the bottom, she stopped again, hearing grunts and the clash of bronze, the sounds of a fight in the anteroom.

Slipping over to the doorway, she carefully peeked in. There was Deiphobos with his back to her. In the soft moonlight from the doorway, she saw a second figure, sword raised, rushing in on Deiphobos. A flash of light hit his face for a second and Helene gasped.

She pulled back, leaning against the wall as her knees crumbled, her breath coming in ragged sobs. Her heart raced, and something inside would not stop turning cartwheels. Menelaos! He had come for her.

Another scream from Deiphobos. Helene caught her breath, knowing who would win this fight. A small, sadistic part of her wanted to see it, the idiot who had claimed her beaten by the best man alive. She rolled over on the wall, bringing her face back toward the doorway, hugging the plaster as she peered around the door frame.

Deiphobos was clutching his ear, his attacker forgotten. Helene saw the next slash coming and caught her breath, watching the flash of moonlight on bronze as it came down. And Deiphobos clutched his other ear. Helene held her breath, heart pounding in excitement.

Another slash, and an arm flopped by his side. Another, and the other arm hung lifeless. He was screaming, head shaking. Another slash and his legs gave way.

Menelaos stood over his victim, his sword held high above his head. With the point down, ready for the killing thrust, he stared down at his enemy, face twisted in battle rage. Helene moved into the doorway, drawn out by the powerful figure, relishing his glory.

For a moment, her eyes met his and she saw a flicker of recognition. Then with a growl of rage, he thrust the sword home and Deiphobos lay still. Ripping his sword from the body, Menelaos flew at Helene, grabbing her arm and pulling her into the room.

Helene cried out in pain, stumbling as he flung her across the floor. When she had righted herself, she found his sword pointed directly at her chest. She held up her hands, pleading with her eyes.

"Please, Mené," she whispered.

"Tell me why I shouldn't kill you right now," he spat.

"Because I want to go home," she pleaded. "With you."

He hesitated, sword point hovering before her face as he studied her. Then he lowered the sword to his side. Moving very carefully, Helene moved in close, eyes locked on his. She stepped even closer, lifted a hand to touch him and felt his shiver.

Then she slipped her arms about his waist and rested her head on the cold bronze of his chest. She stood there for a long moment, heart thudding and breath shallow, waiting. What would he do now?

If only he could learn not to hate her, she would be happy. If he could accept her and take her back, that would be a miracle past all hope. Helene closed her eyes and prayed for a sign.

Then, hesitantly, his arms closed about her. Helene sighed. Maybe there was hope after all. She felt his fingers in her hair, his breath on her neck. Then his hand cupped her chin, making her meet his eyes.

Her vision blurred and a tear slid down her cheek. He brushed it away with one finger, tracing the line of her jaw and moving his finger across her lips.

"Are you sure?" he whispered.

She nodded, unable to speak. Then his mouth was on hers and she gave in to the shuddering need, eager to show him how much she was sure. When he pulled back, she felt shaken and somehow shy, but incredibly happy.

"Are there..." he hesitated. "Did he give you children?"

She nodded. "Three sons. But they died."

"I'm sorry. What happened?"

"I think..." she caught a breath. "The house fell on them, but I think Deiphobos caused it. I think he had his men dig under the walls."

"But that's awful!"

She nodded. "I'm glad you killed him."

He chuckled then. "Is there anything you need? Do you want to gather anything to take with you?"

She shook her head. "All I need is to go with you."

"Then let's get you to the ships."

On a hill outside troy an Achaean soldier dozed by a little campfire. A strange sound broke into his dream and his eyes snapped open. Staring down into the city, he rubbed his eyes. The noise was the screaming of women and the clash of bronze.

As he watched, flames licked at the rooftops, growing fiercer by the moment. Out on the beach, the Achaean camp was awash with light from a thousand campfires, and men yelled and sang.

The soldier reached across and grabbed at his companion's foot, shaking it. His partner slept soundly while he sat on watch, and it took a rather concerted jolt before he jumped awake.

"What is it?"

"Look, Captain," the soldier said, pointing. "Is that what

I think it is?"

The Captain looked, rubbing the sleep from his eyes. "Is the city burning?"

"Looks like it. I think it's finally over. Look, the Achaeans are celebrating by the ships."

"This is it!" yelled the Captain. "After all this time, sitting here on this damned hilltop!"

"So do we light it?"

"Of course we light it! The war's over. Come on."

Grabbing at a stick from the fire, the Captain rushed to the great pyre. Following with his own glowing stick, the soldier almost danced. Pulling the cover off, they thrust their sticks into the centre of the pyre, where the soft kindling had been carefully laid, and watched as it caught alight.

Months ago, they had set that thing, keeping it dry as best they could under its canvas cover. Finally, it would serve its purpose and their job would be done. They could go home. As the two men watched the flames take, the pyre lit up, fire licking up the carefully piled branches to reach for the sky.

Turning, they scoured the dark horizon for the next signal, hoping the sentries on the faraway hilltop were watching. The Captain held his breath for a long moment, watching for any sign. Somewhere out in the darkness, a light flickered. The light grew brighter, and he let out a great cry of delight.

"There it is! It's done."

The soldier laughed. "What now?"

"Now, we follow orders. We get home, as quick as we can. The lord Aegisthus is going to need us."

25

THE RETURNING KING

The queen stared at the remnants of her evening meal, her stomach already rebelling against the small amount she had managed to force down. Klytemestra signalled for the plates to be taken and the tables folded away. Then she settled back into the King's great seat and sighed.

Gissus came and sat beside her, watched with narrowed eyes by Elektra. Klytie wished her second daughter would not be so judgemental.

"Time for bed," Klytie said abruptly.

"Don't be silly Mama," said Krissie. "It's early."

"Well, I'm tired," murmured Klytie.

"I don't think being tired has anything to do with it," Elektra mumbled.

"Elektra, have some respect," said Gissus with a frown.

"You should talk," she spat.

"Elektra!" Klytie sighed, unable to muster a sharper tone.

"Night, Mama," said Orestes, coming to hug his mother. "I hope you feel better in the morning."

"Good night, Orestes."

"I'll go too, then," said Krissie. "Night, Mama."

"Well I'm not going," said Elektra with a pout.

"Elektra, you should obey your mother," said Gissus.

"I don't have to do anything you say, I'm fifteen, I can

do what I like."

"Not while you live in this house," said Klytie.

"Then get rid of me, marry me off, you know you want to!"

"Elektra, please don't."

"Don't think I don't know what happens when we go to bed, Mama. I know you run off to his house. You never sleep here anymore. It's dreadful what you're doing to Papa! I wish he'd come home and punish you."

"Elektra!" cried the queen, stirred to anger.

A clatter of bronze and hurrying footsteps interrupted the argument. "My lady, a signal!" cried the soldier at the door.

"Signal?" Klytie whispered.

"Yes, my lady, the signal fire. It's alight!"

Klytie sat up straight, eyes wide. Aegisthus stood up, hurrying to take the soldier by the arm.

"Show me!" he said.

Klytie dragged herself out of the chair, ignoring her daughter's curious frown. She moved to the door, through the anteroom and onto the porch, Elektra a step behind.

"What does it mean, Mama?"

Klytie shook her head, staring up onto the wall, trying in the darkness to see the men against the evening sky. A dark figure leant over the parapet and called down to her.

"It's the signal, it's alight!" cried Aegisthus.

Klytie gasped, clutching at her stomach, the wind knocked out of her. Her gorge rose and she gagged, almost losing her meagre meal. She barely saw the figure on the wall as it hurried along the parapet toward the stairs.

"Mama, what's going on?"

Klytie gulped air, trying to calm her stomach. "It's over," she whispered. "Troy has fallen." Then she raised her eyes to her daughter's confused gaze. "Elektra, you have your wish. Your father is coming home."

Klytie watched as Elektra thought about what she had said. Her eyes glittered and her face broke out in a smile of triumph. Then she laughed.

"Oh, Mama, now you're going to get it," she crowed. "I'm going to tell the others!"

"Elektra!" Klytie cried, but the girl was already gone.

Then Gissus was there, hands on her shoulders, turning her to face him. She gasped for breath, still struggling to drive the sickness down, shaking her head as she mumbled under her breath.

"What's that?" he murmured. "Klytie, don't shut me out now."

She shook him off, running for the little step into the private rooms. She could hear him following, but she had to get out of sight. She continued toward the stairs and up to her own bedroom. Once inside, she turned to face him, ignoring the tears streaming down her face.

"What do we do now?" she whispered.

"Nothing, yet," he said. "Calm down, my love, he's not going to appear at the gates right now. He could be months away. He might even be dead."

"Oh he's not dead," she shuddered. "He would never allow me that freedom."

He shrugged. "We'll see. We should wait for the official messenger."

"You said months," she murmured. "Could it really be that long?"

"It depends on the winds," he shrugged. "But it could be sooner."

"How much sooner? What's the earliest he could be here?"

"I... suppose, if the winds were good, maybe a week."

"A week?" she gasped, shuddering.

"Calm down, that's not likely. He won't leave Troy that soon, he'll have things to do there first."

"What kind of things?"

"Well, he'll need to divide the spoils, allocate captives to his officers as slaves, and pay his soldiers. It could be a month or more before he sets sail."

"A month?" she squeaked. "No, it can't be that long. He has to get here sooner."

"Sooner? What are you talking about? You want him to come home?"

"No! I don't want him home," she cried. "But he has to come soon or we're both dead."

"What are you talking about?"

"Oh Gissus," she whispered. "I'm pregnant. In another month, I might be starting to show. If I can't convince him it's his, he'll kill me in a heartbeat. Then he'll come for you."

Then, to her great disgust, his eyes lit up, his face breaking into an enormous grin. He stepped in close and pulled her to him.

"Well now," he murmured. "That changes everything."

A week later, Klytie stood at the courtyard wall and watched as the messenger trotted up the hill from the gate. At the lower courtyard, he dismounted and headed for the stairs.

Clasping her hands to stop the trembling, she hurried inside to the megaron, settling herself in the King's seat and dragging her face into a semblance of calm. Aegisthus stood at her side, and her children sat clustered at her feet.

The herald entered without announcement and headed straight for the queen. He bowed and handed her the papyrus scroll.

"My lady, I am come direct from the King, commander of the Achaean fleet, your husband Agamemnon. The letter you hold tells of the fall of Troy and the victory of the Achaeans, and bids you prepare for the King's imminent return."

"Thank you," Klytie whispered.

"My lady, I am charged with receiving your reply."

"Of course," she mumbled.

Handing the scroll unopened to Aegisthus, she sat with hands in her lap and head bowed while he broke the seal and began to read. She tried to close her ears, the tears of anguish falling unheeded, hardly noticing the avid eyes of her children as they listened.

She listened to the low, quiet tones of her lover's voice as he read, not hearing the words, savouring the last moments of her illicit dream as her happiness crumbled about her. When he had finished, she looked up at the messenger to give her reply.

"Forgive my tears," she said, taking a deep breath. "Please believe they are tears of joy. Tell my husband I am glad to receive his news. Tell him..." she lifted her chin, squaring her shoulders and closing down her heart. "Tell him he shall find a fitting welcome. His family await his arrival with eager arms and loving hearts. He shall find his home in order and his wife steadfast in his long absence. Tell him his arrival could not come soon enough."

The herald bowed again and hurried away.

"Oh Mama!" Orestes cried. "Papa really is coming home!"

"Yes, my dear boy, he is."

Krisothemis said nothing, but her eyes sought her mother's with a troubled frown. Klytie tried to avoid her gaze, but the girl would not be ignored. Finally, when Klytie met her daughter's eyes, she saw compassion beyond her years and a deep sympathy she should never have had to feel. Klytie felt ashamed and lost in the light of that over wise gaze.

"Well, Mama," said Elektra with a sneer. "What are you going to do now? What will Papa find when he gets here?"

"Elektra, why must you be so mean?" said Krissie then.

"Alright, children," Gissus said. "Your mama has much to organise before your papa gets home. You must let her be now."

"Come on, Orestes," said Krissie. "How would you like to ride with me?"

Orestes grinned and hurried to the door. Krissie turned back and smiled at her mother.

"Everything will be alright, Mama," she said. "You'll see. Are you coming, Elektra?"

"Coming," said Elektra with a glance at Aegisthus.

Krisothemis and Orestes hurried out, laughing together.

"Stay a moment, Elektra," said Aegisthus softly.

While she stood, half turned on her way to the door, Aegisthus came close behind her, a hand on her shoulder. Klytie frowned, straining to hear as he murmured in her daughter's ear.

"Elektra, I know your disrespect comes from anger and resentment, not from any real hatred. If you really intend to cause your mama harm, continue on your present course. I suspect you do love your mama and would be saddened to see her hurt. If so, you will refrain from your vicious accusations. The last thing you want to see is your mama killed by your papa. You know it would happen, and it would be your fault. I for one would never forgive you. Do we understand each other?"

Elektra sniffed, lifting her chin in defiance. But she nodded, and he released her to scurry from the room. He turned to face Klytie.

"I think it's high time that girl were married," he said.

A round of religious celebration began as the people

prepared for the return of the King. Klytie officiated at sacrifices in every temple to every god and minor deity throughout the city. But watching her, Aegisthus worried.

After every ceremony, she wilted like a flower in the sun. He longed to hold her at those times, but she was determined to put on a show for a people excited by the imminent return of the army.

Late at night, he stood on the wall, staring out over the Argive plain, waiting for her. In public, she shunned all his advances, preserving the image of a good and loyal wife. But late at night, she welcomed him in her husband's bed with a desperation that grabbed at his soul and twisted like a knife in his heart.

Now, they snatched at love quickly and furtively, no more night-long nesting in the privacy of his own home and no more waking together with the sun. Lost in misery, he did not hear the footfall at his back, aware of the soldier's presence only when he felt the knife pointed at his spine.

Spinning away, he grabbed under his servant's robes for the sword he now kept hidden there at all times. But he paused when he recognised the soldier and saw the grin on his face.

"You need to be more careful, my lord," the Captain of the guard warned.

Aegisthus sighed. "Yes, I do. You were right to surprise me. I'm being a fool."

"What's worrying you?"

He leant back against the wall. "The Queen is terrified," he murmured.

"Why? Her husband is coming home."

"Why do you think she's so scared?"

"What are you talking about? I should think she'd be happy."

"You have no idea what that man has put her through."

The Captain cocked his head. "I don't understand."

Aegisthus chuckled. "No, I suppose you wouldn't. Good to know the ruse has worked. Forget I mentioned it."

"No, I don't think so," the Captain frowned. "I've always stood by you, trained you to fight, mentored you. I supported you when Thyestes came back, and helped you reintegrate when he was killed. In all that time, I've never seen you so distracted. You should know by now you can trust me."

"Can I? Even if you knew what I really wanted to do?"

"You think I don't know? You forget I know your soul; the prince trying to break free, denied his birthright. I'm surprised you didn't step up and take power before now, while he was away."

Aegisthus shook his head. "You don't know my heart."

"Then tell me."

"Imagine that the woman you loved was married to a brute, a man who also killed your father and destroyed your life." Aegisthus heaved a sigh. "How would you feel when that man came home and you had to stand back while he beds his wife?"

The Captain raised an eyebrow. "So that's it! I must say, you kept that little secret well hidden."

"Well, now you know. It was her fear that kept her loyal to him for so long, and her fear that stayed my hand. Now, I can't let it go on."

"Does she love you?"

A grin tugged at his lips. "Oh yes, she most certainly does."

"Then I pity you both the days to come."

Aegisthus gave a snort. "Pity? Is that all that's left for me?"

"No, my lord," said the Captain. "You need to know, whatever you decide to do, we're behind you all the way."

*

Klytemestra watched nervously as the maids hurried past, arms full of blood red tapestries and rugs, all taken from various rooms in the palace. She watched as they laid them out in a path, across the courtyard and continuing down the stairs to the lower court.

"Are you sure this is a good idea?" she whispered, wringing her hands.

"You're showing respect to the King," Aegisthus replied. "The people don't have a problem with it."

"But it's too much. He's going to think I'm mocking him, or worse making him act above himself."

"You don't think he's arrogant enough to do it?"

"I..."

"Don't worry, my love," he murmured. "Trust me."

Klytie looked past the lower court and down toward the lion gate. She could hear the excited cries from the lower city that told her the King's retinue was arriving.

She brushed her hands over her tight fitting ceremonial dress, her swelling breasts seeming to jut out in front. Running a hand over her not quite flat stomach, she felt the slight bump accentuated by the snug apron front.

"Stop thinking about it," Gissus whispered. "You look beautiful, he won't even notice."

"I think you underestimate him."

"So he'll think you've put on a few curves. He won't see anything else."

"I hope you're right."

"Look, he's coming," he pointed. "Better get down there."

Klytie took a deep breath and hurried down the stairs. The retinue made its way up the hill, the King carried in a litter at the head of the procession, followed by his personal guard.

Klytie gulped back her rising panic, trying to keep a serene expression. As the litter approached, she guided the men to place it at the end of the red pathway so that the King might step out directly onto it.

"My lord, I welcome you," she said as he stepped out of the litter. "As loving wife and mother of your children I rejoice at your safe return."

He looked around, at the house staff and the children behind their mother, then down at his feet at the crimson carpet, a frown setting on his jaw.

"What's this I'm standing on? What have you done, woman?"

"My lord, I welcome you as king and conqueror, and offer this soft carpet for your war weary feet. No common ground for the slayer of Troy!"

"These rich tapestries aren't meant for a warrior's sandals. You'd invite envy and vicious gossip about me, calling me the man who put himself above the gods?"

"No, my lord, I meant only to honour you."

He sighed. "Well, if you insist, I'll humour you."

"Don't do it, Aggie!" a woman cried, standing in the litter.

Klytie stared, eyes wide.

"Wife, I bid you welcome this woman, who is a prize of war, awarded by my loyal warriors. She's a Trojan princess and worthy of your respect. You'll bring her as a sister into our home."

"Aggie," the woman cried. "I see a river of blood, leading into this house. Please don't go in there."

"Be quiet woman," Agamemnon snapped. "She's pretty, but her wits are weak and addled. Pay her no mind."

With that, Agamemnon made his way across the red pathway toward the stairs.

"I see death, Aggie!" the woman screamed. "Don't go!"

But the King was already heading upstairs. "Come along, Cassandra," he said gruffly.

Klytemestra moved closer to the mad woman. She seemed so wild, so frightened. Perhaps the thought of slavery had addled her wits. Klytie knew what it felt like to be led into a life not of her choosing.

"Cassandra? Is that your name?"

The woman cocked her head.

"Do you understand me?"

The woman tilted her head the other way, staring at her.

"Come inside, I'll help you settle in. My maids can give you clean clothes and food. I promise we won't hurt you here."

"Oh, this house is full of pain," she moaned. "Blood and death, years of horrid murder. I can smell it on the very cloth before me."

"I won't lie to you, Cassandra. This house is cursed. But it won't harm you."

"I see children dead, I see brother betraying brother and nephew slaying uncle. I see blood without end!"

"It's the curse of Atreus. But come now, you're safe."

"Murder will come again!" the girl cried. "Oh I see it, a king dead. Please help me. The prophesy hurts me!"

Klytie felt her blood go cold. "I won't wait out here for a madwoman," she scoffed. "Come inside or stay out here, it's your choice."

With that, Klytemestra made her way upstairs without looking back. Behind her, she heard the girl sobbing her fear, but she followed, feet scuffling on the red carpet.

26

A Crime of Passion

Beside the King, with all his personal guard around, Klytemestra sat in a haze staring at tables laden with food. How long before she had to face him alone? She watched him gulp down another glass of wine, dreading the thought of a drunken Agamemnon letting loose his anger in private.

She looked about for Gissus but he was nowhere in sight. Why did he have to go off now, when she needed him the most? On the King's other side sat the little Trojan princess, hanging off his every word.

Slave, Klytie reminded herself. No princess now, and the girl would have to accept that. She felt sorry for her, but it was the way of the world. Klytie thought of how Gissus had taken on the guise of servant when his own future had been pulled from under him. This girl would have to learn that same humility.

Staring ahead, seeing nothing, lost in her own misery, Klytie hardly heard when the King addressed her. She was dragged out of her fog by a tug at her arm, and a fist clutching into her hair, pulling her hard against his chest.

"Where are your smiles, wife?" he growled. "What has taken your attention so far from your husband that you sit like a stone beside me? Where are your loving caresses and tender kisses, hmmm?"

Klytie forced a smile. "I'm just tired and overwhelmed,

husband," she said. "Forgive me."

"You should be showing the whole world your joy," he growled. "Perhaps you should show me now."

"Show you?" she whispered, looking about for Gissus.

"Come on, then," he said, pulling her up. "Up to bed, wife."

Dragging her unceremoniously out of the megaron, to a chorus of jeers and whistles from the men, Agamemnon took her through the anteroom to the porch. Looking frantically about, Klytie finally saw Gissus standing with the home guard in the courtyard.

She caught his eye, begging for help, and he took a step toward her, but she saw the captain of the guard holding him back with a hand on his arm. Sobbing with fear, she stumbled along, her arm held in a crushing grip.

Once upstairs, Agamemnon propelled her toward the bedroom with a rough push. Staggering into the room, she turned to face him as he closed the door firmly behind them. Trembling violently, she watched as he spun around, a look of absolute hatred twisting his face.

"So, bitch," he snarled. "Who is he?"

"Who is who, my lord?" she stammered.

"Who is the man you can't stop thinking about, hmmm?"

"I... I don't know what you mean."

"Don't lie to me, woman!"

He came at her, ripping at her dress and pushing her back until she felt the wooden frame of the bed against her legs.

"Who is the man you've taken into my bed?" he snarled as he pulled out the lacing of her bodice and yanked her skirt apart. Klytie shook her head, the tears flying.

"There's no man," she cried.

Throwing her clothing to the floor, he pushed her down onto the bed, tearing at his own clothing and clambering up on top of her. With a snarl of distaste, he slammed his fist down on her stomach and she screamed.

"Then who's put this bastard in your belly?" he yelled.

Klytie shook her head. "Please," she whispered.

"Who is he?" he growled, his full weight on her.

"I swear, there's no one," she screamed.

"Don't lie to me! I'm your husband, you belong to me," he yelled as he forced her legs apart. "I claim my right!"

Down in the courtyard, Aegisthus struggled against the restraining hand of the Captain.

"Let me go," he snarled.

"No, my lord, you mustn't go after her. He's her husband."

"I don't care who he is! If he hurts her..."

He caught his breath. Somewhere in the night, faintly over the noise of the feast in the megaron, he swore he could hear a woman screaming.

"Can you hear that?" he whispered. "Listen!"

The Captain shook his head. "I hear nothing but celebration."

"He's going to kill her!" Aegisthus yelled. "Let me go!"

Fumbling under his kiton, he pulled out his dagger. His father's long, ceremonial dagger, almost as big as a sword, sharpened to a fine point. Seeing the blade at his neck, the guard let go.

"I'm sorry, I have to do this," Aegisthus said.

Then it came again, the screaming, a deep long cry of agony peppered with sobbing terror. Gissus ran, feet flying across the cobbles, jumping up the little step into the private reception rooms, taking the long staircase two at a time.

Upstairs he could hear the screams louder now, coming from the royal bedchamber. Hot anger burning in his chest, he ran for the door, slammed against it, forcing it open, the scene on the bed freezing him in his tracks. Oblivious to the intruder, the King heaved and grunted on the bed.

The Queen, crushed somewhere beneath him, let out scream after scream, the sound tearing at Gissus' heart. With a growl of fury, Aegisthus jumped forward, blade raised high.

He ran, straight at the King's bare back, jumping up behind him on the bed and driving the dagger down. A single mighty thrust, and the King shuddered and fell, landing heavily on top of his wife with a long sigh.

Aegisthus stood there for a moment, savouring the death of his greatest enemy, remembering another time that blade had found its mark. Atreus had died in almost the same way by the same hand and the same blade. In his triumph, Aegisthus tasted the sweet tang of revenge.

Then, a whimpering brought him back to reality. With a curse, he dragged at the body of the King, pulling him off the bed. He saw Klytie scramble backward, eyes wide with terror, clutching at the blanket as she huddled at the head of the bed. Gissus dropped to his knees, crawling toward her. She cried out, trying to move even further back, stopped only by the wall behind her.

"Hush, my love," he whispered. "It's alright now."

Her eyes flicked toward him, only now seeing him. Her face crumpled and he rushed to take her in his arms as she sobbed.

"Oh, Gissus, what have you done?" she mumbled.

Aegisthus frowned, his mouth set in a hard line. "Has he always treated you like that?"

"Only when he's angry," she sobbed.

"No wonder you were afraid of him."

"Gissus, what do we do now?"

"Well," he sighed. "First I must get him out of this room. I'll put him in the bath for now."

"Then what?"

"Then... we claim my birthright."

Orestes leant on his sister's shoulder and yawned. At one corner of the hearth, up against one of the pillars, his other sister Elektra giggled in the arms of a soldier, flirting dreadfully.

"You should go to bed," said Krissie.

Orestes shook his head. "I'm big enough to stay up. I'm almost a man!"

"Of course you are, but Papa's already gone to bed with Mama. You don't have to stay up now."

The boy nodded. "Alright then."

Stifling another yawn, Orestes stumbled toward the door. But he was stopped by a strange woman. Orestes thought she might be the one Papa had brought with him.

"You're the King's son, aren't you?" the woman said.

Orestes nodded.

"Do you know where he might be?"

"He's gone to bed with Mama," Orestes said.

"Oh," she sighed. "I just... Maybe you can help me."

Orestes cocked his head.

"I know I'm only a slave now, but... I used to be a princess and... I'd really like a bath..."

"I'll show you," the boy said, taking her hand and leading her out through the anteroom to the porch and into the reception room, heading down the hall.

Entering the bathing room, Orestes stopped, seeing a man already in the small tub, black hair just visible over the edge of the bath. From one side, a servant brought a large pitcher of water and poured it into the bath.

"There," said Orestes. "Papa's having a bath now."

"Thank you for your help," the woman said.

As she moved into the room, Orestes turned to go. But

the woman let out a shriek and he turned in surprise. She was screaming and calling out.

"Oh blood, oh murder!" she screamed. "I saw it and now I see it, he's murdered!"

Orestes stared as the servant grabbed the woman, a hand over her mouth to silence her screaming. He saw a flash of bronze and the woman went limp.

The servant heaved her into the bath and stood looking at her for a long moment. Then the servant picked up the pitcher and spun about, blood drenching the front of his kiton. The boy gasped as he recognised Gissus. He shook his head in confusion and the servant's eyes widened.

"Orestes, wait..." Gissus said, a hand held out toward him.

But the boy shook his head more violently, feeling his knees shaking. As Gissus came toward him, he turned and ran, back to the hall to find his sisters.

Fleeing down the corridor, a bath sheet wrapped about him to hide the blood, Aegisthus ran for the only man he could trust. Sticking his head out onto the porch, he searched for the Captain of the guard.

"I need you, now!" he hissed, signalling to the man.

Slipping back into the reception room, he led the Captain along the hidden corridor beside the courtyard, heading out of the palace complex by the rear exit and down to the barracks.

"My lord, what's happened?"

Aegisthus rounded on him, voice low and urgent. "It's on, Captain, the time has come. It's now or never."

The Captain gasped as Aegisthus pulled off the bath sheet to reveal the blood soaked kiton.

"My lord, what have you done?"

"I need clean clothes, and armour, now!" he said, ripping

off the soiled kiton.

"Of course," he said, reaching for a spare kiton off a shelf. "What are you going to do?"

"You said you'd stand by me," said Aegisthus, heading into the armoury. "Are your men ready?"

"Absolutely, my lord, we've been ready for years."

"The King is dead, Captain. We need to neutralise his personal guard, right now." He scanned the racks for a suitable cuirass. "You know my size, what have you got?"

"Here, try this," said the Captain. He helped him into the plate armour, fastening buckles and tying knots.

"Everything hinges on this night," Aegisthus continued. "I think if you eliminate his captains the men will crumble. Helmet?"

"I think you're right. Here," he handed him a bronze helmet with a high black plume. "Let me tie the greaves for you."

The Captain bent to wrap the cording around the bronze greaves, securing them to his calves. Then Aegisthus held out his arms for the arm greaves.

"Do you have a sword? My father's dagger won't hold up to full battle."

"Right here."

The Captain secured the leather belt and sheathed sword. Aegisthus let out a long breath.

"Well? Am I suitably martial?"

The Captain smiled. "Perfectly regal, my lord. And it suits you."

Aegisthus grinned. "Let's get to it, then."

Orestes ran, to the only place he could think of, back to the megaron and his sisters. He saw Krisothemis standing alone to one side and hurried over to her, clutching at her arm as he whispered what he had seen.

"Are you sure?" she hissed.

"Of course I'm sure!" he cried. "Why would he do that?"

"Let's get Elektra."

"But she's..." Orestes glanced to where his elder sister stood pressed against a hearth pillar, wrapped in the arms of her soldier friend, locked in a drunken kiss.

"This is important," said Krissie, hurrying to her sister and pulling at her arm.

Elektra tried to shake her off, unwilling to break her tryst, but Krissie persisted.

"What do you want?"

"Tell her what you saw, Orestes."

The boy blurted out his story, hands twisting in front, eyes pleading in his terror.

"I knew it," hissed Elektra when he had finished. "I knew Gissus was up to no good."

"What are we going to do?" Orestes sobbed.

"Well, first we're going to get you out of here," Elektra said grimly.

"Why?" Orestes gasped.

"This is a coup, Orestes. Your father's been killed and you're next. It's what happens," she said, turning to her soldier friend. "Are you loyal to my father? Can I trust you?"

"Of course, my lady," the man stuttered. "I'd do anything for you."

"Then let's go."

Orestes followed as Elektra led them from the megaron, through the anteroom and onto the porch, heading for the great stair. But she stopped at sight of the home guard, ranged in the courtyard in full armour. Orestes shivered. They looked so martial, ready for a fight.

"This way," said his sister in a whisper.

Orestes followed her to the right, up the little stair and through the reception room. Heading upstairs, they continued down the upper corridor to another flight of stairs and up onto the roof. They climbed across onto the flat roof of the administration block, running along the line of the north corridor. From there the path to the postern gate was a short jump down the terraced hillside. Elektra turned.

"I'm sorry, Orestes, there's no time to gather your things, you have to go now, right this minute."

"What? You want me to leave?"

"Your life is in danger if you wait even a moment longer than absolutely necessary."

"But what about Mama? I want to see Mama!" the boy sobbed. "Don't make me go."

"Orestes, you must. You must go to Papa's sister, she'll look after you." She turned to her tame soldier. "You'll look after him, won't you? See he gets there safely."

"Of course, my lady, you can count on me."

Elektra bent to Orestes, her hands on his shoulders. "Orestes, listen to me. You must live, to grow up knowing your Papa was murdered. Then when you're old enough you can come back, avenge him and rescue me and Krissie."

"Rescue you?"

"Well of course, we're daughters of the murdered king. We'll be slaves, we won't be princesses any more, and you'll be a prince in exile, waiting for your chance."

"But I don't want to go," he sobbed. "Krissie, don't let her make me..."

Krissie sighed. "I think she may be right, Orestes."

Rushing back up to the palace, through the administrative complex and out into the courtyard by the back stair, Aegisthus and the Captain joined the men of the home guard.

"Fall in!" the Captain called, and the men lined up.

Aegisthus scanned the soldiers before him, his loyal followers, who had been hiding in the shadows for all these years, waiting for this day.

He drew his father's ceremonial dagger, the very instrument that had proven his identity to Thyestes. The weapon that had killed Atreus the usurper and now had tasted the blood of Agamemnon. Blood that still clung to the blade. He raised the dagger high.

"Do you know me?" he cried.

"Yes, my lord!" the men called as one.

"Are you with me?"

"Yes, my lord!"

"Are you ready to fight?"

"Yes, my lord!" came the jubilant cry.

"Then follow me!"

And the men roared. Aegisthus strode up onto the porch, followed by his loyal guard, through the anteroom and into the megaron, bursting in on the revelling warriors. And then the fight was on.

Fighting his way through to the King's seat, Aegisthus turned to see the home guard targeting the captains of the king's retinue. But the common soldiers were slow in throwing down their weapons, the battle raging in the grand throne room.

The king's soldiers, drunk and full from the feast, were no match for the home guard. The fight was over almost before it began. Aegisthus surveyed the carnage. Many men lay dead, the Captain directing the removal of the bodies. Once again, he raised his father's ceremonial sword. All eyes were on Aegisthus.

"Agamemnon the usurper is king no more!" he yelled.

The men of the home guard roared their victory. The survivors of the King's retinue shuffled their feet, held in place by their captors.

"I am the last son of Thyestes," Aegisthus roared. "By right of coup and by the laws of succession I hereby claim my father's throne."

His loyal men cheered, and the old king's guard murmured their surprise.

"Any objections will be silenced and any insurrection will be dealt with swiftly and without mercy. Are there any objections?"

There was silence, only a shuffling of feet and downcast eyes from the followers of the dead king.

"All returned warriors are welcomed into the ranks of the home guard. All veterans will be awarded their due right of settlement. I have no quarrel with men who fought willingly for our homeland. Release them."

The men relaxed, the returned warriors looking about in relief and taking the welcoming hands of the home guard. The men merged, and the soldiers of the King became one force.

"Now, I charge you, go out into the city, join your fellow soldiers in their camps and tell them that a new day has come. You are dismissed."

Slowly the men dispersed, only the Captain and his officers remaining to wait on the King.

"Captain, send for the Queen."

Hurrying downstairs in the company of two soldiers, wild fears tumbling about in her head, Klytemestra listened to the pounding of her heart, in time with her running footsteps.

Entering the megaron, she stopped, staring at the figure on the right wall, seated in the King's place. For a moment, she hardly recognised him, but under that helmet those piercing green eyes called her forward. He looked magnificent, every inch the warrior king.

Stepping forward slowly, Klytie drank him in, heart turning somersaults in her chest, butterflies dancing in the pit of her stomach. This man, this stranger, the man she loved, sat before her in victory, his long lost birthright fully restored, and she gloried in his majesty.

"Come closer, my lady," he intoned, even his voice taking on the power of a king.

Klytie knelt before him, head bowed, breath fluttering in her excitement.

"Rise and take my hand," he said.

She did as ordered, feeling the warmth of the man behind the cold martial exterior, feeling his hand tremble slightly in hers. A smile tugged at his lips as his eyes held hers, stirring a deep longing low in her gut.

"By right of combat, I claim you as my prize," he stated, a twinkle in his eyes. "Will you sit beside me as my queen?"

She longed to throw herself into his arms, eager to show him her answer in kisses, but she held herself in check with an effort and nodded, licking her lips. He lifted her hand to his lips, his hot kiss sending sparks up her arm, continuing through her whole body, leaving her gasping.

"Then join me," he chuckled, guiding her by one hand to the seat at his side. "Captain," he continued. "Bring me the children."

In short order, the girls appeared in the megaron, but there was no sign of Orestes.

"Is the boy asleep?" the King asked.

"No, my lord," said Elektra with a sneer. "My brother is gone."

"Gone?" said Klytie. "Where? Elektra, what have you done?"

"I sent him away, Mother," she said.

"You did what?" Klytie moaned. "Why would you do

that?"

"Everyone knows what happens to the sons when a king is murdered. As soon as he came to me and told me what he'd seen, I found a bodyguard, a soldier loyal to my father, and sent him away."

"But I would never hurt him," said Aegisthus with a frown. "I love you all as if you were my own."

"Where did you send him," cried Klytie, tears pricking at her eyes.

"To my uncle in Phocis, to live in my father's sister's house. Anaxibia will mother him and Strophios will protect him until he's old enough to come back and avenge our father."

"Oh, Elektra," Klytie wailed. "Oh, my poor boy. He should be with his mother."

"I don't care. You lost him when you let that man murder his father."

"He deserved it, he murdered your sister!"

"So you say," said Elektra. "I never saw any proof."

"Enough!" Aegisthus hissed. "Elektra, it's high time you were married. You'll have a house of your own and children to raise. Perhaps that will mellow your tongue."

"I knew it wouldn't be long before you got rid of me."

"What about me, Gissus?" whispered Krisothemis. "What will happen to me?"

"My dearest Krissie, I love you, though your sister would have you believe otherwise. You have a home here just as long as you need it, or until such time as you are married."

Krissie smiled. "Then I will be content."

Through the dark streets of the city, a small cart rumbled down the hill toward the postern gate, pulled by a scruffy old donkey. A man who might have been a soldier or a slave held the reins stiffly, eyes darting about. Under a dirty old blanket, a small boy huddled, big dark eyes gleaming with unshed tears as he peered out between the slats of the cart.

A discordant hum of voices singing, filled with laughter and cheers, floated over the little group, sending shivers down the boy's spine. He swallowed down the lump in his throat, a heavy burden of grief settling over his young heart. While he fled, they celebrated the fall of a king, his papa. Someday, they would pay.

In the early hours of the morning, the queen and her new king finally retired to the royal suite. Hand in hand, they walked up the stairs, speaking only with their eyes. Reaching the privacy of their room, Klytie unbuckled his armour, piling the bronze plates against the wall.

"I thought you looked incredible in this," she whispered. "But I like you better without it."

He grinned. "Are you happy, my love?"

She smiled radiantly. "I don't deserve to be so happy."

"Yes, you do," he said.

She sighed. "What should we do about Orestes? I know Elektra acted out of concern for his safety, but he's my son. Can't we send for him?"

"You know I would never hurt him," he replied. "He's like my own son."

Klytie felt her heart lighten in relief.

"But maybe Elektra was right," he continued. "I think if he were here, he would be in danger, even if not from me."

Klytie groaned as a stone weight settled on her chest.

"He's the son of Agamemnon," said Aegisthus. "Many people will want the law of coup carried out. If it came to that, the soldiers would do it even without my consent."

"Oh, my boy..." Klytie sobbed. "But Gissus, he'll be living with Agamemnon's sister. He'll be raised to hate us, reminded daily of his father's murder. One day, he'll return for his revenge, and the curse of Atreus will come down on your head."

"Don't worry, my love, he would never hurt us."

"I suppose you're right," she sighed. "But what if he forgets me, what then?"

"Hush, my love," he murmured.

"And there's one more thing," she whispered. "I'll never see my sister again. Menelaos will make sure of that."

"Klytie, stop worrying," he groaned, pulling her into his arms. "Everything will be alright."

He captured her mouth with his, silencing her protests, and she began to relax.

"Now, come to bed, my love," he murmured.

With a heavy sigh, Klytie allowed him to lead her to the bed, their bed now. No longer a secret, no longer a furtive, hurried love, she gave herself to him with no thought of consequence. Everything would be alright.

THE END

AUTHOR'S NOTE

HISTORICAL ACCURACY

Writing *The Curse of Mycenae* has been a wonderful experience, returning to my old love (classics) and remembering those uni lectures...

Suggestions that the story is not accurate are largely based on modern retellings in film, which are in themselves usually grossly inaccurate. My story is closely based on the Greek myths beginning with Homer and his contemporaries and fleshed out by the later Greek playwrites, Aeschylus, Euripides and Sophocles.

Every character except one is real, every event is real. Apart from artistic license, this book is as accurate as was humanly possible. Please read on for an account of my research and my justifications for decisions made in the crafting of this book. If you do not agree, I suggest you consult the sources yourself before you pass judgement.

I enjoyed knitting the known events together into a cohesive story. The tricky (and fun) part was working out how the characters get to each landmark event. There is some creative speculation for some of them, but all such inventions are extrapolated from what we actually know from the sources.

This author's note is intended to address a few issues that may have come into question while reading this book. It is not intended to be an essay or a research paper on ancient Mycenae, and any assertions made here can be justified with judicious research if necessary.

CHARACTER NAMES

Many of the ancient Greek names are long and complicated, sometimes difficult for the modern reader to scan easily. It is for this reason that some names are simplified and some major players are given nicknames. In particular, Klytemestra/Klytie is both simplified and shortened, but ironically, the missing 'n' is thought to be closer to the authentic ancient spelling than modern derivations like Kleitemnestra or Clytaemnestra. Minor characters tend to keep their names more or less authentic, since they appear in small doses.

A word about Paris: in Homer, the earliest account of the Trojan War, his name is Alexandros. It is later, in the Greek plays, that he is called Paris. But that is how history remembers him, and it would cause too much confusion to use the 'wrong' name. So, I have used Alexandros as his surname.

There are two invented names, created using authentic naming conventions: Neohippos the minstrel is a real person, but is never named in the sources; the other I will discuss later. Besides these, all characters are known persons found in the ancient sources, so their somewhat difficult names are retained.

One last name that needs a note: Elenos is one of the brothers of Paris. His name, when written in English, is Helenus, essentially the masculine version of Helene. In Greek the H is merged with the E in the Greek letter Eta, pronounced He. To avoid the obvious confusion, I have written his name as it would appear in a direct transliteration of Greek alphabet into English.

The Chronology

As the story opens Helene and Klytie are just beginning their married lives, and can be assumed to be about fourteen or fifteen at the time. When Paris seduces Helene, she already has a nine-year-old daughter and Klytie has her three daughters, so they would have been in their mid-twenties when the war began.

The Trojan War lasts ten years as suggested by Homer, although modern scholars believe this time covered the whole war, not just the siege of Troy. To confirm this, Odysseus tries to avoid the war because of an oracle that predicts he will be away from home for twenty years, which includes the ten-year war and ten years of misadventures on the way home. So by the time Agamemnon is killed, Klytie is in her mid-thirties, which is still young enough to bear three children to Aegisthus, as cited in the ancient sources.

It is generally believed that Achilles was fifteen at the start of the war, which gives us an age for Paris. If Paris presided over the divine beauty contest that followed the wedding of Achilles' parents, he must have been at least a young adult, say fifteen, when Achilles was born, which makes him at least thirty when he seduces Helene.

The sources state that Paris immediately went in search of his prize, but the chronology does not allow for this. I have therefore suggested that Paris took some time searching for her, only discovering her name and location when he finally hears tell of her.

In my story, Tantalus is the eldest son of Thyestes (although his real identity is unclear in the sources), and Aegisthus is the youngest. The twin sons of Atreus, Agamemnon and Menelaos, are somewhere in between.

In my chronology, Thyestes is exiled after the first

coup with his son Tantalus, then a young man of about fifteen, for twenty years. This date is subjective, since no firm chronology is given in the sources, but it makes sense in light of the ages of various characters involved, most notably Agamemnon, who was a child when Thyestes was exiled, and must be fully adult by the start of the story.

This makes Aegisthus about twenty when Thyestes takes Mycenae, Tantalus about thirty-five. So, if Agamemnon is somewhere in the middle, old enough to be amongst the suitors of Helene, and already in exile from Mycenae, he must be at least in his mid-twenties at the start of the book.

The relatively short reign of Thyestes is justified by what Tantalus gains in marriage to Klytemestra: the army of Sparta. Tantalus could not have staged the second coup without the army, and he could not have married Klytie much sooner because she would have been too young.

The third coup by Agamemnon follows hard on the heels of the second, as evidenced by the fact that Klytie's child is only a newborn when he is killed by Agamemnon, along with his father Tantalus, as told by the playwrite Euripides.

KLYTIE'S FAMILY

It's surprising how many Greek myths are connected to this one family. Most notably, Helene of Troy and the brothers Castor and Pollox, who were worshipped in Roman times and survive even today as the Gemini twins of the zodiac.

Through the twins, many other myths are touched upon, such as the journey of Jason and the Argonauts, the rape of the Leucippides, the war against Theseus, and the apotheosis of the twins. Perhaps one of my hardest tasks was fitting these adventures into the chronology of Klytemestra's life.

A note about the mother of Klytemestra and her siblings Helene, Castor and Pollox. Leda is important only so far as she gave birth to these four after being seduced by Zeus in the guise of a swan. Very little is known about her later life, and in all my reading I cannot admit to seeing any mention of her whatsoever. I take this to mean she simply was not there, and have treated her as such.

The identity of Klytemestra's first husband is unclear, being either a cousin or uncle of Agamemnon and Menelaos. His name is also unclear, though he is named Tantalus in the play by Euripides, in which Klytemestra berates Agamemnon for the murder of her first husband and child.

The Character of Agamemnon

There is no doubt in the sources. Agamemnon was a rough, gruff, uncompromising man who showed little respect for his peers and even less tolerance for the opinions of others. Homer's works are full of incidents that illustrate his flaws as well as his prowess as commander of the Achaean forces. He commits murder without a thought and expects to be obeyed.

In a way, he was a man of his times, but it is no great leap to see his treatment of his wife devolving into something darker. Women of Mycenaean Greece had little freedom and no choice in marriage, though they are often shown as equal to their husbands in matters of politics and administration, so long as they never took it to the point of offense against their husbands.

A strong, wilful woman and an arrogant commander of men were bound to clash, and no good recipe for a happy marriage.

ELLA MORTIMER

THE CURSE

The life of Klytemestra is peppered with the tragic history of the royal house of Mycenae, a curse begun in the time of Agamemnon's grandfather, and triggered in the time of Atreus, Agamemnon's father. It is for this reason the book is called "The Curse of Mycenae".

The chronology of the troubled house of Mycenae is difficult to untangle, full of inconsistencies and contradictions. I have attempted to make sense of it within the context of my story. I do not claim it is accurate but I have tried to make it fit logically in all its phases to place the characters in the right place at the right time to perform those key actions that are mentioned in the sources.

THE SACRIFICE

All sources agree, the sacrifice of Iphigenia did occur. The idea that she was transformed into a deer is mentioned in Euripides. I suspect this tradition developed as a rationalisation against the concept of human sacrifice, and to render the following sacrificial feast seem less horrific. I know the suggestion that the girl's corpse became food for the army flies in the face of established scholarship, but it is so obvious as to be impossible to ignore.

It is well known that Mycenaean sacrificial animals were the main course in the following feast. Human sacrifice is not unusual in Greek myths harking back to Mycenaean times. It is well documented that the army stranded at Aulis was starving and close to revolt.

It is not a great leap to suggest that somewhere along the line the corpse was dressed up to look like a deer in an attempt to hide the cannibalistic feast that may have followed. This then could have led to the later tradition that the girl was transformed into, or in fact literally replaced on the altar with, a deer, which then became a feast for the starving troops.

Whether or not you accept this theory is immaterial to the impact the idea has on the rest of the story, and Klytemestra's hatred for her husband is all the more powerful because of it.

AEGISTHUS' FAMILY

Some sources suggest that Aegisthus was conceived by Thyestes when he raped his own daughter with the specific purpose of creating an heir to avenge him. I have not included this event, preferring instead to suggest that Aegisthus was suckled by his sister after the death of their mother.

Soon after, the baby was left exposed to the elements, a common form of infanticide in the ancient world. It has been suggested that the sister did this out of guilt and disgust for his incestuous conception, but I choose to believe that it is just as probable Aegisthus was another victim of the revengeful coup staged by Atreus against Thyestes.

Following a common tradition in ancient Greek myth where heroes exposed to death as babies were suckled by wild animals, the baby Aegisthus survived by drinking the milk of a goat. It was also common for an exposed infant to be rescued by some well-meaning peasant and adopted.

In combining these two ideas, I have created a foster family for Aegisthus, a goatherd and his wife, who fed him on goat's milk and raised him as their own. As an extension of this, I have given him a sister, Philadora, the only purely invented character in the book.

THE LOVES OF ACHILLES

In this story, Achilles does appear to be a rather selfish, sex-obsessed young man. And in the main, this picture is completely accurate. Every woman linked to him in this book is actually mentioned in the sources. In fact, I have even left out a few of his lovers, males as well as females, such as the Amazon queen and, in some accounts, Helene herself. Some scholars even believe his relationship with Patroklos was a love match.

But I do think he grows a little in the course of this story and by the end, he is a little wiser, even if he is killed as the result of another sexual liaison.

The Murder

The earliest sources, including Homer, give Klytemestra a very small part in the murder of Agamemnon. These oldest accounts universally paint her as a puppet of Aegisthus, a fairly weak and submissive woman seduced by an ambitious man. It is only later, in the plays of the 6th century BC that the murder is pinned on Klytemestra.

The manner of the deed is described in two different ways: either the king was killed in the midst of his homecoming feast; or he was killed in his bath later that night. I have chosen to deviate from these. There is still a feast, but why would Aegisthus or Klytemestra suddenly break years of inaction to commit murder in plain sight? There is no motive and no logical reason why it would be planned that way, if indeed they did plan it.

I have chosen to raise the stakes a little, building on their well-documented love affair to create a crime of passion. An event where after chasing her for years, falling in love and having to watch her go back to her husband's bed, Aegisthus finally sees him for the man he is, witnessing the beatings she has suffered and kept hidden.

This is the catalyst needed to break the inertia of years and stage the coup he has been dreaming of his whole life.

He then takes the body and hides it in the bath, where he is discovered by Orestes.

I hope you enjoyed reading The Curse of Mycenae as much as I enjoyed writing it. I trust you found a compelling story about the people who stayed at home when the Greeks went off to war with Troy, with an unexpected new perspective on the great Agamemnon and his much-maligned deserted wife.

Ella Mortimer

The Race of Fire
Revealing Rexa

Miyam was a psychic spy, training to be a member of an elite society known only as the revealers. But that was years ago, before her mother died and her father removed her from her home.

Now, her mundane new life is thrown into turmoil when her father is murdered. Looking for a new start, Miyam joins a dangerous quest to find the long lost king's talisman, and her fate becomes entwined with the revealers once again.

A terrifying invader travels by night, burning everything in its path. A small group of friends strive to save the queen and defeat the enemy. And Miyam begins a personal journey to reconcile her shattered life and rediscover her lost destiny.

Ella Mortimer

The Race of Fire
Awakening Sand

From the secretive world of the revealers a hero will emerge, who will risk life and love to take the battle to the next level.

With the return of the king's amulet, the demonic kalkar appear defeated. But a darker, more malevolent force is now in control, and the world is set to burn. As the kalkar prepare for a new invasion, the princess is kidnapped and the battle begins again.

Sand must find the power to rise above his tragic past, and break the will of the terrible god Kayus, who holds the enemy in thrall. Before the end, Sand faces the ultimate test beyond the veil, to fulfill his destiny and become the Awakener.

Ella Mortimer

The Race of Fire
Rekindling Truth

Legend says the Awakener will bring truth to the world.
But what is that truth and what is he supposed to do
with it? Sand is about to discover that the truth is more
amazing than he ever dreamed.

As Sand begins his predestined task the minds of those
around him seem to fill his head. Meanwhile, the mindless
bodies of the people he hears are slowly being possessed
by something else.

But underneath it all is another voice, carrying the long
dead memories of a forgotten past. A voice that wants his
body for itself.

Sand must embark on a new quest, into the darkest
places in his own mind, through the hidden halls of
history, and to the lair of his greatest enemy, there to
vanquish the voices in his head.

Ella Mortimer

Crystal Runes

Rediscover the magic of rune stones. Based on the oldest known interpretation of the futhark, with English names chosen to reflect the original words and their meanings.

Each rune is paired with a precious stone* suggested specifically to enhance the power of your readings.

*Stones not included.